D1149078

THE
DEAD
CAN WAIT

THE
DEAD
CAN WAIT

ROBERT RYAN

**SIMON &
SCHUSTER**

London · New York · Sydney · Toronto · New Delhi

A CBS COMPANY

First published in Great Britain by Simon & Schuster UK Ltd, 2014
A CBS COMPANY

1 3 5 7 9 10 8 6 4 2

Simon & Schuster UK Ltd
1st Floor
222 Gray's Inn Road
London WC1X 8HB

www.simonandschuster.co.uk

Simon & Schuster Australia, Sydney
Simon & Schuster India, New Delhi

A CIP catalogue record for this book
is available from the British Library

ISBN: 978-1-4711-4749-4

Typeset by Hewer Text UK Ltd, Edinburgh
Printed and bound by CPI Group (UK) Ltd, Croydon CR0 4YY

To Gina

And for her godmother, Christine

Taten statt Worte,
Zähne statt Tränen

'Deeds not Words, Teeth not Tears'
Motto of the *Sie Wölfe* Special Naval Unit 1916–7

'Which is it to-day?' I asked. 'Morphine or cocaine?' Holmes raised his eyes languidly from the old black-letter volume which he had opened. 'It is cocaine,' he said, 'a seven-per-cent solution. Would you care to try it?'

from *The Sign of Four* by Sir Arthur Conan Doyle

THE
DEAD
CAN WAIT

PROLOGUE

The orderlies carried the six bodies down the steps of the sunken ice house that lay half hidden in the grounds of the Suffolk stately home. The commanding officer of the 'special' unit that had displaced the owner and his retinue from the Hall stood at the bottom of the stairs, watching the orderlies manhandle the stiffening forms, grunting with the effort as they laid out the dead on the stone flags. Each of the deceased was tightly swaddled in a waxed groundsheet. *They look like latter-day mummies*, the colonel thought grimly.

The officer lit a cigarette. There was a smell of decay in the air that the smoke would help mask. Not from the six bodies – these poor souls had been dead only a matter of hours – but from the ice house itself, part of which had doubled as hanging rooms for the estate's bag of venison, partridge and pheasant in the years before the outbreak of war. A persistent sharp, gamey tang tainted the atmosphere.

It would be high summer soon enough, and the colonel didn't want the dead men adding to the stink before they could be properly examined. Hence he directed the orderlies to move them to the coldest corner of the subterranean chamber. *Examined for what, though?*

The colonel tried to keep his jaw set and his face impassive as the orderlies neatened up the row of cadavers, moving the legs so they were absolutely parallel, as if this were some kind of Best Laid Corpse competition. Inside, though, his stomach was a bucket of eels. He had been entrusted with the secret project that was intended to bring a swift resolution to the war, to see it all over by Christmas 1916, to consign the horror of the trenches, the slaughter of the Somme, to a hideous but fading memory. Yet out there, in

1

the grounds of the house, in front of generals and politicians and even minor bloody royalty, *this* had happened. Six dead, two others reduced to jibbering lunatics.

Oh, they had managed to cover it up as quickly and smoothly as possible, postponing the test for 'technical reasons', and the bodies were only removed once the viewing stands had been cleared of the dignitaries. Still, it was both an acute embarrassment and a serious setback. *And a damn sight worse for six dead members of the Machine Gun Corps,* he reminded himself. What on earth would he tell the next of kin? 'Died for King and Country' would have to do, wrapped in a bow of the usual platitudes.

The colonel's job now was to keep a lid on this, to get to the bottom of the deaths before someone decided to stop throwing good money – and men – after bad. To save the project at all cost. He dismissed the orderlies, warning them, on pain of the most severe punishments he could threaten, not to reveal or discuss anything they had seen that day. Exile, imprisonment and disgrace awaited those who betrayed his trust.

He smoked on, staring down at the shrouded forms for a few minutes. The flickering oil lamps had turned the groundsheets a glossy, sickly yellow-green. The very colour he himself felt. He could taste bile in his mouth. The colonel tossed the remains of his cigarette onto the stone flags and ground it out with the toe of his boot. He did this rather longer than was necessary to extinguish it.

There was a polite cough behind him and he turned, wondering how long he had had company. It was the unit's intelligence officer, a deep frown corrugating his youthful brow.

'Yes?' the colonel demanded.

'Trenton just expired,' said the young man.

Seven, then.

Seven dead men in one afternoon. *And then there was one.* The colonel muttered a particularly fruity oath. 'Get him brought down here, quick as you can. Who was with him?'

'The new nurse.'

'Well, make sure she keeps her mouth shut. Let's be clear: I don't want anyone outside the main committee to know about this until we are certain what is behind it. I am not letting two years' worth of work go to waste because of an unfortunate' – he looked at the bodies and shivered. The perpetual chill of the ice house was penetrating his bones – 'accident,' he finished.

'But how do we find out what happened out there?' asked the intelligence officer, glancing over his shoulder.

'We have to hope the survivor talks.' The remaining man was the least affected by whatever malaise had struck the eight. He had settled into being merely comatose. 'Hitchcock, isn't it?' asked the colonel.

The younger man nodded. 'And if he doesn't talk?'

The colonel considered this for a moment. 'Then we'll find someone who will make him.'

PART ONE

10–29 JULY 1916

ONE

The sound of the bell was an icicle plunged into his heart. At the first few notes, shivers racked his body and his pulse raced like a rodent's; a prickling sweat broke out, beading his forehead and wetting his palms. A sense of blind panic threatened to over-whelm him as the ringing grew in intensity and then abruptly stopped. The ominous silence that followed was somehow even more threatening.

The gas alarm.

Time to mask up. Major John H. Watson of the Royal Army Medical Corps stepped away from the young lad he had been treat-ing up at the regimental aid post and looked down beneath the trestle table. His gas mask case was not there. He had tripped over it too many times. He had hung it outside, he remembered, on the trench wall. If this was a genuine attack, he needed that mask.

The bell resumed its warning again, seemingly more urgent than before. He heard the bellow of the company sergeant major. 'Gas! Gas! Gas! Come on, lads, snap to it if you want to keep y'lungs on the inside where they belong.'

There was only one other patient in the dugout, and he didn't need a mask. He had breathed his last. The RAMC orderly next to the poor lad, who had been preparing the corpse for burial, was busy struggling with his own rubber and canvas respirator.

'Orderly, when you have done that, get a mask on this man too!' Watson shouted, indicating his own patient. 'It'll be with his rifle. I'm going to fetch my nosebag.'

Watson stepped out from the low-roofed aid station, his feet slithering for purchase on the slimy and worn duckboards. In front of him, on the opposite side of the trench, was a recess, where metal hooks had been screwed into the supporting timbers, forming a primitive open-air wardrobe. From the hooks hung a motley assortment of capes, caps, helmets and coats, but no gas masks.

A figure thumped into Watson and he was spun round, scrabbling to retain his footing. The man, a lieutenant, made goggle-eyed by his air purifier, apologized in a muffled voice and indicated that Watson should protect his face. The junior officer pointed upwards, towards the pale blue of the early morning sky. Like a sly fog, the first tendrils of greyish-green gas were creeping over the sandbags of the parapet. Watson felt his eyes prickle and sting.

Not again. Not chlorine gas again.

It was too late to run through the trenches hoping for a spare mask, so he turned to take whatever shelter the aid station could offer. As he did so, his left foot slipped off the duckboards. It plunged into the thick slime of the trench mud, a glutinous mass that had been festering for nigh on two years. It clasped his ankle and held him firm.

He uttered a crude curse, a bad habit he had picked up from the men. He tried to lift his foot free, but the grip only tightened and the suction pulled his leg deeper into the mire. He would have to lose the boot, a precious Trench Master, ten guineas the pair. *Don't worry about that now, man. Pull!* But the pressure of the ooze was too great to allow him even to wiggle his toes. He held his knee and yanked, but to no avail. The greedy sludge that had taken so many men had him tight.

The gas was rolling down the sides of the trench now, viscous and evil. The gas alarm bell sounded once again and didn't stop this time. Attack in progress. All across the front a cacophony of sirens, hooters, whistles and rattles joined in the warning. *Don't die here, not like this.* But by now he was holding onto the wall, watching the black filth creep further up his trapped leg, his desperate fingers leaving grooves on the rotten wood as he sought purchase.

He looked around for assistance, but every sensible soldier was taking cover. 'Help!' he yelled. The only answer was an imagined snide hiss from the poison drifting towards him. Watson closed his eyes, held his breath, and waited for the vapour to do its worst.

'Major Watson!'

The strident tones of the familiar and distinctly female voice snapped him from his reverie. He opened his eyes. Before him was the coal-grimed window of his surgery and, beyond that, Queen Anne Street, its features blanketed by an eerily unseasonal fog, the traffic reduced to a passing parade of ghostly silhouettes. He wasn't at the front. He hadn't seen, or smelled, a trench for months. Mud was no longer his constant companion and intractable enemy. It was another waking dream of the sort that had haunted him since his return from France.

He turned to Mrs Hobbs, his housekeeper, standing in the doorway to the hall, her face drawn even tighter than her bun.

'Major Watson, did you not hear the telephone?'

The telephone. Not a gas alarm.

She indicated over her shoulder to where the phone sat on its dedicated walnut telephonic table from Heal's. It was a piece of furniture that Mrs Hobbs had insisted was the only proper platform for the new instrument. Not that she actually liked using it herself; they had an agreement that Watson would normally pick up the receiver.

'No, I didn't. My apologies, Mrs Hobbs. Who was it?'

'Mr Holmes.' She said this with studied neutrality.

What, again? Watson looked at the wall clock. It was three in the afternoon and already Holmes had telephoned him four – perhaps even five – times that day, on each occasion repeating some trivial news about having a new water tank fitted at his cottage or some such. Watson had to admit that, to his shame and chagrin, he had taken to drifting off while his friend rattled on about such inconsequential trivia. Especially if it involved bees.

'Is he still on the line?' Watson asked.

'I expect so. He said it was important. He did sound agitated, sir.'

It was always important. And he was always agitated. Watson

glanced outside at the lazily eddying wall of fog, the phantom stench of chlorine still prickling his nose. The senses were no longer to be trusted these days. Neither, sadly, could his old companion be relied upon for coherence.

'If you would be so kind as to tell him I'm with a patient.'

Mrs Hobbs pursed her lips at the thought of uttering an untruth, and closed the door after her.

Watson sat down in his chair and opened the drawer containing a tin of Dr Hammond's Nerve and Brain Tablets, which the salesman had assured him cured men's 'special diseases' arising from war service. He replaced the tin unopened, lit a cigarette and felt the friendly smoke calm him. His statement to Mrs Hobbs had not been a total lie. He did have a patient for company. Himself.

A nagging little voice was hammering away inside, though, even as he enjoyed the tobacco warming his lungs. It was that Holmes telephone call. It was like the Retired Detective Who Cried Wolf.

What if one day it really was something important?

TWO

Miss Nora Pillbody had cycled for a good two miles through the Suffolk countryside before she realized exactly what had been niggling at her.

The day had begun like any normal school-day morning. After a breakfast of porridge, she had loaded her basket with the work she had marked and corrected overnight, and set off from her cottage in plenty of time to take registration. As always, she wondered what excuses would deplete her class that morning – 'So-and-so isn't here, miss, because he needs to help with sheep shearing/haymaking/de-horning the calves/irrigating the potatoes.' There was always something happening on the land that took priority over mere learning.

Once out of the dead-end lane that housed her cottage, her route took her past Cyril Jefford's farm, skirted Marsham Wood, with its shy herd of roe deer, in a long, lazy loop, before she took the old drovers' track that pierced the Morlands' property. This cut a good half-mile off the journey, even if it was a bone-rattling surface, baked dry by the early summer sun. The Morlands had eight children, including three in her school class. With two older boys already in the army and one just eligible for conscription, it was a nervous time for the family.

Miss Pillbody ducked through the shifting, pointillist clouds of midges blocking her way and found time to admire a flash of iridescent green dragonfly, and a Red Admiral warming its spread wings on a fence post. A sparrowhawk hovered expectantly above a cornfield, beady-eyed for potential prey.

She was a few hundred yards from the low, flint-built schoolhouse when it hit her what had been amiss throughout that whole morning's ride. The children. There hadn't been any. Her ears had been full of the calls of skylarks and the rougher cadences of the restless crows, underpinned by the creaking and cracking of the wheat and the buzz of passing bees, but not the usual babble of conversation as her pupils made their way to her schoolhouse.

She had not had to stop to tell Freddie Cox to stop flicking Ben Stone's ear, or coax poor, cleft-lipped Sidney Drayton down from a tree as he indulged in his favourite pastime: spotting and logging the planes taking off and landing at the RFC aerodrome. Or chivy along the Branton sisters, three pretty, startlingly blonde siblings, a year between them in age, always with arms linked as if they were a single child facing the world. With their vile father, mind, it wasn't surprising they needed a united front. Or what about lonely little Victoria Hanson, trudging down the road, feet dragging, trailing an air of melancholy behind her, all big sighs

11

and even bigger eyes that appeared to be perpetually on the brink of leaking?

Where had all the children gone?

She felt a curdling in her stomach as if she had eaten something unpleasant, and her head swam with a sensation akin to vertigo. She had last felt this when the telegram about Arnold, her brother, had arrived. Her mother had passed the brown envelope to Miss Pillbody and she had handed it back, unwilling to be the first to read the news. In the end, they had opened it – and wept – in unison.

He had been nineteen, a full ten years younger than she, when a trench mortar had dropped a shell on him, the baby of the family. He was, she had realized much later, unexpected by her parents, but they had made out he was the son that, after three girls, they had always longed for. People had said Nora and Arnold were very alike, but she couldn't see it. The grief of his death had chased her away from Chichester to the Suffolk countryside, to teaching the children of the estate and the surrounding villages, trying to blank out the war and what it was doing to millions of young men like Arnold.

It wasn't only the children who were absent. By now she should have seen a dozen or more people on the farms. In summer, Mrs Dottington always leaned on the gate after she had collected the eggs from her henhouses, enjoying the sun on her face. Old 'Zulu' Jenkins, veteran of the South African wars, ninety if he was a day, was normally out in the fields, helping – or just as often hindering – his son Johnnie. If not, he'd be sitting on a stump, taking a pipe. And then there were the nameless workers who would pause and doff a cap to her as she rode by.

All nowhere to be seen.

The area outside the schoolhouse was also empty of children, who by now would usually be playing marbles or jacks, or gossiping and sniping. An ad hoc game of boys' football or cricket, perhaps; hopscotch or skipping rhymes from the girls. But apart from a car she didn't recognize, parked across the entrance, the playground was deserted.

She dismounted from her bike, leaned it against the wall and examined the vehicle. She didn't know much about the various makes of car, but from its drab paintwork and stencilled numbers on the bonnet sides, even she could tell it was military in origin.

Miss Pillbody undid the ribbon under her chin and removed her hat before she stepped inside the little vestibule of the school-house.

'Hello?' she asked tentatively. 'Who's there?'

'Come in, please,' came the reply. Inviting her into her own schoolhouse. *The cheek of it.*

She opened the door and stepped through into the classroom, chairs still up on desks from the previous night, the six times table chalked on the board, because she had promised her pupils they would be doing it again first thing.

There were two men in the room, one standing next to the blackboard, the other perched on the corner of her desk. The one on his feet was older, his moustache almost white, a corporal of the new Home Service Defence Forces, who were ubiquitous in the towns and villages of Suffolk and East Anglia. The one seated was an officer, as proclaimed by the gleam on his boots and the swagger stick in his hand. He was square of jaw and dark of moustache, prob-ably a good few years younger than she. *Striking-looking*, she thought, but with a cruel aspect to his mouth and sharp blue eyes that shone with a glacial coolness. His top lip was a smidgeon too thin, she decided, for him to be entirely handsome, but he was certainly attractive. And, she suspected, he knew it. The officer stood and scooped off his cap as she crossed towards the pair.

'Miss Pillbody.'

So he had her name. 'You have the advantage of me, Lieutenant . . .?'

'Booth. Lieutenant James Booth, from the Elveden Explosives Area.' His eyes ran over her, making her feel uncomfortable. 'I must say I was expecting someone older.'

She was in no mood for flirtatious flattery. 'Where are my children, Lieutenant Booth?'

The grin faded to something more sombre. 'They won't be coming to school today, Miss Pillbody.'

'And why not?'

'In fact,' he said, the pink tip of his tongue touching his top lip for a second as he hesitated, 'they won't be coming to school for the foreseeable future, I'm afraid.'

A multitude of possibilities rattled through her mind – were they recruiting children for the war? Was it a disease quarantine? Evacuation because of the Zeppelins? – but none made any sense. 'And why not?'

'I can't say. But we have extended the quarantine zone around Elveden. All the tenant farmers are being relocated for the duration, and the children are going with them.'

'Duration of what?' she pressed. In fact, there was only one week of school left before the holidays, but she wasn't going to let that assuage her indignation.

'I can't say.'

She looked at his uniform, searching for regimental badges, but could spot none. Wasn't that unusual? She wished she had paid more attention to such matters. 'Who are you with, Lieutenant? Which regiment?'

A tight-lipped smile silently repeated his previous statement. Those chill eyes told her not to pursue the matter.

'These children need schooling, you know. A good proportion still can't read or write—'

'All that has been taken into consideration. They will be well looked after where they are going.'

'And where is that? No, don't tell me. You can't say.' She could feel anger rising in her, the sort that bubbled up when she had to deal with locals who told her that their young daughter was going to marry at sixteen and be a farmer's wife and had no need of any further schooling. 'You have no right to do this—'

'But I have,' said Booth, his manner suddenly abrupt. He reached into his top pocket and brought out a folded sheet of paper. 'I have every right under the Defence of the Realm Act. You actually live just outside the new exclusion zone, so you can keep your cottage, but after today you will not be allowed anywhere on the estate until further notice.'

'But—'

'And if you do set foot on the estate, or indeed mention anything that has happened to you today, or speak to any of the locals about this or any subsequent events, you will be prosecuted under this Act.' He unfurled the sheet of paper and shook it threateningly. 'I'm sorry we didn't reach you before you made the journey here, but there has been a lot to do. I suggest you return home to your cottage now. You will be compensated financially, of course, for loss of salary. Perhaps you should go back to your parents in Chichester. I am sure you can find a young man who will snap you up.'

She was furious at both the crass remark and the fact that he had been peering into her life. 'There is more to life than finding a young man.'

Booth raised an eyebrow.

'And there is no appeal against this?'

'None, I am afraid.' He put on his cap. The matter was closed.

He indicated to his driver they were leaving. 'Look on the bright side, Miss Pillbody. Your holiday has come a little early.'

She could think of nothing to say, although she wanted to stamp her foot and wail at him. 'Very well. But I intended to run summer art classes here—'

'Cancelled,' said Booth, bluntly.

'And if I need anything from the schoolhouse at a later date?'

The lieutenant and his corporal exchanged glances. When he looked back at her she felt something icy on her neck and the hairs prickled to attention. 'I'd make sure you take everything you need today. If you come back here, Miss Pillbody, you will be shot on sight.'

THREE

The editor's eyes widened when he saw the person standing before him. 'Next!' he had called and into his office had marched a remarkable sight, a woman, all red hair and leather, dressed as if she were about to tackle the hill climb at La Turbie. Her face – striking enough, but frumpled with fatigue, it seemed to him – showed the dusty outline of goggles. She had clearly ridden a motor bike to the offices of *Motor Cycle Gazette*.

She took off her gloves and held out her hand. 'Mrs Georgina Gregson.'

He took it. 'Daniel Samson.'

'Really?' The editor was in his forties, balding rapidly, with rheumy eyes and protruding teeth. He looked nothing like the lantern-jawed motor cyclists he liked to portray in his publication. This was hardly surprising, as he didn't actually ride himself.

'Yes. Really. How can I help you, Mrs Gregson?'

She unbuttoned her coat as she sat down and took from an inside pocket a cutting clipped from *Motor Cycle Gazette*. 'I have come about this advertisement.' She placed the scrap on the blotter in front of him.

He examined it for a second before he burst out laughing.

'What is so amusing?' she asked.

'You have been outside in the corridor for some time?'

'Yes.'

'So you have seen your fellow applicants?'

She looked over her shoulder, as if the door were transparent. There were, indeed, several others who had answered the same advertisement, although few as qualified as she was, she suspected. 'Indeed.'

'And did you notice anything about them, Mrs Gregson?'

'Well, for the most part, their hands are too clean.'

This wasn't the answer he was expecting. 'I beg your pardon?'

'Some of the fingernails are too clean; they've never touched an engine in their lives. Some are just too smooth. The palms and fingers, I mean. Not a callus between them. No manual work of any description, I fear. There is a chap out there called Collins I spoke to. He's a likely one. Look at his knuckles. He's used a spanner or two.'

'Ah, my point exactly. He's a chap. And you aren't.'

'How terribly observant of you, Mr Samson,' Mrs Gregson replied coolly.

'The position is open only to men.'

She pointed at the advertisement. 'It doesn't say that.'

'It does.'

'No, it doesn't, Mr Samson,' she almost growled.

He snatched up the advertisement and read it. 'It says: "As part of important war work, we are looking for persons with mechanical and engineering skills, preferably with a knowledge of petrol engines and motor cycles." See?'

Mrs Gregson leaned forward. 'No, I don't see. Where does it say "Men only"?'

Samson gave an exaggerated sigh. 'It says "persons".'

'I'm a person,' she said. 'Ask anyone.'

He pushed back in his chair. He wanted this bothersome woman gone. He knew her sort. They did have a page in the magazine penned by 'Motorcyclatrix', who was really Lady Rose Penney, but that was just a sop to the ladies who wrote in complaining that their sex was under-represented in the pages. Mrs Gregson was no doubt one of those who wanted to feminize the pursuit. If they had their way, the sport would become the motorized arm of *The Lady*.

'Well, it's obvious we aren't talking about women. Knowledge of petrol engines . . .'

'I drove ambulances for a year at the front, Mr Samson. I can strip down a Daimler as quickly as the next person. I have rebuilt my Rudge twice. Would you like to inspect my fingernails?' She thrust her hand forward.

'That won't be necessary, Mrs Gregson. Look, I admire you for wanting to do war work. But there is much you can contribute in other fields. You drove ambulances, you say? What about becoming a nurse? Pretty woman like you—'

'I'm done with that,' she snapped. She didn't feel inclined to offer any further explanation as to why she hoped never to see the inside of a hospital ward – or an ambulance – ever again. Like many medical staff who had been at the front, it was the sounds and smells that stayed with her. It seemed the brain could somehow consign the images of the mangled and the dying to some dark recess. But a loud bang would make the heart race, as if it heralded an artillery barrage, and even the most innocuous of scents was sometimes transformed by a mysterious alchemy into the tang of carbolic and the sweet decay of flesh.

'I can't help you, Mrs Gregson.'

She was exasperated now. 'But I understand engines, Mr Samson. I love motor cycles—'

'I'm sorry. My hands are tied.'

'Why? Because of my gender?'

'It doesn't help matters,' he said, a smirk flickering under his moustache.

She stood and buttoned up her Dunhill coat, her fingers shaking with barely suppressed fury. 'Well, we'll see, won't we? I shall find out exactly what is required for this war work and make damned sure' – she paused to enjoy Mr Samson's flinch at the profanity – 'that I get a bash at it.'

With this she turned on her heel and left the room, making sure the door nearly burst through the frame as she slammed it behind her.

Samson picked up the receiver of the Kellogg Interoffice phone and pressed 'Call'.

'Shall I send the next one in?' asked Mrs Beasley at the other end.

'Is it a male?'

'Yes. I'm very sorry about that woman, Mr Samson. I did warn her, but she was most . . . insistent.'

'Not to worry, Mrs Beasley.' He was certain that his secretary was no match for that flame-haired harridan. 'But ask the next candidate to wait a second, will you?'

He opened the drawer of his desk and took out a notebook. He quickly found the emergency number he had been given by the government department that was using his paper to recruit the 'mechanically minded'.

Samson hesitated. The woman might just be full of hot air. If she wanted to do her bit, she could always get a job on the omnibuses. Perhaps he should have suggested that. And yet, she didn't strike him as one who would flit like a butterfly from project to project. More like a terrier that would worry at a bone until it was splinters.

He glanced at the page of the notebook with the telephone number on it. Samson's hand had been shaking when he scribbled it down but it was still legible. Mrs Beasley would have made this Mrs Gregson fill in a contact form, so her address would be out there on her desk. Therefore, he could tell the man at the other end of the telephone where she lived if need be. What would he do to her? Put the fear of God into her probably. As he had Samson.

'Report anyone suspicious,' the dour man had said. 'Or who might cause trouble.' What was the expression he had used? 'On pain of death', that was it. *Call us, no matter how trivial, on pain of death.* A figure of speech. Wasn't it? Although the portly little man who had delivered it hadn't looked or acted like someone who used words frivolously. Mr Grover, he had called himself. A 'servant of the government' was all he would offer by way of identification. The mere memory of those eyes of his, fish-cold, projecting a not-so-veiled threat, made Samson's mouth dry.

For a second he almost felt sorry for Mrs Gregson. But self-preservation was the stronger instinct. He picked up the telephone and waited for the operator. Whitehall 0101. Once he made the call to that number, Mrs Gregson would no longer be his problem.

*

Major Watson's patient was sitting at one end of the gymnasium, which was located in the wing of the former school, now designated a 'special' ward. The doctor stood in the doorway, a nurse hovering one step behind him, and he took some time to observe the soldier before he made his presence felt. The young man, a captain, was dressed in pale blue overalls, which marked him out, so he had heard a nurse say, as 'one of the barmy ones'.

He was at a table, looking down at it, as if reading a newspaper in a library, but there was nothing to be seen other than scuffs and scratches in the wood. Whatever he could see on that surface was visible only to the captain. The man's right leg was pistoning up and down, and his upper body was folded in upon itself, arms crossed over chest, hands gripping the opposite bicep, the whole torso rocking back and forth almost imperceptibly. There was noise, too, a hum from the back of the throat, low and constant, as if he was trying to block out some other sound.

The doctor knew from the notes that the lad had suffered from ataxia, the inability to move, a total paralysis with no physical cause anyone could discern. There was also aphasia, the loss of speech. He also knew that, in a strange way, he was responsible for this boy's condition.

Just seven months previously, in the trenches of France, Watson had helped make the captain a hero, a burden that had led the lad to this 'special' unit in Wandsworth Hospital, designed to deal with those who had been damaged by the war in ways the authorities were only just beginning to grasp. The captain had been variously classified as 'emotional' or 'Not Yet Diagnosed (Nervous)'. Neither truly suggested the severity, or strangeness, of symptoms such a broken man could display. The machinery of war had not killed this one, just chewed him up in its fearsome, unrelenting cogs.

The doctor turned to the nurse at his shoulder. 'I'll be fine by myself.'

'Are you sure, Major?' the nurse asked.

'Captain Fairley and I are old friends.'

20

At that moment the damaged man looked over at him, the head wobbling as if on a spring as it turned. He stared across the scuffed parquet floor of the gymnasium at the figure standing in the doorway, but there was no recognition in the gaze. Just another quack, he would be thinking – if he was thinking at all, the doctor appreciated – with his damn-fool questions and exhortations to pull himself together.

'Hello, Captain Fairley,' Watson said, his voice thin in the cavernous space.

There was no reaction from the patient.

'Mind if I join you?'

The slap of his leather soles on the wooden floor sounded like timpani as he crossed to the table, where an empty chair faced the soldier. He pulled it out and asked permission to sit. When there was no response, he did so anyway. Then he waited.

'Congratulations on the promotion,' he said eventually.

Fairley still studied the desk. When they had met, Fairley had been a mere second lieutenant. Then he had saved Watson's life out in no man's land. Good news from the front was in short supply, so Fairley's story had grown in the telling and retelling. Percival Philips of the *Express* had written about 'The Unsung Hero Of No Man's Land', making sure he was unsung no more, and Reuters had gone with with 'Angel of Mud'. There was a medal. In the months since his brave action, Fairley had become something of an expert on that blasted strip of land between the lines, and had been transferred to an intelligence role and promoted. But while mapping 'the wire' and the German forward trenches, something had happened to Fairley out there, reducing him to this palsied wreck.

'Captain, you do remember me, don't you?' he asked. 'Major Watson. Dr Watson, as was. We met near Plug Street.'

A jolt ran through the man, as if he had been subjected to the electrotherapy that they administered to the worst of the shell-shocked. Watson saw life flicker in the eyes.

'You recall that night?'

'Aye. Major Watson, is it?' Fairley repeated, with an intonation that bore no resemblance to the one he had used when Watson had last talked to him. Then, he had spoken with the cultured, educated tones of a Wykehamist, an alumnus of Winchester College. This voice sounded . . . well, it sounded Scottish.

'Yes, Captain. You've had a pretty rough—'

He didn't get to finish the sentence. With a newfound agility, Fairley leaped, panther-like, across the table, and Watson crashed backwards to the floor under the momentum of the flying body, thumping his head on the wood. Watson's vision tunnelled as he felt the weight of the man on his chest, squeezing his lungs, and, a second later, the long, bony fingers of a madman closing around his throat.

FOUR

Rumours were swirling around London like particles from a dust storm. The wind blew particularly strongly through the HQ of the Foreign Press Association, which was based in a grand town house just off St James's Square. Bradley Ross stood at the FPA's bar, beneath the gilded ceiling, hoping some of the nuggets of gossip circulating in the room might lodge about his person. He needed a good story, soon, or they would pull him back to New York. He didn't want to go just yet. His father was still smoothing feathers ruffled by his incident with the young caddie at the golf club. All sorts of dire retribution had been promised, but, as always, money did the trick. A few more months and it would all be forgotten. Meanwhile, he needed that story.

It shouldn't be difficult. There was a war on, after all. Yet the British were spinning out so much red tape and baffling obfuscation, he felt like he was drowning in lies and half-truths and, in some cases, sheer fantasy.

'You going to the dinner tonight?'

Ross turned to see an unfamiliar face. 'The Savoy? No.'

It was a charity event, men only, and Ross knew it would be dominated by Gabriel de Wesselitzsky, the flamboyant president of the FPA and a man who was, Ross felt, in the pocket of the British. He could think of better ways to spend the ten shillings that the dinner would cost.

'I'm sorry,' said Ross. He prided himself on never forgetting a face but he could not quite place this one. It belonged to a hefty fellow in his thirties, with broad shoulders, blond hair and a wide, friendly face. He was in full evening dress, with a striking emerald shirt stud that flashed and flickered in the light. 'You're with . . .?'

'Movietone. Dirk Alberts.'

Ross thought he might have misheard. 'Dick, was it?'

'Dirk. Dutch.'

The Dutch were neutral, but Ross felt they leaned towards the British side. 'Bradley Ross, *New York Herald*.' They shook hands. 'A camera jockey, eh? You're the guys who are going to put us scribblers out of business?'

Alberts laughed. 'Only when people can carry a movie projector in their pocket. And only then if they ever let us near the war. You need a letter from God countersigned by Haig. So I've been sent here to sniff out a good news story on the Home Front.'

'Find any?'

Ross recognized the little shuffle of feet and the tensing of the body. Alberts' shoulders tightened up towards his ears just a little. Yeah, this guy had a story. But he wasn't going to blab.

'Sorry, dumb of me to ask. Buy you a drink?'

Alberts met Ross's direct gaze. 'Thank you. A Van der Hum and soda.'

Ross whistled up the liqueur and an Old Jamaica for himself from the white-jacketed barman.

'What about you?' Alberts asked.

'Much like yourself. Can't get permission to get close to anything juicy. British got it all sewn up. They got five official war correspondents – why do they need some Yank blundering around telling the truth?'

All five – plus a few special correspondents like John Buchan – allowed their work to be supervised and censored by the British Government. Ross's newspaper wouldn't countenance that.

Alberts swilled his drink around the glass. 'I did hear of one thing that's interesting. Here. In England. Something big.'

'You keep it,' said Ross, feigning disinterest with a wave of his hand. 'Don't tell me anything you might regret.'

Alberts took a large mouthful of his liqueur. 'This isn't a movie-camera type of story. The thing about us lot, we are hardly inconspicuous, are we? You know, a guy with a script and another turning the handle of some big, black box. You don't get undercover cameramen.'

'I guess not.'

'You only need a notebook to get your story. I need a ton of equipment.'

Ross nodded. It was one advantage of the printed word over the moving picture. 'You're making me feel a lot better about newspapers,' he said.

'I think there is room for us both,' said Alberts. 'We are in the same game, just different ways of presenting it. I think this one is on your side of the pitch.'

Ross drank some of his rum. He examined the Dutchman closely, sniffed at his cologne. Was it really only professional companionship he was after? The green of his emerald stud seemed to glow brighter by the minute. Was the choice of colour an accident? Perhaps, as a foreigner, he did not know what it symbolized, in both London and New York. 'So what is it, Dirk? This story.'

The Dutchman gave a sly smirk. 'Just a rumour. No, not even that. A whisper.'

'A whisper of what?'

Alberts leaned in close, and Ross felt the hot, alcohol-laden breath on his ear. 'Something very hush-hush.'

'Where? Here in London?'

'Suffolk, so I am told.'

'Suffolk. Interesting. And would you like to tell me more? Over dinner, perhaps?' Ross asked, his hand coming down on the bar within a half-inch of the Dutchman's. The film man didn't pull away, just stared down at it, wondering if he was interpreting the signals correctly.

'Once we've got to know each other a little better, perhaps,' Alberts ventured cautiously, knocking back his liqueur and bringing the glass down so that their knuckles touched. 'Dinner sounds like a good idea.'

'What about the gathering at the Savoy?' asked Ross, aware of a thrumming in his temple.

Alberts laughed and touched the emerald stud, twirling it between forefinger and thumb. He knew what it meant, all right – that they both belonged to a forbidden fraternity. 'Oh, don't worry, we'll manage somehow.'

Georgina Gregson came clattering down the steps of her lodgings, thanking the Lord that changes in fashion meant skirts no longer had to drag along the ground and so trip you up when descending stairs at speed. As she reached the pavement, the motor taxi standing at the kerb flipped its flag to 'For Hire'. Luck was on her side.

She had a ticket for Sir Henry Wood's 'Promenade Preview' at the Queen's Hall in Langham Place. The last time she had attended one of his concerts, the audience had booed at the inclusion of Beethoven and Wagner, but Sir Henry had won the dissenters round with an impassioned plea that great art transcended national boundaries. This time, though, it was a very safe programme – Ravel, Debussy, Vaughan Williams and Elgar, an Anglo-French musical alliance.

She had bought only a single ticket because she found it easier to lose herself at a concert when she was alone, not having to worry about whether a piece was too modern, or indeed too German, for a companion.

She shouted the address of the hall to the cabby and hitched her skirt as she stepped into the back. It was only when she was most of the way inside that she realized that the rear seat was already occupied.

'Oh, I'm sorry,' she began. 'I thought—'

'Close the door, Mrs Gregson,' said the man, who remained pressed into the corner shadows.

Before she could react, a rough shove pushed her into the interior and the door slammed behind her.

'What is going on? How do you know my name? How dare—'

'You don't recall me, do you, Mrs Gregson?' He leaned forward as he said this, pushing a pink and hairless face into the evening light. 'Grover. Sergeant, as was. Might have added a few pounds since then.' He slapped a stretched waistcoat. 'I knew your husband. Remember you when you were the Red Devil.' He shook his head. 'Never change, do you, you lot? Always causing trouble. Knew it as soon as I saw your name.'

By 'you lot' she assumed the corpulent little man meant suffragettes, of which she had been proud to call herself one. And no, she had no recollection of him at all. She had tried to purge those nightmare months from her memory. The 'Red Devil' had been the gutter press's favourite nickname for her when she had been falsely accused of trying to murder the Prime Minister.

'I'm not sitting here listening to this.' Mrs Gregson turned to open the door but came face to face through the glass with the scowling, bewhiskered face of an aged constable, stooping down and holding the exterior handle so she couldn't move it. When she slumped back in the seat, Grover thrust a piece of paper at her.

'I am detaining you under the Defence of the Realm Act, Mrs Gregson.'

She slapped the document away. 'Really? On what grounds?'

'On the grounds that you have imperilled national security by sticking your nose in where it was not required and then kicking up a stink about it.' He gave a rap on the partition and the cab moved off.

Mrs Gregson racked her brains as to what she had done recently that could possibly—

'Is this about that *Motor Cycle Gazette* advertisement?'

Grover sucked air through his teeth, a thoroughly unpleasant sound. 'There you go again. It would be best if you said nothing until the tribunal.'

'Tribunal? What tribunal?' The word conjured up anonymous bureaucrats in dingy rooms deciding her fate with no recourse to judge, jury or lawyers. She felt a small twinge of apprehension. She knew only too well how the machinations of the legal system could swallow a person whole, even in peacetime. And they were a long way from the days of Habeas Corpus.

'Where are you taking me?' she demanded as the cab gathered speed.

'Somewhere,' said Grover with the hint of a smile, 'where you will feel right at home.'

She could tell what he meant by the amused twinkle in his eyes and she had to fight hard not to give him the satisfaction of tears. They were taking her back to Holloway Prison.

PART TWO

11–15 AUGUST 1916

FIVE

Percy Littlewood finished loading the wooden vegetable crates into the Warwick three-wheeler delivery van a little after eight and set off for the twenty-minute drive through the Suffolk lanes to the Elveden Explosives Area. It was rare for a civilian to have any contact with the requisitioned estate, and over the past few weeks the grocer had learned not to ask any questions and to keep his mouth shut. What they were doing behind the trees was no business of his.

Even in The Plough, when the topic of Elveden inevitably came up and wild speculations began to gain credence with every pint consumed and eyes swivelled towards him, he simply shrugged. He was earning good money delivering food and supplies, enough that he wasn't going to throw it away with idle gossip. He'd seen what happened to them that did let their tongues wag. No, this was a lucrative business, for him at least.

It meant that if the arrangement went on much longer, he could afford to ask Lizzie Cosford for her hand in marriage. Twenty years younger than he she might be, but he suspected the modern woman couldn't afford to be too fussy. A lot of lads Lizzie's own age wouldn't be coming home and, if they weren't careful, England would become a country of spinsters. The newspapers were already full of adverts from desperate young ladies, their fiancés slaughtered in France or Belgium, offering to marry and care for the blinded or the maimed.

There was no traffic on the road and Percy made good time, reaching the entrance to the Explosives Area in just over a quarter of an hour. He stopped at the barrier and the sergeant with the lazy eye went through the motions of looking in the back of the van to make sure he wasn't smuggling anybody in and then waved him on with a warning to unload at the usual place, where he could pick up the order for next Tuesday.

He ran the three-wheeler in low gear down the road that led to the Hall's tree-lined driveway but, as he always did, he yanked at the tiller and pulled off to one side before that palatial building came into sight.

'You'd think they could spare some of those blighters to give a hand unloading,' Percy muttered. But it was always a solitary job, probably in case he engaged any of the soldiers in conversation. He killed the motor and stepped out into an early morning silence. He didn't like the place. He always felt as if eyes were watching him from the undergrowth. Sometimes he caught movement among the trees, heard the snap of a twig or the drift of conversation and laughter, even though he knew the billets were on the other side of the estate. It gave him the willies.

Littlewood quickly unloaded the crates of produce, slipped his bill in the uppermost wooden crate and gave a little laugh. What he was charging them was well worth suffering a dose of the willies twice a week. Then he fetched the sheaf of papers that had been left for him in a wooden box nailed to one of the old oaks. He executed a neat three-point turn and drove back through the barrier, waving at the sergeant as he did so.

It was two miles down the road before he pulled in and examined the orders. As he had expected, there was an extra brown envelope in there, with the words 'Fresh Medical Supplies Required' written on it. Delivering that to Brenda at the post office in Thetford would be worth an extra ten bob, no questions asked.

The envelope, though, hadn't been sealed properly and he lifted it to his mouth to re-lick the gummed edge. And then hesitated. He looked in his door mirror to make sure he was alone on the stretch of road. He took out the piece of paper. It was indeed a list of medical supplies, written in a well-rounded hand.

Lint, seven rolls

Mentholated Balm, three tins

Rat Eradicator (Red Squill Compound)

Accident & Emergency (Surgeon's No. 7)

Gee's Linctus

Scrubb's Cloudy Ammonia (2 bottles)

Sanitary Towels, compressed (one box)

Enule Suppositories (two boxes)

The list went on for two pages. He could get half of the stuff from the chemist at Thetford, but no, this had to be sent to London. And it was something else he was meant to be quiet about. Ten bob, though. He'd swear black was white for that. And the money would go straight into the Lizzie Cosford marriage pot.

He checked the road was still clear, engaged the Warwick's first gear and drove towards the Thetford road.

Had Percy Littlewood been able to translate the code within that humdrum list, a cipher that had been painstakingly worked out between all parties, he might not have kept his mind on Lizzie. For in London, sharper eyes than Percy's would be able to tell that the cause of death of the seven men who died in the training accident was no closer to being solved and that the one survivor was still mute. And the final item, for a case of St Joshua's Tonic Wine to be express delivered – Joshua, one of the twelve scouts sent by Moses to explore Canaan, being the patron saint of spies – would be easily interpreted.

Send your own man in.

SIX

The eight gentlemen of the War Neuroses Committee had filed into the lecture theatre at Millbank and taken their seats, unsure of what they were about to witness. At the front of the hall, at a lectern, stood Major John H. Watson, in uniform, a wooden pointer in his hand. Behind him was a white screen used for lantern projection. Flanking it were several linen-backed hanging displays, each depicting an aspect of the human body – the individuals flayed to reveal the arterial, venous and lymphatic systems, the musculature or the nerve pathways. Next to the podium was a yellowy human skeleton, suspended from a metal stand by a hook in the skull.

Watson examined his audience. There were five officers from the Royal Army Medical Corps, including Crocker, the Deputy Director of Medical Services, and Lieutenant-Colonel Robert Armstrong Jones, Superintendent of Claybury Asylum, as well as three civilian specialists – two neurologists and a psychiatrist. The WNC had been hastily convened to answer questions that had arisen about the incidence of so-called battle neuroses and the treatment of the victims.

Watson felt remarkably under-qualified before them. The length of his own experience of the condition amounted to not much more than eight months. But, he reminded himself, he had one advantage over this illustrious body. Unlike them, he had peered into the dark pit that so many soldiers had fallen into. It was only by luck and good friends that he had not toppled in. But he had felt the tug of despair and anguish, like some dark, malevolent gravity. Only someone who had been to the front, or, like him, even further out into the cesspool of no man's land, could possibly hope to understand what the soldiers were going through, week after week and year after year.

The DDMS was the man to impress here. Watson stole a glance at him. Lieutenant-Colonel Percy Crocker – 'Jumbo' behind his back – was a big man in all departments, with ears you could rig and use as sails.

Once pipes and cigarettes had been lit, Watson cleared his throat. 'Thank you for coming, gentlemen. I hope I can make this worthwhile for you. As you know, I have no claim to be an expert on neurasthenics or psychiatry. I am, by training, a humble general practitioner.'

'Quite,' said one of the officers, as if this settled the matter. Watson moved on, ignoring his comment.

'However, I have had some first-hand experience of conditions on the front line. I have been underneath a bombardment. I say this without any sense of boasting or superiority.' He paused. He wasn't trying to make his audience feel inadequate. He knew Crocker had toured the battlefields, had witnessed barrages, but he was fairly sure the other members of the committee had never left the British Isles. 'It was my own experiences of the after-effects of exposure to modern warfare that led to my interest in the subject of war nerves.' He had to be careful not to say 'shell shock'. It was the deputy director sitting before him who had banned the phrase. 'I experienced nightmares, sudden changes of mood and unwarranted aggression, even towards old, trusted friends, and a withdrawal from the world. The symptoms lasted many weeks after my return home, yet I knew what I had was but a mild bout. When I recovered somewhat, I became concerned by the case of a young man I met out there at the front.'

Watson raised his voice and addressed the technician sitting in the back row of the theatre. 'If we can dim the lights . . .? Thank you.'

Blocks of ceiling bulbs thumped off in sequence, until the only illumination was the chinks of light bleeding around the edges of the blackout curtain and the reading lamp on the podium. Watson heard the audience shift in their seats in anticipation.

'If you will roll the film, please . . .'

The projector, hidden in the closet-like room that usually held the magic lantern, clanked and whirred into life, sending a smoke-laden beam to the front of the theatre. A bright square full of dancing squiggles appeared on the screen.

They were replaced by the image of an agitated man, seated in a bare room, apparently being pestered by an invisible swarm of bees, his arms flailing at thin air.

'This, gentleman, is Captain Fairley. A young man I first met in the trenches in Belgium, when he was a perfectly rational, upright and brave' – he emphasized this last word, pausing for effect – 'young man. This is him a few weeks after returning to England, having suffered a total nervous collapse after being trapped out in no man's land by a German advance and suffering bombardment from both sides, before he could make his own way back to the British lines. This was the second occasion he had been left isolated out there for an extended period. Once is enough for many men.'

He let them watch the tormented captain for a few moments longer, taking in the look on his face that suggested he was party to some invisible horror.

'This, believe it or not, is him after an improvement. Before this he had ataxia and was also prone to fits of violence.' Watson's hand moved to his throat of its own accord before he snatched it away. He thought it best not to mention the physical attack on his person by Fairley at their encounter. It had been a brief spike of rage and within moments Fairley had deflated like a punctured blimp.

'Watch.'

Fairley stood and, still batting at his aerial tormentors, he began to walk, showing the strange, disconnected gait that characterized many of the sufferers. He looked like a puppet whose strings had been cut, jerking and twisting as he struggled to take three or four steps. Watson could sense the discomfort from those watching. Even after a dozen viewings, Watson's own stomach knotted at the sight of the soldier.

The film ended with more squiggles, before it shut off. 'Lights, please,' said Watson.

The audience blinked as the hall was illuminated once more.

'Is that it?' asked Armstrong Jones. 'Has he progressed any further in his recovery?'

'Judge for yourselves. Gentlemen,' said Watson, 'I'd like you to meet Captain Fairley.'

The technician came down the stairs two at a time, a smile on his face, his hand outstretched to greet Watson. He took it and pumped it vigorously.

'I'm sorry for the s-s-subterfuge,' said Fairley, turning to the committee. 'B-b-but we thought it would show the progress I have m-m-made, thanks to Dr Watson.'

'Well, young man,' said Crocker, 'how do you feel now?'

'Better,' said Fairley.

'That is,' said Watson, quickly, 'better than he was. Captain Fairley won't mind me saying this, but he still has moments of . . . let's call it *fragility*.'

Fairley nodded his agreement.

'But, sooner or later, you'll be fit enough to return to the front?' asked Armstrong Jones. 'Not discharged to live on some pension?'

Fairley swallowed hard. 'I suppose—'

'I'm not sure the object of the exercise, the ultimate aim, is simply to return the shell—the damaged soldier to the front, is it?' asked Watson.

A few throats were cleared. 'This committee was set up with that purpose,' said Crocker. 'The number of cases of war neuroses is having a serious impact on manpower.'

'Really?' asked Watson, tetchily. He had to control his temper. 'I thought that was German machine guns. How many died on the 1st of July this year?'

Every man knew the answer to that. News had leaked out slowly about the scale of losses at the Battle of Albert, the first phase of the Somme offensive. But the number of telegrams delivered to families across the country told the story the newspapers wouldn't, at first, admit. Around 19,000 thousand killed, close to 60,000 casualties all told. And that was just day one. And just on one side.

'All the more reason,' said Armstrong Jones, 'for us to send back men who are not physically injured.'

'Ah, but they *are* injured,' said Professor Miller, one of the civilian doctors. He was a wiry man with a thick thatch of steel-grey hair and a mouth permanently tightened in disapproval.

'Exactly,' said Watson, brightening. 'Although not physically—'

'I disagree,' snapped Miller. 'Nearly all war neurosis is caused by damage to the peripheral nerves due to concussion and the carbon monoxide—'

Watson couldn't listen to such piffle. He banged the lectern. 'Excuse me, Professor Miller. That is nonsense. This man had no nerve damage.'

Miller began flexing his hands in the air, as if conducting a particularly intricate piece of music. 'But his walk, his co-ordination—'

'Was not due to physical damage.' Watson turned to Fairley. 'Could you just . . .'

The captain took four confident strides across the room, and the same number back.

'Damaged nerves do not recover like that. Not in this time scale. Would you agree?'

'It's impressive,' agreed Miller, albeit reluctantly.

'What we could not capture in the film is Captain Fairley's voice. Like many patients suffering from war nerves, he began to speak in an entirely alien accent. In his case, Scottish.'

Fairley blushed and studied his feet.

'Scottish?' asked Miller.

'We think that is part of the flight syndrome,' said Watson. 'Of trying to inhabit another body, any body, that might not possess the same memories. One of the captain's first physicians was a Scot. When Fairley left that hospital, he took the man's accent with him.'

'So, Captain Fairley,' said Crocker, 'let's clear this up once and for all. Do you foresee a day when you can return to active service?'

Watson saw the ripple of a twitch spread up one cheek and noted the clenched fist. He knew what that indicated. A sudden flash of memory – often visual, sometimes auditory or olfactory – of the trenches and no man's land had bubbled up, like gas from a flooded shell hole.

'I h-h-hope to be able to serve my country again, yes.'

If any of the committee spotted the evasion, they gave no sign.

'Good man,' said the DDMS with a series of approving nods. 'Good man.'

Watson spoke through gritted teeth. 'Gentlemen, I can't help thinking we are seeing this from different perspectives. We are doing something terrible to our young men, something not widely recognized before this war. We should be concerned about returning them to life, not returning them to that . . .' – he pointed as if the front were just beyond the wall behind him – 'hell out there, to be shot and gassed all over again.'

An uncomfortable silence fell over his audience. Watson realized he had shouted the last sentence. He adjusted his tie.

'Next film, please, Fairley,' he instructed.

'Sir.' The captain, glad to be out of the limelight, bounded up the stairs and entered the projection box again.

'Are you going to share the secret,' asked Professor Miller, his tone more conciliatory, 'of how you achieved such results, Major Watson?'

Watson pointed to the stack of paper on a table near the door. He licked his lips and kept his voice level. 'There are the case notes, which you can browse at your leisure. The fact is that this neurosis is not fixed in its manifestations, but rather is different in every victim. What they have in common is intense shame, anxiety, exhaustion, hatred of the enemy and fear. There is a loneliness, because he has absented himself from his comrades, and a crushing sense of failure to do his duty. And, most importantly, there is the loss of his sense of being a man. This isn't due to weak nerves or a predisposition to the condition.' He caught the eye of Dr Jacobs, a man with a face made up of a series of baggy pouches, who had written extensively on inherent character traits that meant one soldier suffered war shock while his comrade seemed immune. 'In fact, such a syndrome was described in the American Civil War, which in many ways was the first modern conflict, with rail-mounted mortars and primitive machine guns. And Russian officers displayed symptoms of what their German doctors called *Kriegsneurosen* in the war with Japan.'

'Your Captain Fairley was, though, what I would classify as a sensitive type, I think you will agree,' said Jacobs, who had a reputation, along with his mentor, Sir John Collie, as an expert in malingering.

Watson raised his eyebrows and his voice. 'Play the film, please.'

'One moment, Major Watson,' interrupted Crocker. 'Who exactly made the moving pictures of these subjects?'

'A Pathé cameraman.'

'Pathé?' Crocker sounded genuinely alarmed. 'I do hope such images will not be part of the Animated Gazette at the picture palaces any time soon, Major? Think of morale. People might assume this is in some way normal.'

'Charles Pathé is an old friend,' Watson said. Actually, Charles Pathé was an old client of Holmes's, only too happy to lend assistance. 'The films belong to me. There are no copies.'

'Very well,' grunted Crocker, mollified. 'Continue.'

It was a similar performance to the first: a badly damaged man trying to perform simple tasks, buttoning up his shirt, tying his shoelaces, and collapsing in frustration at the enormity of the problem. He then began to walk, but with each step he ducked or swerved, sometimes dropping to the floor for a second, before springing up again. He was dodging imaginary bullets and shells. The final image was of the soldier prone once more, hands over his head, waiting for the phantom barrage to pass.

'This is Corporal Donnelly. Also a Wykehamist, like Fairley. As you know, Winchester College is very well represented among the officer class. But Donnelly preferred to enter the army in the ranks, rather than as an officer. He joined the Royal Irish Rifles and was on day one of the Somme. Under heavy fire, he rescued three wounded colleagues and then went back to destroy the machine-gun position that had killed so many of his comrades, which he did, with Mills bombs and then rifle. There are those who think he deserves a Victoria Cross. I doubt, Dr Jacobs, whether this man was a sensitive type. If he was, we could do with a few thousand more of them, perhaps.'

'It looks like False Evacuation Syndrome to me,' said Jacobs, sniffily. This was his own invention, the idea that a psychological condition, akin to shirking one's duty, could be feigned in order to get back to Blighty. He considered it the new equivalent of chewing cordite to mimic a heart condition and that it was contagious among 'weak-willed' units of the New Army. 'This is just a pantomime act.'

'It didn't raise much of a smile when I was in the audience,' countered Watson.

'And now?' Crocker asked. 'Where is the patient now?'

'Lights,' instructed Watson, as the short film flicked to an end. 'Donnelly was "other ranks",' he continued, careful not to snarl at the committee. 'Not for him the country rest home or the "special" wing. No, he was sent to a "restoration" unit at Netley Hospital, where they live in tin huts and are subject to military discipline, starting with full kit inspection at six thirty in the morning, with route marches, drill and mock combat, all designed, so I was told, to help them "rediscover their masculinity". His family sent him regular parcels of Dr Hartmann's Antineurasthin, which he drank in great quantities. And which, as you know, contains little more than egg white and alcohol. I did intend to bring Corporal Donnelly along today.'

'But?'

Again, Watson found himself fighting to keep a level tone. 'But he hanged himself two days ago.'

The silence was filled by the ticking of the clock at the rear of the hall. 'Ah. That is tragic. But what is your point, Watson?' asked Crocker.

Time to be reasonable, Watson decided. 'We need a different approach to these afflictions, especially for the other ranks. Charles Myers has done some good work in this area.' There was a harrumph from one of the audience. Myers was the army's Specialist in Nervous Shock, and he, too, was beginning to think the 'robust' approach to shell shock was counterproductive. 'These men need to see their family, their sweethearts, to be given constructive work. Not told over and over again how they are no longer men or soldiers.'

The door to the lecture theatre opened and an orderly put his head in. 'Major Watson, my apologies. I am afraid you have visitors.'

'Not now, man!' boomed Crocker. The orderly flinched, reddened, but stood his ground.

'I have a few more minutes,' said Watson, in more modulated tones.

'They say they can't wait. It's about Dora, they said.'

Not Dora. Watson tried to ignore the stab of alarm. Dora was one woman you didn't want leaving a calling card at your door. DORA. The Defence of the Realm Act.

'Will you excuse me, gentlemen?' He pointed at the table once more. 'There are the notes that you might like to look at until I return.'

They were sitting in the foyer of the building, both smoking. The tall, rangy Irishman with the freckled and flinty features and the portly ex-sapper. Coyle and Gibson. Vernon Kell's so-called 'scallywags'. Part of what Watson had known as the Secret Service Bureau, then MO5, and now, for the past few months, MI5. This unlikely duo were secret agents.

Gibson threw down his cigarette and stamped on it. 'Ah, Major Watson. Apologies for the interruption. Would you come with us, please? We have a car outside.'

'Mr Gibson, I am in the middle of a most important—'

'It'll have to wait, Major,' replied Coyle, softly but firmly. 'You have been summoned.'

'Summoned, indeed? By whom exactly?'

Gibson handed over a folded piece of paper. Southworth Professional, Watson idly noted. He flipped it open and read the typed message. 'Watson — come at once with these gentlemen. Bring your medical case. It is a matter of the utmost importance.'

And it was signed, in a shaky but instantly recognizable hand: 'Sherlock Holmes'.

SEVEN

Miss Pillbody, the village schoolmistress without a school, would remember that day for as long as she lived. It was very rare for her to have a gentleman caller. But on that sultry mid-August afternoon, when even her thick-walled cottage cast off its chill, she had two of them, almost tripping over each other on the stone flags that led to her door.

She had just finished a music lesson with Emily Torrent, who was really quite gifted, when the first of them appeared. He was a stranger in all senses of the word, unknown to her and a brighter creature than the village was used to, in his cream linen suit and straw boater. She had just pocketed the coppers and thrupenny bits that Emily had been sent with – a whole florin short, but worth it to hear what the girl could do with Miss Pillbody's neglected piano – when there was a rap at the door.

He raised the boater as she answered and apologized profusely for disturbing her. His accent was equally foreign to these parts.

'You're American.'

'Indeed, ma'am. Bradley Ross. Late of the *New York Herald*. I have rented the little house a few doors down, with a view to writing a book over the next six weeks or so.'

'A book,' she said. 'How interesting. A novel?'

He laughed. 'I'm a writer but not that kind of writer. No, it's on why America should join Britain in fighting Germany and her allies. *The Good Fight* is the working title.'

She nodded approvingly. 'I like it. And will it? Join the war.'

'If I get my pennyworth in, perhaps it will. So, in the American fashion, I am just introducing myself around to my new neighbours.' He grimaced. 'Although it isn't going quite as swimmingly as I imagined it might.'

She laughed at that. Miss Pillbody could well imagine how some of the more insular villagers might react to this bright bird that had landed among dowdy pigeons. 'Can I offer you some tea? We could sit in the garden,' she added hurriedly as Charles, the elderly postman, cycled by and almost fell off, craning his neck to look over his shoulder at them. A story for the pub later, no doubt: Miss Pillbody has *entertained* a man at her house.

'Lovely. But I don't want to put you to any trouble as you must be busy, Miss . . .?'

'It's Miss Pillbody. And I'm hardly busy. Not these days. If you take a seat.' She pointed around the side of the cottage, where a cast-iron table and three matching chairs sat under a quince tree. 'You will have to shake the leaves off, and watch out for any fruit that might have fallen.' She made a mental note to harvest the gravid tree. She had plenty of time on her hands to make jam. 'I wouldn't want you to mark that lovely suit.'

'Pah, don't worry. I'm sure there's a laundry nearby.'

'Mr Ross, there is *nothing* nearby here, as you will soon discover. And what there is, you have to drive the long way around to visit.'

'Yeah, I saw that. They blocked the main road. I have to say they were none too pleasant about telling me to skedaddle. Manners cost nothing, I said. And then this old boy said he'd put his bayonet up my . . . Anyway, tea would be lovely.'

As she waited for the kettle to boil, Miss Pillbody looked at her visitor through the leaded kitchen window. He had big, open features, was broad-shouldered, with a strong thatch of fair hair cut short at the back and sides, but with an attractive fringe across the forehead, and he was a good four to six inches taller than most of the men in the village and surroundings. They were like the local cottages – cramped, dark and mean-proportioned. Only the vicar was taller, and he was from Oxfordshire. It must, she concluded, be the American diet that made for Mr Ross's harmonious proportions.

She looked up at the row of Victorian dolls that held court on the top of her dresser. She caught the lifeless eye of her favourite and asked, 'What do you think of Mr Ross, Heidi?'

As expected, no answer came from the ceramic face, so she took the pot, cups, milk and four Abernethys and two Creolas – all she had left after dishing out the contents of her biscuit barrel to her pupils – into the garden.

Ross was staring at the sky, shading his eyes, watching a tiny dot pirouette through the heavens. 'Is that a Vickers?' he asked. 'The aeroplane?'

'Don't ask me, Mr Ross,' she said. 'I know nothing about that sort of thing.'

'Bradley, please. And I take my tea black, if that's OK.'

'Of course. The plane is from the airfield at Thetford. We get Zeppelins come over sometimes, trying to bomb it.'

'Really?' He couldn't hide the excitement in his voice. 'How often?'

'Not very. And don't worry, they never really do any damage to the village.'

'No, but a good opening for the book. The vile Hun bombing idyllic English pastures with their lighter-than-air war machines. Thank you.' He took the tea. 'So, Miss Pillbody, you know what I do. What about you? You paint' – he pointed to the empty easel set up in the garden – 'and you play piano.'

'I do both, adequately.' In fact, she was quite proud of her watercolours. 'But mostly I teach, or taught, I should say, at the village school.'

'Past tense?'

After a moment's hesitation, she told him about what the locals called The Clearance. It could do no harm. After all, it was common knowledge thereabouts. In fact, some people talked of little else.

'And you have no idea what they are doing in there? In the forest? On the estate?' he asked, reaching for a biscuit.

'No. We are told not to ask. On "pain of death".' She giggled, dropping her voice to a whisper, so low a stray gust of wind could snatch the words away. 'One of the villagers, Jimmy, who worked at the smithy, but was, is, a poacher too, he claimed he got in one night. To the estate. He was after some of those fat birds that aren't going to get shot this year. Stood in the pub, so I heard, telling anyone who listened it was a new kind of weapon. A heat ray. Like in H. G. Wells . . . you know.'

'Golly. Did he have proof of this?'

She shook her head. 'No. It was the drink talking. Then, a few days later, he disappeared. Three weeks he was gone for. They say he's back now, because there are lights on in his cottage sometimes, but he won't answer the door.'

Ross looked puzzled. 'So, they think . . .'

'Somebody took him away and had a word in his ear. A very strong word, Mr Ross. So I think you should leave whatever is going on there out of your book.'

'Sounds like it,' he said, with a frown. 'But you've seen nothing?'

She sipped her tea, aware she had already said too much to this long-limbed stranger. More than she had intended. There was an ease about him that was absent in most Englishmen.

But what if this were a test? What if he had been sent by the military to see if she was a loose-tongued danger? Or was it possible that, although he said he was 'late' of the *New York Herald*, it was a case of once a journalist, always a journalist? Her throat suddenly went dry. She hadn't seen anything. But she had *heard* things. The strangest things. Voices, seemingly disembodied, drifting across the fields. For the most part it was incoherent mumblings, but occasionally a word – or even a vile profanity of the lowest sort – would emerge from the formless drone. And there were more unsettling goings-on – sometimes, those who lived near the railway sidings were forced to draw their curtains and not look out, with guards posted to make sure they did as they were told. What was being hidden from them?

'No, nothing, Mr Ross,' Miss Pillbody said.

Conversation moved on to their respective backgrounds, and she explained about her brother, Arnold.

'Well, it is to reduce the number of cases like your brother that America should come into the war. It'd snap the deadlock in a heartbeat.'

'Let us hope so. More tea?'

'Thank you, but I should be going. If you don't mind, though, I'd like to call again. I just have some questions about how to find a few things.' He looked down at his trousers where a tiny blot of tea had marked one thigh. 'Like that laundry.'

'There you are. Sorry to intrude. I heard voices and . . .'

They both looked up at the uniformed officer who had silently come round the side of the cottage, his cap under one arm, a luxuriant bunch of wild flowers in his right hand. It took a second for Nora Pillbody to place him. 'Lieutenant . . .' The name hovered just out of reach. It had been a good three weeks since she had seen the young soldier. 'Booth?'

'Yes. James Booth.' He looked flustered for a moment, moved the flowers to his left hand and offered the right to Ross, who took it, standing as he did so, and introduced himself.

'Don't let me disturb you,' Booth said, looking from one to the other, although his gaze lingered on her for a second longer. Miss Pillbody remembered how he had appraised her back at the school. Had he liked what he had seen? Hence the flowers?

'Not at all, I was just leaving,' said Ross with a wink. 'Unless they were for me?'

He nodded at the flowers and the Englishman reddened slightly. Ross smiled. 'I thought not.' He retrieved his boater, placed it on his head and touched the brim. 'I bid you good day. Miss Pillbody. Lieutenant.' He walked off, hands in pockets, whistling a jaunty tune.

After the American had left, Booth handed the blooms over.

'Thank you,' Miss Pillbody said. 'Although when we last met, you threatened to have me shot.'

He ran a finger under his collar. 'Yes, well, I am sorry about that. We had to try to get over the, um, gravity of the situation. I brought the flowers to apologize.'

'Are you staying for tea?'

'Perhaps a glass of water? I cycled over. Jolly hot work.'

'I'm sure,' she said. 'But what brings you over here, Lieutenant? Was it just to give me flowers?'

'Well, no. This is a kind of follow-up mission to those left on the fringes of the, ah, exclusion area. I was asked to check you are being treated properly. You are meant to have received compensation for your work.'

'Not a penny as yet.'

'Really?' He frowned as fiercely as he could manage to show his displeasure. 'That's just not good enough.'

It is, she thought, *a rather thin story, but it might be true.* Just because she had two men call in a single day, she shouldn't let it go to her head. 'The education board is paying me fifty per cent of my salary for now. And I am doing some tutoring with those children who haven't been deported—'

'Relocated.'

She waved a hand, irritated by his word games. 'Whatever you call it. They've still been spirited away.'

'And for a very good reason.'

'So you claim. But we have no way of judging that, do we?'

'Not yet, no. But it is a matter of national importance, Miss Pillbody, as I think I said at the time. There's a war on. A little discomfort is to be expected.' He was back to being the harrying intelligence officer she had found in her classroom. He took a breath. 'Still. I'm sorry about your salary. We've had a few cases like this. Farmers not compensated and the like. I'll look into it.'

'Thank you. I'll fetch that water.'

'I'd be obliged. Just one thing.'

'Yes?'

'What does your American friend do? Ross, wasn't it? I mean, he's not a country lad, is he? Not in those clothes.'

'He's writing a book.' Should she mention the journalism part? *Best not*, she decided. 'I'll get the water.'

For the second time that day she examined a male visitor through the window of her kitchen, as she waited for the pipes to cease banging and groaning and the water to run a little clearer. This one was just as striking as the American, in a different way, but his features were screwed up as he frowned, clearly disturbed by something. He was worrying at a fingernail, too, chewing the corner.

Was he really here because he was worried about her finances? Unlikely. It was true that there weren't many single women of a certain class around, so perhaps it was inevitable that such men would find their way to her.

Stop over-analysing, she told herself. *Whatever the men are up to, relax and enjoy the attention.* It wouldn't last. It never did.

EIGHT

Coyle drove them from the hospital into town, handling the big open-topped Deasy with a practised ease. Gibson sat in the back with Watson. The baffled major knew better than to quiz the two spies. All would be revealed. They had allowed him to sum up his lecture and to make arrangements for Fairley to be taken back to his room at Wandsworth Hospital, where he had been moved to a less secure wing.

'We'll need to pay a visit to your home at some point, Major. We've asked your housekeeper to pack a bag,' Gibson said as they crossed the river at Battersea.

'I'll need my copy of the *BMJ*, too.' Watson said absentmindedly. He had been halfway through a fascinating article by a Swedish physician on the use of diet to treat particular forms of anaemia, and there was another on a new anticoagulant for use in blood transfusions he hadn't even started to read. With medical science galloping headlong into new areas, spurred by the terrible casualties of war, it was imperative Watson kept up with the latest developments. 'And my Empire medical kit. The letter asked specifically for it.'

'Of course. But it makes sense to call at Mayfair first.'

'Mayfair? Since when has Sherlock Holmes lodged in Mayfair?'

Gibson didn't answer.

'Shouldn't be detained too long, and we can be on our way,' said Coyle.

'And how many days am I to be packed for?'

'As long as it takes, Major.' Gibson winked at Watson, just to let him know his evasiveness was nothing personal. In fact, Watson liked the chubby little ex-sapper. It was his current profession he found hard to swallow.

They were motoring along the King's Road now and, with all the barracks nearby, there were plenty of soldiers on the street. A brass band comprising injured veterans was outside the Duke of York's, and Watson marvelled at the dexterity of the maimed men in playing their instruments. The ensemble, known as the New Contemptibles, included Jack Tyler, the one-armed trombonist, who had been bought his instrument by readers of the *Daily Mail*. He, at least, had a future of sorts, gaining a fame he could capitalize on in the music halls and variety theatres.

Too many amputees, though, were already reduced to begging while the government bureaucracy sorted out its pension plans. Along with hundreds of other doctors, Watson had lobbied the Admiralty, Chelsea Hospital and the Army Council to have war neurosis or neurasthenia recognized as battlefield-derived damage. So far, they had been promised that the proposed Ministry of Pensions would look favourably upon such claims. But promises weren't feeding families.

Watson turned to speak to Coyle when he heard a loud bang from over his shoulder. A black landau, of the sort he hadn't seen for some years, appeared at their side, the sleek horses dangerously close to the bonnet of the Deasy, the wheels a blur as the polished body of the carriage drew level.

Gibson leaped at Watson, his hands grappling with his head and shoulders. Watson fought back, until he realized what the man was trying to do and allowed himself to be forced down into the footwell. Coyle was shouting something and Watson felt a jolt as the car mounted the pavement. It gave a shudder and halted.

Watson looked up at Gibson, his face inches from his own. He could smell peppermint on the man's breath.

'A little forward, perhaps, Gibson?' Watson said.

The spy sat back up and Watson saw that Gibson had pulled a serious-looking revolver from beneath his jacket.

'Sorry, Major,' said Gibson, yanking him up and adjusting his lapels. Coyle was out of the car, a starting handle in his hand. He was bouncing on the balls of his feet, alert for any change in the scene, scanning faces. The pedestrians all but ignored him. Cars were still an unpredictable nuisance to many people, and there were plenty of drivers who had trouble knowing where the road ended and the pavement began. Coyle, Watson suspected, wasn't one of them. That had been an emergency defensive manoeuvre.

Around them traffic was flowing again. The landau was nowhere to be seen.

'False alarm,' said Gibson with a half-smile. 'Everyone is a bit jumpy, what with one thing and another.'

Watson didn't enquire what the one thing, or indeed the other, might be. He retrieved his hat and straightened his jacket, trying not to show his concern. Experience told him one thing: when men like Coyle and Gibson got jumpy, there was usually something worth getting jumpy about.

They drove down Mount Street, and Watson wondered if the Coburg Hotel was their destination, but they motored on by the grand frontage, watched by the doorman, who seemed disappointed such a grand conveyance was not turning in to deliver guests. They eventually parked outside the premises of

James Purdey & Sons, at the corner of South Audley Street. The window still held an elaborately scrolled, matched pair of shotguns and several beautifully crafted hunting rifles, as well as all the accessories required for a good shoot, but Watson knew that most of the company's expertise was being utilized by the War Department to create new weapons for the battlefields of Flanders. The pheasant, the grouse, the stag, the tiger and the elephant would have to wait. Purdeys were bagging Germans now.

Coyle was still tense as he turned off the engine and the Deasy shivered to a halt. The Irishman slipped out of the driver's door and looked up and down the street, before he signalled Watson to step from the rear.

'You all right, Coyle?' he asked.

'I will be, once we are away from here.' He gave a crooked smile, and Watson could see he had chipped a front tooth since they had last met. There were deeper lines on his face, too, creases that bracketed his mouth, and his freckles appeared to have faded, as if bleached out. 'But it looks quiet enough now. Off you go, Major.'

Coyle stayed with the car while Gibson led Watson back along Mount Street, past a variety of businesses trying to out-do each other with their floral displays, until he reached a recently constructed mansion block. He rang a bell and the concierge admitted them. A young concierge, Watson noted, of army service age. Unusual. There was no sign of anything that might have invalided him out of the army. And he seemed to know Gibson. Another of Kell's spies?

In the lift taking them to the top floor, Watson remarked, 'Coyle seems on edge.'

Gibson nodded. 'That's the way I like him.'

The former engineer, too, had changed since their first meeting in 1914: he seemed to have grown glummer, more careworn over the two years. They had come across each other when they had been involved in an elaborate subterfuge designed to draw out a German spy. That, and a concurrent piece of deception by Sherlock Holmes to try to keep Watson out of the army and out of harm's way. It had caused a rift between the two old friends, although Watson now accepted that Holmes had acted from the best of intentions.

'What have you been up to?' he asked the secret agent.

Gibson looked up at him with a you-should-know-better-than-to-ask expression. Then he relaxed. 'Mostly interviewing or tracking aliens.'

'Looking for spies under the bed?'

'Nothing quite so exciting.' He laughed. 'The vast majority are perfectly innocent, accused by jealous or suspicious neighbours. But Coyle has a nose for sorting the wheat of German agents from the chaff of gossip.'

'I see he has had some dentistry since we last met.' Watson pointed to his front tooth.

Gibson laughed again. 'Yes. The dentist used a revolver barrel.'

'Unconventional.'

'Don't worry. Coyle had the man's licence to practise revoked.'

Watson could only imagine what that meant as the lift halted with a jolt and a bell pinged. He reached for the gate but Gibson gripped his wrist. 'The dentist had a friend called Casement.'

Roger Casement had been instrumental in supplying weapons – Russian weapons sourced from Germany – for the Easter Uprising in Dublin. He had been arrested in Ireland – presumably Coyle had been there – and hanged at the Tower for treason just eleven days before.

'Coyle was involved in detaining Casement?'

A nod. 'Coyle's had a few tussles with his conscience since then. As any man who still has friends and family among the revolutionaries would.'

'Really?'

'Every Irishman is just two removes from knowing a Fenian.'

'But he's sound?' asked Watson.

Gibson looked annoyed at the question. 'Sound as a bell, Major. Don't you go doubting him. Now, I won't be coming in with you.'

'No? Why not?'

Gibson stepped in closer. 'The thing is, Coyle and I have been up to our necks in secrets and not a few lies these past two years. But whatever this is here, today, I'm not privy to it. I am to deliver you and take my leave. So I'll be waiting for you downstairs.' The engineer didn't sound too pleased about this.

'Very well,' replied Watson.

'I've talked too much. I must be getting soft. All I'm saying, Major, is be careful.'

'Why?'

Gibson let go of Watson's wrist. 'Coyle didn't much care for that landau on the King's Road. Truth be told, neither did I.'

'You said that was a false alarm.'

Now Gibson gave a grin, and Watson could see the old mischievousness in his features. 'Shall we go and see if anyone is in?'

He pulled back the metal gate and they stepped out into a cream-and-gold-decorated corridor, the red carpet thick under their feet, the electric lights on the walls glowing softly. There were three doors. Gibson knocked on Number 11 and waited, face before the inspection peephole.

'You've been here before?' Watson asked.

'Once or twice.'

There was a scrabbling of a chain on the other side of the door and then it swung back. A cloud of smoke laced with brandy wafted over them.

'Sir, Major Watson, as promised,' said Gibson to the man before him. 'I'll be downstairs when you have finished, to take him on.'

If the resident of the apartment acknowledged Gibson at all, Watson didn't catch it. Winston Churchill simply grabbed Watson by the arm and all but hauled him into the apartment, slamming the door behind them.

NINE

Miss Pillbody saw the American again later that day, as she sat at her easel in the evening shade. He was no longer so flamboyantly dressed, favouring a dark blazer and grey slacks. There was a tune on his lips, a straw trilby on his head and a book under his arm.

'Miss Pillbody,' he said, raising his hat as he stopped at her gate. 'How was your meeting with the army guy? He's not after your cottage now?'

'No. Just some bureaucratic matters.'

'I bet that's what all the fellows say.'

She gave him a sharp look.

'I'm sorry. Rude of me.'

'No, not at all. Just that there aren't that many fellows left to say anything of the sort.'

'No, I suppose not. Just children, old men and we foreigners left now. May I see?' He indicated her painting.

'Just something to pass the time,' she said, modestly.

He stepped through the gate and stood at her shoulder. 'Nonsense. You have a good eye for perspective.'

'What are you reading?' she asked, hoping to distract him from her blushes.

'Ah. This.' He pulled the volume out from under his arm. 'Tarkington. A novel called *Seventeen*.'

'About?'

'It's frivolous. A boy's first love.'

'American?'

'Very.'

'Wait here, Mr Ross.'

She went inside and quickly scanned her bookcase. Trollope? No. Dickens? Better. Buchan might do it. In the end she selected *Kim*. Kipling never let one down.

She went back outside and handed it to him. 'If you are going

55

to write about Great Britain, Kipling would be a better choice of reading material.'

'Why, thank you.' He took it and placed the two books together. 'I am going to find the village pub. I don't suppose you'd care—'

She shook her head vigorously.

'No. Of course not. No women.'

'No *respectable* women, anyway.' She smiled. 'There is a hotel in Thetford where the ladies might take a sherry without burning all social bridges.'

'I'll remember that. Anything else I should know? About the locals?'

'Well, the menfolk are a bit rough and ready. They'll be suspicious of you.'

'Because I'm American?'

'No. Because you aren't from hereabouts. You don't have to come from America to be foreign. Five miles down the road will do it.'

'I was hoping to get some attitudes about the war from them. Candid and non-metropolitan.'

'They'll be very guarded, I am afraid.'

Ross thought about this. 'What if I bought them all a drink?'

She raised an eyebrow. 'It's against the law to buy other men drinks in pubs.'

'What?' This was one rule he hadn't heard.

'It's true. Everyone ignores it round here, though. But under the emergency regulations, you can't buy another man a drink. It's to prevent excessive consumption. If you do decide to, you have to be careful. Have a word with Mr Sutton. Frederick Sutton. He's the landlord. I teach his daughter Lottie. He's not a bad sort.'

'Thanks for the advice, Miss Pillbody.'

'Nora,' she said, her own name feeling awkward on her lips.

'Nora. Perhaps I'll report back on my adventure at The Plough.'

She nodded. 'I'd like that, Mr Ross.'

'Bradley. In fact, let's go straight to Brad. Can we?'

'I think we can,' she said softly. 'Brad.'

56

'Swell.'

Miss Pillbody watched him stride down the lane, whistling, and she told her thumping heart not to be so stupid and to just calm right down. Handsome Americans weren't part of her plans.

But this one could be, she thought.

Lieutenant Booth was sitting in his office – a former wood-man's cottage, its living area stripped of furniture and refilled with a desk, chair, a safe and a gramophone – thinking about Miss Pillbody and Mr Bradley Ross. What were the odds that a writer would turn up on the edge of the most sensitive site in the United Kingdom? And then go a-calling on the ladies of the village, perhaps looking for gossip. What kind of writer? A 'book', Miss Pillbody had said.

He had sent an enquiry about Ross down to London, and expected a reply within twenty-four hours. It wasn't hard to track foreigners these days. Most were interviewed at some point by Special Branch or MI5. Ross being an American citizen did make it slightly tricky if Booth were to order his removal, but the defence of the realm came first. He didn't want a curious Yank poking around the forest.

Not that there was much to find out. Most of the work had been suspended following . . . The Incident. That was what it had become officially known as: The Incident. Eight men down, seven of them dead. Just the one survivor. And he wasn't talking. Might never talk again, judging by the state of the poor chap.

In the aftermath, Swinton, the lieutenant-colonel in charge of the camp, had managed to avoid a damaging mutiny by reassur-ing his men that the suspension would last until they got to the bottom of the deaths. So, for the moment, all was quiet apart from routine maintenance – normally the little cottage shook day and night and the sound of birds was drowned out by the thrum of heavy machinery.

But what would Ross think when the noises began again? Booth glanced up at the evacuated zone, marked in red on the wall map. Perhaps they should have cleared Snarewold and the other villages too. Anything within earshot.

And what of Miss Pillbody?

Well, *she* was no threat. Might be of some use, in fact. There was precious little in the way of entertainment at the camp. Now that the earl had decamped to Hyde Park Corner, taking his family and most of the staff with him, the only women left were a housekeeper, cook and four maids, all of whom were forbidden to leave the immediate grounds without escort, as well as a nurse, who, while attractive, was well beyond thirty. Flinty, too, by all accounts.

Miss Pillbody was not unattractive and he was certain there was more to her than met the eye. Beneath that placid surface, he suspected, lay something a little sparkier. Like a liquor chocolate, a bland exterior concealing a sharp surprise within. He had felt it at the schoolhouse. It was why he had sought her out with flowers. He could imagine passing time with her, peeling away her layers. A picnic. A bicycle ride. Tea in town. A sherry in Thetford. She would, he was certain, be flattered by his attentions, an officer five or more years her junior, a man with prospects once this part of the project was complete. And along the way he might find out if he was right about her being a tiger masquerading as a tabby cat.

Not that it would go further than a summer courtship. There was Sally back in Bath, the youngest daughter of the local MP. Not quite as easy on the eye as Miss Pillbody, perhaps, but a far more suitable match, socially at least. But it was going to be a good few months until his work was done here and in the meantime he needed some light relief. He knew he had a relaxed charm, when it was required; it was what had landed him the job as Heavy Branch intelligence officer in the first place. That and his father, who was one of the authors of the Government's War Book, which, in 1910, had laid down the minutiae of the country's response to any conflict, from deployment of forces to the censorship of mail.

He countersigned the order on his desk, shipping one of the

men – who had tried to leave the camp three times without permission – to 'a secure and safe location', where he would be held incommunicado until the secret of Elveden was out.

The clock struck seven and Booth realized he was hungry. He stacked his papers, locked them in the safe and prepared to vacate his office. There was rap at the door and one of the signal corporals handed him a telegram. He expected it to be about Ross, but instead it was from the Supply Committee at the War Office.

'Has Colonel Swinton seen this news?' Booth asked the corporal.

'No, sir. You said to show all messages from that sender to you first.'

'Yes. Good man.' His stomach rumbled, but dinner would have to wait. As would thoughts of Ross and Miss Pillbody. Only one thing mattered now. *What the hell was Winston Churchill playing at?*

TEN

Churchill ushered Watson into a long drawing room, furnished with gilt fixtures and fittings that the Sun King might have considered a little ostentatious: a multi-branched chandelier appeared to have been looted from a château, its proportions certainly excessive for the space; a chaise longue glistened with golden threads and tassels; a table of marble sat on elaborately cast legs. *Hideous*, thought Watson.

'Oh, this place isn't mine,' laughed Churchill when he saw Watson taking in the swagged red curtains. 'Like a bloody brothel. It belongs to Harry Clifford; lets me use it when we don't want to do our business in public.'

Churchill then noticed Watson admiring a large oil painting of a sailing ship on a storm-tossed sea, which was still managing to fire a broadside. 'It's called the *Scourge of Malice*,' Churchill said. 'The Earl of Cumberland's ship. Bit of artistic licence there; not sure you could hit a country in that swell. But the *Scourge* was the largest vessel constructed in England at that time. Thirty-eight guns. Struck terror into the enemy. Clifford, the earl, was a privateer, of course, but he gave the Spanish hell in the Caribbean. Drink?'

Without waiting for an answer, the politician poured two glasses of vermouth from a pitcher on a side table, and handed one to Watson.

Watson took it but didn't drink. A privateer. Yes, he could see why Churchill might have a soft spot for the master of the *Scourge*, a man working for his country but not playing by conventional rules.

'Didn't Clifford make a fortune from his buccaneering?' Watson asked.

'And lost it all on horses and jousting,' said Churchill. 'We shouldn't take an analogy too far, eh? But it is relevant in one sense. We intend to strike terror into the enemy in ways they could never have dreamed of. Which is why you are here, Watson. Now, I apologize about all the subterfuge—'

'I have one question first.'

Churchill, who had already drawn breath, ready for one of his legendary orations, albeit to an audience of one, squinted at him. 'What is it?'

From his inside pocket, Watson drew the summons from Holmes. 'Why are you sending me letters purporting to be from Sherlock Holmes?' he said, unable to keep the anger from his voice.

'Purporting?' Churchill repeated cagily.

Watson held up the summons. 'This, Mr Churchill, is a blatant forgery.'

Donal Coyle knew his days as an agent of the British Crown were numbered. He had always been an anomaly in the Bureau, a mongrel, tossed into its ranks because no respectable gentleman would want to become a spy. The SSB/MI5 took what it could get, even if it was a disillusioned Fenian. But those days were over. Gentlemen willingly embarked on all kinds of underhand pursuits now in the defence of the realm. And with events in Ireland taking place, more than ever he was suspect, simply because of his accent.

Coyle knew where his loyalty lay. Well, it lay mainly with his friend Harry Gibson, but also to the department that had given him a home. And to England?

He was no longer so sure.

The Irishman lit a cigarette and leaned against the wall, next to the Purdey shop and just at the rear of the parked Deasy. He stood out here in these streets, with his rough suit and cheap hat. Spies rarely worked in Mayfair. He was dressed for the gutter. It was where he did his best work. There were others, like Langdale Pike, who patrolled the upper echelons for Kell and Co.

Of course, it wasn't just the uprising that had caused him to reassess his position. There had been the letter from his ma, sent through to the secure PO box the service used, telling him that her eyes were going: 'I had to get Marie Coughlan to read your last one to me. They say it's the cataracts . . .'

Perhaps the prodigal son ought to return and help out, see if there was something they could do. His brother was away in America, his sister married and in Cork, and now his mother was relying on neighbours like Marie Coughlan. The cataracts. Her world must be fogging.

Coyle scanned the street, casually watching each car and wagon drive by, while at the same time noting the occupants. So far, nothing had come by twice. Not that there was any reason to expect any trouble. Which was when he expected it most.

He was armed with two pistols. The largest was in his belt – one advantage of a sloppily cut jacket was that it hid a multitude of sins – the other was a small revolver, good enough for close work, in a special leather contraption in his sock. Experience had told him that it was the easiest, fastest positioning for a pistol when driving or as a passenger in a car. It had saved his life twice.

How would he break the news of his return to Ireland to Harry?

They had been together for four years now. And they made a very good team. The oldest in the SSB. But Coyle thought it was time to go home and be among his own people. The ripples from the uprising were still spreading out, agitating the populace. Even those who didn't believe in the armed struggle felt the subsequent executions were cruel and arbitrary. There might be a way to harness that unrest in a more peaceful way than armed insurrection. True, there were people back there who might want him dead but he knew that at least three of them had themselves left this world. He had sent out a few tentative overtures, through his Uncle Sean and—

Black four-seat Shelsey on a Crossley chassis.

The phrase popped into his head, even before he realized what he was looking at.

Puttering beyond the horse-drawn delivery van making its way along the street was a black four-seat Shelsey on a Crossley chassis. A very nice car. Warland Dual detachable rims, too. Probably the 25 HP model. Three occupants, none of them a chauffeur. Smartly dressed, two with dark oiled hair, one fair-haired. One of the former wearing spectacles.

Seen it before, haven't we? But where? Not here, not in Mayfair.

At the hospital. When we fetched Watson. Only driver and one passenger then. The blond one. They've added an extra pair of hands since.

Coyle examined the scene in his mind's eye, almost as if he were watching a Vitascope. It was a trick he had. The Shelsey had driven off before he, Gibson and Watson had. Which meant what? That there had been no chance for these men to act there, which was true. Watson, Coyle and Gibson had exited the hospital cloaked by a phalanx of nurses changing shift, guiding them all the way to the car. If they had picked Coyle up en route and followed him, they must be good at what they did. Damned good.

Then, as sometimes happened when he knew he had to act, his thumbs prickled. It was a strange sensation, almost like the chilblains he used to get as a kid. And, experience told him, it didn't do to ignore his thumbs. Coyle waited until the car had gone by, peeled himself off the wall and ditched the cigarette. He looked back up the street at the mansion block where Gibson was waiting. He had to warn him that Watson's life was in danger.

He had taken four steps when he glanced over his shoulder again, to see the Shelsey had turned and was coming back towards him. He unbuttoned his jacket, all thoughts of leaving the Bureau banished.

ELEVEN

Winston Churchill barely glanced at the letter Watson was holding. 'Would you have come for anyone else?'

'Possibly not, but you could have tried first.'

'I don't have time for "trying",' the MP growled, tossing back the vermouth and heading for a refill. 'How did you know it was a fake? The signature is bloody good. I got it copied from one of his letters.'

Watson had to laugh at that. 'Let me count the ways. The paper is wrong. The typewriter too new. The phrasing—'

'All right, all right. Spare me the smart aleck analysis. Save that for your books.' Churchill's lisp was suddenly very pronounced. He picked up a cigar, abandoned in an ashtray, and puffed it back to life. 'You're here now. It did the job.'

'And Holmes?'

'He's a difficult man.'

Watson tried to make sure the alarm he felt at this didn't show on his face. The fact that Churchill had stooped to forging a letter suggested Holmes was either indisposed or refusing to help the politician. 'He is a very singular man.'

'I think they say that about me, when they are trying to be polite.

We have tried to engage him on several projects, including this one. Anyway, it was you we wanted. Well, *I* wanted.'

'I wish I could say I was flattered.'

Churchill studied Watson for a few moments, his face clenched like a pugilist's fist. 'There have been two great secrets in this war so far,' the politician began. 'One was the plan to get the soldiers off the beaches of Gallipoli without alerting the Turks to what was going on. That was a success, if you can call a retreat from such slaughter a success. And then there is the *Scourge of Malice*.' He pointed again at the painting. 'We are, in a manner of speaking, building our own *Scourge*.'

'To strike terror, you said. Is it some form of ship?'

'What makes you say that?'

'Your background. First Lord of the Admiralty.'

'Hmm.' Churchill gave a flicker of a smile.

'I would imagine you are developing some manner of new water-borne weapon.'

'You're close enough. But for the moment I can't tell you what it is.'

'Then why am I here?' Watson relented and finally took a sip of warm vermouth.

'Our *Scourge* had a malfunction. It killed seven men. Our own men. An eighth survived. Only he can tell us what happened. Until we know for certain what occurred, progress on the device is suspended.'

'Killed how?'

'Well, first they all went insane.'

'Insane?' Watson repeated.

'Yes. Deranged, gibbering wrecks. I know for a fact that you have come across something similar before. A sudden, unexplained insanity.'

'Yes,' said Watson, recalling the affair at Poldhu Bay when the wicked Mortimer Tregennis had used a poison to murder his sister and drive his brother insane.

'But this is of a different nature altogether. There is evidence that they tried to destroy the *Scourge* in some kind of . . .' – Churchill struggled for the word – '. . . frenzy.'

'Could it be sabotage by an enemy agent? If this really is a wonder weapon.'

'It could. But as I said, this is a great secret. Anyone who knows about it and is not actively involved is being detained at what they call a "safe and secure" location. Until the cat is out of the bag.'

'Would that include me?'

Churchill glared at him. 'It might, if I told you much more and you refused to help.'

Watson was offended. He was used to being trusted with affairs of state. In his day, Mycroft Holmes had told him things that could shake the Empire. 'But I wouldn't speak of it.'

Churchill looked annoyed. 'Perhaps. But the story of our bigamist king made an appearance, didn't it? Hmm?'

Holmes and Watson had helped refute an allegation that King George V had been married before, following a hasty affair with an admiral's daughter in Malta, when he was in the navy. An article in a magazine had suggested that George had married his wife, Princess May, bigamously. The defence was able to insist that the King had never met the woman in question. In fact, there had been evidence they had attended balls together in Hampshire, but for the good of the nation, that had been suppressed. However, hints about that cover-up had recently surfaced in some of the more scurrilous newspapers.

'That was not my doing.'

'I would hope not, Watson,' Churchill said, in a manner that suggested there was some doubt. 'But, you see, the nature of this device need not concern you right at this very moment. What we want is for you to treat the eighth man. He won't, or can't, speak. Absolutely struck dumb. What's it called . . . a-something?'

'Aphasia.'

'Quite. Nothing that has been tried, from kindness to cruelty,

65

has broken his silence. To all intents and purposes it's shell shock, just like the conditions you've been treating. Yes, I know all about your work.'

'I'm not the only one in the field,' Watson protested. 'There are others—'

Churchill shook his head vigorously, his nascent jowls wobbling. 'Communists, pacifists and homosexuals.'

'Not all at once, surely, sir?'

Churchill ignored the barbed comment. 'I am being accused of interfering in the project as it is. But someone has to shake things up. I need you to get this man to talk, to tell us what happened and get this war moving again.'

Watson shook his head. 'I cannot get involved.'

Winston glowered. 'Cannot? Or will not?'

'You have seen conditions out there at the front. It is inhumane what we are asking our soldiers to do. Yes, I am dealing with shell shock. And you know what it has taught me? That men can be broken, snapped like autumn twigs. And we are doing it by the thousands. This wonder weapon, will it really shorten the war? Or will it heap misery upon misery?' Churchill made to speak, but Watson waved a hand to silence him. 'Gas was meant to break the deadlock, remember that? The new shells were meant to blast the Germans out of their bunkers. Remember that one, too? The only thing that will end this war is when men like you come to their senses and start talking peace.'

'I don't need a lesson in war from you, Major,' growled Churchill, jutting his jaw in a belligerent fashion. 'I count the dead every day and it never gets any easier. And what you say sounds dangerously like pacifism.'

'Common sense.'

'So you think. And I genuinely think this will shorten the war. You have my word on that.'

'Your word that you believe it will bring about a rapid cessation of hostilities? But you can't be certain?'

Churchill made a snorting sound. 'Of course not. What guarantees are there in wartime?'

'I see more broken men,' said Watson, 'on all sides. I will not be party to that.'

Churchill's voice came from his boots. 'There is one broken man you will be party to, though, I'll wager.'

Watson felt a flame of anger flicker inside him. The reservoir of residual goodwill he felt towards the MP drained away, as if a tap had been opened. He suspected what was coming, but asked anyway. 'What do you mean by that?'

Churchill picked a few strands of tobacco from the tip of his tongue. 'Holmes has had to be detained, for his own safety.'

'Detained?' Watson half shouted in disgust. 'Detained where? And why? He is not a well man.'

'So I hear. Nevertheless, he has been detained and will remain detained until our weapon is deployed. The longer you delay—'

'Are you blackmailing me?' Watson spluttered. 'With the health of an old man who has served his country well.'

Churchill considered this. 'I suppose I am. For a good cause.'

Watson made a disparaging noise. 'A war such as this is *never* a good cause.'

'Sir!' Churchill growled. 'The freedom of this country, of our way of life, is at stake! And you worry about a few windy soldiers. Yes, I will let Holmes rot, and you and half of goddamned London, if it means we can strike a decisive blow.'

The MP had gone quite puce. Watson thought he might suffer a heart attack. Part of him wished it so. Watson took a breath and spoke as calmly as he could. 'Free Holmes and I shall help you.'

'Do I look like a fool?' Churchill replied. 'Where is your incentive then? Get to the bottom of this, I will tell you where he is. You can fetch him yourself.'

'And what if I can't solve the mystery?'

'I think we'll cross that bridge as and when we come to it.' Churchill sensed an advantage and pushed it home. 'But I am not an unreasonable man. Do this for me, Major, and I promise never to interfere in your life again.'

The clock ticked while Watson went through his options. He felt like a chess piece, blocked in whichever direction he moved.

'Am I to be physician or detective?' Watson asked at last.

Churchill gave a sly smile that Watson wanted to dash from his mouth. 'There was a time when you were both.'

Watson shook his head at this misconception of his role in the partnership. 'Do they not have their own doctor at this . . . establishment?'

'Their MO is one of the dead,' grumbled Churchill. 'Went along for the ride to study conditions in—' He stopped himself. 'He was the last to die. They have brought in other medical men, but no plausible theory has emerged so far. The doctors are baffled and the only witness remains stubbornly mute. So, as you can see, a peculiar set of skills is required. Your skills, Watson.'

'When was all this?'

'A week ago.'

'A week?'

'Yes. Time is pressing. How long do you normally need?' asked Churchill. 'To cure these types of people?'

These people. Churchill, like so many commanders, didn't understand what had happened to the damaged men. No doubt he, too, considered their affliction due to a lack of backbone. Even the word 'cure' was wrong. You could never take away their experiences; just get them to live alongside them without it destroying them any further.

'Assuming he has some kind of battlefield trauma? Every case is different. Four weeks—'

'You have five days,' Churchill said in tones meant to brook no argument. 'I heard you worked wonders with that Fairley.'

'That was different, in that I had a previous relationship to build upon. You can't put a time limit on this sort of thing,' Watson said.

Churchill waved his cigar. 'I can. We have to. There is a timetable. Five days, work recommences regardless. At gunpoint, if need be. And, Watson, I am not concerned about this mute's sensibilities. You understand? Get him to speak of that day any way you can.

'And the dead men? Will I have access to them?' asked Watson.

'The dead can wait,' growled Churchill. 'At least until you have made the living talk.'

'In some cases the dead can tell us more than the living.'

'I'm sure you can poke and prod the bodies to your heart's content if you think it'll help. Personally, I think we need our survivor's testimony. You know Suffolk?'

'Not well.'

'We've requisitioned an estate; the work is being done there. Close to the RFC airfield at Thetford. We'll fly you up—'

Watson's stomach felt like it had been pushed off a cliff. 'I prefer not to fly.'

'Understandable' said Churchill, well aware that Watson's wife had died in an aeronautical accident, although he himself was a great believer in heavier-than-air machines, even if he had proven a less than capable pilot. 'But, as I say, time is of the essence. There will be a chap called Swinton to brief you.'

'Ernest Swinton? The writer?' Watson knew his work from before the conflict – dashing jingoistic adventures – and his war journalism.

Churchill nodded. 'Of course you'd know him. Fellow scribbler. Yes, *that* Swinton. He's the colonel in charge of the installation.'

Watson took another gulp of vermouth and then, more to kill time than anything else, strolled across to try the brandy. 'Do I have any choice in this matter?'

Churchill smiled. It wasn't comforting in any way. 'None.'

'And you won't tell me the nature of this weapon?'

'Not until you reach the site. You'll be briefed there.'

'But you know our methods.' The collective noun was cheeky, but Churchill must appreciate how Holmes liked to tease out every detail of a case, more often than not in the drawing room of 221B Baker Street, before racing off. 'Some background, surely, is in order?'

'Not until you are at the location,' Churchill said stubbornly. 'Unless you want to risk spending several months with your old friend on a speck in the North Sea waiting for the *Scourge* to become public knowledge.'

Watson felt another prick of anger. But Churchill had slipped up – at least he knew roughly where Holmes was now. But where in the North Sea? It was a vast expanse.

'And of course,' Churchill said slyly, 'your friend isn't getting any younger or fitter.'

A red mist descended on Watson at the implications of what Churchill was saying. 'I'd like to assure you, sir, that if anything befalls Holmes—' Watson stopped.

Churchill saw puzzlement and alarm flash across Watson's face. 'What is it?' the MP asked.

Watson walked quickly to the window and undid the latch, pulling up the lower half of the sash. 'It sounded like gunshots.'

TWELVE

There was but a cuticle of moon when Bradley Ross approached the ramshackle cottage of Jimmy Oxborrow, the part-time smithy and poacher who had boasted he could get into the estate. He trod carefully, knowing it would be easy to turn an ankle in the darkness. There were no lights showing, no smell of woodsmoke, but one of the looser-lipped lads had sworn Jimmy was living in there. Beer was delivered in pails, apparently, and the odd chicken by well-wishers, and all vanished. Oxborrow was in there. But something had scared him enough so he didn't want to draw attention to himself.

Ross had to stop to relieve himself. He had drunk several pints of beer at The Plough, just to be sociable. It was thin, flat and warm.

Horrible, but necessary. It wasn't till the third pint of that piss that his new friends had relaxed in his company and chatted as if he was one of them.

He buttoned himself up and continued down the rough path to the door of the cottage. He had two bottles of Mackeson with him, one in each of his jacket pockets. He took them out and allowed the pair to clink together, a sound that would raise any serious drinker from the deepest slumber. Then he tapped on the door with a knuckle.

'Jimmy?' he hissed.

Nothing.

'Jimmy? It's Bradley Ross. I'm a friend of Cyril's. He said you liked a drop of Mackeson.' An 'old woman's drink' the gnarled Cyril had called it, but Ross left that part out. 'I'm just going to leave them here, outside. By the bootscrape. OK?'

He walked away, ears alert for any sounds coming from the cottage. There were only the noises of the night, the soft sighing of leaves, the rustle of the fields. He walked fifty yards down the lane and halted. A horse neighed nearby and restless insects sent out scratching and chirping calls. He stepped through a gap in the hedgerow, crouched down and lit a cigarette.

Squatting came easy to him. It had been a punishment at school, forced to crouch with hands on head until pins and needles rippled through your limbs. Later, such practised immobility had been useful when he had learned to hunt. He allowed himself a rare moment of relaxation and felt some of the tension ease from his neck and shoulders.

There was something interesting happening at Elveden, he was sure. He felt it in his waters. The only fly in the ointment was that young lieutenant, Booth. He hadn't liked the way he had looked at him in Miss Pillbody's garden. The man wore no regimental badge, which suggested he might be Intelligence. There were bound to be some of those around on a secret project of this size. And they all looked at you like that. Just like policemen. But Booth was a callow boy, not some wily old operative. Ross was sure he could dodge anything thrown at him by Lieutenant Booth. He had begun his book, *The Good War*, on the ruthless aggression of Germany and its barbarism in Belgium. If Booth should search his cottage, he would find nothing to suggest Ross was more interested in teasing out the secret of Elveden than Allied propaganda.

The cigarette had burned down to his fingers. He stubbed it out in the soil and stood, listening once more for any stray sounds. A fox called in the distance, strangulated and forlorn. Ross retraced his steps back to the cottage, careful to keep in the shadows. He stood at the base of an elm, a few yards from the cottage door, staring into the darkness until he could be certain. Yes, the two bottles of milk stout had gone. The bait had been taken.

THIRTEEN

Coyle had half turned when the first of the bullets sang past his ear and raised a whorl of dust from the masonry behind him. The flash had come from the back seat of the Shelsey. He cleared the Smith & Wesson revolver from his belt and fired two rounds in return, while all the time heading for the shelter of a parked car.

How dare they? he thought. In broad daylight. In the heart of the city. He fired again, and this time he was aware that two shots had been sent in reply. They weren't sharpshooters, but both attempts had come close enough to snap the air like a ringmaster's whip. He risked a look up the street. Harry was there, out on the pavement, also raising his pistol. Bystanders had frozen or ducked into shop doorways. Coyle heard a woman scream. A police whistle sounded, hoarse and feeble at first, now finding its fluting voice.

Coyle had made it to the Austin parked nearby and crouched down beside it. The windscreen shattered, but the glass imploded harmlessly into the car. He had three shots left. He thought about reloading, but now he heard the crunch of gears and an engine revving.

They were speeding off.

He stood and, bracing his right hand by cupping the butt of the S&W, he loosed the remaining bullets at the fast-disappearing motor car. Its rear window vanished in a glistening shower of glinting glass and sparks flew from the bodywork, but it kept going in a straight line, hardly deviating. He hadn't hit the driver.

Should he give chase?

No, they were idiots. He'd clocked them, they'd clocked him; the rulebook said you abandoned the pretence and slipped away. You lived to fight another day. The only damage would have been that Coyle would know for certain that there was an opposition, confirming his suspicions by shooting at him. Amateurs.

He reloaded as he walked, not looking up until he was almost upon Gibson.

His partner was standing, gun limp at his side, staring down at his stomach and the rapidly growing red flower blooming across it.

'Oh, Jesus, no.' Coyle was with him in three big strides, just time enough to catch him as he crumpled to the ground.

The MI5 man was dead before they got him upstairs. The bullet had nicked something major and, from the way the colour drained from his skin and the light faded from his eyes, Watson knew there was massive internal bleeding. *It might be a blessing*, he thought. He had seen too many slow deaths from penetrating abdominal wounds in his time at the front. PAWs could take you quickily and easily, or make you suffer every step of the way towards eventual oblivion. Watson knew which he'd prefer.

Watson, Coyle, Mason the doorman and Churchill, all to some degree speckled in Gibson's blood, stood in silence, waiting on a Lazarus moment that was never going to arrive.

Watson risked a glance at Coyle, but his face was set, granite-like, his breathing rapid and shallow. It was not a good sign. Already the Irishman was figuring out how to compartmentalize his grief, bottle it for another day, setting up the kind of internal conflict that Watson had spent the last six months trying to resolve – teaching soldiers to bear the unbearable.

'I'm sorry—' Churchill began, breaking the silence.

'Shut up,' Coyle snapped. 'Sir, don't say anything.'

Watson had seen Churchill explode at a lesser insult, but the man remained impassive. He had been through enough combat to make allowances. He'd probably give Coyle that one, perhaps another, before reminding him of his place.

'Oh, fuck,' muttered Coyle in a thick voice. 'Fuck it all.'

After a few long moments, Churchill crossed to the pitchers and poured a healthy three inches of brandy into a glass. He offered it to Coyle who took it. 'I was the one who was meant to break the partnership, ye silly man.' He raised the glass. '*Go maire sibh bhur saol nua.*'

The brandy disappeared in a blur of movement and Coyle held out the glass for a refill. Churchill took it with a slow, deliberate movement. Watson could tell Coyle was pushing his luck, treating the MP as his footman.

The Irishman turned to Mason. 'Get back downstairs. There'll be police after all that in the streets. Tell them it was a training exercise with live firing. Any damage will be paid for by the Special Branch. Understood?'

Mason nodded and left, buttoning up his coat to hide the worst of the bloodstains.

Watson looked at the unfortunate Gibson once more. 'You think it was me meant to be laid out there?' he asked nobody in particular.

'I can see no other explanation,' said Coyle. 'I would hazard a guess that, whatever you are planning to do for Mr Churchill here, there are some who would rather you didn't.'

Watson nodded, trying to come to terms with the idea that men were intent on killing him. He had been in danger before, of course. Everyone who ventured into the trenches was in the firing line, but out there, it was mostly fate that decided whether the sniper chose you as the recipient of a precious high-velocity round or if a whizz-bang dropped on your head or the gas got to you before you could get your mask on. To be on a death list, that was something very different. It was personal. Watson wished, not for the first time, that Holmes was with him, for he had spent a considerable time dodging Colonel Moran's bullets.

Coyle took the second brandy from Churchill. 'Who knew that Major Watson was coming here today?'

Churchill thought for a second. 'The Steering Committee for this project. Macfie and Wilson of the Royal Naval Air Service and William Tritton, the senior engineer. Kell, of course. And you two.'

'Holmes?' asked Watson.

Churchill thought for a second. 'Not specifically about today, no. Knew you were to be involved. But he—'

'And they all know about the flight from Hainault?' Coyle interrupted. 'All the same people?'

'Some do,' Churchill confirmed. 'Not all.'

Coyle blew out his cheeks. 'Where were you flying the major to?'

Watson looked puzzled.

'Me and Gibson, we was told to drop you at Hainault Farm airfield,' explained Coyle. 'The RNAS were to take over from that point.'

There they were again, the navy, footprints all over the place. But why take over an estate in Suffolk for naval manoeuvres? Unless it had a large lake. That could be the answer.

'So,' Coyle continued, 'we never knew your final destination. We didn't have to. Then, at least.' Coyle turned his attention to Churchill. 'Sir, I'll be needing to know where you were flying the major to.'

'Why's that?' asked Churchill suspiciously, pouring himself a brandy.

'Because I'm not daft enough to take yer man out to the airfield now the plan is compromised. We'll go by road. In our own sweet time. And before you ask, I won't be telling you the route or the time we will get there. You tell these people to expect him when we arrive.'

'Time is pressing,' Churchill reminded him. 'You don't understand the politics involved.'

Coyle pointed at his deceased colleague. 'I understand something got my friend here killed. And don't you start with an Irishman about how messy politics can get. Just tell me where to deliver the major, please, sir, and I'll get him there in one piece. The rest is up to you.'

Churchill hesitated for a moment and Watson pre-empted him. 'It's in Suffolk.'

The MP glared at him. 'Yes. It's a place called Elveden Forest. It's Lord Iveagh's country estate—'

Coyle began chuckling, although it was a sound devoid of mirth.

'What's so funny?' asked Churchill, irritated at the man's manners.

'I'm sorry, sir. Iveagh, you say? I think I paid for a good portion of that land.' Before Watson could voice the obvious question, he added, 'It's Guinness money, isn't it, sir?'

'It is,' confirmed Churchill. 'And the earl is being very generous.'

'Aye, he is that,' said Coyle in all seriousness. 'A great man for the good works, is Edward Guinness. So, as I say, you telegram your man up there and tell him we're on our way. I'll call in to Kell now and then, just so you know we're still alive.'

As if to emphasize the mortal threat, he took out the pistol from his belt and checked the cylinder. 'We'd best be moving along. I'm going to change cars. The Deasy is too conspicuous now.'

'There is a vehicle that goes with this apartment, garaged nearby,' offered Churchill. 'I've never used it, but the keys are in the hallway. It's a Vauxhall.'

'The Prince Henry?' asked Coyle hopefully.

'I believe so. Will that do?'

'Nicely,' nodded Coyle. 'And another thing, sir.'

'Yes?'

'I'd like to attend the funeral.' He looked down at the dead man. 'Captain Gibson. Royal Engineers.' In death, he would revert to his old army rank. Watson doubted there was an equivalent of full military honours for spies.

'Of course. I'll make the arrangements.'

'Just a moment,' said Watson. 'I'd like to know why he died.'

'You're the doctor,' said Coyle. 'But I suspect that'll be the bullet in his stomach.'

But Churchill knew what he meant. Watson wanted to know what was so important, so secret, as to start a gunfight in central London. Churchill shook his head solemnly. 'That's up to Swinton. I can't—'

'Then you'll have to do without my services. The game has changed somewhat since our earlier conversation.' It was Watson's turn to point at poor Gibson. 'I want to know what cost this man his life and, it seems, might cost me mine. And what is so important that you have imprisoned Sherlock Holmes. If the country—'

'Enough, damn it.' Churchill looked enquiringly at Coyle.

The Irishman gave an exaggerated shrug. 'Oh, don't worry about me, sir, the less I know the better. My job is to get the major to the estate. That's good enough for me.'

Churchill frowned, not a pretty sight as his features folded in on themselves. 'Very well, Watson,' he said at last. 'Follow me.'

'Where to?'

'The library.'

Coyle took off his bloodstained jacket and began to unbutton his shirt. 'And I'll be sending for a change of clothes for both of us, Major. There's no sense in going back to your place, eh? There might be eyes on it.'

When they had gone, Coyle crouched down and held the hand of his friend, the skin already unnaturally cool, the blood on the captain's fingers rapidly crusting over. 'And when I've delivered the major, I'll come back here and I promise you I'll tear this fuckin' town down brick by brick until I find who did this and then I'll crucify the bastards. All right? But forgive me if I don't think on you for a few days, because that'd slow me up, Harry, and you wouldn't want that, would you? Gotta have all me wits about me to make sure the doc gets where he is goin'. Finish the job, that's what you'd want, isn't it?' He leaned over and kissed Gibson's forehead. 'And besides, I reckon I'll be seeing you on the other side soon enough.'

FOURTEEN

Miss Pillbody picked her way gingerly over the shingle, towards a churlish North Sea that refused to shake off its perpetual greyness, even for the summer sun. Small clouds bustled across the sky above her, as if late for some appointment or other, while gulls screeched vague warnings at her. Miss Pillbody turned back and waved, before hitching her skirt a few inches up her calf as she stepped onto the sandier foreshore. Beyond that, the waves licked hungrily around the steel posts that supported the coils of rusty barbed wire, designed to stop small boats being landed.

Booth and Ross were sitting on the low concrete wall of a machine-gun position, which, for the moment, was devoid of both machine gun and gunners. In the dunes behind them were two tall watchtowers, manned by units of the Eastern Command's Home Service Defence Force twenty-four hours a day. Should the Germans decide the Norfolk coast was a convenient place to strike at the heart of London – unlikely, granted – then the HSDF would hold them off until reserve troops could be rushed up from Colchester to reinforce them at positions like these.

'Tell me, are your intentions towards Miss Pillbody strictly honourable, Lieutenant?' Ross asked, examining the extravagantly striped pebble he held between thumb and forefinger.

Booth let out an exasperated laugh. 'Is that any of your business?'

'We Americans can be blunt. We like to know where we stand.'

The colours of the stone he had chosen were remarkable – creams, blues, browns – and he considered taking it home. '*Are* they honourable?'

Booth raised an eyebrow. 'Are yours?'

'I'm very fond of her,' said Ross, tossing the pebble back into the anonymity of the masses and picking up another. *Very fond of the insight she gives me into the village*, he thought. *Very fond at how jealous my presence in her company clearly makes you.*

Booth laughed. 'Spoken like a true, mealy-mouthed cad.'

'I'm not here to stop your fun, Lieutenant.'

'We'll come to that.'

'What?'

'Why exactly you are here.'

Ross took out a silver flask and offered it to Booth. After a fleeting hesitation the lieutenant took it and drank. It was followed by a rasping cough. 'Whisky. Little early in the morning for me. I was expecting brandy.'

Ross raised the flask and took a deep slug. 'Brandy is soporific. This stuff gives you a jolt.' He watched two terns wheel in the sky, their narrow wings impossibly long and elegant. 'So, we find ourselves in a fine pickle, eh?'

They had both turned up to invite Miss Pillbody out on a picnic, Ross on a tandem, Booth in a Morris he had borrowed from the estate. This had amused and no doubt flattered her, and she had come up with what she considered a most pleasing solution – both would take her out. So they had motored to the coast, picking up extra provisions on the way at the market in Norwich.

'Well, don't worry,' said Booth. 'One of us won't be around for much longer.'

'Oh?' Ross ran a thumb over his pebble, feeling the sea-sharpened ridges of its whorled surface.

Booth showed his teeth in an unattractive smile, one that hinted at some sly victory. 'I did some checking up on you. You aren't who you say you are.'

Ross was careful not to betray any emotion.

'You are a writer, yes, but also a journalist.'

Ross relaxed a little. '*Ex*-journalist.'

'But only very recently.' Booth took a smaller hit of the fiery liquor and grimaced with pleasure as it caught his throat.

'Your point being?'

'What are the odds of a hack—'

'*Former* hack.'

'—turning up at one of the country's most top-secret installations?'

'Should you be telling me that?'

'I'm sure you've been in the pubs, Mr Ross. And you know what we did to Miss Pillbody and all the local farmers. Of course it is something hush-hush.'

That phrase again. 'So you don't think I am here because I got off the fence and want to write the book that'll bring America's boys to Europe? You think I want to know what is going on behind your trees and your barriers?'

Booth nodded. 'Yes.'

'So you plan to remove me from the area?

The lieutenant waved at the now-distant Miss Pillbody. 'In a nutshell, again, yes.'

'Can you do that? Legally? To an American citizen?'

Booth fiddled with the cap that lay on his left thigh. It was a moot point, but he wasn't going to reveal that. He certainly didn't want Ross shouting 'foul' at his embassy. 'It's said we hanged Roger Casement on a comma. That the question of whether DORA applies to acts of treason committed outside Great Britain hung on a little piece of punctuation. We made sure it was interpreted the correct way, of course. In your case, we don't need to resort to such a merry dance. In your case, you'd be spying for a foreign power.'

Ross looked horrified. 'But I'm not. That's slander, young man.'

'I think you'll find America is foreign, Ross.'

'Perhaps. But I'm not spying for it or anyone else.'

Booth grunted his disbelief. 'Perhaps not for America in total. But a newspaper? Once a hack . . .'

A voice drifted over on the breeze. They both looked up. Miss Pillbody was waving at them across the undulating waves of shingle.

Ross stood and brushed sand off his trousers. He was angry at being challenged by the youngster. His eyes flicked to the figure of Miss Pillbody, holding on to her hat against the stiffening onshore breeze, her dress pressed against her slim figure. The sea, so placid a few minutes earlier, had begun to show signs of restlessness. The lead-heavy waves, shedding spray as they came, were thumping percussively into the beach. The water's colour had changed too, from gunmetal grey to a more ominous brown. 'If you should remove me from the area, then what is to stop me going into the first telegraph office I come to and telling my former newspaper that I have the biggest scoop of the war? That deep in the Suffolk countryside, the British are developing something hush-hush—'

Booth leaped to his feet, the flask forgotten, fists clenched. 'You wouldn't dare—'

'Two million readers, Lieutenant Booth. But if that was my game, don't you think I'd have done it by now? At least tipped them the wink I had a big story? Asked for some expenses up front? Go and check all the local telegram offices. There'll be nothing from me, I promise you. And the local exchange will confirm no calls to America. Really, I ought to box your ears—'

'You are welcome to try.'

At that moment Miss Pillbody's plaintive voice drifted over to them and they turned to see her frantically waving for them to join her.

'It's probably not the best time,' said Ross.

'Perhaps a postponement?'

He turned to go. Booth grabbed his sleeve. 'Hold on . . .'

Ross waited.

'If I find out you make any contact with a newspaper . . .'

'Booth, truce, eh? Just for today.'

Ross was certain the soldier must be able to hear his heart thumping. It sounded like a bass drum to his own ears. He was very close to being deported. He had to play this carefully.

'I want your word that you will not discuss or approach the estate until we decide what to do with you.'

'Do with me? Look, I am not here for your damned estate, Booth.'

Booth wondered if he should tell him what he had in mind. A few phone calls to check the legality and he could easily have him taken off and locked away on the island they had sequestered for that very purpose. There were no telephones there, no way of contacting a newspaper. 'If you do try, I shall not hesitate to shoot you.'

'You won't have to go that far. I'll promise not to come sniffing around. On one condition.' Ross paused. 'When it gets out what you're doing in there, you tell me everything about it, for this book or another. The inside story. Once it is in the public domain. I'd give you full credit, of course.'

Booth hesitated and then shrugged. 'If I get clearance.'

Ah, vanity thought Ross. He held out his hand and the other took it. Then he gave the lieutenant a shove in the shoulder and Booth staggered back, dropping his hat. Before he could recover, Ross was off, sprinting across the stones as best he could, heading for Miss Pillbody. Booth, who gave no quarter even to his seniors in the 200-yard dash at school, scooped up his cap and set off after him, his whoop drowning out the screeches of the alarmed gulls overhead.

Mrs Georgina Gregson stood and stared at the steamer trunk lying on her cot bed for a few minutes before opening it. She was enjoying the anticipation of being reunited with some old friends. She was hoping the flowery Russian peasant tunic she had purchased from Jollys was in there. And the blue crinoline skirt. Perhaps the striped afternoon dress. And some fresh undergarments – those she possessed were thin and scratchy, thanks to continuous washing and reuse since her detention.

After she had tormented herself enough, she unclipped the trunk's catches and heaved the lid back. Inside, the clothing looked like a rat's nest, all scrunched and intertwined, thrown in without any care or regard. She cursed whichever oaf had been sent to her lodgings to fetch her things. A man, that much was certain. She shuddered at the thought of some unwashed brute rifling her wardrobe and her drawers. *Yes, definitely a man*, she thought, as her eyes fell on a ball of material that turned out to be her ivory silk blouse. A woman would know that the entire caseful would have to be steamed or ironed before any of it could be worn.

She lifted out a pleated Fortuny tea gown, the hem weighted with dozens of glass beads. It had once been her mother's and still smelled of the vanilla fragrance she favoured. Not that she had any need of a tea gown in her present surroundings. Mrs Gregson wouldn't be attending any manner of social event in the near future. She had been plucked out of society, whisked away into a nether world ruled by despots and the Defence of the Realm Act.

Beneath the dress was a small stack of envelopes, all wrapped up in a red ribbon. Within the envelopes were Desmond's letters. He had written her such a precious few of them before—

Two paces took Mrs Gregson across the tiny room from bed to writing desk, where she scooped up and lit a cigarette. She told herself it was the smoke making her eyes water. *Don't dwell*, she told herself. *And don't cry. You are in quite a pickle as it is without collapsing completely*.

After that baby-faced detective had arrested her she had indeed spent a night in Holloway, but in solitary isolation. From there she had been transported in a blacked-out van to the first of a series of 'safe and secure' locations. All the time she had been promised her clothes and the trunk by various guards and warders – after all, she was a detainee, not a convict – but it had taken this long to catch up with her. And hidden in there was all that fate had left her of poor Desmond.

Mrs Gregson stubbed out the cigarette half smoked, picked up the letters and put them to one side, and set about extracting the tangled items of clothing and smoothing them out, laying them on the bed, over the chair and the desk, careful to move the note she had been composing to Major Watson. She had been writing it for weeks now, but she knew it was hopeless: she had no chance of getting to a postbox or post office. And that was terribly frustrating. There was one vital piece of information that trumped all the mundane jottings about Holloway and the dreadful man Colonel Montgomery, who had been in charge of her for a time and did not seem to care that she had but one pair of knickers. No, all that was irrelevant. But if the man she had seen striding the clifftop was indeed whom she believed him to be, Watson must be going out of his mind. She would pay a month's wages to get the information through to the major.

She paused in the act of shaking out one of her Smedley silk and merino vests. Perhaps that was the answer. Bribe someone to post the letter. But no, it would still be opened and read by the local censor. Perhaps if she reduced it to a single, pertinent line, surely nobody could object to that. Ah, but even that would beg a hundred questions. What, after all, could she write?

'I have seen Mr Sherlock Holmes and he too is a prisoner of DORA'?

When, later that night, a hand reached out for the two freshly delivered Mackeson bottles, manna delivered as if from heaven, Ross was waiting. He had crouched low next to the entrance of Oxborrow's cottage, biding his time, breathing slowly, ignoring his craving for a cigarette and the predatory whine of mosquitoes in his ear. Then, after a good forty minutes, something happened. No light showed; Ross simply heard the slight scraping of freshly oiled hinges as the wooden door swung back.

Ross acted fast, gripping the wrist he could just make out in the weak moonlight and dragging the man up to a standing position. Oxborrow worked at the forge assisting the blacksmith and Ross knew instantly that the man was strong, stronger than he in a fair fight, but he had the advantage of surprise. He kept the man off balance and walked him into the dark room, the pair clattering into furniture.

'Shush, there, shush, Jimmy, it's the American. Not the guys from the estate. Shush. Be quiet, you'll have them down on both of us. Calm down!'

Oxborrow stopped struggling and hissed, 'Leave me alone.'

'I just want a word.'

'Fuck off.'

Ross used his second advantage. He tapped the great oaf on the bridge of his nose with the lead-filled cosh. The man gave a yelp as pain exploded in his sinuses and his vision became a veritable Milky Way of celestial bodies. He slumped back into a chair. Ross went and fetched the Mackeson and slammed the door, waiting for the whimpering to subside.

'Mr Oxborrow, I need your help. I am prepared to pay for it. With money enough to keep you in drink for a year. Do you understand? But I need you to answer some questions.'

'You've broken my fuggin' nose,' Oxborrow said in a thick voice.

'No. It just seems like it. It'll feel like there is a cauliflower up each nostril for a day or so. But it isn't broken.'

'Who the fuck are you?' It came out as 'oodafugaroo'.

'I am a journalist. A writer.'

'What kind of writer carries a blackjack?'

'A very determined one who once rode with Roosevelt in Cuba.' A little embellishment never hurt. 'Now, would you like one of these beers?'

A grunt.

'Do you have an opening device?'

'Give 'er 'ere.'

Oxborrow took the bottle and put it between his teeth, levering off the cap, spitting it across the floor into darkness. 'Always carry an opener with me,' he chortled.

Ross waited while the man gulped some down. 'Mr Oxborrow, I would like to know what happened to you when you went on to the estate. Am I right in thinking you know a way in?'

'What's it to you?'

'Word has reached London of a terrible injustice. Families turfed out of their home, livelihoods ruined—' An aggrieved snarl in the throat. 'Schools and churches declared out of bounds. Now, I say the Government, *your* Government, has gone too far.'

'Aye. And it's mine by rights, you know.'

'What is?'

'The estate, like. From my grandfather.'

'Of course it is, Jimmy.' The man was rambling. 'Miss Pillbody asked me to investigate, to see what can be done.'

'But it's army secrets, innit?'

'What kind of secrets?'

Ross could hear the man's ragged breath in the darkness, sense he was thinking things out, considering the possibilities. 'You're not with 'em, are you? Is this like a trial? I told you that I saw nothing in there. Nothing.'

'Relax, Jimmy. I'm not with them.'

The man guzzled the bottle dry.

'Another?' Ross asked.

'Suppose.'

Ross handed it over. 'You know a way in? To the estate?'

A chuckle. 'Course I do.' Ross winced at the sound of teeth enamel on metal. 'Like I said, it's all mine. Know every inch. I should sue that Lord Iveagh. There's a stream . . .' He clammed up. 'You said summit about money.'

'So I did.' In the half-light Ross took out a stack of banknotes. Forgeries, but good ones. 'Fifty pounds there.'

'Fifty pound?' He reached out, but Ross snatched it away.

'Not yet. So there's this stream that you use?'

'Aye.' Oxborrow was sullen once more, now the cash had done a vanishing act back into a pocket.

'You can show me on a map?'

''Tain't on no map. Can show youse for fifty pound.' He laughed to himself and glugged some more stout.

'But you got caught.'

'Not there. I had some old traps for rabbits I went to inspect. Over in woods to the south. Nabbed me straight away.'

'But they let you go.'

'They was all for shippin' me off to some place, but I told them, I saw nothing. Never changed me story. Promised them I'd disappear and say nowt to anyone.' He laughed again. 'And also, those woods with the rabbit, they weren't in the evacuation area. Not really. That's what I said. An' I was right and they knew it. So when I buggered off, they weren't too concerned. They searched the woods, came here once. But they've given up now, I reckon.' Now he gave a low giggle. 'But I never told 'em the truth.'

Ross leaned forward and lowered his voice. 'Told them what? You did see something? In the woods?'

'Not a bloody sausage.'

Ross remembered his training. *You have to ask the right question.* 'But there *was* something?'

He could see the head with its shaggy hair nodding up and down. 'Aye, was something all right.'

The temptation was to hit him with the bloody cosh again. But he kept his temper. 'What was it, Jimmy?'

'Gotta be worth another tenner?'

'An extra sovereign.'

Oxborrow grunted a reluctant acceptance. 'It were voices. All around me. In the trees. Took me a while to work out what they was doing.'

The man paused and Ross resisted the urge to grab him by the throat. 'What are they doing?'

'They's making invisible men.'

'What?' asked Ross, louder than he intended.

'I reckon they's building an army of invisible men.'

FIFTEEN

They hadn't spoken for some minutes when Watson broke the silence. 'H. G. Wells.'

'I'm sorry, Major?' asked Coyle, snapping back into the here and now. He had been thinking of his first meeting with Gibson, when he had saved the Englishman's life. 'What was that?'

'You were wondering what Churchill gave me in the library.'

'Actually I wasn't, Major,' said Coyle. 'Like I said, best a man like me doesn't know too much.' He looked over at Watson, who was sitting next to him in the Vauxhall sports tourer. 'I'm an axe, a club, a pike, a simple weapon, me. Best I don't know.'

'Well, I'm still as baffled as you are as to exactly what they are doing. I just don't want you to think I'm being led by the nose by Churchill.'

'We're all led by the nose by someone, Major. Harry says—' He broke off as he remembered Gibson's fate.

They had spent the night in what Coyle had called a 'safe' house to the south of London. Although Watson was keen to be on his way, Coyle had insisted a night in London would be best.

That morning they had argued over the route, with Watson insisting on several diversions along the way. One had been to purchase a new medical bag and equipment. The other was to head down into Sussex.

As they motored on after a few minutes of silence, Watson cleared his throat. 'I'm sorry about Gibson. I liked him.'

Coyle just nodded, his face impassive. Then he said: 'It was my fault.'

Watson recognized the guilty phase of mourning. 'Coyle, that's not true.'

'Ah, it's good of you to say so, Major. But I know different. I was surprised by them. It's my job not to be surprised. It didn't make sense, coming after you like that. Odd. That was before I knew it was something to do with H. G. Wells.' He let a smile flicker over his face. 'Don't worry, Major, I'm not going to dwell on Harry, not yet. I told Harry he'd have to have a little patience. What I was really wondering is why you insisted we go south before going north.'

They had just left Ashdown Forest, motoring at a steady fifty miles an hour, the wheels humming on newly laid asphalt, disturbing the still, late-summer air. They were not far from Foulkes Rath, site of the tragedy of Squire Addleton, a grisly case yet to be written up and published. Watson pushed it from his mind.

'I have my reasons,' he said vaguely.

'I don't doubt it. I was planning on taking you to Colchester, Ipswich, Diss and Attleborough, coming in above Thetford. Not the way anyone looking out for you might expect. But then, this' – he indicated the twisting road ahead – 'isn't the way *I* expected.'

'No.' Watson looked at the AA motoring map he had purchased at the garage in Reigate, tracing the route Coyle had just described. It seemed a sound plan. 'But I need to investigate something first. Something that is bothering me. Trust me on this.'

'I do, Major. But we'll have to stop overnight somewhere again,' said Coyle, looking at the falling sun. 'We'll get to your destination before dark, but I don't want to be on the roads at night. I need to see who and what is around us.'

'I know an inn or two in Sussex where we can spend the night. Small, anonymous places.'

'Good.' They slowed as the road dipped and turned, twisting through a village comprising two oast houses and a cluster of half-tiled cottages. A few locals stopped to look at the handsome little car with the fishtailed bodywork as it roared by. Watson admired the Irishman's driving. He never seemed wrong-footed by the gears, the one thing about driving that often baffled Watson. Coyle was always in the correct ratio, meaning the engine never laboured. His braking was smooth and controlled, even though he had complained that the system needed upgrading for such a powerful engine.

There was little traffic on the road, barring local agricultural vehicles, and most of them were horse-drawn, and Coyle could let the Vauxhall have its head. Watson had rarely felt safer in a car. It was certainly an improvement on Mrs Gregson, the VAD auxiliary nurse who had acted as his driver in Belgium. They had kept in touch for a few months, but once she had gone back to the front, they had lost contact. He found, sometimes, he missed her forthright and often acerbic take on life. But not her driving.

Coyle's handling of the motor car might be exemplary, but the springing on the Prince Henry was a little stiff for Watson's liking. He could feel a twinge in his spine and another in his left hip. He tried to shift as subtly as he could to the most comfortable position. He didn't want the Irishman to think he had an old invalid on his hands. Well, old, yes. He'd accept that. Getting old was something being denied to millions of soldiers across the globe. He mustn't begrudge the toll of time. But he wanted this body to last a few more years, till peace broke out. Perhaps, then, it would be time to find a spot to see out his final days. Perhaps near the Sussex Downs. But until then, there was much to do.

He felt in his pocket again for the magazine Churchill had given him, taken from a handsome bound set in the library. It was *The Strand* for December 1903. Everything he needed to know was in there, the politician had told him, and had marked a page. At first he had thought Churchill was playing games, because in the same issue Watson had published *The Adventure of the Dancing Men*. But it was another section altogether that he had earmarked. Watson hadn't had time to read it yet, as he had fallen into a sound, exhausted sleep in Norwood. He would when they stopped that night.

Coyle cleared his throat to get Watson's attention. 'I don't mean to pry, Major, but this is something I should know. Is it Mr Holmes we are going to see?'

Watson pushed himself up in the seat a little, ignoring the stab of pain in his hip. 'It is. I tried telephoning, but the machine seems to be out of order. Or so the operator suggested.'

'Why, exactly, do you need to consult him? And could anyone know this side trip is on your agenda?'

Watson put a cigarette between his lips and offered one to Coyle, who took it. Watson lit them both.

'I doubt anyone would predict when I might visit him. We meet sporadically. Then again, my name is forever associated with his. Like Swan and Edgar or Tate & Lyle.'

'Or Burke and Hare,' said Coyle.

Watson laughed. 'Quite. I don't expect him to be here, not if Churchill told me the truth, but I am looking for clues to his whereabouts.' As Holmes himself would insist, he would go over the scene of the crime for clues – for that was exactly what Watson considered the removal of Holmes to a 'safe and secure place' to be. A heinous act. 'I shall be frank, I am worried for Holmes.'

'Why?'

'Churchill thinks this project of his is the biggest secret of the age. But it isn't. There is one piece of news which, if it were to get out, would shock the nation far more than any war-winning device they are dreaming up in Suffolk.'

'And what is that, Major Watson?'

He took a deep draw on his cigarette and let out a stream of hot smoke that was snatched away by the slipstream. 'Sherlock Holmes is losing his mind.'

As Coyle predicted, they reached the little cottage on the South Downs before the dying sun had touched the treeline, but it was a close-run thing. Banks of low cloud blotted the pre-sunset glow into a crimson band along the horizon. To Watson's mind, it looked like a giant sabre-gash in the sky. Perhaps, he thought, as they pulled up at the gate, one day he would stop seeing the wounds of war in everything he experienced.

Coyle sat, examining the little house as the car cooled down, engine and exhaust pipes ticking and creaking as it did so. Watson made to get out but an arm slid across his chest. 'Just a moment, Major.'

Watson looked, trying to see with Coyle's eyes. No smoke from the chimney. No lights – and it had a dark interior even in bright sunshine, so lamps were always lit early – but a letter or note of some description was pinned to the door. The paper was curled at the corners, as if it had been out in the weather for some time.

'Telephone's been cut,' said Coyle, nodding to the wire coils high on one of the corners. 'Let's take a look. Stay behind me.'

They exited the vehicle and walked up the path. As they moved closer to the front entrance, Watson could see the faded writing on the note: 'For the Attention of Mr Sherlock Holmes'. Coyle peered at it, then removed the pin holding it in place, passing the paper back to Watson. He also put a finger to his lips as he pressed down the latch. Watson pocketed the letter. There would be time for that later. A wave of the hand told him to stay put and Coyle, pistol drawn, stepped into the cottage. Watson could feel the chill from within. No fire had been lit and no one had been in there for some time. A pocket torch flicked on, and he heard Coyle moving around, fast and efficient.

Coyle stepped back out. 'The good news is, nobody in the opposition is waiting for us. The bad news is, your friend isn't here. The even badder news is, the place has been ransacked.'

Watson followed him into the living area, lit one of the oil lamps and took in the scene: the unwashed plates, mounds of cigarette and pipe ash, tottering piles of books and magazines, and the remnants of half-completed experiments. 'No, it hasn't,' said Watson. 'In fact, if anything, I'd say he's had a tidy-up.'

Coyle looked perplexed. 'Really?'

Watson nodded. 'Holmes never was the neatest of men.' He crossed over to the fireplace and lifted a threadbare Persian slipper from a hook on the chimney breast. He sniffed deeply, the aroma of the shag tobacco within tingling his senses, then moved to the armchair and sat. 'And he seems incapable of keeping a housekeeper these days. I'll make us some tea in a moment.'

'Aren't you worried?'

'About Holmes? Yes, of course. For several reasons. However, I suspect I know what has happened. When I said Holmes's mind had gone, I didn't mean completely. It's just that he has trouble accessing the higher faculties sometimes. It's as if his brain is stuck in neutral, and he has forgotten how to engage the gears. It started with small incidents: a moment's forgetfulness, an inability to make a connection that, in the old days, he would have seen in an instant. The worst thing was, he became aware of it happening. That's why he retired. That's why he won't get involved with any government schemes. He has a reputation. He wants to die with it intact.'

'I can see that,' agreed Coyle. 'I'm sorry, it's a bloody shame . . . but you know what happened to him, you say?'

Watson nodded. At first, the realization of Holmes's diminishing faculties had upset him dreadfully, but somehow the war had made it seem less of a tragedy. We all wither and die. Even the world's greatest – and only – consulting detective. Now, when he pictured Holmes, he conjured up the man who solved the problem of the Notorious Canary Trainer, the death of Cardinal Tosca, the tragedy of Woodman's Lee and death of Captain Peter Carey. That was 1895. What a year. He could still feel the thrum of excitement as case after case came to the door of 221 Baker Street and up the stairs to 221B. Watson thought the detective at the peak of his physical and mental powers then; it was always that fine vintage, Holmes '95, that he returned to whenever he thought of his friend.

'When his brain is not running properly,' Watson said, 'he behaves oddly. He calls me up, we have a lucid conversation, then he calls me up an hour later, forgetting we have spoken. It's most . . .' He thought of the times recently when he had refused a call from Holmes. He felt his face redden. Could one of them have been something about this business? Could Holmes have been reaching out to an old friend and confidant, only to find himself rebuffed? Watson gave a shiver of shame. '. . . trying. The old Holmes was the most circumspect man alive. The Holmes we have now is a gossip. He could not keep a confidence, even if he wanted to. I suspect that Churchill or his people realized this mistake and had him removed.'

Watson was now certain it had been Holmes who had inadvertently opened his mouth about Miss Mary Culme-Seymour, the young lady the King was meant to have married in Malta in 1890 and neglected to divorce before he married Princess May. It would take only the wrong word to a sharp hack – reporters often pitched up at that very cottage unannounced to interview the legend – for the true facts to emerge.

'You think someone tried to shut him up?'

'Yes, I do. Churchill said those who knew too much were sent to a "safe and secure place". I think that was the phrase. Although he didn't specify exactly where. The North Sea, he said.' Watson held the Persian slipper up to his nose once more. 'The problem is, Holmes would have known too much but could no longer be trusted to keep it to himself.' Watson felt disloyal even voicing this, but he believed it to be the truth. 'Or at least, that is how Churchill would see it.'

'So, Churchill would have gone to Holmes before he came to you? Forgive me, but you were second choice in this?'

'Certainly,' Watson said without rancour. 'We usually come as a package – Holmes's mind and whatever meagre medical skills I still possess. I think once he realized Holmes would no longer be able to bring his powers to bear, Churchill hoped I could supply a spark of the former to join the latter. I am afraid he will be sorely disappointed. Time has taught me that Holmes's abilities are not easily transferred.'

'So you want to find out where he has been deposited?'

'I do. And I shall agitate for his release, DORA be damned. But aren't you charged with such matters? The incarceration of those who pose a threat to national security or some such?'

Coyle shook his head. 'Internment? Not usually. Special Branch or military police, they're the lads for that. I've not heard of anywhere in the North Sea where they are sending folk.'

Watson stroked his moustache in thought. 'But could you find out where it is? Where he might have been taken?'

Coyle nodded. 'Possibly. It might take some time. Harry, he's the one . . .' He paused, struggling with the tense. 'He was the one who dealt with other departments, went in for office politics. Him having a proper accent, an' all. They wouldn't talk to the likes of me – Special Branch was once the Special Irish Branch, y'know.'

Watson nodded. It had been formed specifically to target the Fenians and their bomb plots; the country-specific name had changed when its brief was widened to all international terrorists and anarchists. 'But you are an officer of MI5.'

'That's as m'be. But they're still not keen on talking to bog-trotting micks. Their words, not mine.'

'I'll put the kettle on.'

But Coyle motioned for him to stay where he was. Watson frowned a silent question. Coyle mouthed the reply. 'There's someone outside.'

SIXTEEN

The summer evening had faded into dusk and then thickened into night, and it had grown chill and damp. Rain was in the air. Oxborrow led Ross down the narrowest of country lanes, across stiles, skirting fields, always pressed close to the hedgerow, heading south and then cutting east, towards the black stand of trees that marked the beginning of the forbidden estate.

The poacher said very little, just the occasional whispered warning. The deal was very straightforward: Oxborrow would lead Ross to the access point that would enable him to cross over into Elveden undetected. From then on, he was on his own. Oxborrow had no desire to be put through the grinder again by the goons who had caught him at his traps the last time. He hadn't even been on their land then. Whatever they were doing in there, he said, they were welcome to it. He was just a simple poacher.

And he certainly wanted no truck with invisible men.

Ross was puzzled by that. An invisible army would, indeed, be a fine advantage. But so would getting the Germans to accept a giant wooden horse as a farewell present as the British pulled back. It was about as likely as invisible men. However, something had clearly spooked the poacher out there. When they stopped periodically, Ross cocked his head, but all he could hear was the rustle of wind through branches, the friction of restless leaves and the call of an owl. 'What did you mean, that this is all yours?'

'My dad's middle name was Singh. Dark-skinned, he were. Michael Singh Oxborrow. Descended from them that had it before the Guinnesses. There's a fair few of us from the wrong side of the blanket, to be honest, so I wouldn't get it all. But a sizeable share, I reckon. Come on, then.'

They started off, moving in silence once more. 'Dark here,' muttered Oxborrow. He turned into a sunken path, the night sky reduced to a slit above their heads by walls of hawthorn and hazel. It felt like one of the trenches Ross had read so much about but, thank the Lord, had never experienced.

No matter how dangerous and underhand the life of a spy, there were worse options.

He stumbled on a stone and cursed.

'Quiet now,' admonished Oxborrow. 'We's not too far away.'

It was cold in the lane, a deep, primitive chill, as if summer had never penetrated this pathway since it was first constructed. Ross shivered as he picked his way after the villager, who seemed to have taken on a new fleetness of foot as he skipped over the slow-rotting mulch beneath their feet. Perhaps he could see in the dark or had bat-like powers. It would be handy for a man in his line of work, Ross supposed.

After five or more minutes, a fresh sound entered his

consciousness. The soft burble of water, the trickle of tiny tributaries, the steady drip-drip of wet undergrowth. They were near the stream that Oxborrow had spoken of. Sure enough, Oxborrow slowed and Ross all but walked into the back of him. The soil underfoot was boggy and sticky, the ground beginning to rise, and they emerged from the mud of the lane into a small clearing in a copse of beech trees, which stood like a circle of druids, arms raised in incantation. The gusting wind unsettled them and their branches swayed, as if they were imploring the sky to bring down gods. An opal thread of water pierced the heart of this ring. And something else flitted about. It wasn't the cold of the earth making Ross shiver now. It was the voices.

They were indistinct, overlapping, braided together into a single, transitory hum. But they were male, he could tell that much. The bursts of sound came into the circle of trees from several directions, dancing between the wrinkled, saggy trunks like wood sprites, then fading again. There were moments of clarity, when a single word leaped from the mumble. 'Stupid,' he heard clearly. Were they talking about him? Then, a burst of laughter, rolling like a peal of bells. Then, quite clearly, as if at his shoulder, each word clearly enunciated, the accent top drawer, in contrast to the sentiment: 'It'll make the Hun shit themselves, mark my words—'

He spun and looked for the dark shape of Oxborrow. The man was already backing away. Even in the gloom, Ross could see the paleness of his wide eyes quite clearly.

'Hold on,' he hissed. 'How do you get to the estate?'

'We's on the edge now. You follows that stream, and it goes underground, but a man can crawl through it. You come up to where the huts are. Gotta be real quiet then.'

'Huts?' He hadn't said anything about huts.

'Tin huts, they are. Sort of half a cylinder.'

Ah. The new Nissen huts. One of his previous assignments had been to discover what was being tested at the Royal Engineers' proving ground in County Durham. It had turned out to be prefabricated units for housing people and supplies. There was, he discovered, actually a Major Nissen. Clever, but not a war-winner. What about here, though?

'How many people know about this lane?' Ross whispered to Oxborrow.

The reply was so soft he had to strain to hear it. 'Nobody. No reason to use it. Old Tom Jenkins told me about it and he's dead.'

'And so are you,' Ross muttered to himself.

The razor had been modified from the standard shaving cutthroat, so that the blade flicked out from the handle, but here it locked solid. It was also fashioned to a sharp tip, rather than the gentle curve of the barber's model. At first he thought he'd misjudged it and missed, but then he saw a dark curtain of blood emerge from the gash that ran beneath Oxborrow's chin.

Such was the shock of the moment, it was easy for him to push the man to the ground and clamp his mouth shut while the life force pulsed out of his body. A few convulsions, a series of tremors and he was gone. He would bury him at the base of the hedgerows in the lane.

Huts. That meant soldiers. He lay still, listening for more of the phantoms' talk, but there was none. They had departed. The only sound was the insistent buzzing of a distant aeroplane, no doubt one of the English night fighters sent over to patrol the skies for the German Zeppelins. Lying next to the dead man, he let his own body go limp for a few seconds, allowing the tension to ooze out of his muscles.

Such temporary respites were like a sip of sweet nector in his profession. German spies, indeed, spies of any nation he would imagine, could rarely let their guard down.

Getting into position in the village had meant a stressful few weeks. The tip-off that something potentially interesting to German intelligence was happening in the region had begun with a letter in Liverpool. A mother had boasted to a sister that her son had been transferred to 'something vital to the war effort' in Suffolk.

The letter had been passed to the chief censor to recommend action against the woman and perhaps the loose-tongued son. Ross was one of two or three people in Great Britain who knew that the head of the North-West England censor office was, in fact, a German, albeit one born in Poland. That censor, Silber by name, passed on these broad hints that something very big, very important – very 'hush-hush'– was happening at Elveden to his controller in Holland. So, Bradley Ross had been brought into the field to investigate. *Bradley Ross.*

He had laboured under so many names now, he sometimes forgot his own. It certainly wasn't Bradley Ross, a name he had but recently adopted. Nor Dirk Alberts from Movietone, who, after meeting the genuine article at the Foreign Correspondents' Club, had stolen Ross's identity as being more useful than that of a Dutchman. The Dutch in England were treated with suspicion; most had been interviewed by Special Branch or MI5, as Dirk Alberts had been, twice.

US citizens were inevitably given the benefit of the doubt and so posing as an American made it easier to cover up any slips in his persona. They were still exotic creatures to most of the British, rare specimens from a distant land. Plus, the Allies wanted all that US might and muscle on their side, fighting on the Western Front, so he found people went out of their way to be courteous.

If only they knew . . .

The chances of his being discovered were very slim. The original Ross certainly wasn't going to complain from the bottom of a gravel pit on the outskirts of London. 'Dirk Alberts' had lured him there with the promise of 'hush-hush', as well as something altogether more unsavoury, and taken his life, in all senses.

The new 'Bradley Ross' was really Pieter Dagna, late of South Africa and Germany, and a man whose family had good reason to hate the British down the years. Tales of what Rimington's Tigers, the freebooting British light cavalry, had done to his grandma and mother during the second Boer War was a cornerstone of Dagna history. No bedtime fairy stories for Pieter and Christian and little Hester — just tales of terror and horror drawn from real life.

He shook his head, flinging Dagna back into a shadowy corner of his brain. To survive in his chosen life you had to live in the moment, be who you were meant to be. A writer. American. A British supporter. Not a German spy searching for clues to something so 'hush-hush' that they threatened to shoot schoolmarms.

Whatever was hidden in the forests and meadows of this country estate was clearly a big prize, but he had to be careful. Not for him the firing squad in the Tower of London, which had taken the lives of Lody, Melin, Meyer, Zender and the others. All now at rest, peaceful or otherwise, in East London Cemetery. The last resting place of German spies. He was in no hurry to join them.

The sound of a low-flying plane jolted him back to the matter at hand. An aeroplane. That, he realized, was the next move. Before he went into the lions' den, he wanted to know exactly what was in there. He would request an aerial reconnaissance, with a diversionary bombing raid on the nearby aerodrome to cover the real purpose of the incursion over England.

Perhaps he could persuade Elveden to give up its secrets without having to crawl on his belly into an enemy encampment. But even as he worked out how to get the message across to his superiors, he knew in his heart what the answer would be: 'It's your mission. Just do it and report back.' After all, he was a lot cheaper and more expendable than the pilots and planes of the Imperial German Flying Corps.

Ross gave a sigh and stood, putting his back into the tiresome work of dragging Oxborrow's body towards its final resting place. But not before he'd ransacked the pockets and retrieved the forged money he had given him.

He reached the entrance to the lane and rested, panting from the exertion. He always forgot just how heavy and awkward a corpse could be. When he returned he would come better prepared, with the right boots, clothes, weapons and camouflage. And he would be ready for the shock of those voices. He didn't believe in invisible soldiers. But what if the British were perfecting a weapon to amplify the sound of their army? Some kind of acoustic device. That one, clear phrase came back to him: *It'll make the Hun shit themselves.*

All he had to find out now was what, exactly, those bastards had out there that would loosen bowels on the Western Front.

SEVENTEEN

Coyle put a finger to his lips and pulled the pistol from his pocket. He walked backwards, turning as he went, so that by the time he reached the front door he was facing it, gun held loosely at his side. He listened again, frowning, trying to pick up the slightest sound.

Watson saw it before Coyle did, just an indistinct shadow crossing the glass to the left of the entrance.

'The window!' Watson shouted.

The sound was enormous, blowing Watson deeper into the armchair and making his ears ring. One of the panes shattered, but such was the report of the Smith & Wesson, its fragments cascaded in silence.

Coyle was already out of the door with, Watson thought, reckless abandon. He pushed himself from the chair and went after him.

There were two figures sprinting through the fading daylight, the intruder followed by Coyle, up the slope from the side of the cottage, to where Holmes kept his bees. Coyle was gaining on the stranger and Watson saw him drop his pistol, letting his arms pump him on, until he was close enough to launch himself onto the back of the other man. They landed and rolled into a ball, like an eight-legged hedgehog, before Coyle jumped up and dragged the man up after him.

Except it wasn't a man. Even from that distance Watson could see it was a boy that Coyle was half pushing and half carrying back down the incline, stopping only to scoop up his pistol.

'I could have blown your bloody head off,' he was saying as he came into earshot. 'You little fool.'

The gangly youth was windmilling his arms as he came, afraid of losing his balance as Coyle swept him along. 'I'm sorry. I left Mr Holmes a note on the door and I saw it had gone. I thought he must have come back. I've been worried about him.'

Watson plucked the rain-stained note from his pocket and flipped it open. His eyes went to the signature. 'Bert'.

This was Herbert 'Bert' Cartwright, the young lad who had helped Holmes solve the mystery of the de Griffons just over half a year ago, and helped establish the identity of the man who had been killing Watson's comrades in the trenches. Watson had never met Bert, but Holmes had been trenchant in his praise for the lad.

'You can let him go, Coyle,' said Watson. 'He's friend, not foe.'

'Nearly a dead friend,' said Coyle, shaking his head as he released his grip. Watson could see Coyle was a little shaken, whether by the near miss of the young man or the impetuousness of his actions, he couldn't be certain.

'I'm sorry.' The voice was tremulous and the boy had turned quite pale, but was trying his best to put a brave face on the situation.

'Would you like some water, Bert?'

For a second, Bert wondered how the man knew his name. 'Dr Watson? Is that you, sir?' he asked, straightening his jacket. His voice had that unnatural undulation of the adolescent, leaping registers in the space of half a sentence.

'As was. Major, now. You are Bert, then?'

The youth nodded like a puppy dog. 'We haven't met, sir, but I saw you once. Out on the Downs. Arguing with Mr Holmes. I was just a boy then.'

Holmes remembered that incident and, yes, the boy with the

kite who had witnessed it. A whole two years ago. A lifetime for this lad.

'So when did Mr Holmes leave?' asked Coyle as they walked up the path.

'I was supposed to come and help him with some newspaper cuttings. He is getting very . . .'

'Forgetful?' Watson asked.

'Yes. And clumsy, sir.'

'Clumsy?' The trill of an alarm bell sounded in Watson's head. Holmes, an expert Japanese wrestler, boxer and swordsman, was many things, but clumsy wasn't one of them. In fact, those etiolated fingers had extraordinary delicacy of touch. 'And his manner? Was he his usual self?'

'Not really. Crotchety, I'd say. More than usual, anyway.'

Watson put a hand on the boy's shoulder and squeezed lightly. He wanted his full attention. 'Can you describe him, his physical appearance, the last time you saw him?'

Bert shrugged. 'Same as he always was, I suppose.'

'Are you sure?'

The boy shuffled his feet. 'Well, he was bit heavier.'

'He'd put weight on?'

'Yes.'

Watson had noticed signs of this the last time he had seen Holmes. The rake-thin sapling had thickened in late middle age, a natural part of getting older. Or so he had thought. 'Much?'

A nod.

'And his face? How did he look?'

'Tired,' said Bert. 'He had dark circles under his eyes. I said I'd bring him some tonic. Like my mother takes for her nerves.'

'Did you now. Good lad.' Watson felt the first flowering of shame. *Call yourself a doctor? You've been too long in the minds of soldiers*, he thought. 'Did he take the tonic?'

Bert shook his head. 'When I turned up on the Saturday he was gone. I left a note for him. I come by every so often, see if there is a light on. And there was. And the note was gone. But I didn't recognize that car, so I was worried they'd come back again.'

'Who?'

'The men he said who were badgering him to come and help with the war.'

'Do you know who they were?' Watson asked.

'Oh, yes.'

The sun was slipping away now, the sky darkening to a soft mauve. A brace of bats began their erratic, jerky choreography as they chased down their evening meal.

'Who were they, m'boy?' Coyle asked.

Bert looked at Watson when he answered. 'They were from Mr Churchill, so Mr Holmes said.'

'But you have no idea what it was about? Why the men should come?'

'No. But Mr Holmes did say one thing that was odd.'

'What was that, Bert?' asked Watson.

'He said' – Bert cleared his throat and did such a fine impression that, despite the seriousness of the situation, Watson smiled – '"I once said to my old friend Dr Watson that I thought there was an east wind coming, Bert. But I was wrong. It has shifted. It is now a wind from the west. And if what men are perfecting in their satanic woods but a hundred miles from here should come to fruition, young Bert, the world will never be at ease again. And I for one will be pleased to know I shall not live to see such days."'

They lodged that night at a small inn, just north of Lewes. Watson had impressed on Bert the need for absolute silence on the subject of their visit and the disappearance of Mr Sherlock Holmes. The lad swore he had shared the event with nobody else, had only broken confidence because it was him, Dr Watson, Holmes's trusted companion.

Watson had left him with money to get the window repaired, and contact details should he need help. Bert was still some way from conscription age, but should the war go on, Watson didn't want the young man disappearing into the ranks of the cannon fodder he had witnessed being thrown away in the filth of no man's land.

They arrived at the Torrington Arms just as a summer storm broke. They were welcomed by the landlord who, if he remembered Watson from a few years previously, didn't let on. But he told them there were beds for the night and homemade mutton pie or fresh trout available. A fire might be lit if the temperature dropped.

He and Coyle went to their separate rooms and agreed to meet downstairs for dinner. Watson was given first shot at the bathroom down the hallway and ran himself a deep bath, liberally sprinkled with Du Barry bath crystals. He ached from stem to stern, his ageing body drained by recent events, his mind vexed. A good man dead. A missing colleague detained heaven knew where. He knew he had no leverage with Churchill, no other way of getting to the truth about Holmes's incarceration. You played the game with Winston. You brought something to the table. So, he had to solve the mystery of the seven dead and one insane man to rescue his poor, diminished friend.

Once he had submerged himself up to his neck, he levered himself back up, dried his hands and reached for the magazine that Churchill had given him. He opened it at the marked page and began to read 'The Land Ironclads' by H. G. Wells. Despite the hot water swirling around him, he shivered, as if somebody had opened the door a crack and a draught of icy air was blowing across the back of his neck. And, slowly, like a photograph emerging on silver bromide paper dipped in developing solution, it all swam into focus.

PART THREE

16–19 AUGUST 1916

EIGHTEEN

They spotted the barrier blocking the road from almost a mile away, and the wooden hut positioned to one side, just behind it. They were running south, on a stretch of arrow-straight asphalt, after a long day of hard driving, detours and one overheating radiator. They hadn't spoken much during the final leg of the journey, but Watson felt it was a comforting silence. He hadn't slept that well at the inn, the mutton lying heavy on his stomach and the thought of Holmes even heavier on his mind.

Coyle, too, had suffered an unsettled night. Watson had heard him pacing the floor and talking to himself. At least, he had assumed it was to himself. It could have been to Harry Gibson.

Still, although Watson had felt drained and had dozed for some of the journey, Coyle, being half his age, had shaken off any weariness and stayed sharp for the whole day. He had ensured they were not 'tailed', occasionally doubling back just to see if any other cars followed suit. Eventually, he was satisfied they were alone on this strange trip, and stopped the tricks and feints.

Now, with their destination in sight, Coyle slowed as they approached the roadblock. Already, members of the Home Service Defence Force were positioning themselves across the asphalt, rifles at the ready.

'Friendly,' said Watson.

'There's a machine gun up to the right, too.'

Watson hadn't spotted that, sitting atop a mound between the trees, covered in netting. He suddenly felt like a grouse on the Glorious Twelfth.

'Whatever it is in there, Major, they don't want the likes of me to see it.'

'None too keen on me, either,' Watson said.

Coyle coasted towards a stringy sergeant who stepped into the vanguard. He imagined they didn't get much excitement around there. The sergeant looked like he was keen to pull the trigger as he levelled his Lee-Enfield.

'Halt!' he bellowed, as if any driver could be in doubt as to his intentions. Even without his belligerence, the large red and white pole with 'STOP' written on it was a hefty clue.

Coyle wound the window down and the sergeant stuck his head in, bristly white moustache first. He had to be Watson's age or older.

'This is a restricted area, sir,' he said to Watson.

'I'm delivering Major Watson on the instructions of Mr Winston Churchill.'

The sergeant perceptibly recoiled at Coyle's brogue. 'Are you now? And what's your name, sir?'

'Donal Coyle.'

His eyes ran up and down Coyle's civilian garb. 'And your status?'

'Tired, hungry and heavily armed. It's not a good combination for an Irishman.'

Watson smiled at the guard's horrified expression. 'I'll vouch for him, Sergeant.'

The man looked at Coyle like he was a rabid dog, begging to be shot. 'You wait here.'

Coyle turned the engine off and the Vauxhall gave a grateful shudder. Wisps of steam curlicued from the bonnet.

'You shouldn't joke with these people,' warned Watson. 'It's their one moment of power.'

Coyle pinched the bridge of his nose and squeezed his eyes shut. 'I wasn't exactly joking, Major.'

'No, you must be exhausted. I would like to thank you. For your company and for your efforts in keeping me safe.'

Coyle opened his eyes. 'It still doesn't feel right to me, all this. I hope you will be kept well in there.'

'As do I,' Watson admitted. 'It's a leap in the dark.'

'Are you armed?'

'No.'

Coyle reached down and pulled out the small compact automatic pistol from by his ankle. 'Take this.'

'I'm sure I won't be needing one.'

'Take it,' Coyle insisted. 'I'm done with it now. I've another of the little devils at my digs.'

Watson took the tiny gun, weighed it in his hand – it was astonishingly light – and pocketed it. 'Thank you.'

'You have to be able to count the hairs on their moustache before you pull the trigger, mind. It's got no stopping power. But, as you probably know as well as me, there are plenty of times when just the sight of a gun does the trick. I'd give you the Smith & Wesson but . . . well, I'll be wantin' that one meself. Now, I need to stretch my legs.'

They both got out of the Vauxhall, feeling many pairs of eyes watching their every move. The sergeant had disappeared into the hut. Watson could see the telephone wires stretching away from it.

'What will you do once I'm installed here? Back to London?'

Coyle shrugged. 'I suppose. I have unfinished business.'

The sergeant returned, bustling briskly up to them with a flurry of self-importance. 'You, Major Watson, are to wait here. A car is being organized to take you to your quarters. You' – he turned to Coyle – 'I am afraid cannot enter.'

'Now look here,' said Watson. 'This man has been driving all day. What is he supposed to do? Get back on that telephone—'

'Major Watson,' said Coyle, 'it's fine. I have no desire to cross that line. I have done what I was charged with, albeit a little later than anticipated.'

'You are in no fit condition to drive back to London. And that car needs a rest.'

Coyle nodded at this. Oil, water, brake and clutch fluids needed topping up and there were nipples to be greased and brakes to bleed.

The sergeant softened and said, 'There's a pub in the village about four miles that way. Go back up here and take a right. The Plough. Rooms out back. Nothing fancy. Clean. Good breakfast. Sausages from my brother's pigs.'

Coyle shrugged. 'Sounds perfect.'

Watson and Coyle retreated a few paces away from the soldier and shook hands with each other. 'I meant what I said. Thank you, Coyle. Perhaps we will meet again under happier circumstances.'

Coyle gave a gentle chuckle at that.

'What is it?'

'People like me don't have happier circumstances, Major Watson. I'm not sure you do either, these days. This is about as happy as it gets. I've enjoyed meeting you again. You're a good man. And if you get into trouble, tell Kell to whistle me up. I'll come running.'

'I'm obliged.'

Watson watched the Irishman crank the car back into life, climb in and execute a swift three-point turn, his hand out of the window in farewell as the Vauxhall straightened out and accelerated down the road, a worrying plume of steam in its wake. Watson appreciated what, of course, the unfinished business was. Coyle was going to find out who killed his friend Harry, and make them pay. *That* was why he needed the Smith & Wesson.

Well, Watson could sympathize with his intent. After all, wasn't he, too, acting out of loyalty to an old friend? What else would have brought him to this godforsaken place?

Watson turned back to the barrier. Beyond it, down the road, still as straight as anything the Romans might have conceived, he could just make out a vehicle approaching. And, above the mocking calls of the crows, he thought he heard the faint crack of a gunshot.

NINETEEN

The fracas started with C Company and quickly spread along the dried tinder of boredom and frustration and ignited in the huts of adjacent G Company. By the time Booth arrived the brawl had spread into the open, with clusters of men thumping bloody heck out of each other among the ferns with no rhyme or reason. Some were shouting, but others were just letting out an animal-like roar, as if this were a rutting contest.

Booth stood watching, leaning against one of the forest's hornbeams. He had warned Swinton something like this might happen. Unable to leave the site, with no women and little alcohol, the soldiers grew restless and ornery. It was hardly surprising that steam was let off now and again. And, being men, they did it with their fists.

Booth signalled to Greaves, the military police sergeant. He snapped an order to his men, who weighed in with their clubs, some with a little too much enthusiasm. Booth hesitated as the intensity of the fighting increased, took out his revolver and fired into the air.

The branches above him exploded into life with the shrill cry of alarm and the crash of wings as the crows took flight. The report of the Webley chased through the stand of trees. *It might be a cumbersome weapon*, Booth thought, *but it makes a satisfying bang*.

He then levelled the gun at the nearest soldier. He was a big lad, with a cauliflower ear that suggested a history of brawls, and a thin bead of blood leaking from one nostril. There was the shortest of pauses. 'Next man throws a punch, I'll shoot him dead.'

There was a ripple of discontent among the mêlée. Someone called him a bastard. Booth swung the revolver to point at Gunner Appleton, a bricklayer's labourer, built like a side of beef. He was fairly certain he was the heckler. 'Perhaps you'd like to test me out, Appleton.'

The Somerset man gave a smile and shook his head.

'Where are your officers?'

'At a briefing, sir.'

This could mean anything. The officers were privy to certain privileges, including decent wine and dinners and regular bathing, which were denied the men. 'Sergeant Greaves, every NCO in this pack of animals will be on a charge. Understood?'

'Sir,' snapped Greaves.

'Now, while I have your attention.' Booth holstered his pistol. 'I admire your fighting spirit, lads, but it is misdirected. In the past twenty-four hours, we have been given notice that our little project has received some unwelcome attention.'

The men shuffled to face him now, curious.

'There is a German spy ring operating in the area.'

A few gasped, but most looked at him blank-faced.

He was exaggerating, of course. There was a curious American he didn't quite trust. He had radioed for guidance on the legality of interning Americans. London had said they would 'get back to him'.

'And I have it on good authority they will make an attempt to penetrate the perimeter and ascertain exactly what we are doing here.' Booth clenched his fist and shook it at them. 'I don't have to tell you what a breach of security like that will mean. The element of surprise is everything. *Everything*.' He spat out the word. 'I am going to double patrols. We are going to check and recheck the papers of every man found wandering the grounds. And I am, personally, going to give ten pounds to anyone who finds us a spy.'

There was, as he expected, a cheer at the mention of cash. There always was.

'Now, clean yourselves and your huts up and get cracking. There is a bloody war on, you know.'

He turned to Greaves. 'Put the NCOs on night patrols as punishment—'

Greaves frowned. 'But, sir—'

'They're just letting off steam.' He slapped the plywood model of the new wonder weapon that so much depended on. 'They'll be facing the Germans soon enough in something that isn't made of timber. That'll focus their minds.'

'Sir.'

'Get them organizing their patrols. I want this place sewn up tighter than a swan's backside. Understood?'

'Sir.'

As Greaves turned, Booth smiled. He would offer the same reward to the other companies. Ten pounds. That was almost six months' wages out in the real world for many of these men. He was throwing a net of greed around the camp. If Ross was a bad 'un, he was as good as dead.

The messenger intercepted the lieutenant as he walked the path towards the metal huts housing D Company. 'What is it?'

'Colonel Swinton sends his compliments, sir. He says a Major Watson has arrived.'

Churchill's man. Why did they all kowtow to the Butcher of Gallipoli? Yet Booth was as guilty of it as the next man. The very name Churchill opened doors. Although just as often you ended up catching your finger when they slammed shut. 'Very well. Where have they put him?'

'The Sandgrouse Lodge, sir.'

'I'll be along shortly.'

Booth waved his stick in dismissal, but the lad didn't seem in too much of a hurry to move along. 'Something else?'

'The colonel said to tell you that Major Watson has insisted on getting straight to work.'

'Has he? Good for him.'

'And he is insisting on seeing the new weapon for himself.'

'Is he?' said Booth slowly. 'We'll see about that.'

TWENTY

His name was Hubert Hitchcock, known to all as Hugh. His father was a senior clerk at the War Office, his mother a distant cousin of the Asquiths. He was born in Windsor; educated nearby at Eton, possibly with financial assistance from those relatives. Attended Balliol College, but volunteered for the army before graduating. He was commissioned into the Norfolk Regiment then transferred to the Machine Gun Corps and then its 'Heavy Branch', as the secret unit was called. He was selected, after a brief assessment, as commander of the weapon known as *G for Genevieve*. He was twenty-two years of age.

All that and more was in the file on the table in front of Watson. What wasn't in there was the fact that Hubert 'Hugh' Hitchcock had suffered a catastrophic breakdown.

He sat opposite Watson in the old servants' quarters in the basement of what was known as the Maharani House, a short walk from his rooms, which were located in a rather grand hunting lodge. There were slot windows high in the wall of the basement of the Maharani House, letting in a little of the dusk light, but the space was gloomy, even during the day. Which was, apparently, how Hitchcock preferred it. There was a cot bed, a table and two chairs, a small wardrobe and a bookcase, containing a set of encyclopaedias and a selection of adventure novels, mostly Rider Haggard. Not that there was enough light to read by.

Hugh Hitchcock was dressed in blue overalls. His feet were bare. His moustache needed trimming but he had shaved – or more likely, been shaved – albeit rather spottily. His hands, sporting long, artistic fingers, were lying on the table. Watson consulted the notes. Hobbies: walking, playing the piano. Watson looked at the eyes. He hardly blinked and the pupils were pin-sharp. He also had a strange, coin-shaped mark of reddened, shiny skin on his left cheek.

'Hugh, I'm going to light a cigarette. Would you like one?'

No reply. Watson lit his cigarette.

'Well, this is a bally situation, isn't it? As I said, my name is Major Watson. I am with the Royal Army Medical Corps. I've been sent to try to help you. I am not a head doctor, as they call them. You aren't mad. I don't deal with lunatics. You are the opposite. What has happened to you is entirely natural. Forget any notion of letting people down or some sort of weakness. Poppycock. I just think that sometimes we push our minds beyond a point our maker designed them to go. If one believes in a maker. Do you, Hugh? No matter, it could just be the constraints of our biology we are dealing with. I was reminded when I was driving here. Or being driven. The car began to overheat. We had driven the poor thing hard. And slowly I watched this little gauge that measured the engine temperature. Very clever. My driver said they are quite new. So as the engine got hotter and hotter, so the needle moved over towards this little red zone. What happens if it gets into the red? I asked Coyle – he was the driver. *Sir,* he said, *we have to stop.* And if we don't? *Well*, he said, *the engine seizes.* And can it unseize? I asked. *No, not without stripping it down and rebuilding, checking to see what damage has been done.* It struck me as a reasonable analogy for what our soldiers are going through. They are going into the red zone and instead of letting them rest, we keep going and keep going until we seize their engines. Sometimes it's the body that gives out, but just as often the mind. You've seized up, Hugh, and we have to find out what damage has been done, if any.'

Watson took a sip of water before resuming. 'Have you had any visitors? Would you like some? I can arrange that. But we should start by talking about that day. The day you seized up. That's the key. Forget about all those people who tell you to pull yourself together. Have you had that? Please put it out of your mind. But we have to face that day. You have to talk about it, know what it is, find its shape, before you can box it up and put it aside. And perhaps you never will do that entirely. But you can live with it, of that I am certain. Right now, though, you are frozen. It's there in your mind, isn't it? I would wager it is there in your dreams. We can talk about that, too. Often, I believe, our dreams tell us truths that we find hard to face at other times.'

Throughout this whole one-sided conversation, Hitchcock had remained impassive, his breathing even. Nothing Watson had said had caused a change in facial expression.

'Have you eaten? I'll get you something. And tomorrow, let's take

117

a stroll outside this room. I've only been here fifteen minutes, and it's driving me mad.'

Not the best choice of word, perhaps, but Watson had been hoping for a reaction. Again, not a flicker, just a long, slow blink. Still, he didn't blame him. It wasn't a good joke.

'You aren't mad, Hugh. I'm sure you can hear me. I'll get you out of there.'

Watson waited a couple of heartbeats. 'Did you kill them, Hugh? Oh, maybe not deliberately, but was it something you did? A mistake, that was all? Because you are here. And they are not. Why is that, Hugh? Why were you chosen to survive?'

The only response was a low growl in the throat.

There was a sharp rap on the door before it opened. A shaft of light from the corridor outside fell on Hitchcock. He shaded his eyes with his palms and the growl became a whimper. Perhaps a walk outside wasn't such a good idea after all.

'Sir, sorry to interrupt,' said the soldier, 'but Colonel Swinton would like you to join him for dinner at the Hall when it is convenient. He said no need to dress.' Watson noted the crossed machine guns on the private's uniform.

'Of course. And I'd like Lieutenant Hitchcock here to have something.'

'Oh, he will, sir. Just not while anyone is watching. Clears his plate while I've gone. Nothing wrong with his appetite, sir.'

The private said this with something approaching a sneer. Not sympathy, anyway. As if Hitchcock were faking it, that it was an act he could snap out of at will.

'Tell the colonel I'll be along shortly.'

'Sir.'

Watson turned back to Hitchcock. He put his hand over the sick man's. He didn't try to withdraw it. 'Don't worry, Hugh,' he repeated. 'Whatever happened to you and those others, I'll get you out of there.'

*

118

Watson approached Elveden Hall up the gravel drive, musing on what an unappealing hotchpotch the building was. There was clearly a sombre Georgian country house underneath all the extensions, domes and Italianate pillars that had been plastered on it over the years. It was grand, without being handsome. His opinion altered as he walked into the property. It was still far from handsome, but it became extraordinary.

The house's obvious shooting heritage was indicated by the two small rooms that flanked the immediate entrance. One was full of empty gun racks; the other boot scrapes and hooks for coats and hats. Both had cabinets of stuffed pheasants, partridges, grouse and rabbits on their walls, alongside photographs of gun dogs. Beyond that was the most astonishing hallway, all huge pillars and gilded ceiling, with stars and crescent moons shining down. Ahead was an elaborate, polished marble staircase, and flanking it a series of scalloped arches, supported by pillars bearing a complex coat of arms and inscriptions in what he would later discover was Gurmukhi, the language of the Sikhs.

Although there was European furniture dotted about, the effect was as if he had walked into a maharajah's palace in Lahore.

'Good Lord,' he said to himself, looking up at the constellations on the ceiling.

'Major Watson?' came a voice. 'In here.'

He walked from the hallway, through an arch, into a drawing room even more ostentatious and oriental than the hallway. No inch of plasterwork was free from the carved depiction of flowers, trees, animals – a strange mix of deer and elephants, rabbits and tigers – and yet more foreign writing. Each arch had a dozen mini-arches in its curvature, as if an enormous creature had been nibbling at them, while the columns were deeply fluted, and topped and tailed with elaborate capitals and plinths.

Standing in front of the marble fireplace, which was topped by a gilded mirror decorated with gold and silver peacocks, was a group of five men, drinks in hand.

119

'Welcome to our humble haveli,' said one of them, holding out his hand. 'Colonel Swinton. Pleased to meet a fellow author.'

To Watson's eyes, Ernest Swinton looked like a younger version of Kitchener, with his moustaches trimmed back somewhat. 'As am I,' said Watson. 'I enjoyed the *Defence of Digger's Drift* immensely.'

Swinton beamed and those moustaches twitched. It was a slight exaggeration on Watson's part. It was a workman-like novel in terms of prose, but the military details were exact and the historical setting well rendered. 'Thank you. Of course we all enjoy the retelling of a good Holmes case.'

Retelling? Was he suggesting that Watson was a mere reporter? He dismissed it. Fellow writers often reacted strangely to another's perceived success. Watson would not claim his works were great literature. But there was more artifice in them than a mere recounting of the facts.

Swinton made the introductions, his companions being Lieutenant Booth, an intelligence officer; Major Thwaites; a lieutenant-colonel called Solomon and, most surprisingly, a Frenchman, Colonel Claude Levass.

Booth was a surprisingly young man for an IO, with darting, suspicious eyes and an uncomfortable demeanour, as if something – or someone – had unsettled him.

Thwaites was an old-school cavalry officer – the uniform told Watson he was with the Royal Horse Guards, The Blues, who had fought at Waterloo – well over six foot, still whippet-thin into his fifties, with flamboyant sideburns and whiskers.

'How was your ride this evening?' Watson asked him.

'Very exhilarating,' replied Thwaites. 'You saw me?'

'No. But those fresh marks on your cheek could only have been made by the tips of branches.'

'Or perhaps a lady's fingernails,' suggested Levass, the Frenchman. Levass was smaller than Thwaites by a whole head, dark, almost swarthy, with a pencil-thin moustache, fine cheekbones and a rather winning smile. His English was close to perfect.

Thwaites touched the fine red marks beneath his eyes. 'If only that were the case. But Watson is right, I rode through the thicket at Crisp Hollow with Colonel Solomon here. He had the good sense to duck.'

'I was trying to hang on for dear life,' Lieutenant-Colonel Solomon said. 'With Thwaites every ride is a cavalry charge.' Solomon was a rather hangdog figure, uneasy in both skin and uniform, who didn't seem to Watson to have the bearing of a military man. There were also peculiar flecks on his hands like liver spots that he couldn't quite identify.

'We don't normally dine here,' said Swinton, changing the subject, 'but we like to show off the place from time to time.'

That, thought Watson, *or he doesn't want me mixing with the junior officers.*

'I am afraid his lordship took his cooks and most of his staff with him when he decamped to London,' Swinton continued, 'so we fend for ourselves somewhat. Drink?'

'A Scotch?' Watson suggested.

A white-jacketed orderly detached himself from the shadow of a pillar and fetched him a drink. Fending for yourself was all relative, Watson supposed.

'There you are,' the orderly said. 'With just a splash of water, as you like it, sir.'

Watson looked at the man: fifties, greying hair forced back from a widow's peak and sparkling eyes that suggested life was a huge joke. 'Wright? Billy Wright?'

'Sir. Late of the Army and Navy Club, now mixing drinks at the Elveden Explosive Area until further notice.'

Watson took the drink. 'It's good to see a familiar face.'

Wright gave a cheeky wink in reply.

'That's the official name, by the way,' said Swinton, from over his shoulder. 'The Explosives Area. Anyone asks, it's a munitions testing site. You know the story of this place? Elveden?'

Watson turned. 'I've heard of it. I know it was owned by a maharajah.' He looked around. 'I had no idea he had brought India with him.'

'Punjab, actually,' corrected Booth.

'My Uncle Walter fought in that war,' offered Thwaites. 'Second Anglo-Sikh. Seventy-odd years ago now. He's still alive. Almost a hundred.'

Swinton said: 'The maharajah was a boy king, just eleven years of age, when we won the Punjab.'

'Or, as we say in my country, *stole* the Punjab,' said Levass, his voice full of singsong mischief.

Thwaites glared at him. 'I think the nation that gave us Napoleon should be careful about accusing others of land-grabbing.' He turned to Watson for support. 'Don't you, Major? Eh?'

'Gentlemen,' chided Swinton, as if addressing squabbling children. 'As part of the reparations, we requested the Koh-I-Noor diamond.'

Levass gave a hoot. 'Requested? Demanded, I think. Your Lord Dalhousie smuggled it back under his shirt, as I recall. And brought the boy to England to present it as a gift to Queen Victoria,' he said with an admiring laugh. 'So clever. If anyone ever wants it back, you can just say, "But it was a gift."'

Watson knew some details of the story. The maharajah went on to become a great society figure, friend of the Prince of Wales, and a legendary shot.

'Didn't the maharajah fall from grace by trying to take back his lands?' Watson asked.

'Yes. Fell in with the Fenian Brotherhood and the Russians. Died a broken man in Paris,' said Thwaites.

'I wouldn't feel too sorry for him,' added Swinton. 'There's a fair number of swarthy boys and girls in this part of the world, some with the middle name Singh. He had a soft spot for a chambermaid, did the maharajah. Married one in the end. After his first wife died.'

'I painted his son. Frederick. Prince Freddy.' It was Solomon, speaking in a low monotone. 'Not in this house. He was forced to sell this when his father died. It was at Blo Norton Hall, his house not far from here. He's in France now, with the Norfolk Yeomanry. I saw him when I was gathering colour palettes.'

Palettes? Now Watson had him and the reason for those dabs of faded colour on his hands. 'Sorry, sir, but you're Solomon J. Solomon? The artist?'

The man nodded and gave a pleased half-smile.

'Holmes sat for you, didn't he?'

'Some time ago now.' The painter nodded. 'I think he was displeased with the results.'

'Holmes? Oh, no. Don't be fooled by any bluster. He wouldn't have wanted to seem vain. But he certainly wasn't unhappy with it.' It was a portrait of the detective leaning against the mantelpiece in 221B, his chin thrust out, his brow furrowed, a pipe frozen on the way to his lips. It was so dramatic, you could almost hear that great mind turning over a two- or three-pipe problem. 'It used to have pride of place in Baker Street.'

'And now?' Solomon asked.

Watson wasn't sure what had become of the portrait. 'Storage,' he said diplomatically, 'until a suitable place is found to rehang it.'

'And what of Mr Holmes?' Solomon asked.

Watson looked around, wondering if anyone in the room knew of his fate. Was this apparently convivial company of men part of the conspiracy that had stolen his friend away? But all simply waited for his answer. 'Retired,' said Watson curtly. 'And you, sir?'

'Ah. I am a mere housepainter now.' Solomon turned to Swinton. 'As one of your officers reminded me today.'

'Just for the duration,' said Levass, emptying a sachet of powder into a glass of tonic. 'For my gout,' the Frenchman explained when he saw Watson's professional curiosity was aroused. 'Bicarbonate of soda.'

'To neutralize the acid in the blood,' Watson said. He had never suffered himself, but had seen many patients in agony down the years from swollen joints and skin so sensitive a feather across it could generate intense agony. 'The Greeks, by the way, swear by cherry juice.'

'Do they?' asked Levass as he downed the solution and shuddered. 'It has to taste better than this.'

'And I have had good results with cider vinegar.'

Levass nodded. 'Really? I am much obliged, Major.'

'Although the taste is sometimes worse than the gout.'

A gong sounded, rippling through the house, reflecting sonorously off the marble and the domed ceilings.

'Ah,' said Swinton. 'Dinner. And time to talk business.'

Dinner was served in a rather splendid oak-panelled room in the 'new wing', lined with portraits of Anglo-Irish aristocrats and with none of the more elaborate Indian motifs of the hallways and drawing room, although subtle reminders of the sub-continent remained here and there, like the Sanskrit letters on the ceiling mouldings. There were silver platters, gleaming cutlery, crested plates, crystal goblets and decent wine, but the food was standard mess fare.

Swinton explained: 'There is an officers' mess we usually dine in, above Lord Iveagh's stables, closer to the, um, main training area. But I thought we'd break you in gently.'

Or sound me out first, thought Watson.

'But this is the inner corps of Operation Puddleduck, give or take a couple of engineer chaps.'

'Puddleduck?' Watson couldn't keep the incredulity from his voice. The most secret project in Great Britain was called Puddleduck?

'Well, strictly speaking, that's just this part of the enterprise. Elveden.' Swinton looked slightly flustered, as if someone had been reading his diary. 'Only a silly name.'

Watson wondered just what Beatrix Potter might think about helping to name the most secret project in the British Isles.

'So, what do you make of him?' asked Swinton. 'Hitchcock?'

'Sorry I'm late.' A new arrival came in, breathless, a jug-eared young man with a gaunt, worried expression, dressed in crumpled civilian clothes. He had in his hands what looked to be a rag.

From the scuffed toes of his boots, the grease-spiked hair and his reddened knuckles, Watson concluded the man was a mechanic of some description.

'And I can't stop. I just wanted to say hello to Major Watson. The name's Cardew. I'm one of the engineers on the project.'

Something more than a mere mechanic then, Watson chided himself as he stood to shake the young chap's hand. Cardew demurred.

'Sorry, grease all over it. Came straight from the workshop. The other sponsors have arrived, you see,' he said by way of explanation, the excitement in his voice palpable. 'So we can start fitting them to the main bodies. I am afraid it is going to be a late night. I just wanted to say welcome and hope we can get to the bottom of this terrible business.'

'As do I. But what's a sponson?' Watson asked, although he knew vaguely what the term referred to on a ship. But they were a long way from the sea.

Cardew looked enquiringly at Swinton, who said, 'All in good time, Major.'

'Yes. Well, back to work. I shall see you tomorrow?'

'I hope so. Perhaps you can tell me what a sponson is then.'

'Better than that. I'll show you one.'

'We'll see about that,' snapped Booth.

After Cardew had gone, Thwaites said: 'He's a keen chap. It takes hours to fit those damn things.'

Swinton was eager to get back to business. 'You were giving your opinion about Hitchcock.'

Watson leaned back as his soup plate was cleared. 'I don't quite understand my role in this. As I asked Churchill before – physician or detective?'

'Well, originally we wanted—' began Thwaites, before Swinton glared him into silence.

'I understand. You wanted Holmes, who then would have brought me on board. He for his powers of observation; me for my medical background in shell shock.'

'Something like that,' admitted Swinton. 'I'm sorry, that's not to demean your experience in deduction—'

Watson raised a hand to stop him. 'No need to apologize. It is an interesting case but it is difficult to assess Hitchcock properly on that one meeting when he has uttered not a word. True, the malaise has elements of what we used to call shell shock, but has some peculiar traits of its own. I have a few ideas. Is there a piano in the house?'

'Piano?' asked Thwaites, thinking Watson was suggesting after-dinner entertainment. 'Do you play?'

'It's not for me. According to his file, in his previous life it was a pastime of Hitchcock's. It might help him. A non-verbal therapy.'

'There's one in the music room,' said Solomon. 'I have played it a little. Quite serviceable. Needs a tune, perhaps.'

'And, if we can get him some spectacles tinted against the light, I want to take him for walks.' So-called 'browned' lenses were commonly prescribed for syphilis sufferers, as light sensitivity was a symptom, so they weren't difficult to source.

'In the gardens only,' suggested Booth. 'Not the greater estate. Bit of a flap on beyond the walls. You are liable to get challenged rather robustly. Or worse.'

Watson nodded his agreement. 'And he needs a woman's company.'

Solomon burst out laughing. 'God Almighty, he'll have to join the queue.'

Levass flashed a quick grin. 'I suspect that is not what the major means.'

Watson nodded his thanks. 'Shell shock or whatever term you prefer to use is often perceived as a failure of masculinity. Women, after all, get the vapours and hysteria. Men just carry on. Until they don't. I have had great success introducing women to the environment of the patient. Mothers, sisters, sweethearts . . .'

'Out of the question,' said Booth, with a querying look at Swinton, who nodded his agreement. 'I can't allow it on security grounds.'

'But there are women here?' Watson asked.

'Housekeeper, a couple of maids,' said Swinton.

'And a nurse, I believe.'

Swinton nodded. 'Indeed. You are well informed, Major.' There was a hint of suspicion in his voice.

'I thought I detected the whiff of ether in the hallway.'

Solomon, at least, smiled at the poor joke.

'I also need to see the scene of, um, the crime, as soon as possible.'

'We aren't certain there has *been* a crime,' said Booth. 'Our rule is, despite what Cardew has promised, that as few outsiders as possible see what we are working on.'

Watson turned to Swinton, exasperated. 'Then I am wasting my time.'

'Why is that?' asked Thwaites.

'If this were a murder scene . . .'

He let that hang there for a moment. They would know that he was aware that Hitchcock had seven dead comrades.

'It is no such thing,' said Swinton eventually.

Watson took his time gathering his thoughts. 'Seven men dead. One survives.'

'As a loony,' said Thwaites.

Watson let his distaste at the word show. 'If you take things at face value.'

It took a moment for that to sink in. 'Are you saying that Hitchcock engineered this whole catastrophe? And could be play-acting?' asked Swinton. 'You told us he was shell-shocked.'

'And I believe he is. But was that perhaps not a side effect of his undertaking? He was one of eight men in the same environment. Is that right?'

'Yes,' said Swinton cautiously. 'The same confined space.'

'Seven die, one doesn't. You don't have to be Sherlock Holmes to know where that is pointing.'

Really, Watson, you know I would never leap to such conclusions.

Watson smiled to himself at that familiar, if unreliable, voice in his head. His aim was not to jump to conclusions but to unsettle, to gain the upper hand. Yet he wasn't being entirely disingenuous. It was possible that Hitchcock could be a murderer. It was equally possible that he inadvertently started a chain of events that killed seven men.

'You think Hitchcock——' began Thwaites.

'I suppose nothing,' Watson interrupted. 'But if it were a murder scene, then I would ask to see the murder weapon. To examine it in detail. Something drove this man into catatonia. I believe it is a genuine condition. Not' – he wagged a finger – 'a form of malingering. But how did it come about? I need to know what and where this event took place. I need to see with my very own eyes. Churchill understood that.' He detected a little shiver of displeasure around the table at the mention of the name.

The next course, a shrimp mousse garnished with oysters, was placed before him.

'The others didn't object to not seeing the actual site of the incident,' said Booth.

'What others?'

'The unit's MO, Captain Trenton, was one of the victims. So we rather reluctantly brought two outside medical men in to examine the bodies, and Hitchcock,' said Swinton. 'One civilian doctor from Norwich, one army. We didn't let them beyond the house, of course.'

'Their conclusions?' Watson asked.

'Bafflement,' admitted Thwaites. 'And so we turned to you.'

'Well, Churchill did. Quite how he knew of our predicament I'll never know,' said Swinton, 'but he said he had just the men for the job.'

Men. Churchill had meant Holmes and Watson. And now they had just the one. *The lesser one, they no doubt thought,* Watson concluded.

Tut-tut, Watson, we are two halves of the same kidney.

'So you went along with him in this matter?'

'It isn't easy to argue Churchill down,' said Swinton.

'Quite,' said Watson, without, he hoped, too much bitterness. 'Nevertheless, I can't proceed unless I have your permission to examine every aspect of the case, including the place where the men were struck down. Believe you me, Holmes would say the same thing.'

'How much do you know about Puddleduck?' asked Swinton. 'Is Churchill telling everyone who walks through his door about it?'

'Not at all. He's closed up tighter than one of these oysters back when it had a shell. I know very little for certain. I have made informed guesses. But they are just that. Guesses.' He took a sip of Chablis. The room swam slightly, but not from the alcohol. He was tired. He wanted to get to bed. He wondered how many courses before the inevitable toasts to the King and fallen comrades and the port and cigars. 'But, I repeat, I need to see what killed seven men and drove one insane, no matter how hush-hush it is.'

'Drove *eight* men insane to begin with,' Thwaites corrected. 'Gibbering wrecks. And one by one they died. Some within the hour, the MO in the group took almost half a day.'

'You realize that you may well be confined to quarters if we reveal everything to you?' said Booth. 'Nobody, apart from Churchill and a handful of others, is allowed to be privy to this project and wander the streets.'

Levass swallowed a spoonful of shrimp mousse with an exaggerated gulp. 'We are prisoners of our own making, Major. Very comfortable prisoners, but it could be months before the world knows of what we do. Until then . . .'

'I'll take that chance,' said Watson.

Swinton and Booth exchanged glances once more. 'Very well,' said the colonel.

'Perhaps I could show the major his, what did you call it, "scene of the crime"?' asked Levass.

'I'll accompany you, of course' said Booth quickly.

'Thank you,' said Watson. 'Immediately after breakfast?'

'As you wish,' said Levass.

'Just one thing,' said Swinton. 'There was no crime, Major Watson. This is an unfortunate accident. You'll understand why when you see the conditions the men were placed under. I appreciate your reputation as a sleuth but—'

Watson raised a hand. 'That reputation was not mine. I would never claim it for myself. I am here as a medical man.'

Swinton seemed to relax. 'Very well. The sooner we get to the bottom of this case, the better.'

'Where, exactly, is the machine that did this to them?' Watson asked and pre-empted any questions about how he knew the nature of the device. 'Yes, I know it is a machine of some kind, able to wage war in the trenches. Mere logic tells me that.' *And H. G. Wells.*

Booth answered. 'There is a proving ground in front of this house, beyond the trees. It remains where it came to a halt.'

'And you will introduce me to this nurse of yours? I might need an assistant who has some medical knowledge. What's her name?' Watson asked.

'She's a bit of handful,' said Thwaites. 'We call her the Red Dragon. Not to her face, of course. Real name's Mrs Gregson.'

It was gone midnight by the time Watson got to bed back at the lodge. His meagre valise had been unpacked and there was a jug of hot water and a mug of Horlicks awaiting him. He ran through the evening in his head. Booth had quizzed him on events in London and the assassination attempt. Swinton was interested in Churchill. Levass talked about shell shock and French wine and his time in Mexico among the remains of Aztec civilization. Solomon held forth on his dislike of Vorticism, but how the art movement had a practical application in camouflage. That, Watson realized, was why they had a distinguished Royal Academician in their midst – Solomon was to be the master of disguise for whatever they were developing to unleash on the Germans. It was quite a long way from executing portraits of the great and the good, which was why the 'housepainter' jibe had clearly stung.

Thwaites, on the other hand, was most keen to talk about the adventures of Mr Sherlock Holmes. When Watson agreed to some small talk on the matter, he again studied the expressions of the men around the table, to see if, perhaps, they knew something about Holmes's whereabouts, but they were as impassive as professional bridge players.

Watson had had enough after twenty minutes and switched tack. 'And what is your role in all this, if I might enquire?' he asked Major Thwaites.

'Me?' Thwaites said. 'Tactics. Battlefield tactics. With the new . . .'

'The new weapon,' said Levass. 'Of which we are so proud.' There was a slight slur to his words. 'Aren't we, gentlemen? Although perhaps not Hitchcock, eh? I doubt he's too proud.'

'I think that's enough, Levass,' said Swinton.

Levass turned to Watson. 'You can cure him?'

Watson pushed his wine away. He suddenly felt very sober. 'We'll see.'

That apparently satisfied the Frenchman. Levass's presence was something of a puzzle. The French were allies, of course, but also notoriously loose-lipped. 'It's all classified information until the first glass of champagne' went the old adage. The Frenchman also seemed to enjoy poking fun at what he called 'perfidious Albion', especially over its annexation of the Punjab and the theft, as he put it, of the Koh-I-Noor. He had returned to the subject several times, until Booth had snapped at him, quizzing him sardonically about his own country's colonial record in Indochina, the Caribbean and Africa.

To trust a Frenchman with what Churchill called 'the greatest secret of the war' . . . well, he had to be rather a special kind of Frenchie. And the fact that he seemed drunk and snippy didn't bode well. Watson didn't doubt he'd find out more the next day.

Mrs Gregson's presence at Elveden was perhaps the most surprising revelation. Strictly speaking, she wasn't a nurse, she was a member of the Voluntary Aid Detachment, the VADs. But such niceties were often lost on soldiers. And she was a very competent medical woman, as he knew from their time together in Belgium.

Plus, he reminded himself, *she loves and knows motor cycles*. His patient had been in the Machine Gun Corps – as had the orderly who acted as gaoler – which used sidecars with machine guns on them. Was it her love of those machines that had got her involved?

Watson stripped off his uniform. The warm water on his face made him feel even sleepier. Whatever questions he had would be resolved after breakfast, when he would see Churchill's *Scourge of Malice* in the flesh, or whatever material it was made of.

But he would be there with Booth, Levass and God alone knew how many others. Holmes would never have countenanced that.

He heard voices outside his door and stopped his splashing. He crossed over to listen, but they faded. Back at the washstand, they became clearer once more. They were coming from outside his window. And he was on the second floor.

He pulled back the curtains and yanked up the sash. At first there was only the sigh of the wind, but then he heard them, a number of speakers, talking low and urgently. He looked down at the ground below, but could see nothing in the darkness. There they were again, phantom words floating through the night.

There was the drum of a sudden shower, and he felt raindrops on his head. It increased in severity, pouring down onto lawns and shrubs with a sound like scattershot. The voices were lost to it. He pulled the window down and yawned. *Ah well*, he told himself again, *all will be revealed tomorrow*.

Watson placed the little pistol Coyle had given him on the night-stand and finished his ablutions, eager for the feel of the fresh cotton sheets.

He was just nodding off when he heard the soft tapping at the door and reached for the gun.

That was when the first explosion rattled the windows, throwing sticks of light across the walls and shaking the glass in its frame like chattering teeth.

TWENTY-ONE

Petty Officer Third Class Joachim Kuhn climbed into the observation craft of L.18, the *Admiral Karl Rudolf Brommy*, just as the enormous Zeppelin crossed the British coast. She was cruising above the clouds, and the captain didn't want to bring his precious machine down to within range of the searchlights or artillery. Yet he wanted to make sure they were heading for the correct target. Too many times he had dropped bombs guided only by the glow of city lights through thin, translucent clouds. Tonight, the clouds weren't thin or translucent and, on this bombing mission, he was charged with being more accurate than usual. So, like a plumb-bob, the observation capsule – christened Effi by the men – would be winched down from the main ship to dangle below the cloud cover.

Kuhn opened the hatch in the floor of the Zeppelin's forward control gondola and lowered himself through into the miniature craft slung beneath it. The capsule swayed as he let it take his full weight. As he steadied himself, one of his fellow officers tossed down a pack of Königin von Saba cigarettes. 'Lucky bastard,' he said.

An icy breeze of air was blasting through Effi, which had side windows, but no glass, and Kuhn belted his coat and pulled up his gloves. *Lucky?* He wasn't so sure. But it would go on his record that he had volunteered. And then there were the Königin von Sabas.

Effi was shaped like a miniature 'sausage' observation balloon, with a bulbous nose and four tail fins. Inside, Kuhn had a wicker chair, bolted to the floor, and a table with a compass, charts, a square – so it wouldn't roll away – flashlight, a flask of water and a telephone. There was also a bucket next to the table, next to a hatch in the floor. It could be a long, lonely night in the little craft.

He settled down into the chair. Around him the wind whistled, and the little baby craft vibrated in time with the Zeppelin's engines. Kuhn laid the cigarettes and a box of matches in front of him. Once it was depolyed, Effi was the only place on a Zeppelin one could safely smoke without the risk of a lethal hydrogen explosion.

He checked the compass. Still heading west. Kuhn picked up the phone. 'Captain, this is Kuhn in the observation capsule, testing communications.'

'Receiving you. Thank you for volunteering, Kuhn.'

'Pleasure, sir.' He felt a little stab of pride. The captain, von Schuller, was a legend in the service, a veteran of Zeppelin service, a survivor of the LZ2 forced landing in the Allgäu mountains after engine failure.

'Ready to release, Kuhn?'

'Aye aye, sir.'

The capsule bucked as the quick-release clamps were unclipped by his shipmates in the gondola above. Effi dropped a foot, a jolt that caused his stomach to somersault one way then another. Then the wind caught the little device, causing it to yaw, and he gripped the sides of the wicker chair. A bang as the brake came off the drum, and the capsule was lowered. He looked out of one of the side windows, down onto the cottony clouds that the stars and moon were illuminating. Above him, the umbilical cord of rope was paying out and the precarious little vessel was dropping away from the mothership, the airstream pushing it back towards the giant tail of the Zeppelin.

Once out of the shadow of the airship and its engines, Kuhn could see the cold beauty of the star-rich sky and the ivory moon. Soon, it would be lost to him. Away from the ship, the whole of the night sky seemed to vibrate with the sound emanating from the Maybach engines in their nacelles, slung under the streamlined body. He was surprised they couldn't hear it in London. But he knew the clouds below him acted as an acoustic blanket and most people on the ground might hear only a faint buzz, if that.

'I'm going into the clouds now,' he said, even though he knew the men in the gondola would be watching his progress. And then a darkness enveloped him. He switched on the torch, but it simply generated a milky glow all around him. Effi began to oscillate at the end of her tether. He knew this part. You kept your nerve as the currents and eddies in the clouds threw you this way and that.

Please God, let me live through this. Just one more leave, one more sight of my family, and I promise—

He burst through over a darkened countryside, illuminated only by sporadic lights of hamlets. They were beyond the large conurbations of the coast, the usual targets like Great Yarmouth and Lowestoft, and below him was the flat, featureless – at least at night – farmland of Norfolk and Suffolk.

He consulted the charts and the compass and phoned up the heading, along with a correction. One bright spot of lights had to be the town known as Diss.

'You all right down there, Kuhn?'

'Sir.'

'We must be almost there.'

'Sir.'

'There will be red lights to guide us in.'

'Sorry, sir?'

'According to my orders, there will be three red lights, placed by our agents, visible to you, but not from the ground. If you line those up, east to west, it points directly to the airfield.'

'Very well, sir.'

From the corner of his eye he saw a flash of something, which disappeared as he looked at it. He moved his head, relying on his peripheral vision. It was there again. Red light.

He picked up the phone just as the capsule filled with a miniature tornado, blasting the charts and causing Effi to spin like a compass needle. Kuhn found himself on his hands and knees, the roar of an aero engine drowning out all rational thought except one. He scrabbled for the phone. 'Fighter!'

'Have you seen the lights?' von Schuller asked coolly.

'There is a British fighter down here. It almost rammed me.'

'He can't reach us at his height.'

No, but he can reach me.

'Red lights, Kuhn? Have you seen them?'

Kuhn felt like a tethered goat, waiting for the wolf. 'Yes, I have red lights. And I can see the aerodrome,' he said, looking around for that fighter. It was from Thetford, their very target, for it was from there that the planes with the new tracer bullets were operating, defending the night skies. They had already claimed three Zeppelins.

'Jesus!' he shouted to himself as he heard the thrum of enemy propellers. Then, speaking as calmly as he could manage down the phone, 'I have the three red markers below me and an airstrip coming up. Start your run.'

'Are you sure, Kuhn?'

'Yes, on my mark.'

Where the hell was that fighter? He counted off a minute, as if he really could see the airfield as the Zeppelin was bearing down on it.

'Over target. Bombs away.'

Twelve bombs and three flaming incendiary devices fell in a tight pattern. He could smell the chemicals and smoke even from that height. 'Target hit,' he lied. He would worry about his subterfuge later. He would blame the ground markings, claim that there were decoys on the ground to confuse him. 'Get me up, please.'

'Well done, Kuhn,' said von Schuller, making him glow with shame and guilt. 'The drum is running.'

The cable tightened, drawing him up. As he cleared the last of the thin clouds into the bright heavens once more, he felt a brief blast of the British fighter, spinning his capsule again, and the impression of a dark shape blotting out the stars. The night was sliced by orange streaks, like the dashes in Morse code, which reached up to the black cigar of his Zeppelin. A second stream of dashes joined in. There was another fighter on the prowl. Yellowy flashes came from the gondola. The Zeppelin was replying with its machine guns.

But Kuhn saw a small flame appear at the base of the airship and grow rapidly, looking as if molten lava had burned through the envelope. It spread in an instant, engulfing the nose of the *Admiral Karl Rudolf Brommy*, which tilted, pointing earthwards. Still the evil tracers came, dimming the stars with their brightness as flames cupped the Zeppelin's envelope. Kuhn closed his eyes and gave a small sob, knowing that, where the mothership was going, he was bound to follow.

Bradley Ross had just emerged from the covered stream and into the forest proper when the shower struck. Much of the sting of the downpour was taken out by the interlaced leaves of the protecting canopy of trees, but still he waited against a trunk until it lost some of its initial ferocity. He didn't want to be soaked through and catch a cold. And he was fairly certain if he was taking shelter, then so would any patrol.

The rain eased after ten minutes, during which he pressed his back into the gnarled wood behind him, knees to his chest. He was dressed in black, with a balaclava of the same colour, his skin darkened with coal dust. He was as invisible as he could manage.

Once the shower had reduced to a light, sporadic spray he began to move, the ground springy underfoot, each footstep releasing the smell of damp earth and mulching vegetation. His plan was very simple. He would test the defences, which no doubt Booth would have strengthened, and he would kidnap one of the soldiers and torture the truth out of him. And Miss Pillbody? He hated unfinished business, but in this case there was no alternative. Then it would be motor cycle to Harwich, where he had a contact who could get him across to neutral Holland and the Rotterdam office of the Army Intelligence Service.

Slowly, he rose to his full height, checked his pistol and withdrew his knife: a serrated hunting model this time, not the razor. He moved forward through the ferns, the water flicking off the fronds.

He heard the thrum of an engine and turned towards it, but it was just a car, driving off into the night.

Now, the clouds thinned and the disc of the moon appeared once more, casting a dim, silvery glow over the scene. A light flashed somewhere through the trees, and was gone.

Another set of those strange voices drifted by, but he was used to them now. He no longer thought they were around him. It was just some aspect of the weapon they were developing.

He felt the rifle barrel press against his neck.

'Move and I'll blow your head off, Fritz.'

His throat dried in an instant. 'Fritz? Are you crazy? I'm not German.'

'No?' The speaker let out a long, low whistle and Ross heard more undergrowth rustle. Three men with charcoal-blackened faces appeared. 'This is what a tenner looks like, lads. Turn around slow and put your hands up.'

'A tenner?' Ross protested, doing as he was told. 'What are you—'

'Shut it. Lieutenant said you Hun were creeping around . . .'

Ross had it at once. A £10 reward for capturing any intruder. Booth hadn't trusted Ross not to come looking. Perhaps he wasn't as callow as he looked.

'Yeah, well, your Lieutenant Booth put me out as a mouse, just to see how good you chaps were.'

'What?' said one of the other soldiers. 'What's that prick Booth playin' at?'

'Who gives a fuck?' said the first. 'Get him back, we claim our tenner.'

'Not if he's not a German spy.'

'*Course* he's a German spy.'

'Look,' interrupted Ross, 'if I am a German, how do I know Lieutenant Booth's name?'

'I said it.'

'You didn't. You just said "lieutenant".'

'Did I?' There was doubt in the voice.

'Let's take him to Booth.'

'I'll pay you a tenner each to let me go. I'll tell Booth what happened. But it's a little embarrassing to be caught so early.'

Even in the thin moonlight he could see greed flicker in the men's eyes.

'You got forty quid on you?'

'Fifty.'

'Stick 'im and let's just take it.'

'He resisted arrest,' suggested one, rehearsing their alibi.

Another of them took out his bayonet and slotted it onto his Lee-Enfield. 'Come on. We're all in this. We do it on three.'

'I might be lying,' Ross said. 'I might not have fifty quid on me. Then you'll have killed me for nothing. And Booth will be very, very upset.'

That stumped them. 'But we got nothing to lose. If he's got no money, we just claim the tenner. Say he put up a fight.'

'I think we've got to take him to Booth alive.'

One of them tutted, but it seemed decided.

That's when the trees behind them exploded.

The shockwave threw them all off-balance. Ross jumped backwards, letting himself fall into the ferns. As he fell, he pulled his pistol clear and shot the nearest soldier.

One of the others raised his rifle but before he could fire, his head whipped round from the force of impact in his skull. Only afterwards did Ross hear the sound of the shot. He dropped the third member of the patrol, but the remaining man threw his rifle down and sprinted towards the cover of the forest. As a string of explosions lit up the treeline, Ross fired two shots at the running man.

'Stop that,' someone hissed, as they sprinted by. 'I'll get him.'

Who the hell was that? Ross raised himself up to a sitting position, watching as the figure plunged into the dark of the forest, only catching a glimpse when the yellow light of a detonation briefly illuminated the trees.

One of the fallen soldiers groaned. Ross thumped him with the butt of his pistol. The faux-American was on his feet by the time his saviour returned, breathing hard from the exertion of the chase. The face was wrapped in a dark scarf, so that only the eyes showed, and there was a knitted woollen hat on the head. The body was covered in black overalls. 'Got him.'

'Who the hell are you?'

'Get out of here,' the newcomer hissed. 'I'll clear up your mess.'

Ross started to protest and found he was looking down the barrel of a pistol. He turned and walked swiftly away, shoulders braced for a shot that never came.

TWENTY-TWO

The explosions rippled across the grounds, their sickly light illuminating Watson's room. He crossed to the door and opened it. He wasn't sure who to expect at that time of night, but it certainly wasn't Mrs Gregson, throwing her arms around him and pushing him back into the room, kicking the door closed as she came.

The room juddered and plaster rained down on them. Somewhere a window shattered and the house was alive with the thump of hastily shod feet.

'Dr Watson, am I glad to see you,' she said, and planted a kiss on his forehead. 'You could put the gun down, though.'

Acutely aware he was clad only in his nightclothes, Watson pulled her arms from his neck, placed the pistol back on the nightstand and fetched a gown. 'We should go and help,' he said, pulling the curtains aside. Fires had started beyond the gardens. Something was burning fiercely, throwing up sparks to the heavens. 'What on earth is happening?'

'First, one thing this place is not short of is able bodies. Somewhere out there are several hundred young men. You'd only be in the way.

Secondly, I do believe it is a Zeppelin raid. They have been over before, but never bombed us. Thirdly, the best thing we can do is establish a casualty station for any injured.'

Watson turned and looked at her. She was dressed in a full, dark skirt, lace-up boots and a grey blouse. Her red corkscrew hair was, if anything, wilder than ever, and in the glow of the flames, her face appeared somewhat more lined and drawn than when he last saw her, half a year ago. But then, wasn't everybody's? What hadn't changed was the air of capability and common sense she exuded.

'Of course. I shall get dressed. Then you can tell me what on earth you are doing here, Mrs Gregson.'

'Oh, didn't you know?' she asked acidly. 'Apparently we're making history. I will tell you later. But if I tell you it was my large, self-righteous mouth that got me here, would it surprise you?'

Watson laughed, realizing how much he had missed her.

'I have a first-aid station in the old conservatory, at the back of the Hall. We can work there. I'll turn my back while you get dressed.'

She sat on the edge of the bed, hands folded primly on her lap.

'What sort of first aid do you do here?' Watson asked.

'Burns mostly.'

'Burns? Like Hitchcock's cheek, perhaps?'

'No, not like that. Contact burns. The sort cooks get from hot stoves. Crushed fingers, too. Headaches. Concussion . . .'

'And there is no doctor on site? No MO?'

She turned to speak, then quickly back again when she saw he was still partially clothed. 'There was. I thought you must know. Captain Trenton. He was one of the ones who died in the accident.'

'And he's not been replaced?'

'No.'

'Did you examine the victims?'

'Only Trenton.'

'Yet you were the only medically qualified person on site?' He gave a grunt of frustration.

141

'I don't think they think of me that way. More like a nanny. And . . .'

'And what?'

'From the way they reacted, I think they were frightened by the incident. By the implications.'

Watson could see that. A pet project suddenly going off the rails, perhaps facing closure if it got out that it had killed its participants. There had been cover-ups in the past – the munitions explosion at Faversham was almost certainly the results of sabotage by a German agent, but the Government had blamed the warm weather and 'sweating nitro'. At Netley near Southampton, Watson had heard tell of a terrible death toll during trials of the Super Nautilus class of submarines. The class was never officially acknowledged as existing, but the wagging tongues claimed that three of them rested at the bottom of the sea.

'Do you know exactly what they are doing here?'

Mrs Gregson examined her feet. 'I am kept here, virtually under house arrest.'

'Mrs Gregson . . .' he admonished. He knew her too well to expect her to take 'confined to quarters' lying down. She had the curiosity of a cat. 'You have never gone for an unofficial prowl?'

'Well, I do slip the leash now and then.' She laughed. 'And I've seen one of the machines that killed them and sent Hitchcock mad.'

'One? How many are there?'

'I don't know. You hear them, but rarely see them. I've only really examined this one.'

'Where is this killing machine?'

'About a quarter of a mile from here, perhaps a little more.'

He felt his own curiosity piqued. 'Could you show me?'

'Yes. Although you have to be careful, if you are found wandering around—' Another explosion filled the night. 'Although tonight, of all nights, it might be possible.'

'And you've obviously seen Hitchcock?' Otherwise, how could she know about the mark on his face?

'Once or twice. Poor chap. I had to dress some wounds. And put some ointment on his cheek. He's in a bad way, isn't he?'

'Yes.' Watson cleared his throat when he had finished buttoning up his trousers. 'The worst is over. You can turn around now.'

She did so and smiled at him, her eyes crinkling.

'What's funny?'

'Nothing, Major. Nothing. Just pleased to see you.'

Watson laced up his shoes. 'How did you end up here?'

'I answered an advertisement for people with mechanical ability. They turned me down, because of my sex. I kicked up a fuss. They arrested me for drawing attention to their little project. Initially I was taken to somewhere off the coast, but then they found out I had been a nurse – well, a VAD; I might have not been entirely truthful there. But as I was already compromised, they brought me here. I arrived the day before the accident sent everyone into a flap.'

'Right, let's go and see if there are any injured.'

'Major Watson, there is one thing I should tell you.'

'What's that?'

There was a loud thump on the door. 'Major!'

Mrs Gregson opened it to Booth, and Watson saw the surprise and confusion on his face.

'I just came to escort the major to my casualty station,' she explained.

'Right. Yes. We do have some injuries.'

They heard another series of dull crumps in the far distance.

'Must be using delayed fuses,' said Booth with a grimace. 'That'll make things trickier.'

'We'll be right down,' said Watson.

After he had gone, he turned to Mrs Gregson. 'You were saying?'

'It'll wait,' she replied. 'Let's go and do our jobs.'

They thought Elveden had got off lightly in terms of casualties. Watson and Mrs Gregson had set up in her station – a conservatory that had once held exotic birds from across the world, back in the maharajah's day. Now the perches and wires were empty, the glass cracked, the Indian motif floor tiles chipped.

Thankfully, the place reeked of Sanitas and carbolic, rather than bird droppings and feathers, and was dominated by a well-scrubbed table and two high-backed leather armchairs, taken from the house, which could easily be sterilized, and a variety of cupboards holding medical supplies.

The men sat at the far end of the aviary, smoking as they waited to be called one by one for treatment. A barracks hut had been side-swiped by high explosive, although most of the damage had been done by the bomb's compression wave rather than the blast. There were ringing ears and bleeding noses and concussion, and the worst damage was two broken fingers and a cracked rib. A plywood structure had been hit by an incendiary – that was what Watson had seen sending blazing sparks skyward from his window – but it had been empty. There had been smoke inhalation and singed hair and skin from those who'd battled the blaze, but not much more.

Then, as they were scrubbing down, Booth had appeared, his face vexed and concerned. Mrs Gregson and Watson were busy cleaning instruments and disposing of soiled cloths. 'I thought that was it. We have four more.'

'Bring them in,' said Watson.

'It's not worth it. I mean, there is nothing you can do for them. They're dead.'

'You're certain?' Watson had witnessed battlefield resurrections before.

'Oh, yes. Two of them have no . . . there is extensive damage from explosives. You don't need to be a doctor.'

'You'll need a death certificate,' said Mrs Gregson, rinsing her hands in diluted Lysol.

'I am sure that can wait,' Booth said. He looked at his watch. 'Let's get some sleep. We can assess the damage to the estate more easily in the daylight.'

'Where are the bodies?' asked Watson.

'In our morgue. The ice house.' He pointed to the eastern side of the Hall. 'Next to the lake. We have kept the other seven in there too. It's getting rather crowded.'

'Do you think the Germans know?' asked Watson. 'Know what you are doing here? Is that why you were raided?'

Booth slumped at the very thought. 'Christ, I hope not. I'm telling myself it was just blind luck on their part. And bad luck for them they didn't do more damage. Good night, Major, Mrs Gregson. As I said, we'll know more in daylight. See you at breakfast, Major Watson.'

After he had left, Watson said, 'Mrs Gregson, what was it you were going to tell me upstairs? Before Booth arrived.'

'That island they put me on,' said Mrs Gregson. 'It's called Foulness.'

It rang a vague bell, but no more. 'I'm not familiar with it.'

'There's no reason why you should be. I can't think of any reason why one would visit or even seek it out on a map. But . . .' She hesitated.

'What?'

A deep breath. 'I can't be certain, you understand. I was only on Foulness for forty-eight hours. And I have only ever seen him from a distance, that time when we docked at Folkestone. But I am rather sure I saw Mr Holmes there, too far away to speak to. But he is very distinctive. He looks just like the drawings of him in the *Strand*. A little stooped, perhaps . . .'

'Indeed.' Watson's pulse quickened. 'And this island is where?'

'Foulness? At the mouth of the Thames. In the North Sea.'

Holmes's prison. Now it had a name.

TWENTY-THREE

Ross had barely managed to strip off his soiled clothes and wash his face when there came a rapping at the door of his cottage. *Who could it be, at this hour?* He pulled on a robe and went to answer it, scooping up his pistol as he went. He peered out into the darkness and recognized the pale face of Miss Pillbody.

'Are you all right?' he asked. 'The bombing has stopped now—'

'I know the bloody bombing stopped. I was right under it. Come to my cottage, in by the back way. Don't worry, I've taken care of everything.'

'What?' He could hardly contain his incredulity at what he was hearing. 'What do you mean?'

'Ten minutes.'

He was exhausted and part of him wanted to crawl upstairs and fall asleep on top of the hideous pink candlewick cover on his bed. But that desire was trumped by wanting to know what little Miss Pillbody was up to. So after cleaning off the last of the mud and blood, he dutifully tiptoed round to her house.

She, too, had scrubbed herself and her skin shone in the lamplight. He was amazed by the change in her. Before she had been pretty but docile. Now she looked animated, alive and alert, as if she was on some kind of stimulant. She was in clean underwear, but there was no sign of bashfulness as she told him she would fetch a robe from upstairs.

'There's some disgusting sherry in that cupboard,' she said, 'and glasses on the shelf above. I'll have a large one.'

So would he, he decided.

As he waited for her to finish upstairs, he looked around the cottage, seeing it with fresh eyes. Now he realized how artificial it all was. It was the room one would expect a near-spinster to have, full of hand-stitched cushions and tablecloths, twee porcelain figurines and stiff family portraits, those fiddly watercolours of village scenes and local wildlife, not to mention her collection of strange, rather unsettling dolls. It was a construct, as phoney as the whole Miss Pillbody identity.

'Right,' she announced as she came downstairs, belting a dressing gown. 'You have questions.'

Ross couldn't help but hoot at this. 'Questions? I have hundreds. Who the hell are you?'

'You first.'

'Not a chance. It was you in the woods, then?' he asked.

She nodded, and he shook his head in amazement. 'I'll be blowed. I think you owe me an explanation, Miss Pillbody.'

'All right,' she said, with a ghost of a smile at his incredulity. 'My name is Brandt. Ilse Brandt. I am from Koblenz. But my father was a naval attaché with the German Embassy in London and I was educated here in England for two periods of three years each. I also went to a Swiss finishing school with many English girls. Hence my accent.'

'But the whole story of you, your dead brother, the parents in Chichester. It was so convincing, so heartfelt—'

She frowned at him. 'Do I have to tell you that this job requires you to live the role? You think it, so you believe it, and if you believe it then so will they. One doesn't play a part, one *becomes* that part. Tomorrow morning I will be Miss Pillbody again, with Mama and Papa in Chichester, and a tragically killed brother called Arnold. Ilse will have gone.'

'But what were you doing in the forest?'

'I am with N-A. *Nachrichten-Abteilung*, German naval intelligence. I am supposing your organization is attached to the army?'

He nodded.

'And now I hear the air force has its own intelligence branch and von Kuhlmann of the Foreign Ministry has his own unit. And do they talk to each other?' She picked up her sherry and drank. 'Do they hell. Too many cooks.'

'So you aren't here for Elveden?'

'I am here for Thetford aerodrome. To check air movements and aircraft types, which was easy when I had little boys like Sidney Drayton to do it for me. It is from there they are striking at the Zeppelins, with new planes, new bullets. That raid was intended to put the aerodrome out of action. My mission was to place lights that pinpointed the direction of the field. Looks like something went wrong.'

'That still doesn't explain how you ended up in the forest.'

'I followed you.' More sherry. 'I thought you were a British spy on my tail. Trying to get close. It was pathetically easy to shadow you, you know. And I thought you and that arrogant Booth were cooking up something about me on the beach that day. I assumed it was entrapment, some way of flushing me out. But when I saw you heading for the estate, I realized there was another explanation, as unlikely as it sounded. But the more I considered it, the more it seemed a compelling explanation for you being here. You are an agent of Germany, too. Correct?'

Ross studied his glass and his face reddened slightly under her gaze. 'Well, yes. And Booth *is* suspicious of me.'

'*I* was suspicious of you. So when I followed you from the cottage, I thought you were going to track my lights and extinguish them. Instead you went towards Elveden . . . There was nothing I could do here anyway, except risk being bombed, so I decided to stick with you.'

'I'm glad you did. But aren't the N-A curious about what is going on in that estate?'

'Curious, yes. I have reported it, several times. But they suspect it is an army, not a naval concern. They are far more worried about Zeppelin losses – there is talk of handing over the bombing to the air force. The High Command does not want that. But, once Thetford is out of commission, I am ordered to take a look at Elveden. I think they thought they could use it as a bargaining chip with the army.'

'Didn't that strike you as odd? That they wouldn't want to know about what is happening in the estate. Careless, to say the least.'

'I have considered another explanation.'

'What's that?'

'They already have a spy in there.'

'The navy?' he asked.

'It is widely accepted that the *Nachrichten-Abteilung* is the best intelligence unit in Germany.'

He didn't rise to the bait. It was an infuriating thought, though, this duplication of responsibilities. 'And what will you do now?'

'Until I receive orders about a new raid I shall be Miss Pillbody. Spinster of this parish.'

'But is Ilse married?'

She hesitated before admitting the truth. 'Ilse was married to a Zeppelin captain who died last year doing his duty, bombing British minelayers in the North Sea.'

'I am sorry.'

'Yes, me too.' It was said matter-of-factly, as if she had shed every tear she was going to over her husband.

'It must have been difficult,' he offered.

'Not for long. Before the war I was a member of the radical arm of the *Deutscher Verein für Frauenstimmrecht*.'

He gave a low whistle. Those girls made British suffragettes look like wet nurses.

'That taught me the realities of sacrifice. And, afterwards, after Willi's death, I offered to help the service and was trained at Admiral Hersch's *Sie Wölfe* camp in Saxony.'

'I've not heard of it,' Ross admitted.

'Of course you haven't. It is a unit of young women whose husbands have given their lives for Germany. The She Wolves are designed for infiltration behind enemy lines as nurses, housewives, spinsters, showgirls and schoolteachers. We are a steel fist in a lace glove. Our motto is: *Taten statt Worte, Zähne statt Tränen*.'

Deeds not Words, Teeth not tears, he translated.

'You have no doubt wondered how I could track you and how I could dispose of the bodies with unfeminine impunity? One of Hersch's passing-out tests is the hunting down of live targets. In my case, one of the girls I shared a dormitory with who hadn't quite come up to scratch.'

'What?' He was genuinely shocked.

'Poor Magda couldn't be allowed to go back into the real world, not with what she knew. I know it sounds cruel, but we She Wolves have had any unnecessary emotion or squeamishness purged from us.'

Ross was beginning to feel a sense of relief that he hadn't tried to seduce Miss Pillbody just for the hell of it. It would be like mating with a scorpion. 'I see.'

'Now, your turn.'

So he told her about his South African background, the adoption of the Dirk Alberts identity and then the murder of Bradley Ross to acquire a better cover story. When he had finished he said, 'I reckon Miss Pillbody's is a dull life for a She Wolf. Why don't you help me? With penetrating the secret of Elveden?'

She drained her sherry and considered this. He was right. She was looking forward to seeing the last of Miss Pillbody. 'All right. As long as it does not compromise my mission or put any N-A agent in there at risk.'

'Thank you. Those soldiers, the ones tonight . . .'

'What about them?' she asked, hoping he wasn't going to display a queasy sentimentality about the killing of enemy combatants. He hadn't had the benefit of a Hersch indoctrination.

'How did you take care of them?'

'I used grenades to mask the wounds. They will look like they were killed in the Zeppelin raid.'

'Grenades?' he repeated, dumbfounded.

'Mills bombs.'

'I don't fucking believe it,' he said.

'Fucking believe it,' Miss Pillbody said, unfazed by his crude language. 'I told you the N-A was the best intelligence service. And that the *Sie Wölfe* are trained for all eventualities and contingencies.'

'Do you think they'll be able to tell?'

'Tell what? That we used grenades to disguise the bullet and knife wounds?' She shook her head. 'I doubt it.' She finished her sherry with a shudder. 'Not unless they have got a very good detective up there.'

TWENTY-FOUR

Coyle awoke with a start, not entirely sure where he was. It took a few seconds as the pieces of the last few days fell together and he sorted dream from reality. There had been a bombing raid. That was part of real life. With Fred Sutton, the landlord, his family and the one other guest at The Plough, he had gone outside and watched the glow from the estate, listening to the whump of high explosives and the lighter whoosh of the incendiaries. There was no sign of the culprit, hidden well above the cloud base, but Sutton had sworn he had heard British planes – night hunters, as they called them – go up some time earlier from the Thetford aerodrome.

Coyle rolled out of bed and washed his face and upper body in the cold water he had poured into the enamel bowl in the dresser. When the events finally slotted together, he wished they hadn't. With Harry gone, he felt empty inside. All the passion he had been working up for going back to Ireland had disappeared. It would wait until he had sorted out why his best friend had been gunned down in the streets of London.

He dressed slowly, thinking about the best approach for tracking Harry's murderers as he did so. There were people in London he could stamp on to tell him who had been hired to do what. They wouldn't want to talk. Normally he wouldn't try to make them. It was a sort of unwritten code. But that was gone now. No rules. No English idea of fair play. Just one very pissed-off Irishman with a big gun.

When he went downstairs Sutton was in the kitchen and offered him sausages and eggs. Coyle hadn't realized he was hungry. But the smell made his saliva flow and he asked for eggs, sausages and some bacon and black pudding if they had it. Homemade, Sutton assured him.

'Where did the bombs fall?' he asked the landlord.

'On the earl's estate, so I heard,' was the reply.

Coyle thought of Watson, out there directly under the German bombs.

'It's a big piece of land,' said Sutton, noticing his concern, 'with a lot of trees and very few houses. I doubt there will be casualties, if that's what you are worried about.'

'Well, I hear they get lucky sometimes, those Zeps.'

'Yeah. But mostly they get unlucky. Two eggs enough? And how many sausages?'

'Two.'

'I'll give you three, just in case.'

Afterwards, Coyle went out to the car with his bag and, as was his habit, gave the vehicle a quick once-over. It didn't take long to spot the pool of water under the front end. He checked the hoses and clips, but they were fine. The radiator had burst.

He went back in and explained his dilemma to Sutton. The landlord paused from enjoying his own breakfast. 'I don't know much about cars. What d'you need?'

'A new radiator. Failing that, someone who can solder the radiator core.'

Sutton looked dubious. 'If it was a horse, now, Dingle could do something at the smithy. But a radiator . . . delicate, is it?'

Coyle nodded. 'Can't be fixed on an anvil.'

'That's what I was thinking. There's a garage in Thetford. I could send a lad over on Beezer, the horse. How big is it?'

Coyle traced the size with his hands. 'But it's heavy.'

'So's Beezer. I can get it over this morning. See what they say.'

Coyle could think of no alternative, apart from abandoning the car. And that felt disloyal. It was a good little motor.

'If they can fix it today, I'd pay double.'

Sutton laughed. 'Don't tell him that. He'll charge you four times what the job's worth. Need a hand getting it out?'

'No, I'll be fine. Might need to borrow some tools. Spanners an' screwdrivers an' the like.'

'There's a shed out back. Got most things in it.'

'Any coveralls?'

'Aye.'

'Put it on the bill.'

Sutton smiled. 'I already have.'

Coyle collected the tools and the protective clothing from the shed and set about removing the radiator. He leaned over the bonnet of the Vauxhall and undid the clips holding the top and bottom hoses and the bolts that secured the radiator to the chassis. He lifted it away and inspected the damage to the honeycomb of cooling channels. There were three splits in all, two of them quite small, but the third catastrophic. It needed a proper repair.

He put the radiator down and straightened, feeling a twinge in his back. He walked out from the rear of the pub, under the arch and into the village. As he stretched and windmilled, loosening the muscles in his back, he took in the location of the pub for the first time. It sat in a small, well-tended green, between two of the four roads that radiated from the circle of grass. Opposite was a chapel, dating from the eighteenth century so the stonework proclaimed, a cluster of small shops and the village hall. Behind the pub, up the lane, was the blacksmith's, and that was it. The rest was a collection of cottages, some clapperboard, the rest all pink stonework and climbing wisteria.

Not even a post office, he thought, as he watched the postman arrive, parking his bike and walking his round, knocking on each door, chatting with the occupant. Coyle was about to go inside and wash his hands when he felt a familiar prickle on his neck. He automatically looked around for Harry, check he was safe. But he wasn't.

Idiot, he almost shouted at himself. Whatever and whoever was behind the attack on Major Watson, it was to prevent him coming here, to this part of the world. Which might mean that the people behind it were here, under his nose. Harry's killers – perhaps not the ones who pulled the trigger, but men in the same employ – were likely to be in the vicinity.

He strode back into the pub to tell Sutton that, even if the radiator came back today, he might just be staying on for a little while, such was the charm of the village.

After breakfast, Watson took Hitchcock from his basement quarters and up to the music room, where a Blüthner piano and Mrs Gregson awaited him. The whole way he had his hands clasped over his eyes, keeping out the light. Watson guided him to the piano stool, sat him down and stood back.

'Can you pull the curtains, Mrs Gregson?'

She swished the drapes across until the room was grey.

'It's darkened now,' said Watson.

A dozen heartbeats passed before the patient took his hands away from his face. He blinked rapidly, as if the light was still too bright. Then he lowered the lid of the piano over the keys. He sat there, rigid as ever, staring straight ahead.

'You get any sleep?' Watson asked Mrs Gregson.

'No thanks to you,' she said with a sly grin. 'It's a long time since I saw a dawn like that. Or, indeed, any dawn. Not since . . .'

'Since?'

Mrs Gregson turned her attention back to Hitchcock. 'It looks as if he doesn't want to play today, Major.'

'Perhaps not.' He looked around the room, with its piles of sheet music and busts of eminent composers, not to mention the view onto the garden. The air was perfumed with burning sticks, which released an aroma of oriental spices. 'But it is a somewhat more pleasant environment for Lieutenant Hitchcock than his basement. Will you stay with him?'

'Of course.'

'And talk to him? You'd be surprised how many men miss the sound of a woman's voice.'

'Even mine, Major?' She fluttered her eyelids like a music-hall turn.

'Even yours, Mrs Gregson. I hope not to be too long.'

'Are you going to tell them about what we did this morning?'

He was shocked at the thought. 'No. None of their business.'

Outside, he found Levass waiting for him, along with one of the estate cars and a driver.

'Good morning, Major. Lieutenant Booth sends his apologies. He is detained after last night's bombing raid. Quite exciting, eh?'

'You could say that,' said Watson sourly. 'But for four dead men.'

Levass's face drooped. 'Yes, of course. My apologies. Thoughtless of me. You heard it was destroyed, though? The raider.'

'Good,' was all Watson could offer. He didn't want to dwell too much on men being consumed by flaming gas thousands of feet above his head. Another barbarity of a war that specialized in them.

Levass held open the door and Watson climbed into the rear of the Albion. The Frenchman slammed it shut and came around the other side.

'Area D,' he said to the driver.

Levass leaned back and offered Watson an Elegantes. He refused, not wanting a cigarette to spoil the taste of his breakfast.

'Sir . . .' Watson began.

'You were wondering what a Frenchman is doing here on British soil? With British secrets.'

'I was indeed,' Watson admitted.

'This project is being run jointly with my department in Paris. You know that inventions, they seem to come to people in clusters, as if a eureka moment strikes two, three, four, five at the same time?'

'I'm not sure what you mean,' admitted Watson.

'No, forgive my English. But there are several people who claim the idea for the electric light. Yes? And the telephone. And the internal combustion engine. It is as if God beamed down the possibility of a whole new idea to be picked up in many places. Well, that has happened here. A chain of causation that led, inevitably, to our weapon. In France, in England and in America. But not, as yet, not Germany. As far as we are aware.'

'God must truly be on our side,' said Watson.

Levass guffawed at this, missing the sarcasm. 'I am certain of it, Major Watson.'

God doesn't pick sides, Watson thought. It was highly likely that even now Germany was developing its own secret super-weapon in a setting not dissimilar to Elveden.

Levass banged on the glass screen and the driver engaged the gears. The car swung around the gardens and headed down the grand drive of Elveden Hall, before turning off onto a newly laid gravel track that cut towards a line of poplars.

They passed through them, and a wilder straggle of trees, before the road, now a dirt path, rose and they came to a small crest, where Levass instructed the driver to halt.

They were looking over an open area of what had been arable land, a space the size of a dozen rugby pitches. Watson sat up, examining the once-familiar zigzag and castellated shapes and the curlicues of barbed wire for the second time that day. It didn't look any prettier than it had when he came here at dawn with Mrs Gregson, and the sight still made him sick to his stomach. The after-glow of breakfast was replaced by the imaginary stench of latrines and death.

'Yes, Major. Welcome to France.'

Welcome back to hell, he thought. Watson stepped out of the car, thankful for the breeze on his face. He knew his blood pressure had gone up: he could feel the glow on his cheeks. Ahead of him was a re-creation of the trench system that blighted Belgium and France; a series of Allied trenches, the wire, the awful no man's land, and then the enemy trenches, complete with machine-gun nests. It was eerily deserted, no sound or sight of men.

'It's based on Loos,' said Levass. 'Your Royal Engineers oversaw the Pioneer Corps who constructed it.'

But Watson wasn't listening. He was staring once again at the large, rhomboid, garishly painted riveted metal object at the edge of the clearing, lying at a strange angle, its front apparently having collided with the trunk of an oak, which had been pushed out of the perpendicular. Behind the machine were two wheels that looked to have been taken from a gun limber, but were twisted and smashed.

'So that's a land ironclad?' he asked.

The Frenchman nodded. 'You know H. G. Wells then? He was almost as prescient as Verne. But they are not called that – the machines have been through various names. Landships. The Wilson Machine. But now we call them tanks.'

'Tanks?' It seemed such a small, insignificant word for this great steel beast that had disrupted so many lives, including his own. He had expected the greatest secret of the war to have a more exotic or intimidating title.

'Yes. A clever spy could infer what they might be from the term "landships". "Tanks" is neutral. It confuses anyone who overhears careless talk. You see the writing on the side?'

'HMLS *Genevieve*?' he read. 'What's a HMLS?'

'His Majesty's Land Ship. One of Churchill's naval ideas we haven't yet abandoned. Now look further along.'

Watson peered. 'It's Cyrillic?'

'Yes. It says "With Care to Petrograd". Most of the workers building them think they are riveting mobile water tanks for the Russian Army.'

Watson supposed that, with its solid iron sides and riveting, it did look like a giant cistern.

'That one's what they call a female. Carries machine guns, rather than the male, which will carry six-pounder naval guns. When they all arrive.'

'How many is "all"?'

'That depends who you ask,' said Levass.

'How long has this been in development?'

'The tank? Eighteen months, perhaps.'

As he had when he had first laid eyes on it in the glimmer of dawn, Watson tried to imagine such a monster actually crawling over the land. He could see the revolving treads that were designed to rotate around the periphery of the side panels and thus propel it forward, but he couldn't quite picture it.

'What's it doing over there against the tree?' Watson asked.

'It's where it ended up afterwards. Out of control.'

'After what?'

'After,' said Levass somberly, 'every man inside went insane.'

For the first time in many months, Watson climbed down a ladder and found himself below ground, feeling the familiar chill of excavated earth as he descended. Levass followed, slowly, citing a painful instep from his gout. As he touched the bottom Watson instinctively braced himself for the slop of liquid earth, the scrabble of rats and the smell: the all-pervading stink of putrefaction and sweat.

But there had been no slaughter here, no shells, no gas, no men living like benighted moles in dugouts for weeks on end. This ground had never shaken with a barrage or been raked with machine-gun fire that shredded sandbags and men alike. It was like a museum reconstruction of a Roman garrison or a Viking village – they could show what it looked like, but not how it smelled or felt. It was all too sanitized.

Watson waited for Levass to join him and, after Levass had poured a quantity of bicarbonate on his tongue and washed it down with water, they walked along smooth, unstained duckboards.

'This is the quickest way to cross to the tank,' Levass said.

Watson knew that wasn't true. Levass wanted to show off their trenches.

'How long have you had gout?' he asked.

'Five years or more. It hardly bothers me now I take the powder. Just the pressure on the insole reminds me sometimes. I had to give up riding. The stirrup, you see. That's why I welcomed the tank so much – the iron horse, without a saddle or stirrups. So, Major, do you like our little playground?'

Watson shook his head but didn't answer, too busy spotting

omissions in the diorama. There was no fire step, no sniper positions, no saps built out into no man's land. The genuine trenches and the cubbyholes were always full of boxes and cans, some full of ammunition, others from the last delivery of hot food or drinking water. This wasn't a walk through a trench, it was a stroll in the park.

As he climbed up another ladder and the morning sunshine stroked his face, Watson realized that the soil was all wrong. He stood and brushed his coat; the dirt came off as a fine powder. Sand. In Belgium, from Ypres down to Plug Street and beyond, the clay-rich earth had liquefied to a stinking, gluey mud that was at times as much an enemy as the Germans.

Watson looked out across the reconstructed no man's land, feeling horribly exposed even though he knew no German was looking at him through a telescopic sight, salivating at the thought of adding an officer to his tally. He had left it behind for good, but he was under no illusion – no man's land lay there still, far more horrible and blasted than this construct, a ribbon of darkness meandering across the heart of Europe. If this machine could breach that desolate strip without costing the lives of hundreds for every yard gained, then it might be worth him solving this mystery after all. Perhaps Churchill had been right.

Watson waited until Levass was up top before he crossed to where the tank had smashed to a halt against the tree. Standing in the oak's shadow, smoking a Wills, was Cardew, the young man with the prominent ears who had been too busy for dinner. He was dressed in a brown working man's coat, such as a furniture remover or an ironmonger-shop owner might wear, and square-toed ankle boots. He pushed off from the trunk and threw the cigarette away. 'Hello again, Dr Watson.'

'Major,' Levass corrected.

'Sorry.' Cardew smiled beneath his patchy moustache. In daylight Watson could tell he was around thirty or a little more, with a drawn but open face that suggested trustworthiness and honesty. *It makes a change*, Watson thought. Everyone else looked sly and shifty from the strain of keeping Churchill's great secret. Cardew took a clean rag from his pocket and wiped his palms. 'Slip of the tongue. You'll always be Mr Holmes's friend to me.'

'It's no shame to be recognized as such,' said Watson, taking his proffered hand. 'You said last night that you are the engineer of this beast?' he asked with an inclination of his head towards the machine.

'Only one of them. My full title is Assistant Consulting—' Cardew paused and looked at Levass, fearful of having overreached himself.

'Major Watson has been given full clearance.'

'Assistant Consulting Engineer to the Tank Supply Department. Mr Tritton, my guv'nor, sends his apologies he can't be here himself. There's some quality control problems at Foster's, in Lincoln.' The accent was Midlands, Watson noted.

'You're a motor cycle man?' Watson asked.

'I am indeed, sir,' said Cardew with some surprise, though in truth putting together the Midlands and engineering and coming up with motor cycles was no great feat of deduction. 'I was with BSA initially, did the three-and-a-half horsepower.'

He said the name with pride, though Watson had not heard of it. He needed Mrs Gregson for such things.

'But then when they linked with Daimler, I went to its engine division.' Cardew glanced at the tank. 'Which is why I became involved with this contraption.' His face darkened. 'Although I don't think the engine had anything to do with—'

Watson raised a hand. 'Please, let's not get ahead of ourselves. Who found the bodies?'

'I was the first man in the tank.' He swallowed hard. 'It was . . . well, it was bloody awful, to be absolutely honest.'

'I'm sure it was. Did you notice anything unusual?'

A nervous laugh. 'Apart from eight men gone mad, you mean?'

Watson felt a flash of annoyance at such flippancy but then smiled. It had been a foolish question. 'What position were they in? Lying down? Standing up?'

Cardew mimed putting his hands over his head and rocking back and forth. 'And the sounds . . .'

'What I meant was, did you notice anything out of the ordinary from the usual training sessions? A strange smell, perhaps? Or a noise? Was it hotter than usual?'

Cardew considered all this. 'Not that I recall. But it wasn't a usual training session.'

'How do you mean?'

Levass jumped in. 'A lot of our tanks do not have these sponsons, the side turrets.' He pointed at the bulky protuberances on the flanks of the tank, designed to house its guns. 'They are brought separately and there are . . . delays. So we train the men first of all on the tank without the sponsons, raised up on blocks. So they can familiarize themselves with the gears. Then, we drive them, but also without the sponsons. Then finally, we bolt them on and let them get used to the extra weight. But this was the first test under battle conditions with the sponsons fitted and fully enclosed.'

'Meaning?'

Cardew resumed. 'Normally, we run with all hatches open, to allow fresh air in. It can get a little rank inside. This time we were practising trench crossing under fire. Just a few rounds from Lee-Enfields to give it some authenticity. You see the marks?' Watson nodded as the man pointed out the scattering of dents and chipped paint on the side of the tank. 'It meant for the first time, the tank was fully battened down. Now the men are refusing to run with the sponsons on and hatches closed.'

'For which,' Levass said coolly, 'the French army would have them shot.'

'It's not a direct refusal,' Cardew said. 'But Booth and Swinton know they are planning on cracking at least one opening every time we run. To keep the air fresh.'

Which sounded more like common sense than a matter for the firing squad to Watson. 'And no more deaths so far?'

'None. But we haven't duplicated these conditions exactly.

Colonel Swinton has suspended full battlefield-conditions training for the time being.'

'So describe to me what happened that day.'

Cardew took out his cigarettes and offered them around. Levass took one but Watson refused. He wanted none of his senses blunted.

Once he had his gasper going, Cardew pointed across the clearing to a small wooden viewing platform. 'There were about eight of us watching, wouldn't you say, Colonel?' Levass nodded. 'Colonel Swinton, Major Thwaites, me, Mr Tritton, Lieutenant Stern, Flight Commander Harington – both RNAS – Mr Daniels of the War Office, Lieutenant-Colonel Brough of the Royal Marine Artillery. Oh, nine. Colonel Nicholson of the Royal Engineers was here, too.'

'That's a remarkably wide sweep of interested parties,' said Watson, 'for something supposedly the biggest secret of the war.'

Levass grunted an agreement. 'You know I said that great inventions have many fathers? Well, there are many paternity claims on this one. Not just we French. This machine has been under the command of the Admiralty, the Landships Committee, the War Office, the Ministry of Munitions. Plus we have Tritton, Harington, Swinton, all laying claim to the final form. If this device works—'

'*When* it works,' challenged Cardew tetchily.

'When it changes the war, then it will have many proud fathers.'

'And if doesn't?' asked Watson.

Levass shrugged in his best Gallic manner. 'Then it will be a sad, unloved bastard of a child.'

Watson could well believe it. But if this machine could prevent a repeat of the Somme, he didn't care who claimed parentage and neither would the thousands of Tommies who wouldn't die.

'And your instinct?' Watson asked. 'About its effectiveness?'

'Good,' said Levass, 'if used appropriately. And you? Now you have seen it?'

162

'I have little faith in wonder weapons,' admitted Watson. 'The interrupter mechanism almost gave the Germans the air war, but, eventually, we came up with a response.'

'The trick is to win the war before the enemy can develop a counterattack. Hence the importance of the element of surprise.'

Watson didn't want to be drawn into further fruitless conjecture and so asked, 'Is this the only training ground?'

Levass nodded. 'Yes. Why?'

'It's all wrong.'

'In what way?' Cardew asked. 'It was built by Royal Engineers. It's based on—'

'Loos. I know,' said Watson. Everyone knew Loos; it was the first time poison gas had been used by the British. 'A battle fought almost a year ago, and since that time the shelling and the rain have hardly stopped. Your battlefield is too clean. Someone must have pointed that out. Anyone who has seen the front line will know it's much more challenging than this.'

Levass and Cardew exchanged shamefaced glances.

'What is it?'

'There's nobody here who has actually, well, been at the sharp end,' said Cardew.

'Not in the top brass, perhaps, but . . .' Watson watched their expressions turn sheepish. 'What, nobody on the whole project? Churchill certainly has—'

'Churchill is no longer involved on a day-to-day basis,' said Cardew. 'For better or worse.'

Watson let a sigh of disbelief leak out. Churchill might be a blackmailing monster when it suited him, but there was no doubting his bravery and experience. The man had been out at the sharpest end of all, leading patrols into no man's land, snatching German snipers and recce patrols. He'd tell them in no uncertain terms to rough up their 'playground'. 'I'll talk to Swinton about this later.' A thought occurred to Watson. 'Hold on, Swinton was an official journalist at the front, surely *he* has relevant experience?'

Levass managed a wistful smile at Watson's naïvety. 'Rumour has it, Major, between you and me, that he sat in a tent behind the line, debriefing officers and reading the daily action reports.'

'Thwaites? Battlefield tactics. He must have seen that before.' He pointed to the trenches.

Levass shook his head. 'Sandhurst and books. He was in South Africa.'

'That was another kind of war altogether.' Watson took off his cap and rubbed his forehead. The sun was well up now, and he was feeling hot in his uniform and not a little weary. He had managed three hours' sleep at best.

'But that has no bearing on my immediate task,' said Watson. 'I am here to discover what in that thing drove eight men insane and killed all but one of them. Correct?'

'Yes, Major,' said Cardew.

'Then would you like to give me a tour of the suspect?'

'Of course.'

'I have one question before we proceed,' said Watson.

'What's that?'

'Have you or anyone you know of ever been to Africa?'

'No,' said Cardew. 'Well, certainly I haven't.'

Watson looked to Levass.

'No, me neither. Thwaites has, of course. Why do you ask?'

'Thwaites, yes.' He thought for a moment before pointing to the tank. 'Shall we?'

The metal was hot to the touch, its strange paint scheme of pink, black and grey streaks slightly tacky under his fingers. Levass assured him the 'camofleurs' were hard at work on something more drab, less dazzling, than Solomon's original patterns. But it was mostly Cardew who explained the working of the iron landship.

It wasn't as large as the machines Watson had read about in H. G. Wells, but the sheer bulk was still terrifying. He could imagine the impact of this strange apparition rolling out of the early morning smoke from a barrage, spitting fire as it came.

'This is *G for Genevieve*, a female,' Cardew said, slapping the nose. 'And it weighs just shy of twenty-eight tons. It has four Vickers and one Hotchkiss machine gun. The males have six-pounder naval guns in their sponsons.' He pointed to the turret-like extensions on the side. 'And they weigh slightly more. It is designed, using these tracks, to cross an eight-foot trench. It's thirty-two foot long with that steering gear.' He pointed to the mangled, spoked wheels at the rear. 'Which we are beginning to think is more trouble than it's worth.'

'How fast does it go?' Watson asked.

'Four miles an hour. Which means infantry can keep up with it.'

'That's four miles per hour over even terrain?'

'Yes.'

'Then I suspect the infantry will have no trouble keeping up with it. This thing will have to cross a sea of mud and slurry. What is its journey range?'

'We think about twenty-six miles.'

Watson knocked on the side with a knuckle. 'How thick is the armour?'

'Eight millimetre.'

Watson raised an eyebrow in surprise. 'The German SMK bullets can punch through ten.' The SMK was designed to pierce the boilerplate that British observers and sharpshooters used to protect themselves in the trenches.

'But only snipers have them, don't they?' asked Cardew.

Watson shook his head at the naïvety. 'Not for long, once these appear.' As Cardew well knew, one thing was certain in this war: every fresh weapon gave rise to an appropriate counterstrike. The shock of the new did not last long at the front.

'Can we go inside?' Watson asked.

'You might want to take off your tunic and what have you,' said Levass, pointing at his belt and lanyard. 'It is hot and it is tight.'

Watson did as he was told, while Cardew removed his jacket and hung it on a branch. Levass offered to hold Watson's. 'I've been inside,' he said. 'There is nothing to see.'

Watson took out a torch from his tunic pocket before he handed it over.

Cardew ducked in through the opening at the rear of the sponson and his voice rang when he spoke. 'In you come, Major. Watch your head.'

'And everything else,' said Levass.

Watson took a last deep breath of clear morning air and stepped into the dark interior. He switched on his torch.

'There. Now get your bearings.'

The air was foul, he could taste metal on his tongue, but the inside wasn't as gloomy as he had expected. The internal walls were painted white and there were enough hatches open to show the inside in half-light. His first thought was that it had been used as a storage dump: every inch around him was full of metal boxes. Only as his eyes adjusted did he realize they were full of ammunition for the machine guns. There was another stack of petrol cans. He tried to move and knocked his elbow on a rack holding fire extinguishers.

'The males are even more cramped, what with six-pounder shells,' said Cardew.

Just forward of the centre was the huge Daimler engine, bristling with tubes and wires. Everyone would have to manoeuvre along the two narrow aisles situated on either side of that monster. *Burns*, Mrs Gregson had said. The majority of the injuries she dealt with were contact burns. Now he knew why.

'Is eight the normal tally of crew?' asked Watson, already feeling the strain in his back and neck from being bent double.

'Yes. I know, it seems a lot. You need four men to drive the tank – a commander and driver up there at the front, then two gearsmen on the box back there to control speed and direction of each track.'

'What's that?' asked Watson, pointing at a chicken-wire-faced box, high on the steel wall next to the machine-gun positions.

'Pigeon coop. Each tank carries two pigeons for communications with tank command.'

'Pigeons? What about radios?'

Cardew grinned. 'You'll see. You can't hear yourself think when she starts up. You certainly can't hear anybody else, even over the radio.'

Watson looked around the interior, trying to imagine it once the engine had throbbed into life. He shone his torch on the contraption, tracing four exhausts that vented through the roof. 'Could fumes be blown back in? Could that be a factor in the deaths?' he asked.

'I doubt it,' said Cardew. 'I mean, the engine exhaust isn't nice, but it doesn't cause insanity.'

Watson moved over and examined the vertical exhaust tubes, shining his torch on each in turn.

'Found something?' Cardew asked excitedly as Watson lingered.

'Only that I wouldn't want to be in here for twenty-six miles.' Or, indeed, one. 'How were the men discovered exactly? I mean in what position and where?' Watson asked.

'Most of them were on the floor curled up in balls. Like this.' Cardew put his arms over his head.

'Hedgehogging, they call it at the front,' said Watson. He'd seen men frozen in that position for days, unable or unwilling to come out and face the world. 'And they were alive?'

'You could call it that.'

'And how long did it take them to die?'

Cardew's face looked pained at the memory. 'God, it was terrible. I never knew that there really was a death rattle until . . . I mean, the noise in the throat . . .'

'I know,' said Watson gently. 'How long?'

'Some died within minutes, most an hour or two. The MO hung on for hours. And then there is Hitchcock. Last of them alive.'

'And who declared them dead?'

'Nobody,' said Cardew. He gave a half-hearted laugh. 'It was bloody obvious.'

'Deaths still need to be officially recorded. Along with probable cause.'

'Well, that's the problem, isn't it? We don't know the cause, probable or otherwise. And Captain Trenton, the MO, was on board monitoring conditions and performance. He died. So he was hardly in a position to fill out forms.'

Watson ignored the young man's sarcasm. He knew he appeared like an old-fashioned stickler for bureaucracy in the engineer's eyes. 'And the other doctors that were brought in?'

'Well, as I understand it, they couldn't establish a cause of death . . .'

'So there is no death certificate?'

'No,' said Cardew. 'I do believe the families will be informed they died in action—'

'Good grief, man, that should have been done by now,' said Watson, pinching the bridge of his nose, wanting to be out of this stinking sweatbox. He realized the heat, the claustrophobia and his own tiredness were making him irritable. But the crew's families might be posting letters and making up parcels for men who no longer needed them. It would be a shock when they realized they had been writing to corpses. He owed it to them to solve this mystery as quickly as possible. 'I'm sorry. It's not your fault, I know. I'll sort out the formalities.'

Cardew lowered his voice to a whisper, so Levass couldn't hear. 'Listen, Major, you have to understand that this is being done at breakneck speed. Some would say too fast. The original plan was a thousand tanks, French and British, in one decisive hammer-blow. Then, one hundred and fifty, British only, which didn't please Levass and now . . . we'll have a few score at best.'

'And that's not enough?'

Cardew took a deep breath and his face closed up, as if he was uncomfortable with the truth. 'They will work, sir, but only if deployed correctly. And that is with overwhelming surprise. You get but one chance at that. As you said about the SMK bullets, sir, and I was impressed that a man of . . .' He cleared his throat.

'Of my age?'

'Of your background knew about them. The truth is, sir, as I said, the whole thing is being rushed.'

'Rushed how?'

A seam of anger was laced through the reply. 'The quality of the workmanship and materials, the design, the engine power, the armour thickness, the training of the men, their safety and . . .'

'And what?'

'They've concentrated so much on building complete tanks to show off to their visitors, there are no spare parts. I don't know if you know much about engineering, sir, but I would estimate that fifty per cent of these machines will have mechanical problems at some point. They'll need spares. We haven't got any.'

'I'm sorry to hear that,' Watson said. And he was. Not about the spares. But that young men were being rushed into harm's way without adequate support. The sad fact was that this was nothing new in this war or any other.

'Let's concern ourselves with what happened inside . . . what was her name? *Genevieve*. The tanks won't be going anywhere or surprising anyone if they kill their crew every time the hatches and visors come down.' Cardew nodded his agreement. 'So, I'll need some lights in here, good lights. Can you manage that? And a boiler suit, or some kind of protective clothing.'

'Yes, sir. The tankmen all wear overalls, so we have plenty of spares.'

'Excellent. And I'll fetch my magnifying glass.' Watson looked around at the now-empty space, and heard its anguished ghosts calling him in harsh, metallic tones. 'Something terrible happened in here, Cardew. And we're going to find out what.'

It was late afternoon by the time Watson had finished with the inside of the tank. When he finally emerged, his face was covered in grime, his eyes red from squinting through the magnifying glass, his throat dry and his stomach rumbling from a missed lunch.

Lieutenant Booth, the intelligence officer, was waiting for him, standing alongside Cardew and Levass.

Levass handed Watson a flask of water and he took three big gulps.

'Well, Major,' Booth asked. 'What do you make of our *Genevieve*?'

Watson shook his head to show he wasn't answering questions.

'Can you get me a crew list?' he asked Booth.

'Of course.'

'Did the dead men have anything in common? Background? From the same town or village?'

'No,' said Booth. 'We draw from all over, all classes. All we ask is they be mechanically-minded.'

'But you can get me the personal records of the deceased?'

'Of course. I'll have them sent to your room.'

Watson turned to Cardew. 'There is a bullet hole in the engine.'

The engineer nodded glumly. 'Yes, I am afraid your patient took a pot shot at it when it happened.'

'Hitchcock? Why didn't you tell me? I asked if there was anything unusual. Isn't a man shooting his own engine quite strange?'

'Major,' objected Booth, 'the whole scene was quite strange. And quite traumatic. The bullet was the least of it when it happend.'

'Has it damaged the engine?' Watson asked Cardew.

'I'd have to take off the valve cover and check the valve springs and the pushrods. But not too much, I suspect.'

'So it could be repaired relatively quickly?'

Cardew shrugged. 'I would imagine a day or two at the most.'

'Can you see to it, please? And the wheels at the back?' He pointed at the twisted steering device.

'We can scavenge a new set from another tank. Though they are proving worse than useless. A good driver can steer with just the tracks.'

'Then get me a good driver,' Watson replied.

'What do you want to do, Major?' Booth asked.

'I'm going to fix up *Genevieve* and then we are going to take her back out over there.' He pointed at the phoney no man's land. 'With all hatches closed.'

'You won't find many men keen to do that, Major,' said Levass with a chuckle.

'Well, I shall lead by example,' said Watson, stripping off the boiler suit.

'What do you mean?' asked Booth.

Watson slapped a hand on the side of tank. 'Once *Genevieve* is repaired, I'm going to take her out for a spin.' He let that sink it for a second. 'Anybody fancy joining me?'

Watson decided to walk back to the house alone, to have some thinking time. In truth, he was hoping that a voice in his skull would lay out the solution for him and he could get out of this place with its brutal death machines once and for all. But Holmes, or his mental simulacrum, was silent as he crunched along the pathway between the trees, the sun on his neck.

'You stupid bloody berk!'

The spat insult made Watson spin round, looking for his abuser, but there was nobody there he could see.

'Show yourself!' Watson demanded.

'—calling a berk? Berk yourself.'

That was a second voice. Gruffer than the first. It was a conversation of sorts.

'—gasper. You tight git.' A raucous laugh.

Watson stood stock-still, his eyes shut, letting all his other senses turn down like the wick of a lamp while he concentrated on his hearing. It took more than a minute, his breathing shallow, the beat of his heart loud in his ears until he had it. The disembodied sounds were drifting through the trees like smoke, coming from his right. *Well, you can follow smoke*, Watson thought, *by using your nose*, and determined to try something similar with his auditory faculties.

He set off, away from the path, pushing through a dense undergrowth of fern, nettle and bramble, frequently losing the telltale

171

snippets of chatter and then stopping, until, like a bloodhound of sound, he picked up the trail once more and plunged on, heading due west.

'Have you seen his wife? Ha.'

'Oi!'

The trees grew closer around him. The sunlight barely penetrated sections of it and Watson shivered at the sudden chill as he crossed a gully, dry at that time of year, and scrambled up a sandy bank, grasping at exposed roots for support.

'Game of football?'

'—ckin' likely.'

Now the talk was louder, clearer, coming from over to his left. He skirted through a thicket of hornbeam. Now he could smell cigarettes. There were men ahead.

'I'd like to give him a boot up the backside. No, I would. He suggested I join this new unit. More pay. Special conditions. Oh, yeah, very special conditions.'

'You'd rather you was over in the trenches, would you? Our Alf came back last year, one leg missin'. Won't talk about it even now. But the nightmares . . .'

'Yeah, well, all I'm saying is we should be doin' something.'

Watson kept his breathing shallow as he moved closer. Beyond the close-packed trunks he could see a rhomboid shape, parked just on the edge of the wood. Another tank, albeit one without the side sponsons. The voices were coming from in there.

Then he heard another one, whispering in his ear. Only this time, the hot breath told him it was a real person at his shoulder. 'Do not utter a sound, Major Watson. If you know what's good for you, you will come with me right now!'

Bradley Ross and Nora Pillbody sat in her garden, shadows lengthening around them. On the face of it, they were taking tea, their conversation low and polite. In reality, they were plotting their next move as a newly formed confederacy of German spies.

'Has Booth been around?'

'Briefly, this morning,' said Miss Pillbody. 'He was distracted. I sense some sort of emergency.'

'Caused by us?' Ross asked. He was looking at Miss Pillbody in a new light. Before that night in the woods, the thought of the sexual conquest of Miss Pillbody had been detached, academic. Now, though, he felt genuine excitement about the thought of taking her. He could see that the schoolteacher had been a cleverly constructed mask, a layer of thick paint, like a kabuki performance. Now he could detect the cracks, the little betrayals of her cover that he hadn't noticed before. But, then again, he hadn't imagined her pulling the pins from hand grenades and blowing men's heads off before.

'Are we the emergency?' he repeated.

'I doubt it. The Zeppelin raid, perhaps. They'll be worried that Elveden was the target, don't you think? I doubt our little panto-mime will be discovered.'

'Tell me, Miss Pillbody, do you always carry Mills bombs with you?' he asked.

Miss Pillbody took a dainty sip of her tea. 'Never when I teach school, no,' she said, deadpan. 'At other times, it is an excellent way to confuse any pursuers. You should try them. Lieutenant Booth says, if he can get away he wants me to go picnicking with him tomorrow. He made it clear he would prefer it if you didn't come along this time.'

'He's circling the prey, is he?'

Miss Pillbody raised an eyebrow. 'Oh, I don't think the roles of prey and predator have been fully assigned yet. Do you?'

'How so?'

'We are going about this the wrong way. Sneaking around in that estate, trying to snatch a guard, it is far too risky. And who is to say that if we got one, he would understand what they are doing? A mere guard?'

Ross nodded. 'Good point.'

'But Booth certainly knows what is going on,' she said. 'As any intelligence officer would.'

'True.' Then he understood. He almost felt sorry for Booth. 'You are hoping for some pillow talk?'

She wrinkled her nose at the thought. 'Not at all. When Booth comes here tomorrow, I want you waiting for him.'

'And?'

'And we'll go with your original plan. We'll torture the truth out of him.' She waited while this sank in. 'More tea?'

Claude Levass led Watson away from the echoing voices and the sponson-less tank that he had observed.

'Really, Major, you should not be prying. I saw you swerve off the path earlier and I thought, what is he up to now? Those men can tell you nothing. If you listened to anything they said, you would know that.'

'But the voices,' protested Watson. 'Those disembodied voices – they come from that tank, yet they seem to echo through the forest.'

Levass helped him negotiate the gully once more. 'I should have explained. The tanks without the sponsons on, the open-sided ones we train in? They have a very strange acoustic property. The voice is projected, thrown hundreds of yards away, like some variety trick. The crews use them to smoke in sometimes and their voices drift through the trees. Between you and me, Major, that's how Swinton and the others found out the men were planning on cracking open the hatches during trials – even a whisper can carry for hundreds of yards. The men, they spy on themselves!'

Watson nodded. 'That explains it.'

'Explains what?'

'The voices I could hear at the lodge. They seemed to be outside my window. It was unsettling.'

'You get used to it. Why didn't you ask me? You didn't think it was part of our work here, did you?' Watson said nothing, feeling slightly foolish. His imagination had run away with him a little. 'It is just a by-product as we say in industry. My car is just through here,' Levass said, indicating a snaking path through to the right.

'I sent the driver back, so you will have to take your life in your hands with my driving.'

On the short trip to the Hall, in which Levass handled the motor with a ready ease, they came across Major Thwaites, cantering along a bridle path through the trees. Levass stopped the car to let him pass and the major touched his brim in thanks.

'Where are you off to?' the Frenchman shouted after him.

'Thetford. Errands.'

'Give her my regards,' called Levass.

Thwaites simply shook his head and spurred his mount on.

'There goes history,' said Levass.

'Thwaites?' The man was younger than Levass.

'The horse.' He turned to face Watson. 'Sixteen years ago, the streets of Paris belonged to the horse. London, too. And now? Motor car, motor bus, motor lorry. The cavalry charge has already been made obsolete by the machine gun. In fact, some units of the Royal Horse Guards, Thwaites's regiments, are being retrained as machine-gun battalions. The writing is on the wall. The tank will finish the job. The cavalry will be no more.'

'Do you think that is a good thing?'

'Times change. Several generations ago my people were pirates, yes, pirates. Well, what you politely called privateers. Then, within fifty years, we are respectable businessmen. We must move with the seasons. You can't stay pirates for ever.'

'Well, I think it's a shame,' said Watson. 'About the cavalry.'

'You think so?'

It was Watson's turn to shrug. 'I am an old man. I don't like change.'

Levass gave a laugh, head thrown back, showing his teeth. 'Not so old, I think, Major Watson, eh? What is the expression, there's life in the old dog yet?'

'I don't understand,' Watson said, genuinely puzzled.

'While you were in *Genevieve* I came back for the water and I spoke to Mrs Gregson, just seeing how Hitchcock was coming along. I think you have an admirer there.'

'Hitchcock?'

Levass frowned, not sure that Watson was being deliberately obtuse. 'Hardly.'

'Mrs Gregson? Not in the sense you mean, Colonel.' Watson insisted. 'Though we have been through a lot together.'

'I would imagine.'

Watson didn't reply, simply let Levass drive him the last few hundred yards in silence. He knew it would be impossible to convince a Frenchman of the platonic nature of their relationship.

As he climbed out of the car, they both caught the strains of a piano, being played with some proficiency. Watson cocked an ear to catch the tune, but Levass beat him to it.

'Debussy,' he said, with a smile. 'Arabesque Number One. Someone with good taste among you English.'

'It's Hitchcock, I suspect,' said Watson. 'How was he when you saw him?'

'Catatonic. Mrs Gregson was reading to him. Jerome K. Jerome, I think.'

'If that's him playing . . .'

'She will have worked wonders. I shall come in with you, if I may.'

They found him at the piano, swaying, playing the theme with his eyes closed, rapt. Mrs Gregson was seated by one of the sugar-twist pillars, book in hand, reading by the light of a candle. 'It's a good thing I like Debussy,' she said. 'This is the twentieth time of this one. He did thirty "*Für Elise*".'

'What happened, Mrs Gregson? What triggered it?'

She shook her head. 'I did as I was told. I was speaking to him and suddenly he began playing, dreadfully at first, but slowly getting better and better, as if he were remembering the keyboard.'

'Excellent,' said Watson. He crossed over, leaned close and whispered in Hitchcock's ear, but he gave no sign of having heard.

'Is this a breakthrough?' asked Levass.

'I hope so,' said Watson. 'Has he said anything?'

'No.'

'Eaten?'

'Some bread and cheese.'

'I think we should get him back to his room. He must be getting tired.'

'I shall speak to you tomorrow, Major,' said Levass, 'when we know how the repairs are coming along. Good evening, Mrs Gregson.' He gave a small bow.

Watson listened for a little longer then tapped Hitchcock on the shoulder. 'Lieutenant, I think that is enough for today. We can play again tomorrow.'

A pause, a breath, and then the piece began over again.

'Lieutenant. Listen, I've been inside the tank. Where it happened. I'm going to repair her. Then run her. I am going to find out exactly what happened in *Genevieve*.'

The fingers froze, Hitchcock's head snapped round, his eyes widened with horror. The scream must have been heard all the way to Thetford. Then he began to bang the piano, manically, his fingers jabbing at the keys in a senseless staccato.

Mrs Gregson came over to assist Watson, but he held up his hand. 'No, wait.'

Like a clockwork toy, Hitchcock was running out of energy, the rhythm slowing, until his hands drooped at his sides and he let his forehead rest on the keys with a final, discordant coda.

They were able to lift him to his feet and walk him back to his temporary prison. Once inside, he took three paces to his chair, sat down, placed his palms on the table then let out a long sigh, as if glad to be home. Silent tears ran down his face.

Mrs Gregson promised to bring him supper and read to him. The room was, as always, a few degrees cooler than outside, so she put the paraffin heater on low, just to take off the chill and they left, bolting the door on the outside, although Watson doubted Lieutenant Hitchcock would be much trouble.

'I need some air,' said Mrs Gregson. 'Will you take a turn around the walled gardens with me, Major Watson?'

177

'Gladly, Mrs Gregson.'

There were actually two walled gardens, connected by arches, the second flint-walled one added to the redbrick original as the household grew in the nineteenth century. Each was filled with neat rows of vegetables, well tended in contrast to the somewhat neglected formal gardens, which suffered from the lack of manpower (due to the exile, under DORA, of even the elderly gardeners, Watson assumed). The walls themselves were draped with trained, ornamental fruit trees and patches of decorative clematis.

Above the walls he could see stables and the estate's flint church, unremarkable except for the fact it had twin towers.

'Was the day productive?' she asked Watson.

'Not as productive as yours.'

She prodded him with a finger. 'Don't tease me, Major. All I did was get bored with Debussy. Did you really find something in the tank this time?'

He nodded. 'Actually, it's what I didn't find.'

'I'm sorry?'

'Just a theory at the moment, but there was something missing inside that tank. But I have solved one mystery – actually two.'

'Ah, at last. What are they?'

'Don't get your hopes up.' He explained about the sponson-less training tanks and their magnification effect on the human voice.

'Intriguing.'

'Yes, although the soldiers don't seem to realize that it can be used to eavesdrop on them.'

'And the other mystery?'

'More relevant. I know where that mark on Hitchcock's face comes from. It happened at the live firing practice – when potshots were taken at the tank during the trial, before disaster struck the men inside. It seems that when a bullet strikes the outside of one of those machines, a speck of paint is dislodged in the interior wall or sometimes a blob of welding material. It is hot and travelling fast and it will burn the skin.'

178

'Have you told Swinton or any of the others?'

'Not yet. But I will. I don't think, however, that a burn to the cheek caused his condition.'

'Did you mean what you said? About starting up *Genevieve*?'

'I did.'

'Isn't that rather foolhardy? What if you end up like that?' She pointed over her shoulder.

'That is all part of the risk. I have experimented on myself before.'

'With the blood transfusion, you mean?' When they had been together in Belgium, in order to prove a batch of blood was not lethally contaminated, Watson had infused some into his own veins.

'Yes. And no harm came to me. Not from the blood, at least.'

'That was different,' she said, watching a flight of starlings race around the sky.

'How so?'

'You knew there was nothing wrong with that blood sample, didn't you?'

He grunted an acknowledgment.

'You have no idea what you are dealing with here. Or do you?'

'No,' he admitted.

'So, I have a suggestion.'

'What's that, Mrs Gregson?'

'If you insist on doing this, I come with you.'

Watson had opened his mouth to reply when he saw Swinton crossing the garden towards them. The colonel had a face like a storm cloud and was muttering to himself. Watson saluted and Swinton barely returned it. He was some yards past them when he changed his mind and spun on his heel.

'Major,' he said, 'I am afraid you might not have time to complete your investigations. The orders are for the sponsons to be fitted and men trained as quickly as humanly possible. We are to ship to France on September the 1st.'

'Isn't that rather sudden?' Watson asked.

Swinton nodded furiously. 'Sudden? It's indecent. Experimental machines, and not enough of them, barely trained crews, no spares . . .' He glared at Watson, as if this new development was his fault. 'I detect the hand of Churchill in all this.'

With that he carried on his almost comically fast walk and resumed his one-sided conversation.

'What I don't understand,' said Watson, after he had gone, 'is that if Churchill is so unpopular, why they allowed me in as his . . . envoy?' *Unwilling envoy*, he had almost said.

It was a rhetorical question, but Mrs Gregson replied. 'Because Churchill set this whole process in motion with his Landships Committee. So he feels rather proprietorial towards it. Paternal, you might say. And because Churchill still controls some of the purse strings, and because Churchill could probably scupper the whole project if he so desired. You don't cross Winston in the skullduggery game.'

'As I know to my cost. You speak as if you know his mind,' Watson said, stopping to inspect one of the apple trees. It was showing signs of neglect and needed a good prune. 'But if he knows about things such as the deaths in *Genevieve*, there must be . . .' The truth hit him. That damned ex-First Lord was up to his usual tricks. 'He must have a spy in here, mustn't he? Churchill must have a man within these walls.'

'No, Major.'

'No?' he asked, surprised by the certainty in her voice.

'Churchill doesn't have a man in here.' Her smile, at once mischievous and guilty, told him before she confirmed it that Mrs Gregson was Churchill's eyes and ears at Elveden. 'But he does have a woman.'

TWENTY-FIVE

Coyle was not a man for thinking too much. Introspection did not come naturally. Not since he had been taken under the wing of the Bureau. Now, however, he ran through the day's events, looking for holes in his preparations. He had arranged for the landlady of the pub to do his laundry. He had stripped down his Smith & Wesson and made sure it was in perfect working order. He had written a bland letter to his mother, saying he had lost a close friend, but once he had taken care of that business he would come home for a visit. And then what?

Now he lay on his bed upstairs at the pub, hands behind his head, staring at the cracks in the ceiling, replaying the last few years, beginning from the moment he had walked into the warehouse on Liverpool's Dock Road and seen a corpulent little man tied to a chair, his face showing the marks of a good old-fashioned beating. The victim's head had lolled onto his shoulder. With his eyes swollen closed it was difficult to tell whether he was conscious or not.

Gibson.

Not that he knew who he was back then. Just some British spy dumb enough to be caught. It had been stupid to send him in posing as a gun dealer. But it was the early days of the SSB and the cover story had seemed sound enough – disgruntled and disgraced ex-officer of Irish descent with access to weapons from the Continent and happy for them to be used against the British. They hadn't reckoned with the Brotherhood having ways and means of deep-checking background stories with the British Army, and Gibson's elaborate tale had fallen apart, just as he was promising them a boatful of barely used Maxims and Mausers.

When Coyle had walked into that dusty, echoing space, thick with the clinging smell of mace and cinnamon, there had been three fellow rebels in there. Two were brothers, the Dalys, John and Conor – both short and dark-haired with teeth that seemed to dislike their companions so much they had run in opposite directions – and the third, Eamonn 'Fitz' Fitzgerald. The latter, taller and with striking dark looks helped along by the fine-honed ridges of his cheekbones, was the Witchfinder General of Liverpool and Belfast. His job was to sniff out spies and traitors, and if there was any doubt he always came down on the side of 'guilty'.

'Coyle, where the fuck you been?' Fitz had shouted across the vast spice warehouse as his footsteps echoed on the stone floor. 'Missing all the fun here, lad.'

Fitz had a small table before him and laid out on it were various implements for stabbing, snapping and squeezing the human body. But in his hands was a blowtorch that he was busy priming. Satisfied, he put a Balkan to it and a blue flame roared from the nozzle. A curl of pungent smoke rose from the cigarette.

'There we go.' Fitz adjusted it down to a hiss.

'Who is he?' Coyle asked nonchalantly.

'That's what we are about to find out. Get him awake, boys.'

Conor tossed a pail of water in Gibson's face and he stirred, managing to open one eye. It widened slightly when he saw the man before him and what he had in his hand, but to his credit that was the only reaction. A few moments passed before he managed to get some words from his pillowed lips. 'You are making a mistake.'

'Pah,' said Fitz. 'Youse made the mistake, mister. Well, let's make a few things clear. You aren't getting out of here alive. Not a chance. Next stop will be meeting your maker. But you can get there fast or get there slow.' He tossed his cigarette away and re-lit another one from the torch, almost singeing his eyebrows. 'Jesus, that's warm, now. So, my friend, all you have to do is tell us who sent you and how you get in touch with them. And we'll make it an express train to heaven. Or the other place. What d'you say?'

The fat lips moved. It was like watching two slugs dancing. 'I am Michael Colbert—'

John Daly grabbed a fistful of the bound man's hair and pulled his head back. The leather soles of the agent's shoes scuffed over the floor with the pain. Fitz stepped closer and adjusted the flame so it was louder and longer once more. Then he looked at Coyle.

'Yer fancy a go, Coyle? Human flesh smells just like roast pig, y'know. At least the English do.'

Fitz held out the torch.

Coyle shrugged. 'Why not? Is y'man definitely English?'

'If he's Irish he'll smell like roast beef.' This was Conor, the shorter and stupider of the pair.

The prisoner was scared – who wouldn't be? – but was astute enough not to show it. That was what these lads wanted. Some snivelling. Some pleading. If there was none of that, they'd end it quick anyway. But even the bravest of men were liable to scream for mercy when their eyeballs melted and ran down their faces.

Coyle stepped around the table and held the blue flame close to the Englishman's face. The man could feel the fierce heat now. He closed the one good eye.

'Not too quick, now,' warned Fitz.

'Start with his fingers,' said Conor.

'Or his little English cock,' offered John, to a round of laughter.

Enough, a voice screamed in Coyle's head. *There has been enough of this.*

'You know, John Daly, you always were a little shite.'

Coyle thrust the torch into John's eye, pushing hard as he did so, then letting it go. His left leg kicked back, sending the table flying towards Fitz and his right hand cleared the pistol from his waistband. He shot Conor in the face, but didn't wait to see him fall, and then he swivelled back to Fitz, who had his own weapon raised, pointing at him.

'Now, Coyle, what the fuck was that all about?'

Gibson made the only move open to him at that point. He hooked a toe under the blowlamp that had landed at his feet and sent it arcing towards Fitz's head. He saw it coming, spinning his way, a streak of blue flame, and he instinctively moved to one side. Which is when Coyle shot him dead. Then he turned and did the same to the remaining brother.

Lying on the bed now, Coyle felt a wave of nausea roll over him as the smells came back to him. The blood, cordite and burned flesh mixed queasily with sweet spices. He had never been able to stomach anything with cinnamon in it since that day.

Gibson and he had fled the country and, in gratitude, the

ex-sapper had offered Coyle a job. As a spy. So, he became Gibson's partner. As he moved through their time together in the SSB, their lives intertwined, thanks to those few minutes in the warehouse, his reminiscences eventually came to Gibson's death in the street, gunned down by . . .

By whom?

Men who wanted to prevent Major Watson from heading to Suffolk? Here, in this small bedroom illuminated by the golden glow of a falling sun, in an idyllic part of England, it didn't add up to thruppence. But then, something that did make sense suddenly struck him. It made him sit up, bolt upright. His eyes went to the pistol, laying on the square of cloth on the dresser.

Major Watson hadn't been the target that morning in Mayfair.

He had.

Watson laid out the files of the seven dead men on his bed. He had been through each of them, making notes and cross-referencing with Hitchcock's record. There was little overlap between the tank crew. The commander had been to a top public school, one of the gearsmen to a decent grammar. All were under thirty, the majority barely into their twenties. All had some degree of engineering training – marine engines, motor cycles, motor cars, steam tractors, aeroplanes. One had been a mechanic for the London General Omnibus Company, working on the motor buses that had been running in the capital for more than a decade now.

Apart from the interest in all things mechanical, very little connected them. Had it not been for the war it was unlikely their paths would ever have crossed.

There was a tap on the door.

'Come in!' Watson instructed.

It was Thwaites, the cavalryman. 'Sorry to disturb you, Major.'

'That's all right. I wanted a word anyway.'

'Really? With me?' He sounded genuinely surprised.

'Take a seat.'

'I prefer to stand,' said Thwaites.

Of course he would. The imposing cavalryman stood well over six foot, taller than Holmes, and was a hard man to intimidate when he was on his feet. Not that Watson was in the business of intimidating.

'What do you make of it?' Watson asked him. 'The incident with *Genevieve*?'

Thwaites blew out his cheeks to show his bafflement. 'I have no idea. Strategically, it is a disaster. To lose confidence in the machine at this point . . . you understand that is why Swinton wants to keep it all under wraps?'

'Because he doesn't want the tanks taken away from him,' said Watson flatly.

'Yes.' Thwaites narrowed his eyes slightly. 'Not much gets past you, does it, Major Watson?'

He had to laugh at that. What would Holmes have to say about that statement?

'Swinton will do whatever the high command wants in order to go down in history as the man who unleashed the tank on the Hun. Remember that.'

'I shall. But tell me, surely you should consider the tank the work of the devil? Replacing the horse with a machine.'

'Replacing?' Thwaites's moustache quivered at the very thought.

'Eventually, I would imagine.'

Thwaites was silent for a moment. 'I am fifty-three years old, Major. I have been in the cavalry since I was eighteen and seen action at Kimberley and Paardeberg. My father was in The Blues before me, fought at Tel-el-Kebir. I have two sons, fourteen and twelve; the thought that they might not follow in our footsteps pains me immensely.'

'I understand. Family tradition.'

'Yes.'

Watson sat on the bed. His bones ached from all the stooping in the tank. 'Yet here you are, helping seal the fate of the cavalry—'

'On the contrary,' Thwaites insisted.

'But I hear that some of The Blues are to become machine-gun battalions. Cavalry in name only.'

'Only while we find a new role for the horse.' Thwaites's eyes widened. 'Picture this. Ten tanks abreast, twenty perhaps, sponson-to-sponson, advancing over no man's land, a moving wall of steel, impervious to bullets. Behind them, the cavalry, shielded by the tanks, and behind them, the infantry. When the wire is breached, the horses dash forward, piercing right through enemy lines, a pincer movement, tanks and infantry one side, the cavalry the other.'

Watson could think of many objections. Tanks might be able to cope with trenches; horses had proved rather less adept. And the Germans would change tactics, from the murderous machine guns to lobbing shells over the tanks to burst among the men and horses. But he wasn't there to discuss the tactics of tank warfare. 'You'll need a lot of tanks.'

'And we'll get them.'

'Why did you come to see me?'

'Oh, nothing important.' Thwaites looked uncomfortable. 'It can wait.'

'I'm here now.'

'It's just . . .' He produced a slim volume from his tunic pocket. 'I wondered if you would mind signing this for me?' He handed it across. It was an 1890 Spencer Blackett edition of *The Sign of Four*. 'It seems a little frivolous, now . . .' the cavalryman began.

'Not at all,' said Watson, laying the book down. 'I'd be pleased to. But let me take my time over it. You don't want a smudged dedication.'

'No, thank you.'

'And I am flattered you carry some of my work around with you.'

'Actually, I found it in the Thetford bookshop this evening. Seemed too good to be true. So that's my rather banal reason for coming to your room. But why did you want to see me? Didn't you say earlier you wanted a word?'

'Oh, yes. But I think you've answered my question.'

'Really?' Thwaites looked perplexed.

Watson nodded. 'If you travelled to and from South Africa by Union Castle Line, then you have.'

'I did. But—'

'It is of no consequence,' Watson lied.

'Right. Well, I am keeping you from your work.' Thwaites pointed to the files.

'There's nothing here that speaks to me. Just words on paper.'

'Ah. So what do you do next?'

Watson picked up one of the folders. 'I go and look at the men behind these words. Or what is left of them.'

Before he examined the corpses, Watson called in on Hitchcock, unbolting the door from the outside and announcing himself as he entered. There was no reply. Hitchcock was calm and still, his tears dried, and he was still sitting at the card table, his eyes closed, only a single lamp burning in the corner and a dull glow from the paraffin heater illuminating his room. The fumes from the heater caught Watson's throat and he opened the hinged door at the front of the cylindrical body and peered inside. The flame was yellow when it should have been blue. It was hard to tell in the gloom, but he suspected that the mantle needed a good clean and the wick trimming. He made a mental note to turn it off before he left and get some blankets sent to Hitchcock. The fumes from a badly adjusted heater could be lethal.

'I am glad you are calm now, Hugh. Well, we can do the piano again tomorrow if you wish. But we don't have to. I can see that it upset you somewhat. We could just listen to some gramophone music. It can be very soothing. Holmes used to play, you know. Violin, not piano. Not so much in later years. I think he gave up when he realized he was finding the violin versions of Mendelssohn's *Songs Without Words* trickier than usual. He liked German music. I remember him saying once, "German music is rather more to my taste than French or Italian. It is introspective and I want to introspect!" I'd never heard it used as a verb like that. To introspect indeed. And he loved Sarasate, the Spanish violinist. One afternoon at St

James's Hall, he sat in the stalls wrapped in the most perfect happiness, gently waving his long, thin fingers in time to the music, his languid, dreamy eyes quite unlike the normal Holmes. The music took him to another place, where he no longer had to be the great calculating machine of a detective. I wonder if it can take you out of that place they've trapped you in.'

Watson stopped himself, suddenly aware that he had been speaking of his old friend in the past tense, as if he were already lost to him. He reached up and cracked opened the single, small window. The paraffin fumes were becoming far too pungent.

Watson sat down on the bed and put his head in his hands. 'I don't know about you, Hitchcock, but I am just about done in. Early start, long hours cramped in that tank, a wild-goose chase through the woods. If I'd known this was what fate had in store for me I'd have become a porter at Smithfield or Billingsgate. At least they get beer in the mornings.'

An unfamiliar noise from Hitchcock made Watson look up. As if his neck were a seized joint being freed, Hitchcock's head rotated painfully and slowly towards him. There was so little light that Watson couldn't be sure, but he thought he detected a flicker of a smile on the lips. Yes, there it was, if not a full grin then certainly the promise of one.

Progress! Watson shouted inside. *Progress at last.*

TWENTY-SIX

The ice house that contained the tankmen's bodies sat outside the walled garden, beyond the ha-ha and on the edge of a trout lake that sat behind a grassed embankment. The entrance was a vaulted brick arch with two steel doors, obviously recent additions, and stone steps that led down into a series of rooms, only one of which was clearly an ice store: it was a vast circular space with a floor that sloped to a central drain and racks, now empty, for holding imported Scandinavian ice. The others were larders and game rooms. There was electricity, too, something else newly installed, although only a single weak bulb per room and one over the steps down.

The coffins of the dead were stacked in three pairs and a single in a section of the chamber that, judging from the steel rails and hooks in the ceiling, would have been used to hang the estate's venison. The room was suitably chill for its purpose – Watson had had the foresight to don a thick coat, scarf and gloves – but even so, he could detect the sweet smell of decay from within the plain wooden boxes. Nevertheless, he knew he had to examine at least one of the corpses.

As well as his medical bag, Watson had brought with him a large screwdriver he had found in the handyman's cupboard next to the butler's pantry below the stairs in the Hall.

Each coffin had a name written on the lid in black paint. He chose the single coffin – Pte B. Knowle, MGC – kneeled down, slid the blade under the lid and levered. The wood and nails screeched in protest, and Watson leaned back as the vapours from within belched into the space. He grabbed the lid and wrenched it free.

'Good God,' he said, his voice amplified by the bare brick walls.

Watson had seen plenty of dead bodies before. He had exhumed them, examined them, he knew what death and putrefaction looked like. He was prepared, but not for the sight that greeted him: Private B. Knowles, late of the Machine Gun Corps, was absent from his own coffin.

There were several large stones placed in his stead. The smell was coming from the traces of bodily fluids that smeared the inside. A few flies rose up to greet him, irritated at being interrupted from their liquid feast.

It didn't take Watson long to establish that the others were empty, too, but for a motley assortment of rocks. He took off his gloves and lit a cigarette. It was clear what the motive for removal must be. The dead could still tell tales. Whatever condition those bodies were in, they could have told him, or another professional, something about the cause of death. But what would it betray? What had caused the hedgehogging madness and death? And how had the bodies been moved? Manhandling seven bodies from the ice house was no easy matter, even for a young, healthy man. True, it was tucked out of sight, so a person could work undisturbed. Even so, where could the bodies have been moved to? *Think, man.*

Somewhere close by, I believe.

At the sound of his old friend's voice, Watson sat down on one of the empty coffins. He closed his eyes, imagining himself deep in an armchair in front of a crackling fire, the fumes from his cigarette blending with the smell of woodsmoke and that of Holmes's pipe. The great detective was leaning forward in his armchair, occasionally stabbing with the stem of his briar, his eyes glinting as they sometimes did when his brain examined a problem, turning it over, letting the light play on every aspect, the way a Hatton Garden jeweller might assess a gemstone.

Why do you say that?

It would be a brave man who would run these roadblocks with seven bodies on board a vehicle.

True.

Did you examine the rocks?

Not yet, Holmes. They were quite substantial, though.

I would look to the ornamental gardens. A rockery, perhaps?

Yes.

And the ground outside the ice house. For marks of dragging.

Why?

One man would have to drag a body. Two would carry.

I suppose.

Now, think. Burying seven bodies in haste. Is that feasible?

I doubt it.

So put yourself in this body-snatcher's place. Where would you dispose of the bodies?

Watson started as the cigarette burned his fingers. The room at

Baker Street dissolved to nothing, retreating to that corner of his brain where it was always the 1890s and the streets resounded to the sound of hoofs on cobbles and the cry of costermongers. The sudden cold on his face made him shiver. It was just a trick of an ageing mind, of course, but the echo of these timeslips normally left him with a contented afterglow. Not here. Not when, snapped back to real life, he remembered his friend was not a well man, and had been abducted and taken far from his old haunts to his little cottage, but a prisoner of the very government they served. That was the imperative drive behind solving the murder: finding Holmes. He stood and stamped his feet and watched his breath condense before him.

The lake, of course. That was what the voice in his head had been getting at. The easiest place to dispose of bodies, if they could be weighted properly. More rocks, for instance.

He could imagine insisting the body of water was dragged. Swinton, he suspected, would claim it was a sideshow, something that could wait until the tanks had been deployed. Perhaps he was right. Even a few days in the water might destroy whatever physical evidence the bodies could give him.

Watson walked out into the stone-flagged corridors that led to the other rooms. In the furthest one he found the four victims of the Zeppelin air raid. They were laid out under white sheets, which had soaked up a significant amount of blood. This time he crouched, gingerly, wary of his knees, and pulled back one of the covers. He gave an involuntary gasp. The young man had suffered a terrible injury to his chest, the ribs imploding, driven back to the spine, leaving a mess of lung and heart on the surface. The second had lost most of his head and upper torso, a stub of the severed spine protruding at a strange angle. This man had a large, corpulent belly, suggesting he had been somewhat older. The third was a stomach wound, again the flesh simply torn away to expose the poor lad's innards.

'No air raid did that.'

At first he thought the voice was his phantom companion returned. 'Look at the blast marks.'

He stood and turned to face Mrs Gregson. 'What are you doing here? Writing a report for Winston?'

There had been cross words in the garden, because Watson had clearly disapproved of Mrs Gregson's subterfuge. No good, he felt, ever came of spying. On the other hand, he was somewhat conflicted because without her agreeing to work for Churchill, he might never have seen her again and certainly would not have received the news about Holmes being on Foulness, no matter how vague her sighting. He had confessed to her the underhand methods Churchill had used to get him to Elveden and why the man was not to be trusted. She had hardly seemed surprised.

'Major Watson,' she said now, her voice whip-sharp, 'as we are both employed by the same man, albeit under different circumstances, I find your continued hostility somewhat hypocritical. Churchill plays us all like members of the orchestra. And don't ask which instruments we are, you might not like the answer. Now, Major, I spent two years looking at every single way that an explosion can destroy the human body. After a while you recognize the various patterns. You have to, as it helps decide whether you can save a man. Those explosions were small, concentrated and occurred at very close quarters. There, look.' She pointed. 'The shrapnel.'

Using the tweezers from his bag, Watson reached into the chest of the boy who had suffered the flattening of his ribs and extracted a lump of greyish metal. Mrs Gregson stepped in as he held it up to the bare bulb.

'That's not from any HE shell I have ever seen,' said Mrs Gregson. 'Nor incendiary, I think.' She looked down at the bodies, which although horribly mutilated, showed little signs of charring apart from blast damage. 'It looks like a handle or a lever.'

'From what?'

'If I was a betting woman, I'd say a grenade.'

Watson opened his mouth to reply, but at that moment the lights went out and they heard the ringing clang of the steel doors being closed and bolted from the outside.

Ross rifled through the drawers in the kitchen, looking for implements to carry out their plan. After an elaborate charade of saying goodbye, he had returned to the cottage via the rear entrance. Miss Pillbody had drawn the curtains, so no prying eyes could see she had company – male company – for the evening.

'Would you care for something to eat?' she asked. 'I have some cold ham.'

'Later,' he said, turning to face her. 'Torture him how, exactly?'

Miss Pillbody gave a sweet smile. 'I don't know. I've never tortured anyone. Have you?'

Ross considered this for a moment. He had beaten men to make them talk, but they had broken easily. Booth was an intelligence officer. Surely he would require more persuasion than a fat lip and a couple of missing teeth. 'But you have blown up men with grenades.'

A delicate little shrug. 'That was actually my first time. Needs must.'

Ross rubbed his forehead. He wasn't quite sure what he had got himself into with this woman. 'Are there any tools in the house? Pliers or some such?'

'Not that I have found. There are knives. Blunt knives.'

'I just think we need something that will put the fear of God into a man.' He gave an involuntary glance at the dolls. 'Something to show as much as use.'

'I can't think of anything like that.'

He pointed up at the top shelf of the dresser, which contained her collection of large-headed dolls that stood, staring glassy-eyed into the room. 'We could always frighten him with those. Jesus, they're ugly.'

'They are *autoperipatetikos*,' she said, irritated by his ignorance. 'Walking dolls. My father used to buy me them, then my husband. Now, I collect them.'

'Oh.' *Hideous things*, he thought, but kept it to himself. His own father had collected African ceremonial masks, which had been equally creepy. 'Do you have any more alcohol? I could do with a drink.'

'There's nothing but that sherry. Miss Pillbody wouldn't keep anything else in the house. I was always partial to kirsch in my old life. I don't think it is her tipple, though, do you?'

'No. I'll have the sherry, then.'

Ross sat at the kitchen table, and watched her sort out two small glasses of the sticky amber-coloured liquid. He felt a weariness in his bones. Too many late nights, too much creeping around, too many bodies in a short time. Soon they would have another on their hands.

She sat down and pushed the glass towards him. He took a mouthful and swallowed, grimacing at it went down, leaving a medicinal aftertaste.

'Now,' Miss Pillbody said with resolve, 'stop being so agitated. We have to apply logic here. Time is short. Obtaining the information from Booth is simply the best available option we have. If he won't talk, we'll snatch ourselves someone who will. Then you can get out of here.'

'What about Thetford aerodrome?'

'New orders,' she admitted. 'I am to stand down. After the loss of the ship, the Zeppelin raids are being suspended pending fresh tactics.'

She must, Ross appreciated, have a way of communicating with her superiors. Radio? Pigeons? He doubted she would tell him. 'Such as?'

She gave a long sigh. 'They won't tell me that, of course. But I hear the *Fliegertruppen* has been given permission to raid London with conventional aircraft. Perhaps the time of the Zeppelin is coming to an end. But I have been given clearance by my superior to try to ascertain what is going on at the estate.'

'What about their spy in there?'

A shrug. 'Perhaps there isn't one. Perhaps they consider a two-pronged approach the best option. Perhaps he has been caught and shot.'

'What will you do then? If we break the secret of Elveden? Could you stay here?'

'Oh, don't worry about me. If all goes well, I shall stay on as Miss Pillbody for a while longer. But if we expose ourselves, I'll slip into another life. I'll have done my duty. I will have avenged my husband.' She took another sip. 'If not quite in the way I envisaged.'

A robin started up outside the window, singing as if its life depended on the volume of noise it could produce.

Ross took another small amount of the sherry. 'I'm sorry. I just . . . I never have, I don't think . . . loved anyone. I've hated plenty of people in my time. It's hate that drove me here.' He looked down at his glass and laughed. 'Jesus, what's in this stuff? I thought it was gin that made you melancholy.'

She put her head to one side, as if examining a strange specimen for the first time. 'Just so you know . . .' she began.

'What?'

'I thought about killing you last night.'

It was said so matter-of-factly, as if she were talking about pulling a weed from the garden, that he actually shuddered. 'Why?'

'I thought it would be neater. But then I thought, what if it somehow leads back to me? After all, we've been seen together. I didn't want anyone prying. So, I decided best not.'

He laughed. 'I'm glad.'

'You know, so am I.' She finished the sherry. 'That really is filthy stuff, isn't it?'

'Yup.'

'I think you should slip out the back way and perhaps go and buy us a bottle of something from the pub. I'll do that ham with some potatoes and some greens from the garden.'

'How domesticated.'

'And while you are there, visit the blacksmith. He'll still be in the forge. Ask if you can hire a pair of tongs; say you are having a bonfire or some such and don't want it to get out of control. And a pair of pliers to remove nails from the wood. He won't care; the money'll just go down his throat.'

He stood. It seemed like a plan, of sorts.

'And Ross?'

'Yes.'

'Just in case you are wondering. If it ever becomes expedient, I will do it.'

'What?'

'Kill you.'

He couldn't help but snort at that. 'Jesus, woman, you know how to put a man at ease.' He was still suppressing a snigger when he slipped out the rear, disturbing the vocal robin as he went.

After he had gone, Miss Pillbody washed up the two glasses and placed them in the draining rack, put the empty sherry bottle out in the bin and went to the dresser. From there she selected three of the best carving and boning knives, and set about putting a serious edge on them using a whetstone. The noise released a distant memory of the squeals of pain and the smell of hot blood that filled the sheds when her grandfather let her watch the workers castrate the bulls on his estate. Which gave her an idea.

TWENTY-SEVEN

In the courtyard of The Plough, Coyle bent over the Vauxhall, rebolting the radiator, telling himself to slow down. His haste had already cost him the skin on his knuckles. He had found the letter from his mother and reread the line that should have leaped out at him earlier.

'I had to get Marie Coughlan to read your last one to me. They say it's the cataracts . . .'

He had been so thrown by the word 'cataracts' he hadn't paid enough attention to the name of the woman reading letters to her. Marie Coughlan, née Daly. The sister of the two men shot in a warehouse by one Donal Coyle. They always said the Brotherhood finds you sooner or later. Three dead men on a cold warehouse floor in Liverpool had to be paid for. So they had moved a Daly into his mother's orbit, playing the very long game. And it was true, for years his letters were from no place specific, often given to other agents to post while he and Harry Gibson were on their travels. Anyone looking at the postmark might think him a particularly aimless nomad or a confused travelling salesman. The contents of the letters were deliberately vague as to his location. But lately, blinded perhaps by the fever of homesickness, by the fatigue of a life of subterfuge serving a government that wasn't his own, he must have become careless. And somehow they had picked up his trail. Normally the Brothers would try a snatch, but he flattered himself that they might have thought that too risky. Donal Coyle was a hard man to take alive, at least he hoped so. But he could imagine that the next piece in the newspaper Marie Coughlan would love to read to his mother would be a detailed description of his execution, left to die on the rich men's pavements of Mayfair. He made a note to get a message to Major Watson, to tell him his life was not in danger. Not from roving assassins, anyway.

Coyle finished with the bolts and clipped on the hoses of the cooling system. Using a watering can, he filled the radiator slowly, squeezing the rubber pipes to ease away any air bubbles. When it overflowed he wiped away the excess and examined the radiator core for leaks. He couldn't see any. He got down on his hands and knees, looking for drips. None. But Coyle knew rad repairs failed under pressure and he put on the cap to seal the system, cranked the engine and let it run.

While he was waiting for it to rattle its way to the usual running temperature he lit a Woodbine. What was the next move open to him? He had to get his mother out of harm's way. Because he knew

197

what their next ploy would be. They would get a message to him telling him they had his ma. That she was safe and well – for the moment. And would stay that way, if he turned himself in to stand before a tribunal. A fair hearing, they would say. And they'd give him that before they shot him in a ditch, making sure it was in the face so as to deprive his mother even the comfort of an open coffin. Well, he imagined there was at least one of the Daly brothers who had been denied that privilege too. Only fair. An eye for an eye, literally.

Coyle gave the repair the once-over and, satisfied, turned off the engine. It would get him back to London. Then a train to Liverpool and a boat back home. Would they be waiting for him? Probably. But he had learned a few tricks over the past few years. Gibson had been very adept at changing his appearance. He had used Salvatore, an Italian barber in Clerkenwell, who could transform a man with a fresh haircut, a trim of the moustache, some hair dye if required. It would be worth what he charged.

Coyle closed the car door and walked through the archway to enter the pub. He would tell the landlord he was leaving and settle his bill, maybe have a pint and a pie to see him on his way. But what he saw as he approached the entrance to the public bar stopped him in his tracks.

Swinton and Booth were the first to arrive for drinks, which had been scheduled before another informal dinner to discuss the new timetable for deployment of the tanks. They were to be joined by Cardew, Thwaites, Levass and Major Watson. Swinton poured them each a stiff gin from the bottles on the side table.

'What do you think?' he asked the intelligence officer. 'Is it feasible? This new deployment date?'

'I'm not sure, sir . . .' Booth began.

'I think it is.' It was Cardew, the engineer, dressed for dinner in what passed for the modern way in some quarters: a smart dark blue lounge suit with a collar and tie. 'Although we will have to

198

work day and night. One team to bolt on the sponsons by night, the crews to train on the tanks during the day, first on the statics, then on the fully equipped ones. We'll need a very strict timetable if—'

He stopped when he heard approaching laughter and Levass and Thwaites entered. Both men had slight flushes on their cheeks, as if they had started proceedings early.

'You've heard, I suppose?' Swinton asked them.

'Heard what?' asked Thwaites.

'The tanks deploy in France on September the 1st.'

'Whose idea was this foolishness?' demanded Levass, his mood changing in a heartbeat.

'Haig's, I would imagine,' replied Swinton. The commander-in-chief had sent some of his staff from France to watch early tank tests at Hatfield. They had all been most impressed by how the machines crushed or turned aside the barbed wire. 'Like a rhinoceros,' one officer had reported. A very slow rhinoceros. 'Haig and Robertson, his chief of staff, have been lobbying Lloyd George to unleash the tanks as soon as feasible.'

'To save their faces from the Somme débâcle,' said Levass glumly.

'I think you'll find,' said Thwaites slowly, not wanting to take that slight from a foreigner, 'that the whole débâcle was designed to take some pressure off the French. Those Tommies died so that you could regroup.'

Levass nodded his acceptance of that point.

'And,' said Swinton, 'Haig has the backing of Montagu at the Ministry of Munitions. Operation Puddleduck has become Operation Muddleduck.'

'How many tanks can you deploy in September?' Levass asked.

'A hundred or so,' said Cardew. 'But not many more. And the crews will be novices. Absolute novices.'

'And if we waited until the New Year?'

'Five hundred, perhaps a thousand. More if we had the French ones.' His eyes gleamed. 'Imagine that.'

Levass groaned. 'I can, Cardew. Why, gentlemen, should we use a new weapon at the very end of the fighting season, when the enemy will have time—'

Thwaites interrupted. 'Well, I for one will be pleased when we can stop skulking around and get some serious discussion about who, exactly, should be in charge of these iron horses.'

Cardew smiled. Thwaites liked to use the term to try to claim dominion for the cavalry over the new steel beasts. Cardew was of the opinion a whole new section was required, a Tank Corps, which could sweep away old horse-bound traditions and start anew. But as a mere civilian, he knew better than to voice opinions about any of the armed services in such company.

'I will have to inform my department that the deployment of your tanks with ours looks . . . unlikely,' said Levass. He crossed over and began mixing drinks for himself and Thwaites. 'I shall send people to the testing ground at the Renault factory and try and whip them along. But . . .' He shrugged at the hopelessness of the situation.

'Thank you.' Cardew accepted a gin and tonic from Swinton. 'But we really must make sure we solve the mystery of those deaths. Just for morale's sake. I have repaired the tank's engine. It runs beautifully.'

'And you had no ill effects?' asked Booth.

Cardew shook his head. 'I kept the front visor and the sponson doors open. But *Genevieve* is ready for the test. I told you a few days, I believe,' he said to Booth. 'But it can run tomorrow.'

'Good. Our Major Watson, he seems to think he is on to something,' said Levass. 'We shall see how *Genevieve* performs in the morning.'

'You'll stay for that?' asked Swinton of the Frenchman.

A firm nod. 'I must. If it happens again . . .'

They all stared into their drinks, contemplating the consequences of losing another crew.

'Good. You, too, Booth. I want you on site,' said Swinton.

'Me?'

'All hands on deck. Or, in some cases, in the landship.'

Booth looked crestfallen. He threw his drink back. 'If you'd excuse me, gentlemen, I'll have to change my schedule. I shan't be too long, but please start without me.' He nodded to each man in turn and left the room, boots ringing on the tiles.

A mournful clock tolled the half-hour, followed by the echo of the gong.

'I say,' said Swinton, realizing they were now two men short and dinner was fast approaching, 'does anyone know where Major Watson is?'

Watson groped around in the darkness towards where he had left his bag, careful not to stumble over the trio of bodies or trip on the winding sheets. It wasn't, he appreciated after a few moments, total blackness in the subterranean rooms. Up top were airbricks that scattered a pattern of stripes, ellipses and circles, thrown by the dying light outside, and there was a round airshaft in the centre of the coned ceiling of the ice room.

'What are you doing?' Mrs Gregson hissed, her voice thick with fright.

He tried to keep his own steady. It took all his willpower. *Just the cold*, he told himself. 'I have a torch in my bag, if I can just . . .'

She heard him rattling around in boxes, bottles of pills and various instruments before he gave a small cry of victory. 'Here we are.'

The beam was yellow and ovoid, even at maximum adjustment. The Opalite Medi was designed for testing pupil reflex and peering into body cavities, not lighting up cellars. Still, they followed it, as if pursuing a dancing insect, out of the room and towards the steps that led out of the ice house. Mrs Gregson had only a light gabardine mackintosh over her uniform, and she was already shivering. Her teeth did a little castanet chatter before she clamped her jaw shut.

'Would you like my coat?' Watson asked.

'I'm fine. You are making rather a habit of this, Major.' This was accompanied by a hollow laugh.

'What do you mean?' he asked, as he shone the light up at the closed doors.

'The stables in Belgium.'

He remembered being locked in with a horse while chlorine gas poured under the doors. He had been very lucky to survive unscathed. The poor horse hadn't. 'You were on the outside then.'

'I think I preferred that arrangement.' It came out as a sob towards the end and he stepped in closer. 'No. Just get us out of here, please. I have a rather unpleasant feeling about this.'

'It could be an accident,' he offered, but neither of them really believed that.

Watson moved up the steps and inspected the doors. As he suspected, they had been bolted from the outside. He banged a fist on one of them and shouted, but it felt like the space behind him simply gulped away the sound.

'Well,' he said, 'we'll just have to wait.'

'For what?'

'People know I'm here.'

'Who?' she asked.

'Thwaites, for certain. He was in my room when I examined the files and I told him I had to look at the bodies. And I cleared it with Booth. One of them will be along soon enough. Dinner is in half an hour or so. I'll be missed.'

Mrs Gregson made a strange noise in her throat. It was, he realized, a doubting sound.

'What?'

'Surely whoever knows you were here could be the one who locked the door in the first place.'

She's right, you know.

'Not now, not now,' Watson muttered.

'What did you say?'

'Nothing. Just that you could be right,' he conceded. 'Still, at least there is no gas this time.'

He had barely finished speaking when, from somewhere deep

202

below came the sound of rusty metal breaking free of its resting place, the grind of ancient gearing, and the sudden rush of water. The temperature around them dropped within seconds as a prolonged gurgling came from the main ice storage room.

They were being flooded.

TWENTY-EIGHT

Coyle knew his memory for faces did not match that of Gibson: he had been able to recall a fleeting profile in a crowd from five years ago. But Coyle's abilities were good enough for him to be certain that the man he had seen walk into the off-sales section of The Plough – which he knew simply led into the public bar – was someone he had seen before, across an interview table. He told himself this as he fetched his pistol from the rear of the car, placed it on the front seat within easy reach, and waited for the man to come out.

A Dutchman, he recalled, although no name came along with that piece of retrieved information. He and Gibson had spent a long time looking at foreign nationals through late 1914 and early 1915, paying the more suspect ones a visit. The latter group often included arrivals from the Netherlands and Sweden. They were neutral but it was relatively easy for a German to pass as a native of those countries. Then there was South Africa; again, an Afrikaans accent could mask a spy's imperfect English.

But no, this blond fellow had definitely been Dutch. Was a journalist of some description . . . no, a *newsreel* man. So what was he doing lurking on the edge of one of the most sensitive areas in the whole of the United Kingdom? As he thought about it, Coyle felt his thumbs prickle. He recalled the last time that had happened, out on the street just before Gibson had died.

Five minutes passed, the length of half a cheap cigarette. A few locals went into the pub – elderly labourers mostly, and a woman bent and gnarled by the fields – all using the entrance a few feet along from the one the Dutchman had taken. Two rather better-dressed men emerged from the lounge bar and looked him up and down. One raised his bowler in greeting. *What*, he thought, *if the Dutchman has gone out of a rear entrance?* There was one, he knew.

Coyle reached into the front of the car for his gun, thrust the pistol into his belt and buttoned up his jacket. He needed to check. A dozen long paces took him to the door. He pushed inside and slowed, giving himself time to take in the faces that turned towards him. Yellow smoke glazed the air and the boards were sticky under his feet. The patrons were either sitting at tables around the edge or, mostly, standing in clumps before him, pints resting on enormous beer casks. The drinkers smelled of sweat and rough cloth, with notes of wet dog and fresh sawdust.

The Dutchman was over at the bar, close to the small section reserved for off-sales – by law it should have been partitioned off, but most country pubs paid less than lip service to such regulations. The man had a pint in his hand, a bottle of brandy on the bar in front of him, and was laughing at something Fred Sutton had said.

Coyle pushed his way through the crowd, his eyes fixed on the Dutchman, who seemed oblivious to him. He used his left hand to flick the single button on his jacket undone, just in case. The coat flapped open. *But there will be no trouble*, he told himself. *Just a few questions.*

So why were his thumbs screaming that this was something altogether different?

It was Sutton who caused the balloon to go up. His eyes locked onto Coyle coming though the crowd and he raised a hand. 'All done, Mr Coyle?'

The Dutchman swivelled his head, froth lying on his upper lip like cuckoo spit. His eyes widened when he saw Coyle, who could almost hear the cogs turning in the man's brain as he, too, tried to place the face of the man bearing down on him.

Coyle barged a drinker's elbow as he passed by. Beer slopped and he half heard a grunt of protest. The man grabbed Coyle's sleeve. It was his gun arm.

His quarry saw the pistol in Coyle's belt as the jacket yawned open. He slammed the pint down on the counter and reached for his own weapon.

Coyle used his left hand to push the aggrieved drinker back into his friends. He knew what the movement of the Dutchman — Alberts, that was it, Dirk Alberts — meant. But Coyle had been slowed, knocked slightly off balance by the sleeve-grabber. The Dutchman had an automatic in his hand. The landlord was shouting in his ear, reaching for him, but he was ignored. The weapon boomed, the sound bouncing off the low ceiling, deafening all in the room.

Coyle felt himself pushed backwards, bodies falling onto him as he went — diving for cover or wounded, he wasn't sure — but the breath came out of him in a great roar like an eruption. There was a second shot, and he was aware of a pain across his shoulders and someone leaping over the mass of men on the floor.

'Anyone comes out of this door after me,' the Dutchman yelled, 'and I'll drop him dead.'

Damn, thought Coyle as he felt hot blood seeping around his collar, *I left the keys that lock the switches and the crank in the car.*

Miss Pillbody wondered what the hell Ross was playing at when she heard the banging on the front door. She had pulled herself up to her full height and armed herself with a few choice oaths to hiss at the fool — by the length of time he had been gone, she assumed he must have stopped in for a pint or two — when she yanked the door open. The man before her was clearly surprised by the anger in her expression and took a step backwards into the dusk.

'Miss Pillbody? Good Lord, is everything all right?'

She recomposed her features into something resembling relief. 'Oh, Lieutenant Booth.' Hand to throat. 'My apologies. Some village children have been playing tricks — tapping on the door and running away, that sort of thing.' She gave a nervous laugh. 'I thought for a moment I'd caught one.'

Booth removed his cap. 'No such luck. Just me. I'm sorry, I won't keep you long. Might I come in for second?'

'Well . . .' She leaned out of the house and looked up the road. No sign of Ross.

'If any more children come, I'll box their ears,' he promised, misunderstanding her concerns.

'Just for a moment, then.' She stepped aside and the lieutenant walked in. 'Do forgive me if I don't offer you some refreshment. I have rather a lot of correspondence to get through.'

He smiled. 'I just came to apologize about tomorrow. I am afraid I shall have to cancel our picnic. I shouldn't have promised, there really is too much going on up at . . . at work, as you might say.'

'Oh,' she said, her mouth puckering sourly.

'I hope I haven't offended you, Miss Pillbody.'

'No, not at all. I'm . . . disappointed, that's all. I had a new dress.' In a second she had reconfigured her plans. 'And isn't it about time you called me Nora, Lieutenant?' He smiled at this and nodded. 'Shall we go and sit in the kitchen? I think I'd like some tea after all.'

'I am afraid I am expected back for dinner.'

'Do they know you have come calling on me?'

The frown suggested she was worried about her reputation. 'Oh, no. Not at all.'

'Good. Well, you can talk while I make myself some tea. I insist that we set a new date.'

She closed the door, hardly noticing the clank of the approaching car. They moved through into the dining area, Booth taking in the freshly sharpened knives laid out on the table.

Miss Pillbody put on the kettle and moved so she was within easy reach of the blades. Where was Ross? If he came back soon, they could get on with the grim business now, and have an answer by morning. But Booth was saying something.

'. . . hard to know when I can get away again. There's something of a stew on. Again. All hands to the pumps and what have you. I'd hate to make an appointment and fail to keep it.'

She gave him Miss Pillbody's most demure smile. 'Well, whenever this stew subsides, then. Are you sure I can't tempt you? To tea?'

He was looking up at her row of dolls. It was strange how men found them so fascinating yet slightly repellent. It was the expressions and the oversized heads. These creatures were automata, created for their powers of movement – walking, waving, smiling blinking – rather than the pretty visages of conventional dolls.

She heard the rustle outside the back door first, and ignored it, taking a step nearer the knives. Speed would be of the essence here. She couldn't overpower Booth alone. But the surprise appearance of Ross might just disorient him enough for her to get a knife to his throat.

But it was she who was confused when the door slammed back on its hinges and a wild-eyed Ross burst in with a roar. 'The game's up—' he began, striding towards Booth, who had leaped back when he noticed the gun in Ross's hand and was fumbling with the flap of his holster.

'Bradley!' Miss Pillbody yelled, attempting to drown out Ross's incriminating words. He was about to expose everything.

Miss Pillbody pursued the only course open to her. She snatched up the boning knife and plunged it deep into muscle, blood and bone. There was a startled scream, and Ross grabbed at the handle protruding from his upper arm. The gun fell from his grip onto the stone floor.

'You stupid—' Ross began.

Miss Pillbody covered the rest of his sentence with the loudest scream she could manage.

She knew she had to stop Ross uttering another word. It wasn't as if she hadn't warned him it might come to this. The next knife was a French carver, with a ten-inch blade. She plucked that off the table and struck upwards as hard as she could. The point entered just under Ross's chin and she forced it upward, through the floor of the oral cavity, the fleshy tongue and split the hard palate. A spray of blood spurted from between the lips as Ross, with the strength of a madman, lifted the kitchen table, tossing it at Booth just as he cleared his Webley.

The gunshots were two sharp cracks, close together, which seemed to suck all the sound out of the room. Miss Pillbody watched as the force of the rounds puncturing his chest sent Ross staggering, as much a look of surprise on his face as a man with an impaled jaw can manage. He flailed towards the open kitchen door and fell outside, leaving only his feet sticking into the house. They gave two almighty kicks and were still.

Miss Pillbody turned to thank the man who had saved her by shooting Ross, but was surprised to find Booth sprawled on the floor, pinned by the table, his revolver a few inches from his hand. He hadn't fired the shots. She moved her gaze down the room.

Coyle, who had kicked in the front door when he'd heard the scream, kept the Smith & Wesson raised, looking through the helix of smoke spiralling from the barrel. He had it levelled at Booth who, despite being trapped under the slab of heavy pine, had finally managed to get his gun in his hand.

'Careful now,' Coyle said. 'I'm not sure what's occurring here.' He took a sharp intake of breath and winced. 'And I don't want any fatal misunderstandings.'

Coyle's left shoulder was damaged, although he had no idea how badly. Bones were certainly grinding in there. There was a dead man lying on the floor of the pub, but it wasn't him.

Miss Pillbody began to sob uncontrollably, calling on God's help. Booth carefully leaned across and rested his gun on the dresser, raising his hands as he let go.

'I think we all have some explaining to do,' the lieutenant said.

Using the small torch, Watson located the source of the gushing sound. By the time he had done so, the water was already more than ankle-deep throughout the rooms. He could feel his body heat leaking away through his feet.

'I've found it!' he yelled to Mrs Gregson, whom he instructed to stay on the steps, above the rising waters. His voice rang like a bell.

'You don't have to shout,' she said from over his shoulder.

'Mrs Gregson, really . . .' He shone the Opalite on the sodden hem of her dress. Her feet had already disappeared into the murky swirl. 'Don't you ever do as you are told?'

Oddly the ingress of water seemed to have steeled her. He thought she might go to pieces, but the threat seemed to have summoned up some inner resolve. 'Not if I can help it. And I wasn't that happy sitting there in the dark by myself. I think I heard a rat.'

That was certainly likely. If this place had been used for slaughter and hanging game, and had a drainage system, chances were there were rats. 'I think we'll have met bigger in Belgium,' said Watson. 'And it's not the rats we need to worry about. It's the water.'

Mrs Gregson shivered. 'But are those doors truly watertight? And look, there are airbricks. We'll be able to breathe if we float up.'

Watson didn't offer anything. She knew the answer to that perfectly well.

'But I suppose this water is freezing,' continued Mrs Gregson. 'And this is an ice house. We'll be like those poor blighters on the *Lusitania*.'

'Not quite, but I don't think we'd have too long.' Well, *he* wouldn't. Watson had to face up to the fact that he was an old man, in body if not in mind. Even if he got out, just a short submersion would leave him at risk of a fatal pneumonia.

'Who is behind this, Major?'

'I think we can worry about that later. Hold this for me,' he said, handing Mrs Gregson the feeble light, aware that the water level was now halfway up his calves. He took off his Sam Browne belt and tunic and passed them across, then rolled up his sleeves.

'What are you doing?'

'Shine the light on the water, if you can. Where it is welling up.'

He bent forward and plunged his arms into the cold murk. It

209

smelled heavily of mud and weeds as it splashed on his face. His fingers found the iron grille that covered the drain. Such was the force of water it had lifted a little. It was a decent size, perhaps eighteen inches square. But there was no way he could force himself down there against that flow. And who was to say what was at the other end?

He stood and shook his hands to try to bring some life back to his chilled fingers.

'Well?'

'It must be some sort of scouring system for when they want to sluice the place out. Like cleaning the Augean stables.'

'And where is Hercules when you need him?'

Watson felt stung by the remark, but said nothing.

'I'm sorry. I didn't mean . . .' Her fingertips flittered over his cheek in the dark, leaving warm spots, like glowing footprints.

'It's all right. I'm sorry I'm not a Greek god,' he said.

'What about placing a coffin over the drain?'

'I considered that. The floor is sloped. It wouldn't lie flat enough to seal.'

'We should get back to the steps. At least we can stay dry longer.'

Watson sighed his defeat. 'You're right. I don't have any better ideas.'

But I do, Watson. I do.

They let Miss Pillbody go upstairs to change out of her blood-spattered clothes. A pan of water was put on, so she could wash it off her face. Coyle and Booth put the table and chairs back together and mopped up what they could of Ross's blood. Then Coyle went to the door and stepped over the body into the garden. He had to check the man was dead. He was. Very. He examined the hilt protruding from beneath the chin and winced. It was one hell of a blow. *Never seen a woman behave like that before*, he thought, *not even those in the Brotherhood out for vengeance*. There had been no hesitation in her actions. Brutal, she had been. And that from a schoolteacher?

210

When he came back in, Coyle explained to Booth who he was and the organization he worked for.

'Irish?' Booth asked. 'In the Racket?'

Coyle smiled at the use of the slang word for the intelligence services. The phrase suggested an undertaking that wasn't entirely suitable work for a gentleman. Which wasn't far short of the mark. 'Long story.'

'So it was you who delivered Watson to us at Elveden?' asked Booth.

'That was me.' *And if it wasn't for a broken radiator*, he thought, *I'd be long gone.*

'And how did you come to shoot Ross?' asked Booth. 'I don't understand how you knew he was . . . what he was.'

'Ross? Who's Ross?'

'The fellow lying outside.'

Coyle sat and pinched the bridge of his nose. 'His name is Dirk Alberts. He worked for one of the newsreel companies, Movietone, I think. He was a Dutch national. We – me and my partner, Gibson – we interviewed him as a matter of course and . . . what's wrong?'

Booth had gone quite pale. 'We knew him as Bradley Ross. American. Newspaper man. Up here to write a book.'

For a second, Coyle thought he had made a terrible mistake. Maybe he had got the wrong man? But he remembered the suspect's actions in the pub. Whether Alberts had recalled Coyle from the interview, he couldn't be sure, but the man was certain that Coyle had recognized him. He would have realized that Coyle would discover his subterfuge and, if not exactly put two and two together, do some digging. Ross/Alberts had run through all the possibilities in a fraction of a second and decided his cover was in tatters and he should cut his losses and shoot his way out of The Plough. *And*, Coyle reminded himself, *innocent men don't normally do that kind of thing.*

'I've known a few newspaper people in my time,' said Coyle. 'Dublin, Belfast, London. Hard men, some of them. Never had one pull a gun on me.'

'No, that does suggest you are right.' Booth looked crestfallen. 'He was an imposter.'

'There will have to be police,' said Coyle.

'Here? Why? I can get the body disposed of.'

'There's another body at the pub. Local man. Your Ross, my Alberts, shot him then took my car. I am afraid I stole someone's bicycle to follow Ross without stopping to find out who that poor man was. But dead he is. Now, I can shut news of that down with DORA, but there were plenty of witnesses. We need the local rozzers on our side, calm it all down.'

'Gentlemen?' It was Miss Pillbody from upstairs, sounding frail.

'Yes?' asked Booth.

'Can I have that water, please?'

'Coming up,' he replied.

'I can't lift anything with this shoulder,' said Coyle. Then he lowered his voice. 'Did you ever see a woman react like that?'

'How do you mean?' Booth asked. 'She saved my life. Well, along with you.'

Coyle shrugged and regretted it. 'Pinning the fella like that. It's not natural.'

'Women have instincts we don't understand,' Booth replied defensively.

'Maybe. Not usually with knives, mind.' Coyle could feel a fever starting on him. He needed a clear head to make sense of this and the wound wasn't going to give him that. 'She'll be in shock soon. Realizing what she has done.' Still, it bothered him. The knife through the jaw: he wasn't sure even he'd have had the presence of mind for that. 'It might be in her dreams for a while. And mine.'

'It was remarkable,' conceded Booth.

'But why did Ross come here? Why not just drive away?'

Booth fidgeted slightly. 'I have reason to believe he was quite taken with Miss Pillbody. Paying her court. And perhaps she might have made a useful shield.'

'What, he was going to kidnap her?' Coyle asked.

Booth considered this. 'Well, a hostage might have been useful.'

'Possibly. Don't take this the wrong way, Lieutenant, but I'm surprised you allowed a writer of any kind to operate in the vicinity. Given whatever it is youse doin' over there. Very surprised.' In fact, he almost added, some might say it was foolhardy.

'He was American. Or so we thought. Which made it trickier. But you are right,' Booth said, with surprising self-loathing. 'I was a fool. An absolute bloody fool. Excuse me for a moment.'

He took the water upstairs. Coyle could hear a conversation between the two, but not the words. When he returned, Booth said, 'She's bordering on the hysterical. And who can blame her? I have an idea. I'll fetch Major Watson from the house. He can look at your shoulder and prescribe something for Miss Pillbody. I suspect she'll have trouble sleeping otherwise.'

'Reckon.' But not him. Coyle could feel the energy seeping out of him. He had lost a fair amount of blood, he supposed. He could feel it crusted under his shirt, crackling when he moved. Still his brain tried to go over the facts, but it was slow work, like the wheels were rusty and neglected. 'Why were you here again, Lieutenant? In this cottage when your man burst in?'

Booth was clearly used to being the one who asked the questions and bristled somewhat.

'I'm just curious. Tying up loose ends in here.' Coyle tapped his temple. 'I helped get two men killed tonight. Well, one and half. I don't think that fella there would have survived the . . .' He mimed the knife through the jaw. 'But, it sort of helps if I know why I had to shoot him.'

It was said with the utmost reasonableness and some of the stuffing leaked out of Booth. 'I was here to, well, to cancel an appointment with Miss Pillbody.'

Coyle raised an eyebrow. Even that took an effort. 'An appointment?'

'All right, I, too, was seeing something of Miss Pillbody. Just for a little female company.'

Coyle was silent for a few moments. No wonder they didn't like women on ships: they addled some men's brains. He'd get a bottle from Sutton once all this was done. A bottle of Bushmills was all the company he wanted. 'Did you share a drink?'

'With Miss Pillbody?'

'Aye.'

'No. She was making some tea. We didn't get around to drinking it. Why?'

Coyle moved his eyes from the two upturned glasses that lay next to the sink and said, 'Nothing.' He grimaced as a blade of hot pain ran across his clavicle and up his neck. He could do with that whiskey right now. And his damned thumbs had started prickling like chilblains again. What were they on about now? 'If you don't mind, Lieutenant, you'd best go and fetch our Major Watson, quick as you like.'

TWENTY-NINE

As he came down the stone steps with his orderly in tow, Lieutenant Booth noticed the ground in front of the ice house was unusually soggy, and he could hear water hissing as it spurted in fine sprays through the door seals, like leaking lock gates on a canal.

'That's odd, sir,' said Ridley, the orderly. 'Why is there water coming out of the ice house?'

Before Booth could reply, the full implications of what they were seeing sunk home. Ridley rushed forward, splashing over water-logged ground, drew back the bolts and the two men swung the steel doors open. A torrent of filthy, cold water cascaded over the pair, slopping into their boots. As it subsided Booth shone his torch into the blackness, picking out two shivering figures intertwined on the top step.

'Good grief, man, what happened?'

'Thank God,' was all Watson could manage in reply.

Watson slowly unfurled himself from Mrs Gregson, stood, and led her out into the twilight. Both were shaking hard. Booth turned to Ridley. 'Go back to the house. Bring blankets and brandy, at once, man.'

He guided the sodden duo over to a low wall and sat them beneath its balustrade. Watson's skin was very grey. It looked, from the staining on their clothing, as if the water had come up to their waists. 'What on earth has been going on?' Booth demanded, trying to massage life into Watson's cheeks, while Mrs Gregson did the same with his hands.

'We were in there examining the bodies when someone flooded the ice house,' she said, indicating the stream of water that was still cascading down the slope. 'There must be a mechanism for stopping the flow. A lever or wheel.'

'Wait here,' said Booth, and loped off, flashlight held in front of him.

The orderly returned with blankets and Mrs Gregson began to unbutton Watson's squelching trousers. He protested, but she slapped his hand.

'Ever heard the expression "you'll catch your death"? Well, you will, Major, unless we get you out of these things. What's your name?' she snapped at the orderly.

'Ridley, miss.'

She didn't correct him. 'Now give me a hand, Ridley.'

Using one blanket to protect his modesty, within a few minutes they had stripped all the clothes from Watson's lower half and swaddled him in a second blanket. Mrs Gregson was pouring brandy down him when Booth returned.

'Well? Did you stop the flow?'

'Yes. There was a stopcock system next to the lakeside, housed in a shed. A padlocked shed. The door had been forced.'

'Someone tried to kill us,' Mrs Gregson said. 'And damned near succeeded.'

215

'This is bloody monstrous,' declared Booth. His lower lip wobbled. For a second Mrs Gregson thought he might cry, but he visibly pulled himself together. *Boy for a man's job*, she thought.

Watson mumbled something.

'What?'

'You must get dry, too,' he said slowly. 'You're shivering.'

It was true; her flesh was also severely goose bumped and there was a cyan tinge to her lips. 'I'm not about to get undressed here,' she said firmly. 'Can you walk, Major?'

'Shall I fetch a motor car round? We can get one to that path over there,' Ridley asked.

'Get a move on then,' said Booth, angry at himself for not having considered that. *Too much going on for one night*, he thought. *My head is all over the place.*

While Ridley was gone, Booth asked: 'How did you stop the water rising over your heads?'

Mrs Gregson gave a larger spasm at the thought of the method they had used to block the drain. 'Don't ask. We have some clearing up to do in there.'

Watson again chattered something between his blue lips. He repeated himself once more. 'Tell him. Grenades.'

'We think your three men had been shot or otherwise murdered and grenades used to cover the wounds.'

'Ah.' It was a mournful sound.

'You don't seem too surprised, Lieutenant.'

Booth quickly explained the events at the village and Coyle's belief that Ross had been a German spy.

'C-Coyle's a good man. One of the best. T-trust him,' said Watson.

'Good Lord, what a situation,' said Mrs Gregson. 'So you think this German spy was behind everything happening here?'

Booth helped himself to some of the brandy. 'I have no idea. But I was hoping Major Watson could help his man, Coyle. I came back to find him and the colonel said you were out here with the bodies.

A stroke of luck for you, I suppose. But Coyle's shoulder is in a pretty pickle. And someone needs to check Miss Pillbody, who has had quite the shock.'

Watson nodded enthusiastically but Mrs Gregson said: 'Out of the question. Major Watson needs to be wrapped up in bed, with hot-water bottles and someone to keep an eye on him overnight. He isn't as young as he once was.'

Watson's head moved in protest. 'N-n-n—'

'John Hamish Watson, do not argue with me. I'm the closest to a physician you can get at this moment. And I'm keeping you here.'

They heard the crunch of tyres on gravel and saw the pale ovals of a slow-moving vehicle's lights as it approached along the path.

Mrs Gregson turned to Booth. 'If it's setting of bones, the cleaning of bullet wounds, bandaging or slings, I can do that as well as Major Watson.' The major chose not to disagree with that. She, too, took a mouthful of brandy, enjoying the burn on her insides. 'Give me ten minutes to wash and change and I'll come to the village with you. I can probably sort your Miss Pillbody out as well.'

They entered Miss Pillbody's cottage through the smashed front door. Booth noticed that Coyle's car, the one Ross had stolen, was missing. Had Coyle left? Gone back to the pub? If so he had done so without the borrowed bicycle. That still lay discarded at the gate.

Booth went into the cottage first, shouting, 'Hello?'

It was Mrs Gregson who noticed the figure lying in the hallway, tucked up in one corner, as if it had been kicked there. She bent down and examined the broken body. It was a doll, with a large spherical head and a rather leering expression. Or it would have been, if the porcelain hadn't split, with one side fragmented into a hundred pieces. It was like a miniature Humpty Dumpty.

Booth stopped to see what she was doing. 'That's one of Miss Pillbody's dolls. She collects— oh, God.' He unclipped the flap of his holster and extracted the Webley. 'Miss Pillbody! Nora! Hello?'

He started up the stairs. Mrs Gregson put her head into the living room, and then into the darkened kitchen. 'oh my Lord,' she said softly, when she turned on the electric light. 'Lieutenant Booth.'

He clattered down the stairs. 'Nobody up there. Both rooms empty—'

Then he saw what she was staring at, mouth open in horror.

Coyle was sitting at the table, his upper half bent over it, arms out straight before him, as if he were in supplication to some deity. One hand was crossed on top of the other, and a knife had been stabbed through them with considerable force, pinning both to the table.

Mrs Gregson approached the poor man, telling herself she had seen far, far worse than this. Dispassionately, she took in the hole in the back of the skull, and the matted, singed hair around it. Shot. At very close range. His face lay in a halo of blood, already half-congealed. She touched the body, warm to her fingertips, but not warm enough. She didn't have to check for a pulse, but she did so anyway. Not a murmur.

'Oh my God, they've taken Nora.'

That was the second time she had heard him use her Christian name. 'Nora?'

'Miss Pillbody.'

'And her dolls?' she asked, holding up the shattered toy.

His eyes darted to the empty shelf. 'Good Lord, yes. There were a dozen of them. Whoever took her can't have got far.'

'I'd stay here for a moment, Lieutenant,' she said. 'Go and look upstairs again. Look in the wardrobes. The drawers. Under the bed.'

Puzzled, he did as he was told, while Mrs Gregson examined poor Coyle. His shirt had been partially ripped off his back to reveal the jagged wound in his shoulder. But whoever had done this had not exposed it to dress it; something has been shoved in that hole, she was certain: a knife or a bradle. Coyle had been tortured, the wound, which must have been agony enough, worried and stabbed and pierced to try and extract information from him. She suppressed the urge to be sick.

Booth reappeared. 'You are right. Clothes missing, some drawers emptied, evidence of something dragged from under the bed . . .'

'Could it be a suitcase?

'Yes. She's been kidnapped.'

'Kidnapped? But what sort of kidnappers stop to grab a suitcase and bring the victim's collection of dolls?' she asked, sceptically. 'Or are we looking at . . .'

'What?'

She voiced the thought quickly. 'A second German agent?'

It hit Booth like a physical blow and he stepped back. His face was a picture of misery and shame. 'No. Absolutely not. It can't be . . .'

'Think before you speak,' snapped Mrs Gregson, sharply. 'Anything is possible in this day and age. I've just been locked in an ice house and half drowned. Could she have been an enemy spy?'

Booth ran a forearm across his brow, wiping away a sudden film of sweat. 'I don't know.' He crossed to the drainer. 'Coyle asked me if I'd had a drink with Miss Pillbody.'

'Had you?'

'I hadn't, but . . .' He picked up one of the two glasses and turned it over in his hand, like a pawnbroker appraising trade. He sniffed. There was the faintest hint of a sweet alcohol.

'But perhaps the German agent had, this Ross,' she said. 'Perhaps he had been here before you arrived.'

'I thought he was just, you know, keen on her. A rival, if you will.'

Mrs Gregson really wanted to unleash a tongue-lashing on him, but she simply asked: 'And now?'

Booth swallowed hard. He looked as if the earth was shifting beneath his feet and he steadied himself on the table. 'Christ.' But there was still doubt in his eyes. 'There has to be some other explanation. She was a schoolteacher. I threw her out of the school. No, no. You must be wrong.'

'Give me a moment,' Mrs Gregson said.

She found it in the small parlour, behind the false back of an alcove cupboard. Pillbody had smashed the valves, bent the Morse key and pulled out some of the wires to render it useless. She called Booth through to show him the radio, compounding his torment. She knew he could see a promising future in army intelligence spiralling down in flames.

'What do we do now?' he asked, no longer trusting his own judgement.

'This cottage needs to be searched by experts. *I assume you've done the same with this Ross's lodgings.*'

'Not yet. I'll organize it.'

'I don't think there is much to be gained by leaving poor Coyle there like that.'

'No.'

'He's been tortured,' she said.

'With the knives?'

For some reason, she didn't feel like sparing his feelings. 'At the very least.'

'You're sure?'

'Positive. By your Nora, I would imagine.' *Careful now, you are becoming vindictive, she thought.*

'Please do not call her that.'

Then the dam burst and she found herself furious at this man. Somewhere along the line he had allowed not one but two German agents to get close to him, had let himself see just a woman for stalking, not the wily bitch that must have been hidden under her petticoats. The result of his foolishness was sitting, pinned to a kitchen table, his last minutes on the planet a miasma of pain. Booth wasn't the first man in a position of power who had acted inexplicably over a woman, nor would he be the last, but that didn't make Mrs Gregson any better inclined towards the idiot.

As they walked through to the kitchen, something occurred to her. 'Did Coyle know what was going on at Elveden? About the tanks?'

'Coyle? No, he wasn't even allowed on the estate.'

'There is your answer, then.'

'To what?'

Mrs Gregson gave a long sigh, designed to make the young man feel particularly dumb. 'Coyle was tortured to try to make him reveal what is going on out there. If she already knew, why would she bother to stay around and do that? Obviously she and this Ross had tried infiltrating the place, as the grenades used on those poor soldiers demonstrated, but they must have got nothing. Their next move would be to try to torture the information from someone who knew.' It came to her then what this Pillbody's game had really been. 'Someone like you.'

'Me? But . . .' He pointed as Coyle. 'She did that to him.'

'A piece of improvisation. Second best.'

Mrs Gregson paced around the room, circling the table, her mind trying out various scenarios for size, seeing what fitted together, as if she were doing a mental jigsaw.

When she thought she had a theory that held water, she spoke very softly, as if it was an edifice of building blocks that might tumble if she raised her voice. 'I reckon she was desperate, this Miss Pillbody. The whole thing was falling apart so she took a chance on Coyle knowing what was going on. Why wouldn't he? He's a secret agent. But, before that, before Coyle recognized Ross in the pub, I suspect they would have gone for you. After all, you were a better prize. You worked there. You had seen everything at Elveden. Tell me, Booth, how do you think you would have stood up under torture?'

Booth remained silent, trying to digest all this and pondering the answer to that last question. Who knew? was the retort he came up with. He might be spit-in-your-eye, do-your-worst defiant or he might be whimpering like a baby within five minutes. The truth, he suspected, was somewhere in between.

'Can't shift this. How strong is this Miss Pillbody?' Mrs Gregson was trying to pull out the knife that secured Coyle's hands to the table.

'Let me,' said Booth, glad that this woman was at last displaying an inadequacy. 'Stand back.'

It took him three heaves. On the last one he thought something might pop in his neck, such was the force required, but he wasn't going to fail in front of Mrs Gregson, who seemed to damn him with every withering glance and curl of the lip. The blade came free with a horrible squeak that reminded him of the swineyard. 'There.'

He moved around the table and pulled the upper body back, towards the sitting position, accompanied by the crackle of dried blood.

Mrs Gregson heard the ping, and thought it must be a sprung hair clip of some description, but the comma-shaped piece of metal flying through the air was much heavier than any such device. Then she saw a larger, bulkier object rolling off the table, towards Booth, just as he realized what had been hidden under Coyle, his dead weight keeping the handle in position.

'Grenade!' he yelled.

Afterwards when she replayed the scene in her mind over and over again, Booth would show no hesitation, as if he was acting on pure instinct. It was possible that was the case. But it was possible he knew that any enquiry would censure him into disgrace and he saw a chance to redeem himself, even if it cost him his life. But time in her recollection was distorted, slow, so she couldn't be certain of his motives.

She was later told that the grenades that they discovered were all of the older type, with the long six-second fuse, so Booth would have had at least some time to consider what he was doing.

Consciously or instinctively, either way, Booth dropped to the floor after the Mills bomb, spreading his arms out, so that the grenade was pressed firmly against his sternum.

'No!' she cried, not even thinking of the alternative.

It went off with a loud but oddly muffled bang, the force lifting Booth up hard enough to crack his skull on the underside of the table, and to send the lifeless Coyle and chair barrelling into Mrs Gregson, flinging her away like the doll she had found in the hall.

The combination of living and dead bodies absorbed the blast, saving her life, so that she awoke half a minute after the detonation, ears deadened, her face stinging from debris, but more or less physically intact.

She pulled herself upright. The bulb had blown in the explosion, for which she was grateful, because it meant she couldn't make out the ruined remains of Lieutenant Booth too clearly. Her anger against him was gone. He had selflessly saved her life which, she supposed, wiped the slate clean. *But*, she thought dispassionately, *it seems that this Miss Pillbody has a facility for dispatching her admirers that a preying mantis could only envy.*

Then, as there was nobody there to witness her despair and terror, she put her head in her hands and sobbed.

THIRTY

Watson awoke with a start, a whirl of images crowding his brain: some fractured remnants from his dreams, others stark memories from the previous day and the rising water in the ice house. The latter generated an enormous shiver, which ran from his crown to his toes, accompanied by a long, ululating groan.

'I have some tea, when you are ready. How do you feel?'

'Alive,' he said with some surprise, as he pushed himself up the pillow.

'That's something.' Mrs Gregson, kitted out in a fresh nurse's uniform, was sitting next to his bed, the morning sun setting her hair aflame. She had pulled the curtains back. That was what had woken him so suddenly, scrambling his thoughts. He blinked the fragments of dreams from his vision and looked at her. Her eyes were red and underscored with purple.

'Are you all right?' he asked. 'What's wrong?'

'I should have let you sleep. But there is much to be done.'

He remembered the tank test, which Booth had told him had been rescheduled for that very day. 'Of course. I'll take the tea, thank you.'

She passed it across and he shuffled up in bed to receive it.

'And we have to deal with the ice house,' he began. 'Does anyone know—'

She shook her head. Watson's idea had shocked her at first. It was so out of character. But, as the water had risen, she could come up with no viable alternative. They had used the dead bodies of the three grenade-damaged men to block the drain, forcing the one with the large stomach halfway down, piling the others on top and then one of the rock-filled coffins on top of them. It hadn't stopped the flow, but it had reduced it to a persistent trickle. Otherwise, by the time Booth had found them, they would have been fully covered, only their heads above water, gasping for air and with hypothermia guaranteed. But it had been a macabre solution, one for which she hoped God would forgive them. Although, increasingly, she was beginning to believe there would be no reckoning in the afterlife. Ascribing blame for the last few years of carnage would tax any god.

'I am afraid that the bodies in the ice house are the least of our problems,' she admitted. 'We can file that under "needs must". No, there have been other, much more serious developments.'

Watson took a gulp of tea. 'Such as?'

It came out in a rush, sentences tripping over each other, pauses only for breath. But it was coherent none the less and she gave him a full account of the previous night, along with her interpretation of events, always stressing where she was making wild assumptions and leaps in the dark. By the time she had finished, his tea had grown cold.

'That's all,' she said, and slumped a little, exhausted from the effort.

'All? My goodness,' Watson said, struggling to come to terms with the carnage in a sleepy village. 'And Coyle, dead? It is hard to believe. Such a . . . I liked him. And Booth. That grenade was an evil trick. It could easily have been you.' The thought of Mrs Gregson's narrow escape caused something akin to physical pain in his chest. And Watson was taken aback by the severity of the reaction. It took a few moments for him to compose himself. 'The damned tank hasn't even gone into action yet, but look at the number of lives it's already cost.'

She straightened a little. 'We lost that many before breakfast, at one time, Major. When we were at the sharp end.'

That was the truth. But, somehow, that endless convoy of dead anaesthetized you to the horror. They had names, they had – for the most part – faces, but they came along to the wards, the mortuaries and the charnel houses in such vast numbers it was hard to imagine they'd ever been fully formed human beings, with lives to live, sweethearts to find, children to bear, old ages to enjoy, before the war swerved their destiny onto such a hard road.

Watson looked into her face and appreciated that by invoking the Western Front and its horrors, she was trying to put the gruesome events in the cottage into some kind of perspective. *What a world,* he thought, *when a woman has to rationalize the murder of four men in a single evening, and her own close brush with death, by summoning up memories of an even worse slaughter.* One thing was certain, he hoped he never ran into this Miss Pillbody.

It was later, when Watson had quizzed Mrs Gregson further on the details, that he asked her something that had been bothering him.

'You never did tell me why you stopped nursing. Why you came back from the front. I don't blame you, everyone has their limit.'

'Mine was called Desmond.'

Watson handed over the teacup and saucer. 'Desmond?'

'Major Desmond Ward-Maine. He was at Gallipoli, part of strategic planning. I met him at . . . well . . . it doesn't matter now.'

'It does to me. I think it does to you. Can you bear to tell me?'

Mrs Gregson took a deep breath. 'Desmond was married. He told me that right from the off, when I met him at the hospital. He wasn't seriously injured, but stayed for a few days. We got along, and you know how it is over there. Overworked, lonely, frightened . . .'

'And the nurses don't have it easy, either.'

She gave a bleak smile.

'We contrived to meet, whenever we could. Once a week sometimes, more often once a month. But he would write. Lovely letters. Mostly.'

'Mostly?'

'Well, sometimes he would get on his high horse about Gallipoli. He said if the public knew the truth . . .'

'Which was?'

'Oh, the usual. Lions led by jackasses.'

'He could have been in serious trouble for that.'

'His letters never came through the censors. And not just for the political content. He could be quite . . .' – she fanned her face with her fingers – 'passionate. So for the most part the letters were personal.' She swallowed hard, steeling herself. 'We were . . .'

Watson spoke softly. 'If you tell me you were lovers, I won't be shocked, Mrs Gregson.'

'Once,' she said flatly. 'In a damp French bed with an artillery barrage going on that broke the bottle of champagne he had brought along as Dutch courage for one or both of us.' She gave a short sniff. 'Just the once. I didn't ask him to leave his wife and son. Didn't expect anything else. Well, perhaps to do it another time without the shelling and with champagne.'

'But there wasn't?'

'No. You've heard of Gommecourt?'

'I don't think so,' he said, his voice barely a whisper, his stomach knotted in anticipation of what was to come. It was a familiar story in its arc, yet the agony came freshly minted with each version told.

'Just south of Arras. It was an attack by the Midlanders and the Londoners on a German salient there, around what was left of a château. As usual, the Germans were well dug in. There was wire, of course, and it was uncut by the shelling. And Gommecourt was particularly muddy, so progress was slow. Desmond—'

Watson slid out of bed, pulled down his nightshirt, and stood behind her, hand on her shoulder. 'I think I know the rest. I shouldn't have asked.'

Her hand rested lightly on his. 'You don't know the rest, Major. They brought him to my hospital, my ward. It was as if someone up there was mocking me. "You dare to make love to this man? Well, what do you think of him now?" He was in such pain, such pain. So I gave him morphine. And more morphine. And more. Until . . .' She let out a sob. 'I murdered him.'

Watson squeezed Mrs Gregson's shoulder. It felt hard beneath his touch. 'Or I think perhaps you simply hurried him along on his way. Godspeed.'

'That wasn't the . . .' – she swallowed hard – ' . . . that wasn't the worst part, Major.'

'Things like this have happened hundreds, thousands of times. You remember when I first saw a mortally wounded man at the front? I tried too hard to save him, neglecting other patients, when—'

'I wrote to his wife.'

The words were like the toll of a bell. Silence followed, just the dying echo of the short sentence in the corners of the room.

'Why?'

'I wrote to her as his nurse. I told her he died a peaceful death. That he was a brave man who did his duty time and again. That he loved her and his child and spoke of them often.'

'That was a kindness.'

She snorted. 'It was selfish. An attempt to prolong my contact with him, no matter how . . . second-hand.'

'But nobody would think badly of you for it. You didn't mention—'

'No,' Mrs Gregson protested. 'No, of course not. What do you take me for?'

A woman grieving for her lover, he thought, but didn't voice it.

'She asked to see me when I was next home on leave. Just to hear about his death first-hand.'

'To feel a connection.'

'So I thought.' She twisted in her chair, so she was looking up at him. 'The moment I spoke to her about Desmond, she knew. I could see it in her eyes. She knew everything. How? How can that be?'

'Mrs Gregson, you are perhaps the most worldly woman I have ever met. And I mean that as a compliment. Even Sherlock Holmes would tip his hat to your powers of observation and deduction. I say that as one who often fell woefully short of his standards, but . . .'

'But what?'

'The moment you said his name, Desmond, I, too, knew you had been lovers. Don't ask me to analyse why. Holmes would speak of inflections and cadences and grace notes. I just hear the warmth. My second wife used to speak of a pilot . . . oh, I am sure nothing happened. But there was a quality to her voice that caused me to feel the green worm turn in my heart. Admiration, tenderness. As I say, it might have been an infatuation with the image of the man – the dashing aviator, lord of the skies, defier of death, versus a quotidian doctor—'

'Hardly,' she protested with a small snort of disbelief. 'The famous Dr Watson? Quotidian?'

'Oh, I was by then, save the occasional summons by my friend. I am sure her infatuation would have faded over time, but then . . . well, as you know, she was killed. But believe you me, the secret passion is harder than you think to keep just that. How did she react? The wife?'

'She was perfectly pleasant to me. Polite. I had no inkling at the time. Then, she wrote a letter to the Director of Medical Services, copied to my hospital matron, accusing me of . . . Well, she made out I had gone to see her to gloat.'

It was difficult to condemn the widow, just as it was to censure Mrs Gregson. Such actions always seemed the right course at the time. He still regretted the occasion that he and Holmes had fallen out so badly over his own medical service, yet both of them had been convinced – were probably still certain – that they had been in the right. 'I'm sorry.'

'I was dismissed from the VADs, of course. The family was well connected, after all. I thought never to nurse again. I tried to enroll in something more . . . mechanical, as you know.'

'To my mind, you did nothing wrong. You did not confront the wife with evidence. I am sure you never confirmed her suspicions? No, I thought not. I would wager that, even now, she is wondering if she imagined it and did great harm to a good nurse.'

'VAD,' she corrected automatically.

'Mrs Gregson, you are as much a nurse as anyone with a piece of paper to show they are a Queen Alexandra sister. Now, I have a question.'

'About Desmond?'

'No. I think that is enough of that.' Watson was ready to change the subject, to move on from her obvious pain. 'About Churchill. How do you get messages to him?'

She rubbed her forehead, as if shining away all thoughts of Desmond.

'Through the delivery chap, Littlewood. He drives the grocery van that comes every morning. I use it to bring in medical supplies, but sometimes the list I give contains a message.'

'And Littlewood radios or telephones that to Churchill?'

'Not directly. He doesn't know it's coded. It goes through the postmistress to London, where I suppose it's deciphered by Winston's lot.'

'I see. Can you get a message to her?'

'Yes. I'll send Ridley to the village.'

Watson took a piece of paper and a pencil from his pocket and began to write. 'I need him to tell her to send an SOS through whatever channels she uses to contact London. In plain English. Churchill is to send a team of Kell's men up here, double-quick. And for this man to come as well.' He passed the note over. 'And I want Coyle's body shipped back to Ireland and his family. Then they have to seal that village and investigate what, exactly, the two Germans – if they *were* German citizens – were up to. I think you might be right, the spies hadn't guessed what's going on here. Hadn't penetrated the estate, at least. But therein lies the puzzle.'

'How do you mean?' she asked.

'If the Germans didn't get in and do it, what exactly killed the men in that tank?'

'And,' Mrs Gregson said with great deliberation, 'who was it who locked us in the ice house?'

Swinton was waiting for Watson at the foot of the stairs. 'I have postponed the tank test for the time being.' He held up a piece of paper. 'I have a most extraordinary missive here from Mrs Gregson, about the goings-on last night. We've lost Booth. Booth! And her allegations—'

Watson cut him short. 'She has told me all about it. You can trust Mrs Gregson.'

He looked doubtful. 'If you say so.'

'She had the presence of mind to report everything to you.'

'Yes, well. Somewhat hysterically, I would say.'

Compared to standard army reports, perhaps, Watson thought. But then it was incredible how dry the army could make the deaths of thousands of men seem.

'I need you to brief us on exactly what happened in that village last night. I assume you know all the facts?' Colonel Swinton said.

Watson looked over his shoulder, wondering if it was best that Mrs Gregson did it. After all, she had been there. But he decided not to make her relive it again. And, clearly, his account, even if second-hand, would be held in higher regard than any woman's. 'I know enough.'

'And the business in the ice house?'

'I can make informed guesses about who did that.'

Swinton rubbed his chin. Watson could see he had

shaved – or had been shaved – hastily and that he was worrying at a few bristles on his jaw. 'Watson, what the hell is going on? Are we compromised?'

'Up to a point. The Germans will now be even more curious about what is happening at Elveden. I suggest you make security even tighter. This is your operation, Colonel, but my advice is to press on. After all this time and effort . . .'

'Levass told me you were sceptical about our wonder weapon.'

'Part of me still is. But I don't want men such as Coyle to have died in vain, Colonel. If Churchill is right, if you, Levass and Cardew are right, and it will change things for the better, then I think we should proceed. What time was the tank test scheduled for?'

'Three o'clock.'

'Then I suggest you reinstate it. I want you to gather together all your best tank crews, please. At the trench test site.'

'Why?'

'I need to ask for volunteers to restart and drive that damned tank. And I am going to see if I can coax Hitchcock to watch.'

'Really? Is he up to that?'

Watson shrugged. 'Last night I thought I saw something, a spark, as if I had broken through—'

He stopped when he heard shouts of alarm coming from outside.

'What's that?' asked Swinton.

'I don't know,' said Watson, as calmly as he could. 'But it doesn't sound like good news.'

'In here, sir.' The corporal, hoarse from all his yelling, stepped aside and let Watson walk into Hitchcock's cell.

'I brought him his breakfast,' the soldier said, his voice shaking, 'and he was like that. I didn't—'

'Hush now, Corporal. Nobody is blaming you. When did you last look in?'

'Midnight or so. Sleeping soundly, he was.'

'You brought him the blankets as I asked?'

'Well before that, sir.'

'Can you leave me?' Watson asked. 'Ten minutes.'

The corporal seemed glad to acquiesce and, when he had gone, Watson pulled the door almost closed. He crossed over and kneeled beside Hitchcock.

'Poor Hugh,' he said softly to the figure on the floor next to the bed. The dead man was lying on a pile of the blankets, curled up, his hands interlocked behind his head, knees drawn up to his chest. Hedgehogged, just like the others. 'I let you down, didn't I? I'm sorry, old chap. Looks like that bloody *Genevieve* has the full complement now. All eight of you.'

Watson touched the body. Still warm. He gently moved a limb. Rigor mortis hadn't taken him yet, so if they moved quickly they should be able to uncurl him from that undignified posture.

He stood, wincing as one knee clicked, and looked around. Not sure what he was looking for, he began to examine every inch of Hitchcock's cell.

After ten minutes the door swung open, but it wasn't the corporal. Swinton exclaimed when he saw the coiled shape of the dead tankman: 'For crying out loud. Hitchcock too? I thought you said you'd had a breakthrough, Watson!'

The major didn't reply immediately, just licked his thumb where he had burned it on the paraffin heater.

'Colonel, I want Hitchcock laid out in a cool cellar,' he said eventually. 'And I want him guarded, day and night, until I can organize a full post-mortem and pathological investigation. I'd like to do a preliminary examination within the hour.'

'You don't think he was . . . ?'

'Murdered? I don't know.' Watson gave a last glance at Hitchcock, crunched up as if expecting a barrage to fall on his head any second. 'But, for the moment, all I'd say was that this man died of very unnatural causes.'

*

232

While he was waiting for the body to be moved and straightened, Watson found time to examine the ground around the ice house. It was, as he expected, churned into mud from all the water that had flowed out of the doors when he and Mrs Gregson had been rescued. There was nothing to be gained from going over that ground. Stooping low, he moved away from the ice house, following the soggy ground until it dried a little, just before the flagging of the gravel path. There, he identified his own boots, but the rest of it was an incoherent riot of hobnails and heels, with only a severely square-toed imprint and Mrs Gregson's Glastonbury motoring boots standing out from the rest.

'Sir!' It was the corporal, hailing him from the steps.

'Yes?' asked Watson, straightening.

'Lieutenant Hitchcock is ready for your attentions now, sir. In the cellar of the main house.'

'I'll be right over. Someone with the body now?'

'Sir.'

'Good. Give me five minutes.'

The tankman was laid out in the wine cellars of Elveden Hall, a series of rooms that were secured by a heavy oak door. There was a guard outside, as requested, and the key to the area – which still held some of Lord Iveagh's best bottles – was with Mrs Joyce, the housekeeper.

They had laid Hitchcock out on a gnarled old table, scarred from candle burns and the ring-marks of countless bottles and glasses. He was still dressed, but covered in a sheet. Although there were electric lamps, they were dull affairs, with a light reminiscent of a tallow candle, and Watson lit two ancient oil lanterns. He had looked for Mrs Gregson to assist, but she was nowhere to be found. No matter, he wasn't going to do a full autopsy.

He pulled back the sheet and looked down at the husk of the tankman. Watson muttered a small prayer, but mainly from habit. He knew from his conversations with Mrs Gregson that they shared an increasing disbelief in any deity. Like every man at the front, he had prayed when he was in the trenches. Who wouldn't call on help from a supreme being while hell was unleashed around you? And like almost every man at the front, he had come away wondering how God could allow such monstrous happenings. Unless it was pure malevolence on the part of a supreme being, who enjoyed watching his creations destroy themselves in evermore complex and ingenious ways. Perhaps, after all, it was the devil up there, pulling the strings of war.

Can you smell that?

Holmes was never one for pointless philosophical musings. He wanted *facts*, and facts about God's motives were few and far between. And yes, Watson *could* smell something. Feeling like a self-conscious bloodhound, he sniffed at the corpse, running from head to toe. As he neared the feet he recoiled slightly. He knew that smell, even in its feeble form, as here. Why hadn't he noticed it before? The damp and the paraffin heater in the cell, perhaps, the perfumed sticks in the music room, might have masked it.

Hitchcock had on Derby pattern shooting boots, rather than regulation issue 'ammunition' boots, but that was hardly surprising; many men – especially officers – customized their footwear if they could get away with it. Watson undid the laces, loosened the tongue and its gusset and eased one off. As he rolled the sock down he saw the telltale discolouration and now the smell made him hold his breath.

Gangrene.

Not gas gangrene, the curse of Flanders Field, thank the Lord, nor trench foot, but the old-fashioned sort, familiar from his kind of war in the last century. *But how did that form?* Hitchcock had not been wounded, had not been standing in a trench in icy, filthy water or wearing boots that had crushed his feet.

A thought occurred to him, and Watson looked at the man's fingers. The tips were discoloured. Two of them were black. That was why he cried when he played the piano. The pain. Not the tune. The pain. Idiot!

Go easy on yourself. This isn't what you were expecting.

Ha! Good of him to say so. But Holmes always expected the unexpected, thrived on the twists and turns of a case. Gangrene. How had *Genevieve* done that? He wished he had his medical books with him.

Not Genevieve. *Not the tank.*

There was a footfall behind him and he turned, startled. It was Thwaites. 'Sorry to disturb you, I . . .' His nose wrinkled. 'Good Lord, what is that stink?'

'You've never smelled gangrene before?'

Thwaites shook his head, his moustaches oscillating. 'Not for a long time now. Festering bullet wounds, mostly.'

'No bullet wounds here.'

Thwaites cleared his throat. 'Colonel Swinton sends his regards and says, when you are ready, we can begin the new test of *Genevieve*.'

'Of course.' He held up his hands close to his face. The aroma of necrosis seemed to have clung to his skin. 'I'll just go and clean up.'

Thwaites looked at Hitchcock's body once more, at the swollen, blackened toes on the single uncovered foot. 'Did that bloody tank really do *that*?'

Watson flicked the sheet back over the corpse. 'That's what we are about to find out.'

THIRTY-ONE

Thirty-two men gathered in the shade of an oak on the edge of a partially cut field of rye, next to the trenched area that had been used to recreate a version of the Loos battlefield, and where the lozenge-shaped *G for Genevieve* now sat, an innocent, harmless lump of metal. Until someone fired her up. Watson had commented on the rye, it being an unusual crop in the district, but Swinton had told him that the maharajah had loved rye bread, and that the tradition of making it had continued. The harvest, though, had been abandoned for security reasons, and now the over-tall plants lolled drunkenly in the breeze.

Most of the group that gathered to hear Watson were dressed in the overalls that were most convenient for operating a tank. Many wore caps with their original unit badges on them: mostly Machine Gun Corps and Royal Artillery. It was clear that the 'Heavy Branch' had been put together in such a rush that nobody had had time to think of uniforms or badges. Yet in Watson's experience, the *esprit de corps* of any new service – the Royal Flying Corps was a case in point – was vital to its success. And a singular identity was a vital part of that. From his conversations, it appeared everyone was working towards the one big 'reveal' when the tanks were unveiled in action. Few people, it seemed to him, had considered the weapon's long-term future or the sort of unit that would man it, apart from Thwaites, the cavalryman. *Genevieve* and her ilk wouldn't be a secret for ever. What did they do with them then?

Swinton had arranged for a series of ammunition boxes to be lashed together to make a small stage for Watson to address the troops. Watson was dreading this. He was well aware that he was no great orator. He could deliver a lecture and a clinical appraisal to a packed room, but here he was asking for men to risk their lives. He had to appeal to their hearts and minds, their patriotism and sense of duty. And to what end? He wasn't sure.

Cardew, Levass and Thwaites were clumped together near the makeshift podium. Cardew had a grease-stained face, as he had been putting the finishing touches to *Genevieve*. As usual, there was a rag in his hand. Levass was smoking a small cheroot, enjoying the sun on his face, while Thwaites slapped his leg with his swagger stick, as if impatient to be elsewhere.

From the far edge of the field of rye came a low thumping sound, and all felt it transmit through their feet. A second, higher note as an engine revved, then a thump as gears were engaged. As a man they turned to see what was making the noise, which was soon joined by the threshing of plant material. Above the agitated necks of the plants they could just make out the landships coming towards them, like agricultural machinery reprogrammed to destroy, flattening the crop before them, sending up a column of grain and chaff. The pair of tanks didn't exactly burst out of the rye field, more pushed the stalks aside like curtains: heavy-set Wagnerian sopranos of riveted metal making an operatically grand entrance.

Even though he had seen one before, Watson felt a surge of panic as the pair turned and wheeled towards him, those linked tracks rotating hypnotically, whisking the soil into a yellowish dust, as if intent on crushing him and grinding him into the ground. If he were a German soldier, he'd run.

They juddered to a halt in unison, the doors in the rear of the sponsons swung open and most of the crew de-tanked, leaving the drivers, visible through the open front visor, in place.

This pair had, according to instructions, been running with all ventilation open. The two were slightly different: one had machine guns, like *Genevieve*; the other had wicked-looking naval six-pounders poking from the side sponsons, so it looked like a ship's turret turned on its side, one on each flank. A female and a male. The male had a cage-like structure over its top, sloping away from the centre in an inverted V, as if it were a shallow roof awaiting slates. It was, Watson decided, a device to deflect grenades and bombs.

Cardew walked over, rubbing his dirty hands on the rag. 'What's this, Major?'

'Colonel Swinton allowed me two more, one male and one female. These are our controls, Mr Cardew.'

'Controls?'

'Controls. The question is, was what happened in *Genevieve* a function of that one tank, or will it be repeated in each of the machines? There is only one way to find out. If the problem is *Genevieve*'s alone, well, you know better than I, but I am sure she can be stripped down and rebuilt. If it is all the tanks . . .'

'It'd put us back months,' Cardew said glumly.

'Yes,' said Watson, 'because Haig won't be best pleased if you send him what turn out to be mobile coffins, will he?'

'I should think not. The whole idea is for the tanks to kill the enemy, not the poor buggers inside,' agreed Cardew. 'Excuse my French. How will you decide who goes in which tank?'

'We'll draw lots, apart from two places.'

'Which are they?'

'There are two men I want in *Genevieve*.'

Cardew laughed. 'Let me guess. Me and you?'

'Indeed. I shall look for any medical anomalies. You for mechanical defects. One of the crew will be wearing a gas mask and have extras ready to hand out at the first sign of trouble.'

'A gas mask?' Cardew asked. 'So you think it's the engine fumes?'

'I don't know,' said Watson, truthfully. 'But we'd best be prepared for all eventualities. Now, I have to ask for volunteers to run with all hatches closed over the testing ground.'

'I'd better warm *Genevieve*'s engine up to the same temperature as those,' said Cardew. 'Otherwise we won't be comparing like with like.'

'Good idea,' conceded Watson. He turned to Swinton and nodded that he was ready to proceed.

'Gentlemen!' Swinton bellowed. The assembled soldiers snapped to attention. 'At ease. I would like to introduce Major Watson of the Royal Army Medical Corps. He has been brought in to get to the bottom of what happened in *G for Genevieve* recently – events that have given rise to wild speculation and rumour. Major Watson is a man of science and a man of medicine. Also, a few of you might have heard of him in a previous career, Dr John H. Watson of Baker Street.'

Someone actually applauded, a rather lonely sound in the open air, but there was a murmur of recognition. Watson waited for the inevitable disappointment when they realized they had the cart but not the horse. Sherlock Holmes cast a long shadow, even when he was incarcerated in some high-security prison.

Watson stepped onto the ammunition boxes, rewriting his words as he went. The opening seemed feeble; he needed something with power, something to stir the blood.

'Soldiers of the tanks! Sailors of the landships! It seems you might have made enemies. Good! It means you are doing something right.'

The words boomed over the field and Watson, like every other man, looked in the direction of their origin. For one moment it seemed as if the sycamores had spoken, but then, from the shadow of one of them, stepped a familiar figure. Winston Churchill. Behind him was Mrs Gregson and, next to her, leaning slightly on her, was a beaming Captain Fairley, his face still pale and drawn, but shell-shocked, Watson hoped, no more.

Churchill, too, was grinning, loving the theatricality of his entrance. Watson had expected – indeed requested through the post-mistress – the captain, but Churchill coming was a total surprise. And how on earth had the pair got to Elveden so quickly?

'Can I have the floor for a few minutes, Major?' he asked Watson. He lowered his voice. 'Before you ask, I still have friends in the RNAS.' Of course. He'd have flown up with pilots of the Royal Naval Air Service. 'You solve puzzles, you cure men. Me, I make speeches. Mrs Gregson told me the gist. Do you mind?' Watson shook his head. 'Excellent. And I hope there are no hard feelings about my technique for getting you up here? Perhaps you appreciate now—'

'You did what you thought was necessary,' said Watson flatly.

'As I always do.'

Churchill puffed on his cigar as he surveyed the tankmen before him. At once the atmosphere had changed. The wily politician, well fed and red-faced, had the air of a Roman general about him. The soldiers, still at ease, now seemed taller, and leaned forward, as if to catch every word, every nuance of what the former First Lord of the Admiralty was going to say.

'I am not going to take credit for that marvellous creation.' He pointed the glowing end of the cigar at the two parked tanks, still clicking and creaking as they cooled. 'But I will take some credit for nursing it to life. I am the midwife, not the father. Yet I still fill with pride when I see it. Yes, it's crude and noisy and slow. But so am I sometimes.' A ripple of laughter. 'But I can build up a head of steam for those who get in my way. When I know I am right, there is no force in the world can stop me saying so. God give me strength to admit my failures and I do, I do. But the tank, gentlemen, is not one of them. I will not allow it to be one of them. It will take its place alongside the horse, the lance, the musket, the Martini-Henry, the Maxim, the aeroplane, the submarine and the dreadnought as a weapon that changed the face of war. And that weapon is ours, it is Great Britain's.'

A cheer. Watson stole a glance at Levass, who, as expected, was frowning. Surely he couldn't expect subtlety at a time like this. Then Churchill wrong-footed them both.

'And, of course, it also belongs to our gallant Allies in this struggle – France.' Levass inclined his head in acknowledgement. 'But our problems are here, now, not in France or Belgium. What we ask you to do is no less than going over the top, just as brave, just as valuable. You are fighting for our way of life. I say this machine can save our way of life and, if used properly, can save millions of your countrymen's lives. Tommies crouching in the trenches, with bullets flying over their heads and gas in their lungs, don't know we are trying everything to break out, to push the Hun back where he belongs and keep him there. This is our Kraken, our fire-drake, the monster that will put ice into our enemy's hearts. I say to you this day, we did not want this war. But once a country is so unfortunate as to be drawn into a war, no price is too great to pay for an early and victorious peace. There will be losses, there have been grave losses. There have been, I hear, eight men lost on this very ground, before a shot in anger has been fired. But looking at those losses squarely and soberly, you must not forget, at the same time, the prize for which you are contending. It is civilization. It is the British Empire. It is your home towns and villages, your wives and children. That is why we need victory. We are fighting with a foe of the most terrible kind, and we are locked in mortal struggle. To fail is to be enslaved, or, at the very best, to be destroyed. Not to win decisively is to have all this misery over again after an uneasy truce, and to fight it over again, probably under less favourable circumstances and, perhaps, alone. Why, after what has happened, there could never be peace in Europe until the German military system has been so shattered and torn and trampled that it is unable to resist by any means the will and decision of the conquering Power. That is why we need a decisive victory. When I speak of victory, I am not referring to those victories which crowd the daily placards of any newspapers. I am speaking of victory in the sense of a brilliant and formidable fact, shaping the destinies of nations and shortening the duration of the war. Beyond those few miles of ridge and scrub on which our soldiers, our French comrades, our gallant Australians, and our New Zealand fellow-subjects are now battling, lies the downfall of a hostile empire, the destruction of an enemy's fleet and army, the fall of a world-famous capital, and probably the accession of powerful Allies. The struggle will be heavy, the risks numerous, the losses cruel; but victory when it comes will make amends for all. You deserve to get from your leaders, be they military or civilian, the courage, the energy, the audacity and readiness to run all risks and shoulder the responsibilities without which no great result in war can ever be achieved. And, in return, we ask the same of you. Long speeches are not suited to the times in which we live, and, therefore, I shall detain you only a very few moments more. I have known Major Watson a great many years. He has worked, for no fame and no reward, along with his illustrious colleague, Mr Sherlock Holmes, for the benefit of this great country time and time again, for which we thank him. We have had a small setback here at Elveden. I say to you, let us pick up the tattered flag from the field, and go forth once more, as proud members of the greatest nation and the greatest army this earth has ever known! You want proof of this? No nation has ever at any time in history found such a spirit of daring and sacrifice widespread, almost universal, in the masses of its people. Britain has found millions of citizens who, all of their own free will, have eagerly or soberly resolved to fight and die for the principles at stake, and to fight and die in the hardest, the cruellest, and the least rewarded of all the wars that men have fought. Why, that is one of the most wonderful and inspiring facts in the whole history of this wonderful island, and in afterdays, depend upon it, it will be taken as a splendid signal of the manhood of our race and of the soundness of our ideals. Major Watson, you have the, um, floor.'

The applause was loud and ringing, with men clapping until their hands stung, and Churchill doffed his hat and puffed some more on his cigar as he sucked up the adulation along with the smoke. He leaned over to Watson and whispered, 'Bit long-winded, I am afraid. Just rehearsing for an address tomorrow. Hope you don't mind. But I think you'll get your volunteers.'

And when Watson asked for them, as far as he could tell, every hand went up.

The three tanks stood on the edge of the faux battlefield, the bodies within rattling from the vibrating hulls. Apparently starting the engines was sometimes tricky, if not downright dangerous – a naked flame to the carburettor – so Cardew had suggested Watson and most of *Genevieve*'s crew stay outside. Watson chatted to Fairley while he waited. 'What do you think?' he asked Fairley, pointing to the wire and the trenches.

'Impressive. Gives me the willies, still,' Fairley admitted.

'Me, too. But?'

'Too neat, don't you think, sir?' Fairley said, confirming Watson's initial diagnosis. 'Men have been fighting in these holes for two years. Shells have knocked them into strange shapes.' He kneeled down. 'This is sand, isn't it?'

'Very sandy soil, yes.'

'Good drainage then. No mud.'

'Not much, no,' agreed Watson. The unholy trinity of trench, machine gun and barbed wire had a fourth horseman – the sticky filth that covered the land out there. 'Also I detect a lack of machine-gun emplacements on the German side.'

Fairley peered. 'Well, I'll have to take a closer look.'

'Will you? I want you to map out a proper defensive German position. How the machine guns will rake the tanks. I know they look shocking at first, but the Germans will recover. I want you to stay here and help Thwaites and the others put the tanks and their crews through as genuine a war as possible. Import mud if you have to. Collect farm slurry; it can't smell worse than the trenches.'

'Lord, no.'

Watson looked Fairley straight in the eye. 'There isn't a man here who has been through what you have been through, seen what you have seen.' He laughed. 'Smelled what you have smelled. With them, it's all from books and newspapers and Mafeking. Can you do this without . . . well, without a relapse?'

'Say what you mean, Major,' Fairley grinned, and for the first time in months Watson saw the chirpy Wykehamist who had helped him survive out in the mud of Belgium. 'Without going doolally again?'

'It's not a term I like to use. But it will mean re-creating and reliving the conditions out in France and Belgium, both in the trenches and out in no man's land. It has to be authentic.'

'I can do it, Major. And I will. And thank you.'

Watson frowned. He knew what the thought of charity could do to a proud soldier. He spoke as brusquely as he dared. 'For what? I'm sorry, Captain, I'm not doing this for you. You just happened to be the best man for the job.' He pointed at the tank crews clambering onto and into the machines. 'I'm doing it for them.'

Fairley smirked, not convinced. Watson summoned over Thwaites and introduced the two men. 'Major Thwaites here is an expert on cavalry tactics,' said Watson diplomatically, 'but has not had direct experience of the trenches. I do believe you two can learn from each other. Now, if you'll excuse me.'

Watson looked around for Mrs Gregson, but couldn't see her. Churchill, however, had pulled away from the other officers and was lighting another cigar. Watson quickly moved him even further away.

'Sir,' he said. 'I'd like to thank you again—'

Churchill cut him off with a wave of the smoking torpedo in his hand. 'Needed to come up and knock some heads together. You've heard the new timetable?' Watson indicated that he had. 'Bit of a stretch, if you ask me. Look, Major, this sideshow here, just get it finished. So we lose a few men. How many do you think will die in those tin cans once they start rolling? Eh?'

'I dread to think.'

'Sort this mess out, Watson. For the good of the nation.'

'I have a request.'

The eyes narrowed behind the pungent veil of fumes. *He looks like a suspicious bull walrus sensing a rival on the ice*, thought Watson. 'Yes?' His lisp made it sound like a snake's hiss.

'Holmes. I know you have him locked up in Foulness—'

'He is not locked up,' protested Churchill. 'Far from it. He is very comfortable. And you get this fixed, we get the tanks out in the open, it won't be for much longer, eh?'

'That's still weeks. The man is fragile—'

'The man is an irrelevance now,' said Churchill gruffly. He pointed with his swagger stick of a cigar. 'The landships. That's what is important.'

The cruelty of the words stung. Holmes had done great service, as Churchill himself had just admitted in his speech, yet here he was being cast aside, forgotten. No sentimentality there. Watson expected to feel anger, but he didn't. In Churchill's world, you were one of a trilogy: friend, foe or someone useful. The only other category was 'irrelevance'. Not worth a second thought.

'Major Watson,' shouted Cardew, 'our commander says he's ready when you are.'

'Coming.'

'Good luck, Watson,' said Churchill.

'I want him off that island.'

'All in good time.'

'Good time is what we don't have. He needs medical attention, sir.'

'Well,' said Churchill, waving his cigar at the tanks, 'when this trial is all over and you know the solution to our problem, you are more than welcome to join him at Foulness. Doctor.'

With that, he turned on his heel and moved off, trailing clouds of cigar smoke like a Havana-powered locomotive.

Watson cursed the man's intransigence and his slippery ways, straightened his shirt and strode over to the machine he now remembered he had called a steel coffin.

THIRTY-TWO

Once she reached Ipswich in the dead Irishman's car, Miss Pillbody had gone to the post office to telephone the emergency number she kept sewn in the lining of her bag. Her call had been answered at once, by a rather offhand and imperious woman. Miss Pillbody explained that she had a serious toothache and that her own dentist was on holiday. The name of that dentist? Warren. She was given a time and address, and told that Mr Delaney would do his best to fit her in.

The address was in Great Yarmouth, one of the main crossing points for the Zeppelins. She suspected this dentist was in the same line of work as she was. A woman driving a car had already attracted too much attention, so she abandoned the Vauxhall near a totter's yard behind Ipswich station where, she was sure, it would be watched and eventually taken behind closed gates and either stripped or repainted, renumbered and resold. *Pity*, she thought. It was a nice motor car.

She caught the train to Yarmouth. Soon she would have to abandon Miss Pillbody, just as she had the Vauxhall. She didn't care. Like the Zeppelins, the school teacher's time would be over soon enough.

The address of the dentist was near St George's Park and she took a taxi from the station. She was exhausted and in no mood for walking. She had just the one pair of shoes with her and precious few clothes in the hastily packed Morocco leather bag. Most of the space was taken up with her dolls, all but one of which she had managed to wrap in newspaper and stow relatively carefully. Just the automaton called Lola was missing, the head smashed beyond reasonable repair. Ah, well, it could be replaced. One day.

She turned up at a suburban house, the lower half of which had been converted into a dentist's surgery. She examined the road, noticed a fancy, fast-looking car parked on the opposite side of the street. Trouble? Were they one step ahead of her already? Well, if so, it was too late now. On the other hand, she had started seeing trouble everywhere. She needed to relax. She was like an over-wound watch.

When she entered the hallway she almost gagged at the smell: a mix of chemicals and boiled food. To her left was a door marked 'Waiting Room', and she entered to find a sharp-faced, middle-aged woman sitting at a desk. The telephone at her elbow suggested she had been the one who had answered when Miss Pillbody had called.

'Can I help?'

'Miss Lilywhite,' she said. 'I called for an emergency appointment.'

'Take a seat.'

Bentwood chairs were arranged around the periphery of the room. She sat and examined the hunting prints that adorned the walls, wondering who on earth thought scenes of stags being torn to pieces by hounds would soothe anyone waiting for an extraction or a filling.

She could hear muffled sounds from the surgery, behind the door with a plaque proclaiming that a dentist lay beyond it. No screech of drill, just a conversation peppered with a few jovial laughs. A wall clock solemnly ticked the seconds away, punctured only by the occasional sniff of the receptionist.

After ten minutes the surgery door swung back and a portly, red-faced chap walked through, one side of his face swollen, speaking as if he had a mouth full of golf balls. The dentist, a spindly man dressed in a frock coat, was all smiles, and slapped the man on the back.

When the patient had left, with some incomprehensible farewells, the dentist turned to her. His thyroidish eyes, which looked as if they hadn't been seated properly in their sockets, unsettled her. 'Miss Lilywhite? What seems to be the problem?'

'Toothache.' She touched her jaw with her fingertips and grimaced.

'Well, if you'll come through, we'll take a look, shall we?' He turned to the woman. 'I think, Mrs Atherton, that will be all for today. I can manage Miss Lilywhite on my own.'

'If you are sure, Mr Delaney.'

'Absolutely. You toodle off and enjoy your evening.'

The woman gave a look that suggested she hadn't enjoyed an evening since the last century but, nevertheless, she began to gather her things together. Delaney, who was a good head shorter than Miss Pillbody, ushered her into his surgery. Here the stench of overcooked food disappeared, replaced by ether, rubber and chloroform. A black leather dentist's chair took centre stage, in front of a window made opaque by yellowing net curtains. A cabinet of horrors was open next to it on one side, full of evil-looking implements, with a pair of tall, metal cylinders and accompanying valves and hoses sitting on the other.

'Put your bag there. Take off your hat and have a seat,' Delaney instructed.

'I haven't got toothache,' she replied.

247

'A check-up never did anyone any harm. And if anyone should burst in' – he snicked the lock to make this unlikely – 'or peek through the window, the scene will be of patient and dentist at work.'

She did as she was told and settled in the chair, the leather of which had cracked so that it looked like a map of a complex estuary. It creaked under her weight.

Delaney washed his hands in a small sink, his voice low. 'You were only to contact me in an emergency.'

'This is an emergency. The station is blown.'

'Blown?' he asked, as if unfamiliar with the term.

'There was another agent operating in the area. From the army.'

Miss Pillbody could see him in the periphery of her vision, drying his hands. With his widow's peak, gaunt features and Victorian clothes, he looked more like a mortician than a medical man.

He moved to stand behind her. 'And the Zeppelin bombing mission?'

'Unsuccessful. They missed by a country mile. Actually, several country miles. But there is something else.' She explained about Elveden and the secret testing site. Delaney listened intently, his frown deepening as she spoke. She explained that, although given permission to ascertain what was happening at Elveden, she had failed, thanks, she made clear, to Ross.

'And you have no inkling of what it might be they are developing on this estate?'

'No. I did try to extract information from a British agent, but he wouldn't crack. I suspect he had very little to tell, and he just didn't want to give me the satisfaction of co-operating.' There was grudging admiration in her voice. 'But my recommendation . . .'

Delaney raised the bushy eyebrows that sat over his protruding eyes. Recommendations were his department.

'My suggestion would be that the place is firebombed to destruction. Just in case.'

'I'll pass this along.'

'I'm serious. They should start the raids again. Five Zeppelins. Ten. The air force—'

'I said I would pass it along,' he said firmly.

'And what about me?'

He approached her, rolling up his sleeves. 'Open wide, please.'

'Oh, for goodness' sake—'

'Come along. When did you last have your teeth looked at? It's a golden opportunity. Besides, I am going to do all the talking from now on.'

He reclined the seat and she allowed herself to follow it down. Delaney switched on the overhead light and then picked up a curved probe.

'Open wide.'

He peered into her mouth. 'The emergency run home is through Liverpool.'

She repeated the name as a gargle.

'Yes, Liverpool. Harwich, Plymouth, Dover, they are all watched closely. In Liverpool they look for Irish troublemakers coming in, not our people going out. Take tea at the Adelphi Hotel any Saturday or Wednesday afternoon. Ask for a table next to the statue of a dolphin. The Greek for dolphin being Delphis, you see, it is something of a mascot for the hotel. Does this hurt?'

She flinched a little.

'I thought so. A small cavity and one that, rest assured, will grow and grow, but we can put paid to its expansionist plans. A waiter will approach and ask you what room you are staying in. You will say Room 505. He will reply that there is an important message for you. Your instructions for the next meeting will be in that message. Understood?' He straightened up. 'I shall have to take out the decay and fill with amalgam. I follow Black's seven-step principles of cavity preparation and repair. The best there is. But we will need to inject you.'

'I don't like needles.'

'I won't hurt you, although I can put you out if you wish. Just a little gas and air will do the trick. Then, when it's all over, we can talk about lodging here before organizing the train north.' Delaney gave a tight smile. 'Once we have buffed you back to pearly white.'

Miss Pillbody's teeth were aching from his probing, and she could feel a little hotspot of pain in her lower left jaw. He had disturbed something.

'Very well. If you must.'

The dentist moved into her field of vision and nodded solemnly, showing her that she had made a wise decision. 'I shall prepare the inhaler,' he said, moving over to the cylinders of nitrous oxide and oxygen cylinders, and their rubber hoses with the attached black mask. 'And I shall use Novocain as an anaesthetic. Let me assure you, you would not get better treatment in Harley Street.'

'Let us just get this over with.'

'You must be relieved.'

'About what?' she asked.

He shrugged. 'You know, all the subterfuge.'

She hesitated before answering. 'It's what we are trained for.'

'I suppose.'

She felt an unease growing. Who could be relieved at having to abandon a mission?

The dentist unravelled the hose from the machine, adjusted some valves, placed the mask close to his own cheek to check the flow, and turned to her. Was it the shake of the hand? Or the sly look in the eye? Or perhaps that flickering smile of anticipation? Something betrayed him and she would never be able to put her finger on it. She could hear Hersch's voice in her ear: 'An agent at the end of his or her mission is often considered expendable. Some operatives like to tidy up loose ends. Don't let that happen to you. You are too valuable to the Kaiser.' She thought of poor Magda, her roommate, and the mixture of terror and surprise on her face as Ilse had slit her throat. A young woman, discarded because she couldn't quite make the mark.

'We didn't discuss a fee,' she said, pushing the mask away.

'Oh, I won't charge you a penny,' Delaney said cheerily.

That clinched it. Whoever heard of a dentist doing something for nothing?

As the rubber nosepiece was lowered towards her once more, she reached out to the tray of instruments and grabbed the first implement that came to hand. She swept at him, intending to slash his face to buy herself some time. But she had selected one of the hook-ended probes. It sank into the corner of his eye socket with a squish.

He gave a squeal, and tried to pull away, but she held firmly onto the probe and, with a terrible sucking sound, the eye plopped from the socket. She released the handle, leaving both eyeball and instrument, which had penetrated the tough sclera of the eye, dangling onto his face.

Delaney screamed and thrashed, pausing only to call her terrible names as a mixture of blood, tears and something viscous ran down his cheek. He stumbled over to a mirror and shrieked at what he saw.

He began to open drawers, looking for something to do serious damage to Miss Pillbody, his vision swimming, the pain boring straight down the optic nerve into his brain. When he had located a large, saw-bladed knife, he turned. But the chair was empty. Miss Pillbody was standing over her bag. From it she had pulled Coyle's Smith & Wesson. It was pointing its snout straight at him.

'Is all that true about Liverpool?' she demanded.

'You stupid fucking cow—'

'Is all that true?'

'Of course it is. Of course it is!' He took two strides towards her. 'Look at my face—'

She didn't want to look at his face. She shot him twice in the chest. As the noise died away and acrid gunsmoke replaced the smell of dental chemicals in the air, Miss Pillbody wondered if the Vauxhall was still where she had left it in Ipswich. She needed to get out of East Anglia fast.

*

Mrs Gregson found Lieutenant Halford, the man who had been selected from the mass of volunteers to supervise the test drive, walking around *Genevieve*, examining the exterior for signs of damage and rattling the treads to ensure the tracks were correctly tensioned.

'Congratulations,' she said.

'Oh, thank you, Nurse. Although I think commiserations might be in order.' He turned and shouted to a tankman on the far side of the machine. 'Taffs, check there is no slack in that track, will you?'

'Aye, skip.'

'Commiserations?'

'I tell you, that Winston could make a grouse vote for the Glorious Twelfth.' He slapped the side of the tank. 'Almost made us all forget what happened to the last blokes who rode in *Genevieve* here.'

'That's exactly what I wanted to talk to you about.'

He had her attention now. Like many of the tankmen, his face was peppered with grease and oil, but, underneath, there seemed to be a handsome if gaunt young man, with curly dark hair and choc-olate-coloured eyes, although one of them was quite bloodshot. 'Is that giving you trouble?' she asked.

'What?'

'Your left eye.'

'Got a bit of grit or metal in it.'

'See me later. I'll irrigate it for you before it does any more damage. Not much use as a tank commander with one eye, eh?'

'No. Look, Nurse, I've got to get on here.' He half turned. 'I will call by after this is over, but—'

'But you need me on board.'

He stopped walking away. 'On board?'

'In *Genevieve*. During the test.'

He shook his head and laughed. 'It's not a joy ride, miss.'

Careful, now, she thought. *Don't bite his head off. He's just a boy.* 'No, it's a situation where men might die. Oddly enough, that's become something of a speciality of mine. Anything happens in old *Genevieve* here' – it was her turn to smack the riveted side – 'you'll need swift medical action.'

'Shall we start her up, gentlemen?'

It was Cardew. The two volunteer gearsmen picked up their cranks and stepped inside *Genevieve*, followed by the driver.

'I have to go. Look, if a doctor is needed, we'll have Major Watson with us.'

'You've seen the major lately, have you?'

Halford glanced over his shoulder to where Watson was deep in conversation with Fairley. 'What do you mean?'

'He's not a young man,' Mrs Gregson said, feeling disloyal but pressing on. 'Nor will he be the most agile member of your crew if an emergency does arise. I am only stating the obvious facts.' The latter was more a justification to herself than to Halford.

'That's as maybe—'

'You need me. It might mean the difference between life and death for all your crew. I saw what happened to the last lot of young men who were in there. It wasn't very pretty.'

'You've made your point.' Halford scratched his cheek in thought. 'Look, if the major agrees—'

She put a hand on Halford's shoulder. 'No, no, Lieutenant. I've got a much better idea, we can—'

The engine rumbled into life, the metal plate next to them began to vibrate loudly and four small, black clouds spat out of the exhausts.

'What did you say?' Halford asked.

Mrs Gregson leaned in close to Halford to complete the conversation.

THIRTY-THREE

Watson felt like he was entering the biblical fiery furnace as he stepped awkwardly through the low door in the rear of the right-hand sponson. The air was broiling, thick with exhaust and petrol fumes, and several of the men had pulled their coveralls down to their waists, so they were effectively working in their vests. Rather than the usual army steel helmets, they were wearing the new leather ones, which perched on top of the head.

Watson was glad he had heeded the warning not to wear his tunic – he had on a summer-weight shirt, with tie, and had already rolled up the sleeves. With so much flesh on show and so many hot pipes, he had to be careful not to suffer one of the contact burns that Mrs Gregson had described.

The fact that so many cogs and rotating elements were completely unshielded made Watson wonder how many digits and hands would be lost before the war was out. Such accidents were easy enough to avoid under test conditions; he imagined things would be different when war exploded all around. And, as he knew from his earlier inspection, the two big cylinders at the front of the interior contained petrol. An even more horrific scenario filled his mind. Immolation was not a nice way to die.

'Is it always this noisy?' he yelled at Cardew. The engineer cupped a hand to his ear. He said something back, but it was like watching a mime. Watson looked around. With no need for gunners, there was a slightly depleted crew. At the controls was Lieutenant Halford, next to him Sergeant Taffs, the driver. At the rear were two gearsmen, Privates Mead and Stenby, whose job it was to engage the secondary gearbox and keep everything thoroughly greased. Sitting in the sponson saddle seats on each side, where two gunners would normally be, were Cardew and, opposite him, a private, who was wearing a gas mask as instructed. Watson hadn't been introduced, but the private's role would be to throw open the sponson doors and front visors if the crew became disoriented or deranged in any way. Spare gas masks were hanging on the ammunition racks next to him.

Even over the thudding of the engine Watson heard the clang of metal on metal: the commander was banging the side of the hull with a spanner, as if ringing a dinner bell. All the visor hatches were pulled shut, leaving just the light from the small vision slits, covered with glass prisms, to illuminate the white interior. Tiny festoon lamps offered some feeble assistance, but it was as gloomy as a cellar. Watson swallowed hard, trying to contain a flash of incipient claustrophobia, his instinct to throw open the hatches once more and suck in unpolluted air. Was he going insane already?

The madness, Watson, would be to think this was in any way normal.

True, very true. He took a deep breath of the foul air and tried to relax. Cardew indicated the spare saddle seat next to him, and Watson shuffled over and perched on it. Cardew slapped his thigh in reassurance.

There was a loud squeak as Taffs pressed the clutch and engaged gear. The engine revs dropped as the driver let the clutch back in. More fumes belched. The note changed as Taffs gave it more juice and the gearsmen engaged the sprockets with their secondary gearboxes. Watson's stomach lurched as the tracks rotated around the circumference of the rhomboid and the inside of the machine became even more cacophonous, something Watson hadn't thought was possible. Now his eardrums seemed pressed deep into his brain, as if they might meet in the centre. Cardew, seeing his distress, handed over two small blobs of India rubber. Earplugs. Watson nodded his thanks and screwed them in. The racket dropped to just below absolutely unbearable.

The tank jerked, steadied, then moved forward, the vibration and jolts from the unsprung chassis already shaking Watson's spine.

Here we go, he thought, *on the Landship of Fools.*

From beneath her gas mask, Mrs Gregson was watching Major Watson intently. He looked distressed and pained but, she supposed, beneath the rubber and canvas covering her head, so did she. Sweat was running down her forehead and fogging the eyepieces. The bulky overalls, designed to cover her curves, were not helping. Even though she only had basic underwear on underneath, it was like being inside a mobile Turkish bath. Thank goodness she had thought to deploy her acoustic swimming earplugs; at least the noise wasn't too deafening. But the vibration was horrendous, making her feel nauseous, and she seemed to be thrown about like a sack of spuds every time the tank hit a bump. How could men fight in this thing?

She had considered simply following the tank on foot, ready to step inside if it got into trouble. After all, it apparently couldn't go much faster than a brisk walk. But, in the end, Mrs Gregson had decided she had to be closer to Watson. She was concerned about him. Hence her shameless petitioning of Halford to allow her on board.

As he had in Belgium, Watson was acting as if he were a far younger man, as if, for the first time in human history, the slow deprivations of age did not apply to him. True, he didn't look his age – even though she had no idea exactly what that was, but anyone who had fought at the Battle of Maiwand was no spring chicken – however, she knew that his energy levels were lower than those of the youngsters who surrounded him. The man who had come back from the ice house had the pallor of death upon him and a pulse that barely deserved the name. She had expected him to need a week in bed. But here he was, risking his life in this steel beast. Which demonstrated, she supposed, that Watson still possessed remarkable recuperative powers.

There came another banging on the hull and Mrs Gregson saw the two gearsmen busy themselves on their charges. The tank gave a judder, almost like a mechanical shiver, and then she felt it turning. She took a peek through the observation slit above her head. They were changing direction all right, heading off towards the wire. The pretend no man's land. But there would be no pretending if this great, galumphing beast tipped into one of the trenches and became stuck fast.

Even over the roar of the engine and the whine of the tracks, they heard the shriek of the wire as it was crushed. Some of it sprang free and lashed against the thinner metal of the sponsons, like the tentacles of a dying creature. Then the world tipped, sending those not holding on stumbling forward. Mrs Gregson cracked her head on a machine gun and almost ripped the mask off her face as pain flashed around her cranium.

Walking behind, she concluded, *would definitely have been the sensible option.*

Now they were nosing further down again, like a submarine diving, she would imagine. The engine misfired twice, probably as petrol sloshed in the tanks or the carburretor's float chamber, starving the Daimler engine of fuel, before a laboured change in tone announced more power and the nose began to lift, slowly at first, but then with a constant, deliberate speed. She guessed what was coming next. The tail dipped, flinging them back the other way, but this time she kept her skull clear of any protruding objects. She skinned both sets of knuckles, though, and a blackened nail.

Genevieve's nose pushed upwards and then fell again with a great smash that blurred the world around Mrs Gregson. She shook her head to try to clear her vision, already limited by the little Perspex roundels in her gas mask.

After frantic work from the crewmen, His Majesty's Land Ship *Genevieve* was back on level ground and Halford, the commander, thrashed his spanner against the hull. This was not instructions, but a little victory drum roll – the cumbersome *Genevieve* had crossed the first trench. Mrs Gregson smiled to herself at his childish delight. It was Halford who had smuggled her on board. Nobody else had the authority, and it had taken all her persuasive powers to convince him that women in tanks weren't bad luck. How could they be? None had had a chance to ride in one yet. Although, she admitted, it was a dubious privilege to be a pioneer in this moving Hades.

Genevieve baulked and swayed now, bouncing over the contours of the no man's land. Mrs Gregson scanned Watson's face for any sign of alarm. Would he realize where he was? That he was crossing a replica of the grim place where he had lain, trapped in the filth, waiting to die from a German sniper's bullet?

But she could see he was more concerned about the compression blows transmitted through his spine and examining the crewmen for signs of distress. She saw something flit over his face: a little tremor. His eyes were staring straight ahead, and he had stopped appraising the crew. He had also ceased blinking. No, he wasn't taking in what was happening around him – he was watching something else, an internal show, playing in his brain, projected onto the backs of his eyes. A spasm of horror crossed his features and he began muttering to himself. Watson was in trouble.

She rose from her seat, and so did Watson. His mouth gaped open and then he shouted something, the words lost. From beneath his shirt, he pulled out a small, compact gun and fired, a noise loud enough to be heard over the machine. The bullet bounced off the floor, sparking around the tank. Cardew was already wrestling with him.

Mrs Gregson stepped around to the other side of the Daimler, the heat of the engine block soaking through her like liquid. Watson was still thrashing, the gun waving in the air. Another shot might injure any one of them as it flew round the interior. Mrs Gregson did the only thing she could think of. She pulled off her gas mask and helmet and shoved her face into Watson's, forcing him to recognize her, while yelling his name at the top of her voice. Watson's mouth dropped open once again and, his eyes wide with madness, he relaxed his grip on the gun and pitched forward into oblivion.

THIRTY-FOUR

Ian Ackland had thought being in the British Secret Service would be far more exciting than it had turned out to be. He had expected danger in foreign lands, but had joined just two months before the schism that created two separate agencies, one for home and one for abroad. He had been deemed most suitable for work within the British Isles.

Even that held out hope of Richard Hannay-type adventures: dinner at the Café Royal, drinks at the Ritz, gambling at Brooks's interspersed with daring train dashes, narrow escapes and uncovering spy rings. But Ackland, cursed with a congenital limp that kept him out of the army when he came down from Cambridge, was probably not considered train-dash material by the people at the top.

It was true that Colonel R., the man who had recruited him at a hotel in Northumberland Avenue, had warned him the job was 'ninety-five per cent tedium and when you are in the midst of the five per cent, you find yourself praying for tedium once more.'

It hadn't all been dull. He had once found himself helping Gibson and Coyle, the department's old hands, arrest two men in Hull. They claimed to be cigar salesmen. Gibson had suggested that any genuine seller would have better luck in ports with cigarettes and pipes; ordinary seamen did not go in for cigars – that was the Admiralty. It was the kind of detail a real agent noticed. So, after tracking them from Plymouth to Portsmouth to Hull, they had pounced.

One of them, Janssen, had bolted, and Ackland and Coyle had given chase and tackled him to the ground. True, it had been Coyle who had spotted Janssen's little derringer and torn it from his grasp, but Ackland had proved a man with a gammy leg could still manage a fair turn of speed. And it had got the blood racing.

Which was more than could be said for sitting outside a dentist's surgery in Great Yarmouth. 'A whisper' was how his director had put it 'that he is up to more than teeth pulling'. A whisper. But then, it was a whisper and a hunch that had brought them to Janssen. The spy, and his associate, had later been shot at the Tower.

Two flashes lit up the surgery windows.

Ackland sat up straight behind the wheel. Had he imagined things? He had seen the woman with the luggage – odd for someone visiting a dentist – arrive and Delaney's secretary leave. He spooled back over the past thirty seconds. Had he heard anything? There, buried beneath his reminiscences of Janssen, was something. Gunshots? No, surely not. Perhaps some piece of dental equipment malfunctioning?

The door to the house opened and the woman with the bag hurried down the steps, pausing to look left and right, her eyes hesitating as they raked his Armstrong-Whitworth, before she walked at a brisk pace towards the main road to the north.

Ackland sat frozen with indecision for a moment. Should he go in and see what had happened inside? But how would he explain his interest to Delaney, the dentist? It might tip him the wink that he was being watched. His director would be furious. No, follow the woman. Whatever had occurred involved her. *Who goes to the dentist with luggage?* he thought once more. Unless they were planning on a trip. Perhaps that was it. Delaney was a travel courier, handing over tickets and passports to enemy agents. A woman? Well, it wouldn't be the first time. Hadn't Basil Thomson of Scotland Yard's counter-espionage branch arrested that Dutch woman Margaretha Zelle at Falmouth? With little proof that she was a foreign agent Thomson had had to let her go, but he had circulated a memo warning that the Dutch dancer known as 'Mata Hari' – Zelle's stage name – should be considered a suspicious person.

And that stare, as she examined his car, it had made his skin itch with apprehension. There was something both professional and predatory in it. She might not be Mata Hari, but she was someone he should be interested in.

The Armstrong-Whitworth was fitted with the new electric starts, normally only found on Rolls Royces and such marques, but they were temperamental, and Ackland muttered a little prayer as he pulled out the choke an inch and pressed the starter button. The cold engine groaned as it turned, seemed to die, then accelerated until it caught, leaping about like an eager puppy. The woman was about to turn the corner, so he engaged first gear and, without waiting for the engine to warm up fully – he could hear the chief mechanic barking his disapproval – pulled away from the kerbside.

At the corner he paused, waiting for a horse-drawn brewer's dray to cross in front of him. He could see her down the street, still hurrying on, but looking over her shoulder, then at the next junction, anxiously scanning left and right and then back in his direction. Had she spotted him? No. A cab – she was looking for a taxi. And he would be stuck behind, and blinded by, the enormous high-sided cart with its barrels of beer.

Ackland let out the clutch, floored the accelerator and spun the wheel. For a second he thought he had overcooked it, as the tyres shrieked in protest and the back end seemed to float around the corner, but, after a brief fishtail, he was on the opposite side of the road, causing bicycles to swerve as he rushed past the dray, cutting in just in front of the horses as another vehicle filled his windscreen. He glanced in the rear-view mirror and saw one of the animals had started to buck, but he had no time to worry about that.

He halted again at the next corner where he had seen her standing. This was a much busier road, full of omnibuses and motor lorries, as well as cyclists and motor cyclists. He scanned both ways, but could see no sign of her. There were several taxis in the mêlée, so she could easily have hailed one while he was busy overtaking. Ackland banged the steering wheel with his fist in frustration.

Ah, well, next best thing. Back to the dentist, see what had transpired there. He would feign toothache to gain entrance. He began a laboured three-point turn, and was just at the apex, wrenching the wheel around, when the door was yanked open.

The Armstrong-Whitworth juddered and stalled as he was pulled out from behind the wheel into the street. A big, ruddy-faced fellow with thick white moustaches was tossing him around like a rag doll. It took a moment before he realized it was the drayman.

'You little bleeder,' he said, pulling back his fist. 'Look what you done to my horse.'

He couldn't see what he had done but he could hear one of them complaining loudly.

'I am an officer of the law—'

The drayman hit him with a fist the size of a shovel and Ackland went sprawling to the ground, his face a massive circle of pain. He tried to reach into his pocket.

'Watch out, he's got a gun,' someone shouted, most unhelpfully.

The drayman kicked him and stamped on his right hand, even though he had no intention of reaching for his weapon, but his Scotland Yard-issued ID.

He let out at yelp of pain and then: 'You bloody fool! I'm a policeman.'

'You are a menace, that's what you are.'

The drayman hauled him to his feet, just as he heard the engine of the Armstrong-Whitworth kick back into life. Nicely warmed now, it gave a willing roar and the slightest of grinds as the gear was selected. The sporty machine came back at the two men at high speed, cracking into both of them and sending them into a heap in the gutter. Ackland's skull bounced off the kerb and he went out cold. The big drayman raised himself on one elbow, just far enough to appreciate that it appeared to be a woman who had run him over and left the driver for dead.

'There, that's all done.' Mrs Gregson tied off the bandage she had put on Cardew's hand. 'I'll have another look at it later. Normally I would let a burn like that get some air, but I suspect you aren't going to keep your hands away from oil and dirt, are you?'

They were in the old aviary, and Cardew's hand represented the last of the various burns, cuts and scratches she had had to deal with after the tanks' test runs.

'It's my job,' said Cardew, flexing his fingers, 'to get filthy.'

'You make it sound like you are a chimneysweep. Couldn't you wear gloves?'

Cardew gave her a look that suggested she'd recommended he don a feather boa. 'We need the lightness of touch, Mrs Gregson. Skin on metal. It can't be beaten.'

'Except when the metal is hot.'

'That's an accepted hazard in my line of work. How is Major Watson?' Cardew asked.

'Getting better.'

'He had me worried there for a while,' admitted Cardew. 'What do you think caused—'

She shook her head. 'I am sure Major Watson is asking himself that very question right now. And if I know him, he'll have an answer soon enough.'

Cardew nodded. 'You know, just before the test Thwaites, the cavalryman, came to me and—'

There was a rap on a pane of glass in the open door to the make-shift surgery. 'Shop!'

Lieutenant Halford, now changed out of his overalls and into the uniform of the Royal Artillery, walked across the tiled floor towards them. 'Sorry to interrupt. I remembered I promised to get this done.' He pointed at his left eye. 'It's scratchier than ever.'

'We're just finished here,' Mrs Gregson said, and Cardew rolled down and buttoned his sleeve. 'But you were saying? About the cavalryman?'

Cardew shook his head. 'No, don't worry. Probably nothing. I'll tell Major Watson when I see him. Lieutenant Halford, you have the chair.'

After Cardew had left, Halford sat down. Mrs Gregson took a white enamel kidney tray and a saline irrigation pump from one of the cupboards.

'I'm glad I let you persuade me to allow you on board,' said Halford. 'I reckon you saved Watson and the rest of us.'

She smiled. 'Perhaps.'

'Oh, no doubt about it, Nurse. Top-hole behaviour. Thank you.'

'Call me Mrs Gregson. Can you tilt your head back?'

He did as he was told. 'And where is Mr Gregson?'

'France, I believe.'

He moved his head forward. 'You believe?'

'Mr Gregson and I parted company some years ago.' Why was she telling him this? 'It was expedient to keep the title.'

'Ah. In which case, one good turn deserves another.'

'Hold still. And hold this there.' She got him to position the dish under his chin and began to squirt the sterile saline into his eye. 'You wear goggles, don't you?'

'We do, but sometimes with the goggles and the prism slits, you can see bug—you can't see anything. So you lift them off. So how about this good turn?'

A jagged black particle like a miniature coal lump washed out of his conjunctiva and into the dish. 'Ah. I think we might have the culprit. What good turn?'

'I let you in the tank. My good turn. Now you let me take you to dinner. Your good turn.'

'Blink.' She dabbed at his face with a cloth, mopping up the water. She was pleased to see the flush of red beneath his ears. At least he had the decency to be embarrassed by such a barefaced proposal. *When did boys get so bold?* she wondered. The war, of course. 'We aren't allowed off the estate. How can you take me out to dinner? Not that I am considering the proposal.'

'Let me worry about how and where. We can—' His face contorted into a look of puzzlement.

'What is it?'

'Did you hear that?'

'Hear what?' asked Mrs Gregson.

He cocked his head to one side. 'Sounded like a scream. From over there.'

She followed his finger. It was pointing through the window of the aviary to the distant Sandgrouse Lodge where Major Watson was billeted.

THIRTY-FIVE

Watson sat at the desk in his room, drafting a memo to the Ministry of Munitions and to Winston Churchill. He had headlined it: 'Some

Medical Observations on the Conditions Inside the Landships' and 'Most Confidential'. He wasn't sure he would get a decent hearing, but it had to be said. Not because of his own behaviour and collapse, but because of the atrocious atmosphere within the 'bus' or 'car', as they called them, that the brave young men who manned them would have to fight under. It had been known for a long time that carbon monoxide could cause confusion and death; he himself had been called to many deaths, from infants to adults, caused by faulty heaters or fires in closed rooms. There must be a better method to eliminate the CO and CO2 that the engine belched into the interior.

Added to that, the heat generated by the Daimler caused petrol to evaporate from the internal tanks – there was no external way for pouring petrol into them – so it vented from the screw filler caps straight into the already foul air, stinging the eyes and attacking the throat. And then there was the heat; he estimated it might reach 120 degrees Fahrenheit. Put together with the horrendous racket and lethal machinery, it was an act of torture to subject British soldiers to it.

Watson was no engineer, but he thought there must be a way to shroud the engine and the gear machinery and make sure the exhaust fumes cleared the car's body. And a silencing system, perhaps. And petrol tanks that didn't turn the whole bus into a potential fiery deathtrap. He didn't fancy trying to get out of the narrow escape hatches and doors in an emergency. And, of course, the inside was full of thousands of rounds of ordnance, likely to start exploding.

But this wouldn't be what the commanders on the Western Front wanted to hear. They weren't concerned about the niceties of the machines. They just wanted them lumbering forward out of the morning mist and smoke, panicking the Germans. And they wanted them before the winter rains, fully tested or not. After all, life in the forward trenches was no picnic for millions of men. Why worry about the comfort of a few hundred tankmen?

Watson sighed. He doubted it was all that cynical, or at least hoped it wasn't. They were desperate for something to shorten the

265

war, to save lives, and they were only too happy to clutch at this metal straw.

There was a rapping on the door.

'Come!'

Cardew put his head around the door, his face full of concern. 'Can I see you for a moment, Major?'

'Yes, of course,' said Watson, laying aside the papers. 'I have a few questions about *Genevieve* anyway.'

'Are you're feeling all right?'

'Never better . . . Well, that's not true, but a dose of clean air seemed to clear my brain in no time.'

Cardew ran a hand through his hair. 'Thank goodness for that. What are you writing?'

'I'm lucky it's not my will. If it wasn't for you and Mrs Gregson . . . what on earth was she doing in there, anyway?'

Cardew laughed. 'I think she used her female wiles on the commander. You've not seen her?'

'She is avoiding me. I think she is concerned that I'll bite her head off.'

'And will you?'

Watson laughed. 'I suspect even a circus lion might come off second-best in the head-biting stakes with Mrs Gregson.'

'And are you avoiding this?' From behind his back Cardew brought out a bottle of brandy. He fished in the pocket of his jacket. 'And two glasses.'

Watson nodded. 'As a doctor, I shall not hesitate to prescribe myself a little medicinal tot.'

'You've eaten?'

'Some soup from the housekeeper.'

Cardew set about pouring two glasses on the side dresser. From over his shoulder he asked: 'What do you think happened out there, Major? To make you go——'

Watson cut him short. 'Insane? It's interesting, isn't it, that the other tanks we ran today had no such mishap?'

The 'controls' had run for a full hour, hatches fully battened, and although the crews were grateful to get out, and showed some signs of mild asphyxiation from the fumes, none of them had suffered a mental collapse.

'Curious, I suppose,' said Cardew.

'I'm just writing my report. Do you have any theories?'

'Me? I'm just an engineer. But between you and me, before the test I did see Thwaites—'

Watson cut him off. Thwaites was not the culprit in this. 'Oh, more than a mere engineer, I think. You are a policymaker.'

'How do you mean?' Cardew asked warily.

Watson put his pen down and turned to face the man. 'When you decided to delay the introduction of the tanks, why didn't you go for mechanical sabotage? Instead of targeting an innocent crew?'

Cardew stared at him as if he was still in the grip of the madness. 'Major Watson! Really!'

'I am not sure you intended to kill the men in *Genevieve*, did you?'

Cardew sipped his brandy but remained quiet.

'You did everything as one should. But for one thing. It was what was missing from *Genevieve* that was important.'

'Which was?' Cardew asked, his curiosity getting the better of him.

'Dirt.'

'Dirt?'

'And grease and soot. When I first inspected *Genevieve*, I found one of the exhaust pipes spotless. The others were as I described – filthy. But this one had been wiped clean. By a rag, I suspected, from the smears. Who do we know who always carries a rag?'

'When you first . . .?' Cardew asked, puzzled.

'I slipped out for a little inspection before the official one. At sunrise, with Mrs Gregson. Often better that way, to have the scene to oneself. But later, when I inspected the interior with you, all were polished clean. So that they matched, I suppose. How is the hand, by the way?'

Cardew looked down at Mrs Gregson's dressing.

'*Genevieve*'s exhaust was damned hot just now, wasn't it? But after I had my little turn, you had to wipe it again to check that the drug wasn't still active, affecting me and then, who knows? Perhaps you.'

'This is nonsense, Major. Something has scrambled your brain.'

Watson shook his head. 'No, it can only be you, Cardew. You don't want your machine wasted in dribs and drabs. You want to wait until there are thousands. Didn't you say that?'

'Yes, but . . . so you weren't affected in the tank? You didn't take leave of your senses?'

'I am afraid that little incident was a charade.' Watson couldn't keep the pride from his voice. 'The first bit of real acting I've done since my days at Blackheath Football Club.'

I thought that was a Christmas pantomime, Watson.

'Not counting a few impersonations for Holmes. It did the trick, anyway. I even fooled Mrs Gregson, and that is no simple matter. Although I think my rapid recovery aroused her suspicions. But I wasn't after plaudits for my performance. What I really wanted was to see what you – or someone – would do if there still seemed to be a residue of the poison. What you did was rewipe the hot exhaust pipe at the first opportunity. And burn yourself into the bargain.'

Cardew shook his head as he imagined an innocent man might. Yet, Watson noticed, something was glistening on his forehead. His eyes flicked to Watson's brandy. Watson had no intention of drinking it, for he suspected it was intended to hasten the return of his mysterious symptoms. Watson would become another of *Genevieve*'s victims.

'But even before that, I had my suspicions. Square-toed boots are very distinctive around a military base. The ground outside the ice house was rather churned and soaked by the water, but a close inspection of the soil nearby showed several impressions of square toes. It was you who locked us in the ice house.'

Excellent, Watson, excellent.

Cardew's only response was another shake of his head.

'What was the concoction you used?' asked Watson. 'In the tank?'

'Major, I fear your brain is definitely scrambled.'

'I thought at first it might be the devil's foot powder,' continued Watson. 'You, though, are probably too young to recall "The Adventure of the Devil's Foot"? The so-called devil's foot root? It is an extract of *Physostigma venenosum*, the calabar bean, although I held that detail back from my account in the *Strand* lest others be tempted to use the terrible drug. But, I reasoned, that is found only in Africa, and not South Africa, but chiefly along the banks of the Ubangi, which forms the border between French and Belgian Congo—'

'I have never been to Africa!' Cardew protested.

'No. Nor has anyone here, as far as I am aware, not the central part of the continent, anyway.' Thwaites's experience didn't count; he hadn't travelled overland through the continent but by ship to and from Cape Town. 'And with the Cornish sample destroyed, the only other example in this part of the world is in a laboratory in Buda. So I considered the matter further. Not the devil's foot, then. Something European, perhaps. How did you hit upon the idea of using ergot? Was it the local rye fields, gone to seed, infested with the stuff? And to find a way for the vapour to work amid all those competing fumes . . . part of me is impressed. But you are a man of science, a seeker of solutions, aren't you?'

Cardew said nothing now, just gulped at his brandy.

'Did you know at the beginning of your scheme that it causes vaso-constriction? Affecting the brain and the limbs, causing gangrene. That was why you had to dispose of the bodies, wasn't it? The doctor was the last to die, so had the most advanced gangrene symptoms. And poor Hitchcock. At first I thought he was weeping at the piano because of the pain. I now think it was something worse for a musician – he couldn't feel his fingers. The fingertips were losing their sensitivity. That is why he banged the keys. The gangrene was coming, so I suspect you pushed him along with a little more of your devilish concoction, hoping we wouldn't examine him too carefully.'

'Poppycock.'

'Perhaps. Hitchcock, I can't be sure of. But I did notice that the paraffin heater in his room had been on – I turned it off when I left him and ordered more blankets. It had also been wiped clean. Was that how you delivered it? No matter. Your quarters and workshop are being searched as we speak, looking for this foul poison you have created.'

'I didn't . . .' Cardew gulped. 'I wouldn't. What you suggest is monstrous.'

'And so is what is at stake. I have put myself in your shoes. We have one chance with this machine and you wanted to make sure it was the right one. What are eight deaths versus the millions out there? Eight men die every minute somewhere in this war. And I am sure you had other plans to stall the progress. But I ask you again, did you mean to kill the men in the tank? And what other schemes have you put in place?'

Cardew sucked in his cheeks and began to chew at one of them.

The door swung open and framed Swinton, and behind him two military policemen. 'Well?' Watson asked.

Swinton, who had taken the precaution of wearing gloves, held up a glass bottle, the size of a jam jar, half-filled with a black, oily liquid. 'In a panel behind the bed in his quarters. Along with what appears to be a coded recipe for making it.' He looked at Watson. 'What is it?'

'I suspect a suspension that uses ergot of rye. *Claviceps purpurea,* possibly, or another species. It infects various cereals and, if digested, causes ergotism – *ignis sacer* or St Anthony's Fire. The symptoms are intense burning of the limbs, hallucinations, gangrene and death.'

'Cardew—' Swinton began, his voice trembling with rage.

'Just a moment, Colonel.' Watson turned his attention back to the young engineer. 'I think we are about to hear all the details.'

'Not from me,' snarled the young man.

'It is your best hope,' said Watson.

'You'll never know the truth.'

'Oh, I think we will,' said Swinton, stepping aside to allow the military policemen into the room.

'Not from these lips.'

In one clean movement Cardew swept up Watson's neglected brandy and swallowed it in one. He stood, staring at the Major for a few seconds and then gave a little laugh and a cough. 'The poison doesn't . . . doesn't have to be delivered as fumes, Major. It . . .' – he took a step back – '. . . it can work dissolved in liquid. As you were meant to discover.'

Watson jumped from his chair and ran towards the man, intending to make him sick, but Cardew clamped his left hand over his mouth and scurried backwards. From his pocket he extracted the pistol he had confiscated from Watson in the tank.

'Get back,' he threatened through his fingers. 'Or I kill the major.'

Watson raised his hands to show he was coming no further. 'Look, Cardew, the tank will be deployed within weeks with you or without you. It's too late to stop now. Churchill, Haig, the other desk-wallahs – they don't care if a crew is killed or goes mad. They'll just get another one. The dead men are an irrelevance. You are a clever lad. Don't throw it all away.' He risked a single pace forward. 'We can plead temporary insanity. All those hours working with the machine, the stress of sleepless nights, the damned fumes . . . make yourself sick, now. The toxin can't work that quickly. Good God man, you don't want to die of madness and gangrene.'

Cardew's features relaxed. He let his left hand drop and spoke clearly. 'You know, you're absolutely right.' He put the gun to his forehead and pulled the trigger.

The report was almost as loud as Watson's scream.

THIRTY-SIX

Miss Pillbody had no real idea where she was. She had arrived in Liverpool in time for afternoon tea at the surprisingly opulent Adelphi and had sat next to the dolphin, as instructed. A waiter had asked for her room number, she had given the correct response and received a note with her pot of tea instructing her to go to the basement of a shop called Blackler's. There she had been bundled out by two workmen and loaded into the back of a delivery van for a short but bumpy ride. One of the men sat with her, rifling through her bag until he found the pistol and pocketed it without comment.

She was so tired, she almost didn't care what happened to her. Only her *Sie Wölfe* training – the long marches on no sleep and little food, and the nights of mock interrogation – kept her going. And that training told her to pick her moments. When resources are low, marshal them carefully and strike when you have a good chance of succeeding, not merely to demonstrate courage or defiance. So when the van stopped and her escort produced a blindfold, she offered no resistance.

She was helped down from the van and shuffled through a door, up a flight of stairs and along a corridor. When the blindfold was removed she was in a rather shabby hotel room. Her bag was placed on the bed, and the two men departed. She heard the key turn in the lock.

The temptation was to lie down on the bed and sleep. It had been a long, fraught journey from Great Yarmouth, by car and then train. Then she caught sight of the colour of the pillows and thought better of putting her head on them. She examined the windows, but they were screwed or nailed shut. The grimy panes looked out onto an airshaft. All she could see were a number of similarly unwashed windows on the opposite wall.

She sighed and sat in the only chair, a rather upright and scuffed object placed next to a mismatched and equally careworn desk. She closed her eyes, trying to empty her mind of the last forty-eight hours. But there was one question that kept returning: had the dentist really been out to dispose of her? Were his instructions to remove any potential loose ends, as she had become? Or had her fevered imagination made her liable to over-react? She would probably never know the truth. What she did know, judging by the documents in the car she had stolen, was that the dentist had been under observation. So, with the British on his tail, he was no great loss.

She must have nodded off, because when she opened her eyes again a man was entering the room. He had on a black frock coat, waistcoat and striped trousers and had a pair of pince-nez dangling round his neck. He had a beaky expression that reminded Miss Pillbody of a vulture. The hair was heavily oiled and he smelled of strong tobacco. He inclined his head towards her. 'Good evening.'

'Good evening,' she replied.

He glanced at the bed and decided to remain standing. 'I apologize for the manner of your arrival.' He gave a snort of laughter. 'Indeed, for the place of your arrival. I'm sure you're used to somewhat different surroundings, Miss . . .?'

She didn't answer. She wasn't sure who she was now. 'I am here to report.'

'Really? I think news has travelled ahead of you. Or at least snippets of it. You remind me of one of those hurricanes they have in the Caribbean.' She could detect a faint accent now. This man wasn't English. 'Leaving a trail of destruction in her wake. An agent in Suffolk, a dentist in Great Yarmouth . . .'

'A compromised dentist.' *And perhaps a dead British policeman as well*, she thought, *under the wheels of his own car*. It was quite a tally she was clocking up. 'And I did what I had to do. As an agent of Germany.'

'Forgive me, but I have no way of knowing that. You could be an agent of the British Crown.'

'And so could you.'

'I am, my dear. A very senior agent of the Crown. I am the Chief Postal Censor for the north-west of England. I see all the sensitive material written in Liverpool, Manchester and beyond. And I act on those pieces of information that might be of benefit to Germany and the Kaiser.'

She laughed. If that was true, it was a remarkable placement. 'Why are you telling me this?'

'Oh, because if you are who I think you are, then you might be useful to me. If not, you'll leave this room in that bag of yours.' He glanced down at it, and she shuddered.

A mournful horn sounded somewhere nearby and received an answer to its call. They were close to the river. Easy to dispose of a body, whole or otherwise.

'I am an operative of the *Nachrichten-Abteilung*, German Naval Intelligence,' she said. 'My last assignment was to guide a Zeppelin over Thetford aerodrome. Unfortunately, another agent, operating in the area, was recognized as a spy and compromised my position. I was in Great Yarmouth with Delaney. When I left, I realized he was being observed by British agents or police.'

'How did you escape?'

'I . . .'

'Careful now. I am not stupid. I have some facts to draw upon.'

This could have been a bluff, but she stuck as closely to the facts as she could. 'I shot Delaney when I realized he was under observation by the British.' It was only a small lie, a transposition of timing. 'He would have been no further use and could have betrayed both me and you—'

The man put his hand up. 'I am not judging. Probably very wise.'

'I managed to lose the British agent and then stole his car.'

He looked impressed. 'Most resourceful.'

'Which I spent the night in, in a country lane. I then abandoned it and took several trains to Liverpool.'

The man tapped his lower lip with an index finger. 'I am afraid I shall have to verify some of that. Can you give me the name of your handler at Naval Intelligence?'

She pursed her lips. What did he take her for? She had said too much already. 'I can. But I won't.'

He smirked. 'Hersch has a weakness for *femmes fatales*.'

This man doesn't know the half of it, she thought.

'I shall check with him. Is there anything that would confirm your identity?'

They locked eyes for what seemed like many minutes before she said, 'Tell him that he shouldn't make love with Rudy in the room. It is very distracting.'

'Rudy?'

'His schnauzer. He barks at the most inopportune moments.'

The man nodded, vaguely affronted by such candour. What sort of training was seducing your agents? Or perhaps it was the other way round. 'You really are quite a remarkable women. I shall try to get confirmation as soon as possible. In the meantime . . .' He looked around and wrinkled his nose. 'Try and make yourself comfortable. Is there anything I can bring you?'

She was distracted by something at the window that had caught her eye. 'I'm sorry?'

'Can I bring you something?'

'I haven't eaten anything for quite some time.'

'I'll see if we can send something up.'

'Thank you.'

As soon as he was gone, she got to work on the window.

Watson sat on a bench in the walled garden, letting the low evening sun warm his face. He just wished it could heat up his bones, which seemed permanently chilled. He ached all over. The strain of his few days at Elveden had taken its toll: the freezing water, the hellhole of a tank and the suicide of a young man right in front of him – *a man who had intended to feed him a poison to drive him mad, and thus further confuse the situation*, he reminded himself. Thank goodness he made sure the engineer had not been allowed unaccompanied access to the other two machines, or he might have poisoned those too.

Watson could hear the noise of the landships, blowing across from the trench system, their Daimler engines revving and protesting and sometimes juddering to a halt. Coughs and splutters marked desperate attempts to restart them. But it wasn't his concern now. He was sure there would be no more madness among the crew, well, not of that sort. The terrible conditions would afflict those in the belly of that beast in other ways, though. He was still going to file that report on conditions inside the tanks from a medical perspective.

'What are you thinking?'

He looked up at Mrs Gregson, who handed him a tall glass of something that looked like a urine sample. 'What's this?'

'Medicine. For your nerves. Don't ask questions.'

He sipped. It was a whisky with ginger. It made his insides glow. 'Thank you, Nurse,' he said.

'May I?'

He shuffled along and she sat next to him. She placed a hand over his, as hot as an iron, it seemed to him. He hesitated for a moment before he put down his drink. A smile played over her lips and she squeezed.

'What is it?'

'I'm worried about you,' said Mrs Gregson.

The sound of an explosion rolled towards them and Mrs Gregson looked startled.

'It's perfectly all right. Fairley is insisting they try to duplicate the conditions with a few big bangs.' He watched a thin rope of smoke climb upwards, like some fakir's trick. 'Worried how?'

'Have you looked in the mirror?'

He gave a small chuckle. 'Best not, I think. Except for shaving.'

'Are you eating?'

'My appetite seems to have deserted me,' he admitted. 'But. Well . . .' The sight of the young man's blood and brains on his wall – he had moved bedrooms – came back to him every time he sat with a full plate before him. 'It's early days.'

'When did you know it was Cardew?'

'I didn't. Not for certain. You might have noticed this, but I am not a great detective.'

Come now, Watson—

He ignored the imposter.

'There was only ever room for one of those in the team. But I was certain it had to be someone on the technical side, someone who thought the tanks had to be delayed. I had the shoe imprints, but that was not conclusive. The wiping of the exhaust. But, to be frank, it was what the Americans call a hunch. Holmes always hated hunches. But it was the best I had.'

'Will they work? The tanks over there? Will they shorten the war?'

He shrugged. 'They are slow, noisy and unreliable, and an awful lot of expectation has been placed on them. In truth, I don't know. But I am no longer as dismissive as I once was. It might take just one decisive breakthrough to get this war moving again and out of the trenches. That alone would be worth it. Anything that breaks the stalemate will save lives.'

'And what now? Swinton won't let us just waltz out of here. Not with the unveiling of the machines so imminent.'

Watson coughed, and he heard something rattling in his tubes. So did Mrs Gregson, who squeezed his hand until the fit passed. 'No, I suspect not. I thought I'd volunteer for quarantine at this place, Foulness.'

'Please, no.' He was aware of their hands as a single entity now and he had to admit he was enjoying the sensation. He reminded himself not to enjoy it too much. A man of his vintage . . . that way lay humiliation. Yet he found himself envious of her Desmond, of the intimacy they had enjoyed, no matter how fleeting. But the man must have been half his age. Watson extracted his hands from the nest of fingers and put it from his mind.

'I have to go. Churchill told me I was welcome to join Holmes. As his doctor.'

'Now Winston has no further use for you. Typical. Foulness is a dreadful spot, Major. Too damp for a man in your condition. Why on earth would you do that?'

Watson turned and looked at her, fixing his eyes on hers, so she would know he was being absolutely serious. As he spoke, machine guns chattered manically in the distance.

'Because if Sherlock Holmes is there, I am going to get him out.'

And then he began to cough again, a raspy, hacking thing that reddened his face and scoured his throat to rawness, over and over until he feared it might never stop.

'Well,' she said, so softly he didn't catch her words, 'you'll be needing a nurse then.'

The two men who had abducted her came up with a tray of food. She knew it was a pair even before they arrived, because of the footfalls on the stairs. She sat, hands folded in her lap, at the small desk, to the right of the door. There was a knock.

'Come in,' she said, raising her voice just enough to be heard.

The key turned, the door pushed back slowly and the bearded one stepped through. He held nothing in his hands but a pistol, which he kept down at his side. He looked around the room and, satisfied, nodded.

The second man entered, carrying a tray with a pot of coffee and some sandwiches on it.

'Can I have it here, please?' Miss Pillbody asked, indicating the desk.

'If you move away,' said the one with the tray. 'The guv says you're a bit of a live one.'

She stood and took three paces back to the wall. The tray-man nodded and approached quickly, as if he wanted to get this over with. The speed was just right for her purposes. His ankle caught the steel wire she had unravelled from the crude curtain runner and stretched out across the room.

He staggered forward, the tray tipping in front of him. The beard started to laugh, thinking it was mere clumsiness. Miss Pillbody moved in, caught the tray and the coffee pot. She spun the steel disc of the tray towards the gunman, who took it full in the throat, and brought the coffee pot down on the tray-man's head, then flung the remaining contents into the beard's face. Then she was across the room, careful to jump over her own booby trap, and her knee went into his groin. He let out an awful squeal. She was wrestling the gun from his hand when she heard the applause. Miss Pillbody turned to find the postal censor clapping his hands, an admiring grin on his face. 'Oh, very good, very good indeed.'

She let the bearded man slide down the wall with a groan.

'I've done a little checking, Frau Brandt. It seems you are who you say you are.' He looked down at his two dazed men and shook his head in disgust. 'And, you know, I think you'll do very nicely with us. Very nicely indeed.'

'For what?'

'New orders.'

'From?'

'Hersch himself. Oh, don't worry, you can confirm it personally with him.'

'And they are?'

'To forget Thetford and Elveden for now. We suspect security there will be doubled or tripled in the wake of your activities. I am not attaching blame to you, you understand. But we need to get someone inside a place where tongues will be much looser about what is going on.'

'And where is that?'

'Have you heard of an island called Foulness?'

PART FOUR

1–16 SEPTEMBER 1916

THIRTY-SEVEN

The two men sat in comfortable silence on the sea wall, gazing across the mudflats that led out to the North Sea. Each had his pipe. Both were well wrapped against the early morning wind that was knifing down the estuary. This was an illicit meeting, forbidden by military decree, but when two men meet on a beach, each in need of a few minutes' contemplation, no man-made law could stop them taking a few moments to enjoy some silent companionship over a pipe or two.

The sun was up, but the strange fog of the last few days had reduced it to a pale disc, like a giant coin hoisted into the sky. The tide was running out, revealing patches of *Zostera*, out beyond the samphire. Small groups of brent geese were roaming over the shoreline, picking greedily and honking their pleasure at having the harvest all to themselves. Beyond them the sea was a line of glinting silver, slowly being drawn back behind the masking veil of mist. Gulls came and went from this shroud, as if being made to vanish by a magician who could then make them reappear at will. Something about the light and fog seemed to magnify them; to the men on land they appeared as big as rocs. As the sea retreated, it revealed spindly outcrops, the remains of ancient wrecks, some impossibly old, perhaps Vikings who had foundered during their raids, or Romans seeking passage to Londinium, the captain bewildered by a sudden fog.

'Early this year,' said one of the men, the older by a decade and owner of a full white beard. He pointed with the stem of his pipe to make sure his companion understood he was referring to the geese, which had recently arrived from Siberia.

The other nodded and sucked in a mouthful of hot smoke, as

content as he had been for many a day. His mind, so often as foggy as this seascape, was pin-sharp. He did not believe in premonition, but something told him there were events afoot, happening off this island, that would soon impinge on him. But he had no control over whatever was brewing. So he didn't fret about it.

Fifteen minutes passed without another word and the world seemed to shift, as if the moon was not only taking the tide out, but dragging time to a near halt. *Perhaps that was why they had chosen this place for the exiles,* he thought. It seemed to exist beyond the every-day, as if the mirages playing their tricks with sky and water out there were reality, and England, a few scant miles behind and in front of him, was but a dream. It seemed inconceivable that a war was going on, consuming vast amounts of energy and men. If the belligerents could just sit here for a few hours, they might realize the futility of it all. That in a thousand years, when they were all gone and the machinery of war rusted away, the brent geese would still come for the eelgrass and the waders for the worms and molluscs.

For all its closeness to the heart of a great Empire, he realized, this island ran on wild time, the clock of the wilderness unregu-lated by man.

Behind him, on the road some hundreds of yards away, he heard the noise of a vehicle, breaking the spell. There was the squeal of brakes and the sound of rough voices swelling and falling on the breeze. The army had finally woken up. There would be a patrol; recriminations at being so close to an islander.

His pipe had breathed its last anyway. He tapped it out, stood, a rather creaky event these days, and nodded to the older man, whose face above that magnificent crescent of beard was browned and lined by many hours spent at such spots, whatever the weather.

'I'll be here tomorrow,' the islander said. 'Live just there.' He nodded to a building that appeared little more than a wind-beaten shack close to the causeway. 'If you fancy another chat . . .' He held out a hand, every bit as wrinkled as his face. 'Jack Whent.'

The other grasped it, feeling bone and gristle and a lifetime of work on the land, beneath his fingers. 'Sherlock Holmes.'

If the name meant anything to Jack Whent he didn't let on. Just another inclination of the head before the eyes swept back out to the shimmering confluence of sea and sand.

The U-boat had spent the day skulking just below the surface, a few miles out from the area of the Thames Estuary known as the Black Deep. The crew didn't care for inaction. While you were hunting, you had no time to think of the ridiculousness – and peril – of navigating the most crowded seas in the world in a flimsy metal tube. Inaction gave pause for thought. However, the day was dying and the slow hours had finally passed.

'Creep speed,' announced the captain. *Schleichfahrt* would move them forward by running the electric motors at 100 r.p.m. It was agonizingly slow – less than three knots – but it ensured they didn't generate much of a sound signature. 'North-north-west. And take her up to twenty. Very slowly.'

'Aye.'

They were heading for the Black Deep now. It was one area that saw plenty of commercial traffic and so had only been very lightly mined. He just hoped that the visibility had improved since their previous sortie the day before, when a fog bank had obscured the mainland and islands completely.

Schepke instructed an increase in speed to four knots and consulted the Royal Navy charts on the map desk. He issued a change of heading, running south-west. Ahead of him were two passages, the Sunk and the Trinity, both of which led to the Black Deep. Schepke knew that two fresh wrecks had settled close to Trinity. He headed for Sunk, bringing the boat up as he did so, ever alert for the scrape of hull on sand.

'All stop, level the boat,' he said. 'And bring her up to periscope depth.'

The U-boat rose smoothly through the water as the ballast tanks were pumped out.

'Eight metres.'

'And up periscope.'

It was still there, that damned haze, plus it was dusk, which blurred the world even further. Full night was preferable to the transition period from day to darkness; dusk was when the half-light played tricks with the human eye. He spun through 360 degrees. Nothing: no landmark, no fix. No, wait. A light. A buoy? Possibly. Then another light: a brief flash and gone. He couldn't be certain. He had to see in person, not through a salt-encrusted lens.

'Bring her right up. Chief, you'll have the con. Run the diesels. Biel' – he indicated the IWO, the first officer of the watch – 'you come up with me. Bring the signalling lamp.' Schepke grabbed his thick woollen jacket and put it on, wrapping a scarf around his neck.

They felt the swell now as the currents caught the boat, and spread their legs to secure their footing as U-48 rolled. The new saddle tanks made her wallow more than the original model. The IWO scurried up the ladder and undid the hatch, stepping back as a bucketful of water poured in. Then he clanged up the steps into the English night. Schepke followed, Leitz binoculars at the ready. As he climbed up he felt the cold of the evening stab at him. Breathing was like a sprinkle of tacks in his nose.

There was the lonely ring of a bell echoing over the water, audible even above the chuff of the diesels, running to charge the batteries. The unpredictable mist and the encroaching night meant they could see very little beyond the hull. Schepke put the Leitz to his eyes and peered into the blackness, looking for the signal from shore that he had been told was vital to the war effort: he was to decipher the optical Morse code from the island and radio the information back to base and await further instructions. But there was no light to shine his signalling lamp towards. 'See anything, Biel?'

'No, sir.' Then, looking over his shoulder, 'What the hell is that?' Something else was drowning out the diesel rumble.

Schepke turned and saw the looming shape appearing from the bank of fog. It was big and solid and heading straight for them. 'Dive! Dive!' he shouted down through the hatchway. But as the thump of the closing ship's engines, suddenly pushed to full throttle, reached him, he knew in his heart it was too late. The Black Deep was about to claim another wreck and thirty-six bodies.

Colonel Robert Montgomery belted his British Army Warm overcoat tighter around his torso and peered across the reed beds, through the haze that was hanging over the River Roach. Normally he would have seen the smoke stack of the converted pleasure steamer that was heading his way from Burnham-on-Crouch, but the damned fog in the air had blanketed the island for days now. He had grown used to being scoured to his very bones by the North Sea winds, but some freak of autumn weather had banished them. Now the breeze blew from the west, bringing with it the fumes and the filth from the chimneys of the brick works at Great Wakering, busy working day and night for the war effort. Montgomery wasn't sure which was worse: the icy blasts of gales from Siberia or the grit and sulphur from the mainland.

He heard the plaintive horn of the *King of Burnham* – once called the *King of Bohemia*, but rechristened for patriotic reasons – a signal showing the vessel had turned from the Blanklet into the narrow channel through the reed beds that was the River Roach. It would be around a mile away, making its stately progress with the tide.

Montgomery was standing on the quay, the main docking spot on this godforsaken island of Foulness, waiting to greet it and his two new arrivals. He only hoped that, as well as the new detainees, they had plenty of groceries from Luckin Smith and meat from Osborn's, as well as the case of brandy he had asked for.

Montgomery had not expected, when he volunteered his services, to end up with such a posting. He supposed that at fifty-one and with slightly arthritic hands, he couldn't expect a front-line commission. But Foulness – never was a place so well named. It was a large pancake of an island, so flat the navy had insisted the windmill be demolished in case it was used for sightings by enemy submarines. They had wanted the church steeple dismantled too, but the islanders had revolted at that. Now the spire was draped in netting and camouflage, which to his eye made it stand out even more.

He would be glad to see the back of this land, with its wind-stunted trees and endless drainage ditches and sea walls constructed over the decades to stop the land returning to where most of it belonged — under the waves. It was his successful time as assistant governor of Aylesbury that had suggested him for the post of warden of the most unusual prison in wartime Britain. There he had gained a reputation as a tough but fair modernizer, as opposed to the actual governor, who had been there since the time of the murderess Florence Maybrick and other celebrity prisoners. Not that the men and women scattered across Foulness were called prisoners. 'Detainees' was the preferred term. They had undergone no trial, had had no opportunity to plead their cases. Someone, somewhere had invoked DORA in every case, and they were transported to Foulness to be held until such time as they no longer presented a threat to national security.

Which, he was reliably informed, would be within the next six weeks. Which meant he could leave this featureless fortress for ever and with an unblemished record. No prisoner — detainee — had ever been lost. Well, not strictly true, there had been two deaths out in the Black Grounds, the thick muddy gloop that ran along the southern part of the shoreline. There were ways across it, but you had to know what you were doing. The couple, who had by all accounts fallen in love, despite both being married to others, had tried to make it off the island at low tide. Both had become stuck fast and drowned in the incoming tide. They were discovered, arms wrapped around each other, when the sea retreated. Nobody had tried the same trick since.

He heard his men behind him shift as the prow of the *King* nosed out of the mist, giving one more sound of its horn. 'Look lively,' Montgomery shouted, and several members of his Pioneer Corps shuffled forward to catch the rope.

'Ahoy, Colonel Montgomery,' shouted Rippingale, the skipper, from the rail of the craft. The engines were straining now as the reversed propellers churned water to bring her to a halt.

'Captain!' Montgomery yelled back. 'Is all well?'

Even from that distance, he could see the gloom on Rippingale's face. 'I wouldn't be saying that, sir.'

'Why not?'

'I'm afraid we lost one of the prisoners.'

THIRTY-EIGHT

'Watson! There you are,' exclaimed Holmes, as if his old friend had just returned from an afternoon at his club. 'The brent geese are back, feeding on the eelgrass. Just the males and the young females, for the moment. The mothers and gosling will follow. We've lost most of the swallows, I am afraid. The peregrines are increasing, though, day by day. Did you know sparrowhawks change colour as they age, from yellow to orange to, in old age, deep red? And look, look, at this. The spotted, pied and red-breasted flycatchers. Four warblers – sedge, wood, garden and willow, the water rail—'

'Holmes,' Watson said wearily. 'Might I sit down first before you name every bird on the island?'

It had taken Watson a few weeks to shake the malaise that had come over him following the death of Cardew. That, and his immersion in icy water, had taken its toll. If not for Mrs Gregson's solicitous care, he might not have made it at all.

'Of course, of course, my dear chap. Put your case down. I have some brandy somewhere. Are you all right? You look quite done in.'

Watson slumped into the armchair that Holmes had cleared of papers and looked around the room. Holmes had been given one of the signal cottages, built during Napoleonic times as part of a chain that ran around the south coast of England. It was a neat, white, wooden single-storey structure, now bereft of its flagpoles. Holmes had covered the walls of the small living area with charts of his bird-spotting activities. Interspersed were a number of rather good watercolours of some of them, including a fine kingfisher.

Watson then turned his attention to his former colleague and what he saw pained him. His weight had, indeed, ballooned, and the smoking jacket he was wearing was stretched taut. His moon-like face was pale, the eyes underlined by thick brackets. Gone was the rake-thin parcel of nervous energy that Solomon had once captured so well. The man was ill, anyone could see that. So why hadn't he, a doctor, noticed? Because he had neglected to visit. A criminal negligence by a man meant to be his friend.

You had your own problems, Watson: the waking nightmares, the terrible sounds and smells haunting you, remember?

'I'm sorry, Holmes, what was that?'

Holmes looked puzzled. 'I didn't say anything, Watson.'

So the phantom voice had always been just that – a figment of his imagination, mere ventriloquism. It wasn't the voice of reason but psychological comfort. Ah, but it had served him well. He had the real thing before him now and a duty to restore the great man to what he had been, or as close as he could manage.

'Do you have a kettle, Holmes?'

'A kettle?' Holmes looked at the wall charts, thinking Watson meant a bird. 'A kettle?'

'For tea.'

'Ah, yes. A kettle. Of course.'

'Can you put it on?'

Holmes slipped through to the tiny kitchen and Watson heard him clanking about with the range, opening and closing the cast-iron doors. 'It's gone out,' he shouted. 'Won't be long.'

Watson sighed. It would be some time before he could get enough hot water to feed Holmes the beef tea he had brought. 'You have taken up painting?'

Holmes's head appeared in the doorway. 'No, no. Miss Deane did those. Rather good, aren't they?'

'Miss Deane?'

'Another ornithologist. Met her out in the samphire beds.'

'Local?'

'Good lord, no. We aren't allowed to mix with them, not really. Only about thirty left on the island, anyway, just to keep the farms going. No, like me, she has been cast here into this pit.' He lowered his voice, pointing to the sheets of paper pinned to the walls. 'I know it looks strange, Watson, but my birds keep me from the abyss.'

The phrase sent a chill through Watson's tired body. He looked at his old friend, could see the concern in his eyes. The lapses in memory, the confusion, must have plagued him these past months. He no doubt thought he was tipping over the edge into dementia.

'My old friend, with luck there is no abyss waiting,' Watson said, and closed his eyes.

He was exhausted after being robustly questioned for more than an hour by Montgomery, furious that Mrs Gregson – whom Montgomery knew from her previous stay – had apparently disappeared overboard into the mist. It was a blemish on his record and he wanted someone to blame, and Watson and the skipper were the two firm favourites. Montgomery had sent out search parties to look for signs of her. Watson, though, knew she wouldn't be found.

'It awaits us all,' said Holmes gloomily.

'Pernicious anaemia,' said Watson.

'What's that?'

'You are not mad, Holmes,' said Watson, forcing himself to open his eyes. 'I believe you have pernicious anaemia. At least, as soon as we get you to a hospital we can check my diagnosis.'

The weight gain, the pale skin, the confusion. It all pointed to an aggressive form of pernicious anaemia.

Holmes frowned. 'Isn't that fatal?'

'In some cases, yes. But a study by Swedish scientists has concluded its effects can be reversed by diet.'

'Diet? How so?'

Watson reached down and opened his case. From it he fetched two jars of beef tea and a large, string-tied parcel from Osborn's. Already he could smell the contents, the rich iron tang of animal blood. 'Holmes, I do hope you still like a lightly cooked liver.'

For a delicious few minutes, Watson felt time had rolled back twenty, thirty years. With two chairs pulled up in front of the cast-iron stove that heated the cottage, a mug of beef tea each, a pipe for Holmes and a cigarette for Watson, he felt the same comforting glow of familiarity that marked his times at Baker Street. Holmes, too, seemed content, his eyes hooded, a smile on his lips, as if in a relaxed reverie.

'Tell me what you have been up to, Watson,' he said softly. 'Spare me no detail. What brings you here?'

'You do. I intend to give you some of my blood.'

A chuckle. 'That's very generous of you, Watson.'

'I am a universal donor. It won't work miracles, but it will keep you from that abyss you mentioned.'

Holmes's brow furrowed. 'To be honest, it is more like a black fog. You have the necessary equipment with you? For this . . . transfusion?'

'I do,' Watson said, slightly taken aback. 'You aren't going to try to dissuade me?'

'As with the fairer sex, medical matters are your department, Watson.'

The major thought back on all the arguments over Holmes's use of cocaine and the days without food when he was in thrall to a particularly vexing case, and how he rarely won any of those arguments with the detective. This was a changed man, at least for the moment. Well, he was going to seize on this new compliance.

'It is just the start, Holmes,' Watson warned. 'I have to get you off the island and to hospital for tests.'

'I hear that Montgomery has only ever let one person off the island. A woman. That took the influence of Mr Winston Churchill himself.'

'I know, Holmes. That was Mrs Gregson, and Winston had his own reasons for removing her.'

'Can we get word to him?'

'Churchill is busy with the Gallipoli inquiry. He won't give us the time of day. So, as we speak, Mrs Gregson is organizing our escape.'

Holme's eyes were wide open now. 'Your Mrs Gregson? From the de Griffon case?

'Yes, she is the woman Churchill took off Foulness, for his own reasons, of course. It is a rather long story, Holmes.'

'The best always are.' Holmes leaned forward and, with some grunting, threw another log into the stove. 'And we aren't going anywhere for the moment, are we?'

And so, for the next hour, Watson explained to Holmes all that had happened, from being intercepted by Coyle and Gibson, through the unmasking of Cardew, to Mrs Gregson finding a spot to hide on the *King of Burnham*, while Watson insisted to the captain that she had jumped overboard rather than return to Foulness. He hoped, by now, she had managed to slip ashore onto the mainland. Several times Holmes asked him to repeat a section, as if he couldn't quite grasp it.

'And so you volunteered to come here to be with me, rather than stay at Elveden?' he asked finally.

'Yes, once I recovered. I think they were glad to see the back of me.'

'And these "tanks", where are they now?'

'On the way to France.'

'In great numbers?'

'I fear not. Not as many as young Cardew would have liked.'

Holmes said nothing, simply leaned back and closed his eyes.

'And these toxic fumes,' he said eventually. 'You didn't discover how this engineer could have created them?'

'No. Swinton insisted on keeping the coded formula as evidence for any eventual inquiry. He has had no luck breaking it.'

'Pity. That you didn't bring it, I mean.'

Holmes, of course, might well have had more success with the cipher. 'Quite so. Of course I should have made a copy. But I suspected something to do with ergot of rye—'

'Ergot? It would take someone with a sophisticated knowledge of chemistry to extract the active substance. Did he have this?'

'I have no idea, Holmes.' Another familiar feeling crept over Watson, not one of contentment, but of dread. He could feel himself being drawn along by Holmes to a place where the ground shifted under his feet and all certainty fled. He tried not to snap, but his exhaustion got the better of him. 'What is it, Holmes?'

'Levass. Not too common a name.'

'It might be in France.'

Holmes pointed the stem of his pipe at Watson. 'You know of *La Bouche?* The Buzzard? A famous French pirate. Real name Levassuer. Believed to be part of the inspiration for the novel *Treasure Island*. His family disowned him, especially after he was hanged for piracy, and shortened their name to Levass.'

'Fascinating,' said Watson, with more sarcasm than he intended.

'It is. Because a certain Jean-Paul Levass became one of early nine-teenth century Paris's top perfumers. His son expanded the business into pharmaceuticals and chemicals. And his grandson still runs the business, I believe.'

'Colonel Levass?' Watson felt a hollowness in his stomach. Hadn't the Frenchman mentioned something about his family being priva-teers? 'It wasn't Cardew after all?'

'I didn't say that. But perhaps the two shared a common aim — to delay the deployment of this super weapon until it had a better chance of success. I must say I have some sympathy with that thought. Although not with their methods, of course.'

'Of course.' Watson wasn't really concentrating on the words, he was replaying his memories. The bodies in the ice house. It would have taken more than one man to move them from their coffins. He had thought that at the time. Yet when Cardew was unmasked, he had shut that inconvenient fact away. 'So you think——'

'All I am saying is that there was one man among those you have described with the expertise to create this diabolical psychoto-mimetic. Levass is famous for his expeditions to central and South America searching for new drugs. You must have read his account of his time in the jungle? *La recherche de Dieu l'usine*?'

Watson had neither read nor heard of anything of the kind. 'He mentioned Mexico, I seem to recall,' he said vaguely, 'Over the first dinner.'

'Then perhaps he came across the *semillas de la Virgen*.'

Watson's Spanish was rudimentary, but he managed the transla-tion. 'The Seeds of the Virgin Mary?'

'A powerful hallucinogen used in religious ceremonies. It comes from a species of morning glory. And you mentioned fear of light? Datura is also widely cultivated in Mexico. A hallucinogen that causes dementia and, as a side effect, intense photophobia.'

'Well, Hitchcock certainly had that.'

'It also causes rapid post-mortem necrosis of the extremities. Which can be mistaken, if I remember correctly, for gangrene.' Holmes raised one eyebrow.

'Really?' said Watson glumly, feeling like a chided schoolboy.

'But any worldly toxicologist worth his salt would know what it was. After all, it is mentioned in Mathieu Orfila's *Toxicologie générale*. As a Spaniard, Orfila had travelled extensively in Central America. I would contend that it was why the bodies were disposed of. The methodology and the necrosis would have pointed to Mexico or similar.'

'Wouldn't the killer know that from the start? That it would leave telltale signs?'

'Ah. You are forgetting von Hohenheim's famous maxim.'

Watson, on the back foot, racked his brains. '*Sola dosis facit venenum?*'

'Excellent, Watson, excellent. The dose makes the poison or "*Alle Dinge sind Gift und nichts ist ohne Gift; allein die Dosis macht, dass ein Ding kein Gift ist.*"'

The man was showing off now. Holmes, Watson appreciated, was enjoying himself. This was one thing he had clearly lacked for these past weeks and months: an audience. It was improving him by the second.

'"All things are poison and nothing is without poison",' translated Watson slowly. 'Only the dose makes a poison.'

'Yes. It is possible, Watson, that we have an accidental murderer on our hands. He may have meant merely to incapacitate the tank crew but miscalculated the toxic effects of the vapour. It is devilishly difficult to control the dose of a gas.'

Despite feeling both annoyed and humiliated, Watson couldn't help but look at his friend with renewed admiration: even Holmes's clouded mind was superior to his own. 'So I was only half right,' he said glumly. 'It was Cardew and Levass, working in tandem.'

'Ah, but without me you only had half of the usual resources,' said Holmes with a wan smile. 'And you did well. A fifty per cent solution is better than none.' There was a twinkle in his eye. 'Although as you know, I used to favour a seven per—'

'That's as maybe,' said Watson quickly, not wishing to be reminded of Holmes's cocaine preferences, 'but we need to warn the Heavy Branch about Levass. They have a singularly evil cuckoo in their nest.'

'Indeed they do. But there is no communication with the mainland, Watson. No telephones. Only a radio, controlled by Montgomery.'

Watson clenched his fists in determination. 'Failing word arriving from Mrs Gregson that she has succeeded with Churchill, we have to get to that radio, Holmes.'

'What? All in good time, old chap, all in good time. Shall we eat?'

Watson sensed Holmes had left him again, his intellect smothered by an animal instinct. He was hungry.

At that moment there came a loud hammering on the door. 'Ah, that will be Miss Deane,' said Holmes with a grin. 'Let her in, would you?'

THIRTY-NINE

Colonel Swinton looked across the bleak landscape of the field outside Yvranch in Picardy. Once it had been productive farmland. Now it was pitted into troughs and churned into peaks, so that it almost looked an ocean, frozen in mid-swell. The creatures responsible for this desecration were lined up in a row, their engines grumbling into life. Next to Swinton was Lieutenant-Colonel John Brough, the man designated to take these machines into battle. He was in his forties, a veteran of the Africa campaign against the Germans, which had left him gaunt and sallow. Doctors suspected malaria, but Brough was the sort of soldier who got on with the job rather than worry about such a mildly inconvenient illness.

'Haig will be coming tomorrow,' said Swinton, as they trudged towards the tanks. Crews in overalls were busy fussing over the machines, making sure the tracks were properly tensioned and the exhausts weren't blocked – there were several suicidal species of birds that liked to build nests in them. 'Best make sure the men smarten up.'

'It's dirty work, Swinton. You know that. You can't run tanks and look like the Household Cavalry. When is he coming?'

'The nine o'clock show.'

'Bloody circus.'

Swinton wasn't sure he had heard correctly. 'I beg your pardon?'

Brough stopped walking. He was a head taller than Swinton and he leaned in and towered over him. 'I said, it's like a bloody circus. Show times nine and two. Crush that boulder. Knock over that tree. And they come and smirk. Like we are clowns performing for them. We need to be training for war, not performing for the top brass on a whim.'

Swinton nodded. 'You have made your thoughts on that very clear. You and Clark.' This was Major Philip Clark, Brough's second in command of the Heavy Branch – now known also as the

'Fighting Side' – who also despaired of the 'pony show', as he called it, of displaying the tanks to the generals and colonels who had to be persuaded that the machines could fight alongside men.

'Any news on when we will be used?' Brough asked.

Swinton did indeed have news, but he ducked the question. 'Within a few weeks.'

'And we have how many more cars coming over?' The tanks were shipped, in great secrecy, from their proving grounds at Elveden and the new base at Bovington by train and boat, all the while shrouded in canvas and classified as 'Water Tanks: Mobile'.

Swinton cleared his throat and gave the most optimistic number of machines he could expect. 'Thirty.'

'So, we'll have no more than a hundred completed tanks. Well, reckon on a third of them breaking down. That means we can field sixty or seventy. I'm not sure that's really enough to show what they can do. But I, for one, can't wait to get stuck in.'

A tank lurched forward from the line, moving into the clearing and giving a little pirouette as the driver tested the running gear. The rear steering wheels were up, Swinton had noticed. Drivers disliked them and found them unnecessary, because the best operators could do incredible things with just the tracks and gearboxes.

'You won't be getting stuck in, John,' said Swinton softly, his voice full of regret.

'What do you mean?'

'I'm sorry to be the one to break the news. Haig is going to tell you tomorrow. I thought I'd better prepare you, just in case you do or say anything foolish. You are being transferred.'

'What? Where?' The yellowness of the skin had been replaced by a creeping redness.

Swinton sighed. 'Not certain. Blighty, so I hear.'

Brough spun around so that Swinton could not see the expression on his face. After a few moments' composing himself, he turned back. 'And Philip gets my post? Well, he's a good man—'

Swinton shook his head. 'No, Clark is tarred with the same brush.

You should have just got on with your circus shows, John. The Brass don't like being told when they can and can't see their new toy.'

'Yes, that's the trouble, isn't it?' Brough said with suppressed fury. 'They think it is a toy. Wind it up and watch it run. So who will take charge?'

'We think Elles, eventually.'

'Sound choice,' admitted Brough. Elles was an engineer by trade and had been involved in placing the orders for the early tanks. 'He'll understand the challenges.'

'Unfortunately he is working on the strategy for the next big push. Haig won't let him go just yet.'

'Then whom?

'Frogatt-Lewis.'

'Flogger Lewis?' he said. The man was well known as a martinet, the worst kind of stick-in-the-mud army officer, who thought striking miners should be shot and hanged from the lift gear, and suffragettes sent to nunneries for life. His view of military discipline was even more unyielding. Clearly, someone wanted to smarten up the corps. Haig, he suspected, always a stickler for appearances. He would, no doubt, rather the tanks gleamed than worked. 'Apart from the madness of changing commanders just before a first engagement, what on earth does Flogger know about tanks?'

'Not much at the moment, but we've been given someone to babysit him who knows more than enough. Good chap.'

'Who is it?'

'The French tankman. Claude Levass.'

FORTY

Miss Deane turned out to be a rather charming and efficient woman, somewhere in her late twenties or early thirties, with fair hair drawn tightly into a bun; a rather shiny, well-scrubbed face; and dark, unbecoming clothes, a severity offset by a warm smile. She insisted on cooking dinner for all three of them and listened intently as Watson explained his diagnosis of Holmes. Holmes seemed less engaged than previously during the course of the meal, often shooting off on strange tangents. Miss Deane, however, was both indulgent and adept at steering the conversation back from its various precipices. She was also very modest about her painting skills, which Watson thought somewhat better than the 'mere dabbler' status she insisted upon.

After dinner, Watson performed the transfusion, taking some of his own blood, citrating it and injecting it slowly into Holmes. It took more than an hour in all. Afterwards, Holmes fell asleep in the armchair and Miss Deane said she would show Watson to his lodgings. He had been assigned the Dutch House, a small cottage once occupied by a dyke engineer from Rotterdam who had helped redesign the sea walls in the previous century. She took an oil lamp from Holmes's window ledge to help guide their way. She promised she would put his old friend to bed before she retired to her own place in the Workhouse, where all single women were housed.

'Thank you,' said Watson, 'for looking after him.'

'It's my pleasure. I enjoy his company. And you think you can cure him?'

Watson shook his head. 'I can't promise that. But I might be able to manage the condition.'

As they picked their way down the lane by the lamp's jaundiced light, Watson asked her how the pair had met.

'He found me painting on the beach one evening – well, I was out in the samphire – and he talked about the landscape of the island. How strange it is, how long it has been occupied. He pointed out the Broomway—'

'The what?'

'The Broomway. It's a path, out at sea on the sands.'

'Tidal?'

'Yes.'

'And it goes where?'

'Careful here,' she said. 'The road is very uneven. Look, your cottage is down there.'

He peered into the gloom and could see the silhouette of a thatched roof against the almost starless night sky.

'Only ten minutes to curfew,' came a voice from the darkness.

Watson could see the figure, a Home Service soldier, he assumed, sitting in a makeshift guard post at the end of the garden. 'Don't worry . . . Corporal Deal, isn't it?'

She has better eyes than me, Watson thought.

'Yes, miss.'

'I'm just dropping off Major Watson here and I'll be back along presently. Is that all right?'

'Make it snappy, miss. The old man isn't too happy at the moment. What with being a woman down, as it were.'

'Really?'

'Best ask your gentleman friend about that.' He also sounded none too pleased.

As they walked on, Watson explained in more detail about the need to get Holmes off the island for medical tests. He didn't mention the tanks or Levass, who had made it more urgent than ever that they escape. Someone had to get to France and warn them what they had in their midst. Even if that someone, heaven forbid, was Major John Watson.

'How long have you been here?' he asked.

'A few weeks.' She waited for the inevitable follow-up question. 'Do you wish to know why I was exiled?'

'Not if you don't want to tell me.'

'I have a brother . . . oh, it doesn't matter. I was careless, that's all. I fell foul of the GPO and the police came knocking one morning. I am, apparently, a risk to national security and the defence of the realm.'

'Well, in a strange way I am pleased you are here. For Holmes's sake. I feared I would find him rather the worse for wear.'

301

'Oh, I doubt I have much to do with that. I get the feeling he doesn't really care for women. The fact that I like observing and painting birds is far more important than my sex.'

'I am not sure I can argue with that.'

'Although the fact I can make a half-decent steak-and-kidney pie seems to have caught his attention, too.'

They both laughed at this. Holmes had always enjoyed his food. And, inadvertently, she had been feeding him the kind of sustenance that might help with his anaemia.

'This is you, here. Do you want me to come in and light the fire?'

'Miss Deane, do you cosset *all* the men on the island?'

She giggled. 'Only the famous ones, Dr Watson. Good night.'

'Good night. Oh, Miss Deane, one more thing. This Broomway. What else did Holmes say about it?'

'That it goes to the mainland. And that it is the most lethal road in Britain.'

The combination of darkness and fog had been extremely kind to Miss Gregson. Nevertheless, she waited in her hiding place – a storage cupboard near the bow on the starboard side of the *King of Burnham* – until she was sure the boat had been secured for the night.

As she crept along the deck, peering through the darkness for any sailors still on board, she reflected on how well their ruse had worked. Dr Watson was only meant to have yelled, 'Woman overboard!' and thrown a life belt into the creek. But his frenzied removal of his jacket and his clamber onto the rail, apparently moments away from making a dive into the murky waters below, had convinced captain and crew that Mrs Gregson must really have leaped rather than return to Foulness. They had hauled him down, struggling. Watson's subsequent wailing and gnashing of teeth had, to her ears, verged on the melodramatic, but it seemed to do the trick. No onboard search was made, and even at Foulness her escape bid was accepted at face value. All she had had to do was wait until the *King* returned to Burnham and bide her time.

There was a chain across the top of the gangway to the pier and she was careful not to rattle it as she unclipped it and stepped through, closing it behind her. There were voices onboard, the sound of glasses clinking and laughter, but as far as she could tell any crew was sensibly inside, rather than out in the fog.

She hurried onto dry land and headed for the quayside exit, which would take her out to the bottom of the high street. Up there, then along Station Road, and she should be in time to catch one of the last trains to Liverpool Street. And then—

'Miss?'

The man loomed out of the mist and cut off her path, planting himself in front of the ornate gates that stood between her and freedom. He was in his fifties, clean shaven and in the uniform of one of the Home Service Defence units. The guard was holding an old Martini-Henry rifle of greater vintage than he. 'What are you doing here, miss? It's all out of bounds when the gates are locked.'

'Mrs,' she corrected, pointing back at the *King of Burnham*. 'I just took my boy, Sam, his supper.'

'You didn't come through here.'

'I did.'

The man narrowed his eyes. 'I never sees you.' He looked her up and down.

At least she wasn't in any sort of prison uniform, but the coat she had been allowed was two sizes two large and the collar moth-eaten. She didn't look her most elegant. She could almost be . . .

Mrs Gregson coarsened her voice. 'All right, you have me. How much?' She thrust out one hip.

'How much for what?'

'Your share of what I just earned with the tars, m'lovey.' She stepped closer and the guard retreated a little. 'I made some money with the sailors tonight. I suppose it's only fair to share it about a little. Half a crown do the trick?' She began to rummage in her bag.

'Oi, none of that. I'd be no better than you if I take a whore's money. I should take you over to the harbour master—'

'And explain how you let me in to do some business while you turned a blind eye. All for half a crown?'

'I never—'

Mrs Gregson hit him with her fullest, devilish smile. 'Look, you are flustered already. I don't think he'll believe you, will he?' She stepped in even closer and stroked his face.

'Stop that!' He raised his rifle, threatening to push her back. 'I ain't even got half a crown on me.'

'You have now,' she grinned. 'Best check your pockets.'

'You little minx. Get out of here,' he snarled. 'And don't let me see you round here again, you tart.'

He fumbled a set of keys from his webbing and unlocked a small access gate, all but pushing her through.

'Night,' Mrs Gregson said, cheerily, before letting the mist swallow her. The thought of him searching every pocket of his tunic and trousers for a phantom half-crown put a skip in her step as she headed up the hill.

At the station she bought a second-class ticket to Liverpool Street and waited the seven minutes for the Great Eastern Railway service, which arrived trailing its own mini-smog, the sparks from the fire flitting off into the night like escaped glow-flies.

It was only after she had taken a seat in an empty compartment that she allowed herself a sigh of relief. Done. She had with her Desmond's letters, describing all that was wrong with Gallipoli, letters she felt Churchill would pay handsomely to keep from the public.

There came the blast of a stationmaster's whistle from down the platform and the train gave a jerk.

And all she would be asking Churchill for was the release and rehabilitation of Holmes and Watson. It was as good as in the bag.

With a rising sequence of chuffing, the loco took up the strain and the service began to move forward. Mrs Gregson closed her eyes, weariness threatening to snatch her away, when the train slowed and then halted. They had barely left the platform. Then there came the creak of wood and the squeal of metal couplings and they were on the move once more. But backwards this time. They were reversing into the station, where, as she lowered the window and peered out into the soup of smoke and fog, she could just make out the distinctive silhouettes of the waiting policemen.

The cottage smelled of damp and mildew, but once he had lit the lamps and got the fire going, Watson began to feel better-disposed towards it. Besides, he expected he wouldn't be there for long. Not if Mrs Gregson had anything to do with it. Her plan was simple: to recruit Vernon Kell of MI5 to her cause, using the letter Watson had given her, and to buttonhole Churchill until he gave way on getting Holmes off the island. Not an easy task, but Mrs Gregson had realized she had one weapon for her campaign: Desmond's letters to her, blaming the High Command for the strategic and tactical failures of Gallipoli and singling out Churchill in particular. They might just make the difference between censure and exoneration for the former Sea Lord. It was blackmail, a crime Holmes held to be particularly abhorrent, but in this case it was all for the greater good. And, Watson thought with some satisfaction, it was turning Churchill's own weapon of choice against him.

Watson went upstairs to inspect the bed, stripped off the sheets and located new ones in the cupboard. Slightly musty, but they'd do. Back down in the kitchen he found supplies of Camp coffee, tea, mouse-nibbled biscuits and Bovril. He would need more than that. There was, according to Miss Deane, a small shop next to the George and Dragon. Sadly, the pub had been shut down for the duration.

He had just set about making coffee – it would have to be black – when he heard the rap at the door. He half expected Holmes, but it was Montgomery. Without asking if he could come in, the colonel shouldered his way past Watson, sweeping off his cap as he did so. He was tall enough to have to stoop in the low-ceilinged cottage.

'Making yourself at home, Major?' Montgomery asked.

'As best I can. Coffee?'

'No, thank you. Don't let me stop you.'

Watson made a cup of the glutinous brown liquid of, mostly, chicory essence. He liked his hot, although there were those who swore it was best served cold.

'What can I do for you, Colonel?' he asked, after the first sip.

'Just checking you have everything you need.'

'Not quite.'

'Oh?'

'Mr Sherlock Holmes is not a well man. I suspect pernicious anaemia.'

Montgomery tutted his sympathy.

'I would be grateful if you could arrange a transfer to a hospital.'

'I have seen him striding about. He doesn't seem ill to me.'

'Mr Holmes has a most unusual constitution. But he is not a young man. We can slow down the effects with diet and blood transfusions. But I would like confirmation—'

'I can't let anyone off the island.'

'Even on compassionate grounds?'

'Security. You have heard of the Black Deep?'

'No.'

'Fifteen miles from here is a remarkably deep sea trench. Deep for this part of the world, at least. Once a day, specially built boats leave from East London and make their way out here. When the tide is exactly right, they open the valves in their holds and London's sewage comes out as a thick sludge, turning the sea black.'

'I can't see exactly—'

'Two days ago, one of the boats had a mechanical failure. It dropped anchor while the crew carried out emergency repairs. It is dangerous out there. Many a ship has broken its back on the sands. When it was ready to go, at dusk, it saw the most remarkable thing. A German submarine, U-48, surfaced in front of it. The British captain had the presence of mind to order full steam ahead and it rammed the boat before it could fully submerse. We don't know if it sank it, but, judging by the damage to the sludge boat, significant contact was made. We

306

believe that U-boat was sent to find out what is going on on this island. There are channels in the sands that a small boat can navigate. I suspect the U-boat was trying to land a raiding party. To be honest, nobody will be kept here indefinitely, I can say no more than that. Have some patience, Major. But while we suspect imminent enemy action, my orders are to keep this place locked down tight. No exceptions.'

'It seems rather draconian.'

'I'm sorry.'

'Do you even know the great secret that this island is meant to protect?' asked Watson.

'No. I don't need to and I don't wish to. It would be one more burden.'

'But what if I told you there is a man who wants to make sure the whole project founders at birth?' Watson swept his arm in a semi-circle. 'A man who wants all this subterfuge to be a waste of time?'

'Go on.'

'He is a Frenchman, yet far from an ally. You could stop him simply by sending a telegram.'

'To whom?'

'Churchill. Just say "Arrest Levass". He'll understand.'

Montgomery frowned at this. 'On what grounds?'

'On Mr Sherlock Holmes's say-so.'

'And that will be enough to put this Levass behind bars, will it? The word of a man that you yourself have admitted is not entirely well? It will secure an arrest?'

Watson could see that it might not. An accusation without hard evidence, a piece of conjecture by Holmes from a second-hand account. 'Perhaps not. But it is worth a try. It will certainly pique his interest.'

'I'll think on it.' In actual fact he had already made up his mind. Montgomery didn't want Churchill back, sniffing around. The man made trouble wherever he went. And at that moment, he knew, Churchill was fighting for his political life and reputation, giving evidence to the Dardanelles Commission, trying to prove Gallipoli was not his fault alone. And the idea that one man – a

Frenchman at that – could derail the British war effort was ridiculous. Montgomery suspected this Levass business was simply a ploy by Watson to get his friend off the island.

'That's all I ask.' Watson didn't press the point. He still had the ace of Mrs Gregson up his sleeve.

'But I warn you, I am not inclined to grant you any wishes after today's shenanigans.'

'What do you mean?'

'I know you have already tried to make me look a fool.'

Watson said nothing, fearing what was to come.

Montgomery finally let a smirk play over his face. This is what he had come for: a gloat. 'You see, we picked up your friend at the station, on board a train for London. Seems she made a guard at the docks suspicious and he reported her. Mrs Gregson is in the Workhouse under lock and key. And that's where she'll stay until charged under the Defence of the Realm Act.'

FORTY-ONE

Holmes and Watson discussed their options over some excellent devilled kidneys prepared for Holmes by Miss Deane. She confirmed that Mrs Gregson was being held, under guard, in a room on the top floor of the building known as the Workhouse.

'What's to be done?' she asked.

Holmes pointed a forkful of kidneys in Watson's direction. 'Watson, your thoughts?'

'We have to get off the island, get you to a hospital.'

'Don't you worry about me,' said Holmes. 'You have bigger fish to fry. You must warn the Heavy Branch about Levass.'

'But surely it is too late for this man to stop the machines being deployed,' said Miss Deane.

'What if he sabotaged the landships enough that all sides think they are a failure, until he is ready to show the world his own, Gallic version?' replied Watson.

'But the French are our allies,' said Miss Deane as she poured them all tea. 'Surely he wouldn't—'

'Miss Deane, men – mostly men – often perpetrate the most terrible crimes on the flimsiest of pretexts,' said Watson. 'Levass believes he is right, and everyone else is wrong, and there is no telling what he might do.'

She sipped her tea. 'I suppose so.'

'I intend to see Montgomery this morning,' said Holmes, 'to try to convince him of the peril of the situation.'

'I wish you luck,' said Watson glumly. 'A most intractable chap, he seems to me.'

'I fear you are right, Watson. But the alternatives?'

There was a moment of contemplation, and the taking of more kidneys, around the table.

'Holmes,' said Watson eventually, 'there is another option. This Broomway that Miss Deane mentioned. Perhaps I could—'

'Ha! Do not even consider it, Watson. You know what locals call it? The Doomway. The most lethal road in the entire United Kingdom. I, for one, cannot think of another that has claimed more lives.'

'How so?'

'It is called the Broomway because the route was marked with bundles of twigs. Like sweeping brooms. Hazel, I believe. Well, most of those have long gone, replaced by wooden posts. Posts that are not easy to spot in a mist or a sea fog. And there are precious few landmarks to steer by. The glutinous Black Grounds that fringe the pathways have claimed even those familiar with the route: postmen, farmers, priests, horses and sheep. Why do you think they put so few patrols on the south side of the island? Nobody in their right mind would attempt to navigate it, especially not with this mist. And the tide. You have seen how flat the land is? The tide races in faster than even a young man can run. You would be food for crabs.'

'You make it sound worse than no man's land,' said Watson with a shudder.

'Apart from the fact there are no shells or snipers trying to do you harm, I believe it is, Watson. No, you would surely founder and die.'

'I see.'

'I, on the other hand, with my admirable sense of direction, can get you across.'

'Holmes—' he began.

'Miss Deane, fetch me a piece of paper, if you will. And a writing implement. I believe there are some in the drawer in the kitchen. These kidneys, might I say, are the finest I have had in many a year.'

'Did you hear about the submarine?' Watson asked while she was gone.

'No. Pray tell.'

Watson repeated what Montgomery had told him, about the sludge cruiser.

'What was a German submarine doing here?' asked Miss Deane, returning with the requested items.

'Up to no good, I assume,' said Holmes, dismissing the tale from his mind. 'Now, let me show you.' He took the stub of a pencil and a sheet of lined paper. 'The Poet Laureate, Robert Bridges, once wrote a monograph on the forgotten and ancient roads of Great Britain. Rather better than his later poetry, in my opinion. He traced the Broomway back to Roman times, I believe.'

Holmes drew a rough shape on the paper. 'This is Foulness. Approximately. And here, to the south-west, the mainland at Wakering Stairs. Now the path actually runs offshore from the island, some hundreds of yards. The trick is to find the solid paths, the causeways, which feed into it, like the tributaries of a stream. They come from here, here and here. These are in some ways the most lethal part of the journey, because people try to cut corners to get to the Broomway. But that is a fatal mistake – these are the tracks where people die when they stray. Go either side of that

310

solid ground, which you can usually detect by the remains of ancient wattles, wooden boards, laid over the mud, and you are in the Black Grounds. And you won't be coming out of that sinking mud.' He gave a theatrical twirl of his hand, a gesture retrieved from long ago, and lowered his voice. 'Not alive, Watson, not alive.'

'But you couldn't do that journey. It looks far too dangerous, Holmes. And you are not a well man.'

Holmes dismissed this with another wave of his fingers. 'I shall have you to lean on, Watson. And Mrs Gregson.'

'Mrs Gregson is under lock and key,' Watson reminded him. 'And I don't see why we need involve her in such a treacherous undertaking.'

'Oh, I can get her out of that room, gentlemen,' said Miss Deane. 'There is an attic that runs the entire length of the building. It wouldn't be hard to break through a patch of ceiling if someone could devise a distraction.'

'A nice fire, perhaps,' said Holmes with a wry smile, recalling, thought Watson, the ruse he had used in the story they called 'A Scandal in Bohemia'.

'Well, there is a kitchen,' Miss Deane said.

'Once unleashed, fire is difficult to control,' said Watson. 'We don't want casualties.'

'True. We must plan this carefully,' said Holmes, his eyes blazing with excitement. Watson was inclined to take his pulse to make sure he wasn't over-doing it, but he knew he mustn't fuss. The sense of purpose burning within Holmes was both gratifying and infectious.

'And when we get to Wakering Stairs?' Watson asked. 'What then?'

'We find a motor car,' said Holmes, as if Watson was being particularly dim. 'And drive it to London. A few words with Kell at MI5 will put us in the clear, I'd wager. And then we send word to the tankmen in France that they have a viper in their midst.'

'Steal a car?'

'Borrow one, Watson, borrow one.'

'But I have no idea how to *borrow* a car,' admitted Watson.

'No, but from what you tell me, your Mrs Gregson does. That is why she is vital to our plans. We need to spring her from her trap. A prison breakout, if you please.'

They both turned to look at Miss Deane.

She flushed slightly under their gaze, then took a deep breath. 'Very well, I will help break her out, gentlemen. But on one condition.'

'What is that?' asked Holmes.

'I can come with you.'

'In which case,' announced Holmes, 'we will be needing four stout walking sticks, even stouter shoes, a brick or stone and a large spool of thread.'

FORTY-TWO

The stutter and then roar of the six tank engines cut through the silence of the dark woods as the four-man starter handles turned. Already the attuned ear could hear that one of them was running rough, its rhythm erratic and the exhaust note strained. *So five will move forward from Yellow Dump*, thought Levass, *the great invention edging ever closer to the front line, albeit it in painfully small increments.*

He walked through to the edge of the once verdant, now ruined and splintered forest, where the machines sat, their drivers waiting for the Daimler engines to reach their operating temperature. The wilier mechanics would have lit a small paraffin fire under the gearbox or diff to help thin the oil and speed things along. They were all learning the little tricks and foibles of the machines. Another six months . . .

'They need to be in place by dawn. Shouldn't they get a move on?'

It was Colonel Cecil Frogatt-Lewis, newly installed commander of the Heavy Branch and a man who had little sympathy for the waywardness of complex mechanical devices. He and Levass were touring each of the muster sites of the tanks that had so far made it to the forward areas. The attrition rate had been appalling. And now, as the sick engine missed several beats and fell silent, it appeared they had lost another. Levass saw figures moving through the gloom, torches in hand, heading for the stricken 'bus'. The mechanics would try to get to the bottom of the fault, but experience told him that repairs inevitably took several hours. And he had been adamant to Frogatt-Lewis that the tanks should not move in daylight hours and must remain camouflaged when stationary. He hadn't come this far to let a clever German spotter realize what kind of new weapon they had.

'What's that smell?' asked Frogatt-Lewis, sniffing the air like a bloodhound. 'Flowers?'

'Gas shells,' said Levass. 'It leaves a sickly sweet smell even after it has lost its potency.'

'I see,' Frogatt-Lewis replied, instinctively changing to shallow breathing.

'Captain!' Levass yelled.

The commander of the small group of tanks, a weary-looking lad in his early twenties, with a grease-stained face, trotted out of the darkness and saluted. 'Sir?'

Levass recognized the man from Elveden. He had driven *Genevieve*. 'Halford, isn't it?'

'Captain Henry Halford, yes, sir.' He had been promoted from lieutenant on arrival in France. The new rank still sounded strange to his ears.

'You only have an hour until dawn,' said Frogatt-Lewis, returning the salute. 'You need to move up.'

'One of the tanks—' Halford began.

'Leave it,' said Levass.

'Leave it?'

'No time. Where are you moving to?'

'Memetz Wood.'

'That's four miles away,' said Levass.

313

'So I believe,' said Halford, with just a hint of insolence.

'And you average less than three miles an hour.'

The young man nodded. 'If we push them any harder, the fuel consumption is enormous. It's like pouring petrol into a hole in the ground. We stack the steering gear with spare tins, but as it is . . . it's a worry.'

'We are aware of that.' Levass also knew that U-boats had sunk several tankers full of fuel destined for the greedy tanks. 'Take any supplies off the crippled tank and distribute between the remaining five. We'll get you all the fuel you need up to Memetz.'

'Sir. Thank you.'

'And one other thing,' asked Levass. 'You've been to the front?'

'Not yet, sir.'

'I have, recently, for the first time. I thought I was prepared. I had heard all the stories. In half a mile the landscape will change. You think this wood has had shell damage? Wait until you see what artillery has done up ahead. There will be craters like you have never experienced. And there will be bodies. You'll have to go over them. Are you prepared for that? You won't know if they were friend or foe, men or horses. Death has mixed up their bones like it was making a soup.'

Halford blanched a little. 'We'll do our job, sir.'

They heard the low rumble of guns, even above the tank engines, and Levass caught a glow on the horizon a false dawn of shellfire.

'Good luck, Captain. What's your tank called?'

'*G for Glory*, sir.'

Frogatt-Lewis grunted. 'Well named. It will be a glorious dawn.'

Levass couldn't resist a snort.

'And, son . . .' added Frogatt-Lewis.

'Sir?'

'Wipe some of that muck off your face, will you? And that helmet is all very well when you are engaging the enemy, but I expect a cap when outside the tank.'

This, Levass knew, was nonsense. Any time you drove a tank

there was a danger of skull hitting bulkhead. Swapping caps every time one de-tanked was just impractical. 'Understood?'

'Sir.'

'Off you go.' When the lad had left, Frogatt-Lewis turned to Levass. 'Did you have to put the wind up him quite so much?'

Levass said nothing. The 'wind' was but a gentle blowing on the skin compared to the hurricane of horror that awaited him. He remembered that troublesome Major Watson being shocked that none of them at Thetford had seen real trenches, genuine no man's land. He understood now. No second-hand description could prepare you for the sight and smell of the real thing.

Within fifteen minutes the first of the tanks, led out by a warrant officer holding a lantern aloft, jerked out of line and began its tortuous progress towards the shelter of the next wood. The black-and-white Cubist-style paintwork really did disrupt the vision, and, as intended, it was hard to make out where the machine ended and night began. However, the square, silver cans of extra fuel glowed dully at the rear of the machine, remaining faintly visible as the tank turned into the textureless blackness of the sunken road that led north-west, to battle. They needed to be painted in a dull finish.

'Driblets,' muttered Levass.

'I beg your pardon.'

'It's what Haig calls it. Use the tanks in driblets.' He couldn't keep the scorn from his voice. 'In three months we will have eight hundred French caterpillars. In four months there will be a thousand of those. A thousand Mark Ones. Imagine!'

'Careful, Levass. I may not know much about tanks, but I know Haig, Rawlinson and Butler. Brough went because he disparaged the plan of a few tanks and plenty of infantry. Isn't that so?'

Levass sighed, aware that his views could get him sent back to Paris. And that wouldn't do. 'Just thinking out loud. I feel sorry for the men. Untried machines, untrained crew, not enough tanks, not enough time, not enough petrol, not enough range. And Haig expects a miracle.'

'The Prince of Wales told me he doesn't expect much from them,' name-dropped Frogatt-Lewis. The prince had indeed been to see the tanks perform, crushing gun carts and knocking over trees in the tame-bear shows they put on at Yvranch.

'The Prince of Wales is not running this show,' said Levass. Which was just as well as the young man didn't know the meaning of the words 'secrecy' and 'discretion' — the very night of the demonstration he was sending his father drawings and specifications through the regular post. Luckily they had been intercepted and carried across by Top Secret pouch. Anybody else would have ended up on Foulness.

'And that promise you just made. How are you going to guarantee them fuel, Levass?' Frogatt-Lewis asked. 'I've been badgering GHQ about it these past few days. We have to take our place in the priorities, apparently.'

'We'll use French fuel. There are dumps at Maricourt and Albert. I can press on the *Bureau Central Interallié* to organize French drivers and lorries to bring it forward. If you wish, I can organize its distribution to each company.'

'Really?'

Levass nodded. 'The battle here was to give us French some breathing space. The least we can do is give you some petrol.'

They waited until the last of the dazzle-painted tanks had pulled away and turned into the lane that would take them to Memetz Wood, where they would be parked among whatever was left of the trees and re-netted, leaving only the forlorn crippled machine, abandoned like the little boy in *The Pied Piper of Hamelin*. They could hear the ringing of tools on machinery as the mechanics got to work stripping down the uncooperative engine.

'Where next?' asked Frogatt-Lewis.

'La Briqueterie near Trones Wood,' said Levass. 'C Company are bombing up.' This was one of the best of the Heavy Branch groups, men who had been trained from the very beginning at Thetford. 'Then to Rawlinson at Heilly, to explain our tactics.' Sir Henry

Rawlinson was the Fourth Army commander and Heilly was his new forward HQ. He was demanding to know how the tanks would be used on the day and what they meant for his infantry. It was a good question.

'Very well, let's see how they are getting along at Trones Wood. Should get to Heilly in time for breakfast, eh? One thing Rawlinson doesn't skimp on.'

'Unlike his tanks.'

'Levass! Enough. Driblets or not, we do whatever GHQ wants. It'll be their heads, not ours.'

Levass smiled as Frogatt-Smith headed for the staff car. Now he had control of the fuel supply, he could do with it as he wished. Heads might roll, but the tank might just live to fight another day. In its thousands.

FORTY-THREE

Dawn was just a vague blush of a promise when the four pilgrims set off for the mainland. Getting Mrs Gregson out through the ceiling had been far easier than anticipated, once Miss Deane had left a half-bottle of Holmes's brandy where the guard couldn't help but notice it. His snores kept most of the women in the dormitories of the Workhouse awake all night, although by the early hours they had softened to a mere low rumble, with the occasional rising snuffle.

Mrs Gregson and Miss Deane slipped out into the night, crossing the fields and the plank bridges over the ditches. With the moon playing peek-a-boo with the clouds and only the stars to guide them, it was a treacherous crossing. At one point Mrs Gregson's foot slipped into a slimy ribbon of water. She felt it slop over the top of her Glastonburys.

'Oh, damn!'

'Ssshhhh,' said Miss Deane, at which point her sole, too, slipped on the rotten board and she went ankle-deep into mud.

'Oh, double damn!'

'Shhusshh,' hissed Mrs Gregson, and the pair spent a few minutes snorting away suppressed giggles.

Having freed themselves and waited to ensure their noisy submersion had not attracted anybody, they squelched on.

'I have some spare stockings you can have,' said Miss Deane. 'The boot will dry out soon enough.'

'I think I've picked up a fish. Something is moving in there.'

'Don't be ridiculous,' said Miss Deane.

'No?'

'No. It's probably a frog.'

Mrs Gregson gave a small squeal and clamped her hand over mouth. The pair hurried on. When they reached Holmes's signal cottage, an uncharacteristically cross Watson was waiting. 'We could probably have hired the band of the Coldstream Guards to come across with you. It would have been less noisy.'

This only made them laugh more.

Watson closed the door behind them and, while they stripped off wet shoes and stockings, he fed them brandy.

'I'm going to get some dry socks from my room,' said Miss Deane. 'I'll be as quiet as a mouse.'

'Don't be long,' warned Watson.

When he returned from seeing Miss Deane out of the front door, Mrs Gregson hugged Watson tightly, which caused Holmes some amusement.

'I'm sorry I got caught,' she said. 'I should have been more careful.'

'Nonsense,' said Watson. 'We knew it was a risky undertaking.'

'Keep your voices down,' said Holmes with a hiss. 'Have you quite finished with him?'

Mrs Gregson nodded. 'For now.' She held out her hand. 'Mr Holmes, so very pleased to meet you properly at last. Georgina Gregson.'

He took her hand. 'The pleasure is mine. Watson speaks highly of you.' There was a twinkle in his eye. '*Very* highly. Ah' – he released his grip on her fingers – 'I see you are naturally or instinctively left handed,' he said. 'But you use the right for most things, except . . . the violin?'

'The cello,' she admitted. 'But I haven't played in years. Not since before the war. How . . .?'

Holmes glanced at Watson with a little smirk of triumph. 'The thumb musculature, Watson. It stays very distinctive in one who has played since they were a child. Now, drink this.' Holmes offered her a tumbler of brandy. 'Miss Deane has made up some food for us. I have it in my knapsack. Do you really need that bag?'

Mrs Gregson was busy examining Holmes's wall of bird sightings. 'What?' She looked down at the tapestry carpetbag she had brought. 'Sorry, yes. I can manage. Who did this painting?'

'Miss Deane. Really, Mrs Gregson, we aren't here to admire the art,' snapped Holmes impatiently. 'Here.'

Mrs Gregson took the brandy from him and drank it down, suppressing a cough as it seared its path to her stomach. 'How long is this crossing?'

'From where we join it,' Holmes replied, 'it is just over three miles. In bright daylight, perhaps an hour or an hour and a half, shore to shore. But we have to cross the island to the starting causeway first. And we can't use the roads. And it will not be fully light for the first part of the journey. Three hours at least.'

Watson looked at his wristwatch. That meant it would be around breakfast time before they reached the mainland. Probably about the time that the balloon would go up about their disappearance. There was one thing that might work in their favour. Montgomery might think nobody would be crazed enough to try to navigate the Broomway. 'It will be tight,' was all he said.

Mrs Gregson suppressed a yawn. 'Then we had better get started.'

A movement behind her indicated Miss Deane had returned. She handed a pair of thick woollen socks to Mrs Gregson. 'Best I could manage.'

'They'll do. Nice geese,' she said.

'Thank you.'

'I don't mean to be rude,' Mrs Gregson said, as she rolled on the socks, 'but you are coming because . . .?'

'Because it was the price of your freedom, Mrs Gregson. And because without Mr Sherlock Holmes, Foulness will become even more unbearable.'

There was a tartness to the reply, but Holmes ignored it. They were all on edge. 'We each need to select a walking stick,' he said, pointing at the ones he had collected. 'Ladies first, I believe.'

The initial leg of the journey took them out across the cluster of buildings that made up the hamlet of Churchend, heading east, threading through the darkened cottages, away from where they knew there were sentry posts along the main spinal road that ran – with various diversions – north to south across the island. A low moon threw a slanting light, forming a latticework of shadows across their path. It made focusing difficult and within the first five minutes each member of the group had stumbled at least once. It wasn't difficult to imagine the owl that hooted at them was laughing at their clumsy progress.

'I didn't want to do this,' said Holmes, rummaging in the old knapsack he had found in a cupboard in the cottage. 'But needs must.' From it, he produced a torch. He had wrapped it in some flimsy material ripped from the cottage curtains to diffuse the beam. It gave enough light to show them the dark snakes of the drainage ditches and the planks for traversing them, but still progress was slow. Watson noticed that the streak of paleness in the east was strengthening to something more definite.

Something darted from a hedgerow, a fox, and Holmes stopped suddenly, causing the others to collide into him. He hushed them quiet.

A door in one of the nearby cottages opened, throwing a blade of light across a garden, and they heard a grumbling voice. The four fugitives paused mid-stride, not daring to breath. The man relieved himself loudly against the wall, too lazy or befuddled by sleep to even make the outhouse. The stream slowed to a trickle and the man grunted and went back inside.

From far away a foghorn sounded, like the long lowing of a cow. There might be mist or fog out at sea, perhaps even a haar, the dense North Sea fogs that rolled across the waters and land, like a nomadic, earth-bound cloud. Or like the fog bank that had rolled over Dartmoor that fatal night, many years ago now; a distance that gave Watson vertigo to think of it, of all the time that had passed. The thought of the hound, the fog, the terrible fate of Stapleton in the mire made Watson's throat go dry. *You won't be coming out of that sinking mud. Not alive, Watson. Not alive.* Perhaps this was a foolish undertaking after all.

'We must pick up the pace,' urged Watson.

'And risk turning an ankle?' Holmes replied. 'Caution is needed on this stretch. We head for the farms at Rugwood, then out to Asplins Head.'

'We can cut across here,' said Miss Deane. 'See? Over the fields. It will save us some time. I used it when carrying my painting equipment.'

'Very well,' said Holmes. 'Lead on, Miss Deane.'

Watson heard Mrs Gregson mutter something under her breath, but it was lost on the wind.

Levass watched the sun come up over a shattered landscape. The village of Heilly no longer existed, apart from mounds of dusty rubble and domestic debris, such as twisted bedspreads and splintered cooking ranges. Every road and lane had abandoned vehicles or smashed carts thrown carelessly to one side. The air was thick with the aroma of breakfasts and the fumes from the cooking fires of thousands of men, hidden from view in trenches or farmhouses, scattered over hundreds of square miles. It was likely at least some of the smoke and smell was coming from German stoves, a few miles away. But in twenty-four hours' time there would be no bacon, sausages, corned beef, Maconochie or cigarettes for breakfast. It would be a tot of rum and over the bags, as the opposing armies got back to the business of killing each other.

Both sides knew something was coming. The British guns, practising their range, had continued right through breakfast, but had fallen silent at last, as if to allow Levass a chance to enjoy a cigarette and some tentative tweets of birdsong in peace.

He was leaning on the staff car, trying to empty his mind of the madness of the meeting he had just attended. Sixteen tanks to XIV Corps, to be split into twos and threes. Eighteen to XV Corps. Eight to III Corps. Six to fight with the Canadians, in two groups of three. The rest to be held in reserve. What rest? That total was more tanks than they had working. Each tank commander would be given map references and timetables and be expected to rendezvous with his infantry support at his 'point of deployment'. A creeping barrage would signal the start of the push, slower, more thorough than the disastrous one of 1 July, which had failed to cut the German wire. The idea was that any German coils that remained untouched on that September morning would be crushed into the mud by the tanks.

'And what will the barrage do to the ground the tanks are meant to cross?' Levass had asked, much to Frogatt-Lewis's displeasure.

The gruff General 'Tommy' Tankerton had turned his eyes on him, his comically huge moustaches quivering. 'The tank will be deployed. We were promised machines that could cross any ground. Well, we shall see.'

Levass had pointed out a memo to GHQ from Swinton, stating that there would be little prospect of a second chance of surprise.

Tankerton had dismissed him. So they were committed. All the effort that he and Cardew had made to slow down the progress had been dashed on the thick skulls of ambitious and pig-headed generals. Levass regretted the men who had died in the tank at Elveden. Their death was accidental – he had intended a temporary insanity – although, for a while, he thought that perhaps it would do the trick anyway and the tank project would be delayed until spring

'17. But no, Churchill had managed to infiltrate Major Watson into their ranks. And, thanks to the doctor and his busy-body investigation – and Cardew's guilty conscience, which had led him to taking his own life – the tanks had come to France anyway.

Now he had twenty-four hours to make sure the great machine was not wasted in these driblets.

He finished his Elegantes, threw the stub into a pile of rain-rotted webbing, and went in search of a mimeograph machine.

By the time they reached the causeway at Asplins Head, Holmes had visibly deteriorated. His breathing had been laboured for half an hour and air was now whistling in his tubes. His pace length, that great Holmesian stride, had reduced to a shuffle, and as they reached the shoreline he leaned on one of the low walls that ran down the crude harbour where in peacetime the Thames barges had docked to collect the island's harvest.

'Holmes, I think we have to reconsider.'

'Give me a moment. Please.'

Watson stepped away to allow him some room. The two women were looking out to sea. The waning moon showed a black causeway made of crushed brick and stone, which led down to an expanse of mud, silvered with rivulets of what looked like mercury in the dawn light. There were shapes, picking their way across the flats: the first of the sandpipers and oystercatchers were out, the proverbial early birds, scuffling for breakfast.

'How is he?' asked Mrs Gregson.

'I fear the burst of energy he has shown since my arrival might have depleted his reserves. The efficacious effect of the blood transfusion has faded.'

'So we stay?' asked Miss Deane, with some alarm. 'On the island?'

Watson looked back at his friend and then across to the sea. The causeway was clear enough, with its twin row of poles perhaps six feet apart. But some yards offshore, where the causeway gave way to mud and sand, it was bathed in a silver, impenetrable light. It was hard to know how dense this fog actually was, thanks to the tricks of the new sun. But it didn't look promising.

Holmes beckoned Watson over. 'I know what you are thinking. And you may be right. I might survive the journey . . .' – he paused for breath – '. . . but I will slow you down.'

Watson indicated the strange luminescence hovering offshore. 'I am not certain any of us can make that crossing.'

'Nonsense. Look in my knapsack. The ball of twine.'

Watson helped him shrug off the burden. He opened it and found the rough string.

'You tie this to a good-sized rock. Pick one from the foreshore. When you are at a pole and you can't see which direction to go, you leave the rock and pay out the string.'

'Like Theseus in the labyrinth?'

'Precisely,' Holmes wheezed. 'But there are no Minotaurs out there. Just the Black Grounds. So, if you can't find the next pole, you retrace your steps back to the rock and try again. The poles are thirty yards apart at most, so you will know quite quickly if you have gone astray.'

'Holmes, I can't leave you. There must be another way.'

'You don't have too long, what with the tides. You must warn Churchill about Levass.'

'You are more important than all that.' But was he? Was one man more important than the lives of all those young tankmen, even if that man was Sherlock Holmes?

'My friend—'

'I am not your friend, Holmes.'

The detective looked at him askance. 'No?'

'Not at this precise moment. I am your physician, and I should have realized that. We shall go back and use other skills to enact the result we desire.' Although Watson wasn't entirely sure what those skills might be, he didn't want to risk watching Holmes expire out on the inhospitable fringes of the North Sea. 'And attempt another transfusion, perhaps.'

Somewhere on the island a dog barked at the coming dawn, a plaintive, lonely sound. It was followed by the uneasy bleat of sheep. The whole of Foulness would be waking soon. Holmes saw the concern in Watson's face. 'If you go, I can throw them off the scent. Tell them you stole a boat, headed for Burnham—'

'No. I am not leaving you, Holmes,' Watson said firmly. 'If anything happened—'

'Mrs Gregson and I can go,' said Miss Deane.

The two men turned to look at the women. Watson shook his head. 'The same objections apply. Two women out there? On those sands? I would never forgive myself.'

'Dear Watson,' said Holmes with an unexpected warmth, 'it is so good to see you again. Have I said that?'

'Not in so many words, Holmes.'

'How remiss of me. Well, it is true. I heard you say you thought the blood you so generously gave me was responsible for my renewed vigour. My dear chap, it was the *sight* of you. And the thought of one more adventure out there . . .' He pointed with his staff. 'But it is not to be. Is it?'

'Not this time, Holmes. Not this time.'

'Then perhaps it is time to bully our Colonel Montgomery.'

'I thought you had tried to persuade him,' said Watson.

That old, familiar arch of a quizzical eyebrow once more. 'Not to the very best of my ability,' Holmes admitted. He took a deep breath. 'I fear I held back somewhat. A little part of me wanted to try the Broomway, you see. But perhaps you are right. Another pint of your blood, some beef tea and I am sure we can crack this fellow another day.'

'Are you strong enough to start heading back?' Watson asked Holmes.

'You aren't starting anywhere,' said Miss Deane. 'Give me the twine.'

The tone of her voice made Watson turn towards her. The sight of the compact pistol in Miss Deane's hand suggested they had fallen into a terrible trap.

*

It must, thought Levass, *have been like this in the days and hours before the great battles of centuries ago.* Crécy, Poitiers, Agincourt. When the French fought the English for control of their own country. The weapons might have changed, but perhaps the tank was just a new version of the longbow or the flintlock: something that altered the balance of power for a short time, until some sort of equilibrium was re-established in firepower.

He was at Memetz Wood, where four of the original six tanks were now safely bivouacked among the twisted trees under a gloomy low sky that deterred all but the bravest aviators. The men were striding around and clambering over their metal charges, recalibrating tracks and packing and repacking the ammunition, the food, the water and the fuel they would need for the dash – if that was the right word – across no man's land.

Levass found Halford, the young captain in charge of the unit, sitting on a metal ammunition box next to *G for Glory*, smoking a cigarette. His face was even grimier than the last time they had met, while his hair, freed from the confines of the leather, stuck up at wild angles like the grass of a badly neglected lawn. He stood up as he saw Levass approach.

'Sir.'

'At ease, Halford. This is unofficial. Had breakfast?'

'Sir.'

'How was the crossing this morning?'

'Eventful. We have two broken ribs, a broken nose. Two cases of what I hope is temporary deafness and a bad outbreak of nerves.'

'Will he be all right? The nervous chap?'

'I gave him a bit of a talking-to, some rum, told him to get some sleep.'

'Driver?'

'Gunner.'

Levass nodded. The tankmen could find another gunner if need be; drivers were all but irreplaceable. 'And you lost a tank, I see.'

'HMLS *G for Gorgon*. Threw a track and rolled into a ditch. She's still there. Salvageable, I would imagine, if one can pull her out. I've sent a message back to HQ. And now we six are four. And *G for Ginny* has a gearbox that's whining like a stuck pig.'

Levass handed him a sheaf of papers, all produced on a Banda machine. 'Excuse my handwriting.'

Halford blinked some dust from his eyes and focused. It was headed 'Notes For Tank Commanders'. He read some of it out loud.

'Tell all your men everything you know or think you know. Take all the petrol cans you can carry. Fill up at every available opportunity . . . rush in among the enemy, firing every available gun . . . under no circumstances must your tank fall into enemy hands. Call off an engagement if this is at all likely or possible. If in danger of capture, pour petrol on all papers and orders and set fire to them . . . loose off all your ammunition . . . destroy the machine completely . . . pigeons are not to be used except in an emergency.'

'That all seems straightforward enough, sir,' Halford said.

Levass detected some doubt in his voice. 'But?'

'You make it sound as if abandoning the tank has more priority than engaging the enemy. Sir, I'm sure you didn't mean that—'

'Of course not.'

'Just that . . . they'll have to carry me out of that thing feet first once we start rolling. Someone has to show what it can do. Yes, they are noisy and temperamental, filthy and stinking, but, by God, you should see the face of infantrymen when we pass. And it's on their side. Imagine how the Hun will feel. I know we'll do well. Given the chance.'

That was one thing they could agree on. 'Given the chance.' Levass doubted they would be given that chance. 'I am sure you will,' he said, and clapped Halford on the shoulder, feeling a flush of warmth for the brave young man.

'If you can give a copy of the memo to each commander . . .'

'Of course.'

'I'll leave the fighting talk to you. But, do stress the part about capture. We don't want the Germans getting their hands on one of these.'

'No. Although I hear rumours they already have their own.'

Levass shook his head. 'Rumours. War runs on rumours the way those tanks run on petrol.'

'Talking of which, you said something about fresh supplies of fuel. We've burned through over fifty per cent of ours.'

'New stocks will be along later in the day. If I were you, I'd fill up with the new stuff when you get the opportunity.'

'I will, sir. Thank you. And for taking the trouble to do this.' He held up the mimeographs.

'It's no trouble,' said Levass. 'After all, we all want the same thing.'

'To get out of this alive, you mean?' asked Halford, with a cheeky grin.

'To get out alive on the winning side,' corrected Levass.

'Cup of tea? Or coffee, sir?'

'No, I'm going to all the deployment points, to hand out this document.'

'Beg pardon, sir. But I have a question.'

'Which is?'

Halford cleared his throat. 'You're French, sir. Why aren't any of our chaps making the effort to do this sort of thing? We hardly see anyone, except they come to countermand the previous day's orders.'

Levass shrugged. 'You'll have to ask them that. I couldn't say.'

'Very diplomatic. Well, on behalf of the lads, thank you. We could do with a lot more like you, Colonel Levass.'

FORTY-FOUR

It feels like some sort of Canute-like suicide, thought Watson. Every brain cell told him he shouldn't walk out into that mist. Not with a fading old man on his arm. Or at gunpoint.

But the quartet trudged down the causeway, Mrs Gregson in the lead, holding a hefty stone and the twine, followed by Watson and Holmes. Miss Deane brought up the rear, her gun pointed at their backs. As Holmes had explained in cool, reasoned tones, shooting them on the island would raise an alarm. The crack of even a small pistol would run and run over that flat land, with nothing to impede its progress. And plenty of soldiers, stirring in their bivouacs, would recognize it for what it was. So Holmes had bought them time. But to what end?

The dark path of crushed rock and stones disappeared beneath the remarkably firm sand, like a stream plunging underground. The sand was decorated with the curled tubes of casts left by the animals that lived beneath. Here and there Watson could see fragments of age-blackened wood, almost fossilized, which must be the remnants of the ancient wattles.

Holmes, leaning heavily on his stick, pointed at a pile of cockleshells scattered around the base of one of the marker posts. He bent down and picked up a handful. 'Look, Watson. *Glycymeris glycymeris*. The dog-cockle. Believed to be inedible, but there is evidence hereabouts that the Saxons had a recipe for softening them—'

'For God's sake, keep walking,' said Miss Deane, recognizing the delaying tactic.

Holmes tossed the shells over his shoulder. 'One should never miss the opportunity to observe,' he said loftily.

They carried on towards the shifting silvery cloud, diffusing any light that the new dawn was offering. The going was tough, Watson soon appreciated. The sand was hard enough, but heavily ridged, so the chance of turning an ankle was a very real one. The uneven surface was as dangerous as cobblestones. Furthermore, Holmes, his face worryingly pale but for two spots burning bright, high on his cheeks, was leaning heavily on Watson. This ungainly four-legged creature stumbled after Miss Deane, who had moved ahead and was walking crab-like, best to keep an eye on both Mrs Gregson at the vanguard and the two old men.

They reached the point where the Broomway ran parallel to the shore, which meant they had to turn west – to their right. Miss Deane, pistol still held at her waist, bunched them together.

'I reckon the sound of any shot will get swallowed by this muck,' she said to Watson and Holmes. 'So you two keep up, or . . .' She let that fade. 'Off you go,' she said to Mrs Gregson. 'We'll be right behind.'

'You know,' whispered Holmes, 'that once we are far enough out, she won't hesitate to shoot us?'

Watson nodded. The younger man trapped inside his ageing body had already urged him to take decisive action: to leap on Miss Deane or – heaven forfend – strike her down. But he detected something steely in this woman, a viciousness that suggested she would not hesitate to put a hole in him if she was under threat. And the way she moved, alert, agile, cat-like, suggested she had physical resources that might outmatch his own, while the chances of his being able to disentangle himself from a wheezing Holmes quickly enough to act were slim. His only hope, he realized, lay with Mrs Gregson.

'I can't see the next post,' said Mrs Gregson, stopping in the midst of a shallow pool.

The party peered ahead into a shifting wall of luminescence, tinged with streaks of yellow. Fumes from the brickworks, no doubt.

'Take the end of the twine,' snapped Miss Deane, 'and keep walking until you find it. Tug when you have. And, please, don't do anything stupid.'

They watched as Mrs Gregson tramped forward in the direction they hoped was correct. If she couldn't find a post, she would simply retrace her steps. But Watson wondered for a moment if she would simply carry on, abandoning them out there. It would be the sensible move.

Watson glanced over his shoulder. The mist was closing behind them. The floating lines and whorls projected onto his retina – the 'floaters' of ageing eyes – made it hard to focus, and he imagined figures just behind the curtain of fog, ghosts of all those who had been swallowed by this most treacherous of pathways.

They heard a shout and the string twitched.

'Come on, you two,' said Miss Deane.

They found Mrs Gregson next to a stumpy black stake, older than the ones they had passed so far.

'You're certain that is it?' Miss Deane asked.

'You can just make out the next one. There.'

All Watson could discern were more of the slowly moving cellular shapes that inhabited the vitreous humour in his eyes. He blinked, but the focus wouldn't come.

'Lead on.'

But Mrs Gregson put her hands on her hips. 'I am right about you being a German agent, aren't I? It's Miss Pillbody, isn't it? From the village?'

'It doesn't matter who I am.'

'The woman who killed Coyle. And Ross. You are the German spy, aren't you?'

Holmes muttered something under his breath. All Watson caught was the note of despair.

'How did you know?' Miss Deane asked, not bothering to deny it.

'The paintings. I knew I had seen that style before. But I couldn't place it. Didn't think it was important. But I'd seen one in your cottage, hadn't I?'

So *this* was the woman who had tortured and murdered his poor friend, Coyle. Watson felt something rising in his throat and must have tensed.

'Careful,' whispered Holmes, sensing impetuousness.

'Lead on,' Miss Deane repeated.

'What do you hope to achieve by this?' Mrs Gregson demanded.

Watson looked down at his feet. Had the water deepened? Was the tide moving? It was probably no time to be lingering.

'She knows about the tanks,' said Holmes. 'That's what she has achieved.' His voice was full of remorse, for he had told her about the landships and allowed her to be in the room while Watson filled in the details. 'We should continue.'

Mrs Gregson nodded and began the slow trudge to the next pole. As Holmes managed to spread his load more evenly between his stick and his friend, they fell into a ragged rhythm, making better progress into the shifting mist, the smell of the brickworks growing stronger, the occasional gull appearing from the veil to mock, or perhaps warn them, with their screeches.

After some time, Mrs Gregson stopped and pointed to a new kind of pole, one that resembled the sunken mast of a great galleon. Miniature versions of it could just be glimpsed, running left to right.

'Is this it?' Mrs Gregson asked.

It took Holmes and Watson a few moments to catch up and another thirty seconds before Holmes could speak. 'Havengore Creek,' he gasped.

'What?' Miss Deane demanded.

'It's a channel. For boats. Not for us. We go on.' He pointed ahead. 'That way.'

'So we are not too far?'

'Another thirty minutes, perhaps a little longer.'

They waited while Miss Deane performed some mental calculation. 'Keep moving.'

Apparently Holmes did not have half an hour in him. He began sliding further down Watson's body, slumping noticeably with each step. A gap opened up between them and the two women. Miss Deane looked back and beckoned them on with the gun. At that point, Holmes fell to his knees, a wretched noise coming from his throat.

Their captor took a step back in their direction. 'Get up.'

Watson crouched and loosened Holmes's collar. His friend nodded his thanks.

'He cannot.'

'He has to.'

'Let me lie for a moment,' croaked Holmes, laying himself across the riffles of sand. His clothes began to wick up moisture.

'Holmes, you must not—'

'Langdale Pike,' he muttered.

'What?' Langdale Pike was the pseudonym of one of the most notorious gossip columnists in London.

'If she is intent on London . . .' — he gulped for air — 'Pike can stop her.'

Watson feared his mind had gone. *How can a scurrilous pedlar of half-truths stop this woman?* 'Very well, Holmes. But we aren't finished yet.'

It was a faint smile that flicked over his lips. 'I've said it before, Watson. You are the one fixed point in a changing age.'

'Up!' Miss Deane was standing over them now. 'Or I'll shoot you where you lie.'

She raised the pistol. Holmes closed his eyes in acceptance. Watson cursed the tired knees that made a leap at her impossible.

There came a gurgling sound from beneath her feet and, before their eyes, the channels in the Broomway began to fill. The tide was coming in.

Miss Deane took a step backwards, her shoes splashing on the water rushing to cover the temporary road once more. She laughed at their predicament. 'Good luck, gentlemen,' she said. 'I doubt we will meet again.'

'Major—' Mrs Gregson began, but Miss Deane poked her in the ribs and the pair trudged on. They were soon lost to the fog.

'She has calculated you will not leave my side,' said Holmes.

'She is right. We still have a chance of out-pacing this.'

'You might. Just. You can save yourself.'

Watson gripped Holmes's shoulder. 'Nonsense. We'll try together.'

'It would be sensible for you to go,' insisted Holmes. 'Logic dictates it.'

Watson was in no mood to be dictated to by friend or logic. 'And leave fifty per cent of myself behind?'

More water lapped at his shoes. He remembered the phrase about the speed of the incoming tide. *Faster than even a young man can run.*

And certainly quicker than two old crocks could make it to safety.

Watson put his hands under Holmes's armpits. 'We'll go together, Holmes. Or die trying.'

FORTY-FIVE

Mrs Gregson took a step back towards the two men struggling upright on the sand. Miss Deane pointed the gun at her. 'Stop. We go on.'

'No.'

The pistol was raised to eye level. 'I need you, Mrs Gregson, but not so badly I'll risk all while you help two men who are already dead. Walk on. Or you can stay here with them.'

'I'm not sure you'd shoot me in cold blood.'

'No? Think back, Mrs Gregson. Think back to that cottage in Suffolk. I do believe you saw something of my handiwork there. In fact, my grenade almost got you, so Major Watson told Holmes. You think being a woman will somehow protect you? Besides, I don't have to kill you.' She inclined her head to the swirling dark waters, now greedily reclaiming the land. 'All I have to do is shoot you in the knee. Then the tide will have three of you.'

'You are murdering two of the finest men who ever lived. They don't deserve this. Holmes and Watson—'

'Move or die, Mrs Gregson. Move or die.'

Reluctantly, Mrs Gregson backed away from the terrible sight, turning as soon as the mist reduced the figures to floundering wraiths.

'He won't leave him, you know. Watson won't leave Holmes, even if he could make it. They'll die together out there.'

Miss Deane nodded. 'I'm counting on it.'

By the time they splashed their way up the causeway at Wakering Steps the water had reached thigh level. Both women had fallen silent, lost in the effort of fighting the force of water trying to topple them over or push them off course. Mrs Gregson's bag had been an early victim of the surge. Now she only had the clothes she stood up in. As if mere dresses were important. At least Desmond's letter was safely tucked in her bodice. Mrs Gregson tried not to think about Watson or Holmes, hundreds of yards behind them, unable to go forward or back, the sea rapidly claiming them.

She scrabbled up the rough ramp to the sea wall, aware that she was losing sensation in her feet. Mrs Gregson wasn't going to show weakness in front of this appalling woman, though, not after what she had done to her friends.

Miss Deane, too, was puffing and panting, but she still had a grim and gritty determination about her. She had, for example, managed to hold on to her own bag, although it was soaked through. 'No time to rest.'

'What do you intend to do now?'

'Find a car. Head to London.'

'And betray your country?'

'There is nothing to betray. I'm not British. I only sound that way. I'm as German as the Kaiser.'

'German?' Mrs Gregson had assumed she was a turncoat Englishwoman, not an actual enemy national. 'That explains why you don't care about them.' She pointed out to the causeway. Was the mist lifting? She could see three sets of poles now. A moment ago it had been one. 'Two fine Englishmen—'

'I don't care, no,' Miss Deane replied, puzzled that anyone should expect her to be concerned about a pair of old, useless men. 'I know this country has some sentimental attachment to them, but the world has moved on.'

Mrs Gregson's teeth began to chatter. 'We should get warm. We'll catch our deaths.'

Miss Deane found that amusing. 'Come on.'

Mrs Gregson began to walk up the path. The wind had changed direction, she realized, and the strange fog was dissipating. She could see fields, and some buildings appearing ahead.

'Where's the town?' asked Miss Deane, alarmed by all the countryside coming into view.

'I have no idea,' said Mrs Gregson.

'There must be one near. Come along, step it up.'

Miss Deane hustled her along the uneven pathway, which showed signs of the passage of vehicles, but there were no actual cars or lorries to be seen.

'They'll have noticed our absence by now,' said Mrs Gregson.

'Shut up.'

'I would imagine they will start putting up roadblocks.'

The thump from the butt of the gun made Mrs Gregson cry out, but Miss Deane had enough presence of mind to jump back after she had delivered it. Not once had Mrs Gregson been in a position to overpower her. She touched her scalp and sucked in air. 'You've drawn blood.'

'Just keep your opinions to yourself.'

They trudged on, squelching as they went, the low sun growing in confidence as the milky mist faded, leaving just the smoke from the distant brickworks to haze the sky. Soon Mrs Gregson had that strange sensation of being too hot in all her clothing while shivering uncontrollably.

'There. What's that?'

It was parked outside a low agricultural building. An army truck, with canvas sides and an open cab, its paintwork new and shiny. For a second Mrs Gregson dared hope it meant that there were people – specifically, armed men – in the vicinity but as they swerved off the road and crossed into the yard nobody appeared. Mrs Gregson touched the cowling of the engine. Stone cold. It had been left overnight.

'This will have to do,' said Miss Deane.

'A woman driving a lorry? How far do you think you'll get?'

'Nonsense, plenty of women are driving now. Ambulances and the like.'

'Not dressed like that,' said Mrs Gregory.

Miss Deane glanced down at her ruined dress. 'We'll worry about that later. Can you start this thing?'

Mrs Gregson didn't answer. The crack of the gun and the heat of the bullet snapping by her ear made her jump.

'I'm running out of time and patience. Can you start it?'

She sensed a new note of desperation in the woman's voice. She must be under pressure to risk taking the shot. Mrs Gregson had the horrible realization that she might be entering the last few minutes of her life. 'Yes.'

'Then do so while you still have two knees to walk with.'

'You're going to kill me anyway.'

Miss Deane sighed. 'You know, I haven't decided one way or the other. But you're doing a damn fine job of persuading me.'

Mrs Gregson lifted the fluted cowling and peered into the engine. She slammed it shut. 'Some have self-starting systems. Not this one.' She climbed into the cab and leaned under the dashboard. She found the crank. Then she pulled out the wires from the ignition and, stripping the ends with her teeth, wound them together.

She emerged with the crank and offered it to Miss Deane. 'Do you want to do the honours?'

'Don't be ridiculous.'

Mrs Gregson gave a thin, superior smile and inserted the business end of the crank into the engine. The kick-back on the lorry could be fearsome, she knew, so she made sure she wrapped her thumbs away, so as not to break one.

'You might want to give it some throttle and choke when it catches. It is cold.'

Miss Deane moved around to the driver's side. Standing on the running board, she found the choke and pulled it out a quarter of an inch. Then she put her left foot on the throttle, while hanging onto the open door, her pistol still pointed at Mrs Gregson. 'Go on.'

Mrs Gregson, who had started many an ambulance, grunted at the resistance. The handle moved a fraction of a turn and stopped.

'What is it?'

'It's a pretty new lorry, by the look of it. I wouldn't be surprised if the rings aren't bedded in yet.'

'Put your back into it.'

Mrs Gregson glared, spat on her hands and leaned everything she had into turning the crank the fast half-turn normally required. The engine made a desultorily chuffing sound. 'Throttle,' she said. 'When it catches. Not too much or you'll flood the carburretor.'

Another two attempts and the engine caught, tentatively at first, then gaining in confidence. A well-timed blip of the throttle from Miss Deane and the whole thing settled down in a satisfied purr. Mrs Gregson, pleased not to have broken a wrist, pulled the crank free.

'There you are. What now?'

'Strip, please.'

'What?'

'You said it yourself. I'd look silly in this truck in my Sunday best. But those peculiar leathers of yours . . .' She stepped down and waved the gun. 'Take off your clothes.'

FORTY-SIX

Jack Whent had lived all his life on Foulness. He was born in 1829, seventeen years before the first school was opened on the island. So he had missed that, never really learned to read or write, just enough sums to know the price of feed and how much to sell his mustard to Colman's for. He had been to the mainland for extended periods three times in his life, one of those as baby when his mother feared the scarlet fever had him and they had taken a pony and trap along the Broomway to the hospital at Great Wakering, another to get married, and a third to travel to the Lake District with his father to buy sheep.

His brother had been a farrier and a blacksmith, put out of business by the tractor and dead of drink soon after. His wife had died of TB. His son had Old Marsh Farm now, but Jack didn't care for Jinny, the wife. She was an off-islander – no problem with that, his own wife was from Burnham – but she acted as if she had fallen among Stone Age people.

The Whents were still farmers and his son made a good job of it. But Jack and Jinny in the same room was always a recipe for a good row. So he preferred to live at what she called The Seashack, but which he knew as Perrin's Cottage, after the harness-maker who used to live there. Another business gone, taken by mechanicals.

Jack was happy at Perrin's, but he didn't sleep much or well. If he was still slumbering when the first birds started up, it was unusual. So it was no surprise he was propped up in bed, stoking the first pipe of the day, when he heard the sprinkle of stone or the like on the salt-darkened windows of his home.

He slipped out of bed, the smoke forgotten, and walked over to peer out, see if it wasn't some local children playing a joke on old Jack. The new generation seemed to have lost all respect for their elders. His old dad would have strapped some of them for even looking at him the way they did.

Outside, though, was still dark and visibility poor, not helped by the mists. *No urchins would be out in that. Not at this hour.* But as Jack turned away to give some more attention to his pipe, he caught the sound of voices. Sharp and brittle at least one of them was. A woman? Then fading. Someone was going out on the Broomway. They had to be mad.

He slipped back into bed, finished the preparation for the smoke and lit it. Mad, they were. He'd walked and ridden that road hundreds of times to pick up supplies from Wakering. Knew it like the back of his hand. And he wouldn't walk it in this mist. Not unless his life depended on it. You could find yourself walking straight out to sea in a heartbeat, convinced you were heading for land. Well, you were. Kent. On the other side of the estuary.

As the first tendrils of smoke warmed his lungs, he gave a small, exploratory cough and he closed his eyes. How many more mornings would he have like this at his age? Hundreds, if he was lucky, no more. Why cut short his quota by going out there in filthy weather? Couldn't see hand in front of face, let alone the poles. He had seen those sands swallow whole ponies and traps. There were at least two motor cars he knew of under the mud. And God alone knew how many bones. It would be madness to go out there. A man would need his head testing.

With a sigh he threw back the covers once more. *What was that old saying about curiosity and cats?*

FORTY-SEVEN

Mrs Gregson stepped out of the leather breeches and skirt combination and threw them at Miss Deane. She plucked them out of the air and tossed them into the lorry's cab. Mrs Gregson had hoped there might be an opportunity to tackle her while she changed, but she obviously intended to do that down the road.

'Turn around and kneel.'

Mrs Gregson, dressed now in her Braemar winter-weight all-in-ones, shook her head. 'No.'

'Turn around, kneel down. I'll make it quick.'

Mrs Gregson felt a surge of anger that made her clench her fists. It was better to go down fighting than to be meekly executed like some lamb in an abattoir. 'No.'

'So be it.' Miss Deane cocked the pistol, the ominous click audible even above the engine. 'You aren't the first woman to die at the hand of the *Sie Wölfe*. By the way, who did take the grenade at the cottage?'

'Booth.'

'Ah. No great loss then.' She took a breath and levelled the gun.

Mrs Gregson took a step forward just as a rock bounced off Miss Deane's skull with a dull ringing sound.

The spy's eyes rolled in her head and she staggered sideways, the gun falling from her hand. Mrs Gregson leaped for it, her fingers closing around the butt when a mighty kick caught her under the chin, sending her skidding on her back along the ground. The sky was full of daylight stars, and she could taste the iron-sting of blood in her mouth.

As she leaned up on one elbow, the gears of the truck ground and it pulled away, gathering speed as it careered onto the road with an ungainly swerve.

She was aware of figures approaching at some speed, but she plucked up the fallen pistol and stood. As the lorry crunched into a higher gear, she took aim and fired, pulling the trigger until the hammer clicked on empty cylinder after empty cylinder.

She flung the useless weapon after the disappearing silhouette, then turned to the shapes at the corner of her vision and saw Watson approaching, bedraggled and limping, but alive at least. She threw out her arms and clasped the major to her body, squeezing the air out of him. She gave him a kiss on the cheek, cold and bristly on her lips, but she didn't care. Only after a few moments did she remember she was dressed only in her underwear. She pushed him away, holding him at arm's length.

'I am so glad to see you, Major. And you too, Mr Holmes—'

But it wasn't Holmes. It was a wrinkled old man, his face as weathered as driftwood, bracketed by a great crescent of a white beard.

'This is Jack Whent. Islander,' said Watson. 'A man who can throw a stone with enviable accuracy.'

She felt a terrible sense of foreboding. 'Is Mr Holmes all right?'

'He's restin' up at Molly Birkin's place,' said Whent. 'He'll be a lot warmer'n you at the minute.' He shrugged off a tweed backpack and fetched a blanket from it, whether for warmth or to spare her modesty, she couldn't be sure. She was grateful for it, whatever the reason.

'Your mouth,' said Watson with concern. 'There's blood.'

She slapped his hand away. 'It's nothing. I'll have a sore jaw tomorrow. I don't quite follow,' she said. 'What happened out there?'

'Holmes was not as ill as he seemed. I recall he once said to me: "I have my plans. The first thing is to exaggerate my injuries." '

'That would be the affair with Baron Gruner and the Chinese pottery?'

'Yes,' said Watson, surprised but pleased she had remembered a story he had yet to write, told to her one night in Belgium. 'Well, this time he wasn't as disabled as he seemed. He was using his stick to search for some of the old rotted withies that mark a path from land to the Broomway.'

'I told him about it, in passing, like,' said Whent. 'That there was, is, a path that ran not to Wakering Stairs but to Haven Point. It was so called because if you make a sprint for that, the tide wraps around that causeway, but doesn't cover it till a good fifteen minutes after the rest. A haven, see? It's narrow, though; you gots to know what you doin'. Luckily I do.'

'But what made you follow them?' she asked.

'Some bloody fool threw some cockles against m'window in the darkness.' The old man laughed. 'An' I heard voices. Who'd be crazy enough to take the Broomway in a swale like that? I had to see. So I followed, in the mist, like. Thought someone'd spotted me now and then, but I hung back until I found Mr Holmes and his friend here on the sand. I brought 'em ashore, took Mr Holmes to Molly's and came across here fast as we could. We heard the lorry start up and reckoned it was you two. I saw that woman looking to make mischief and thought I'd better stop her. 'Tweren't that long a throw.' Whent sucked in a lungful of air. It was the longest speech he had made in decades.

Mrs Gregson still had questions, but they could wait. 'Well, thank you, Mr Whent. What now? That woman is on her way to London. She is about to tell the Germans about the tanks.'

'I'll wager that woman is on her way to the first telephone box,' corrected Watson.

'Probably not one till Great Wakering,' said Whent. 'Only army stuff at the camp over yonder. She won't get in there.'

'But if we can gain access, we can get the duty intelligence officer to shut the local exchanges,' said Watson. If they could convince them of the nature of the emergency, that was.

'You can do that, can you?' asked Whent, not familiar with telephones.

'DORA can.'

Even Whent had heard of that. 'Good ten-minute walk,' he said, looking Watson up and down. 'Maybe fifteen.'

Which probably meant at least twenty. 'We have to warn France about the tanks, as soon as we can,' said Watson, his exhaustion driving him close to despair. 'Many lives depend on it.'

'Hold on a second,' said Mrs Gregson, hurrying over to where the pistol had fallen. 'Even an empty gun has some persuasive power.'

'What is it?' asked Watson, wondering why she needed the pistol with no bullets.

But then their older ears heard what Mrs Gregson's younger ones had already noted: the rise and fall of a thrumming engine as it negotiated bends. A motor cycle was coming.

FORTY-EIGHT

The tankman and the infantryman read the new instructions by sputtering candlelight in the dugout near the parked tanks. Halford, the young tank commander, had a stack of notes in his pocket about start times, direction of attack and infantry support – the first few typed, the second lot hastily scribbled as tactics shifted. He was now down to just two tanks. Two more of them had come to grief in a wide, sunken lane called Monkey Valley, which was part pathway and part shell-cratered swamp. One had broken down four times before it gave up the mechanical ghost; the other was stuck fast in mud that doubled as the strongest glue in the world.

Halford's own tank, the 'male' known as *G for Glory*, was running superbly, and he had managed to scrounge sixteen extra gallons of fuel off a Royal Engineers convoy, so he was keeping the extra French juice in reserve. In truth, Halford didn't like the sound of it. He had been laughed at when he said that, but his father had raced at Brooklands before the war and he knew about the noise that various grades of petrol made as they sloshed in their tins. This new stuff sounded thin.

He looked at his watch. Four in the morning. An hour until his tank rolled forward through the shattered, leafless tree trunks that surrounded them, towards the place called Chop Alley – he didn't want to ask where the name came from – and onto no man's land. The new orders said his tank was to be in the vanguard, arriving a few minutes ahead of accompanying infantry. Halford's would be the first ever tank to see action against an enemy. A mixture of pride and trepidation swirled inside him at the thought.

'So,' said Lieutenant Archie Cross of the 6th Battalion, The King's Own Yorkshire Light Infantry, 'you will have a man in front of you to guide you through this part.' He pointed at the trench map. 'Just to the beginning of no man's land. There are craters here and here that need careful skirting. After that, you are on your own. You will head diagonally across here towards Delville Wood here. There is a German outpost there, protruding into no man's land. It has a wide field of fire. Our objective it to destroy that post, then swing across to support the main thrust of the attack towards Flers, where you will liaise with the second tank. The artillery has been instructed to leave a corridor in the rolling barrage to allow you safe passage. During the attack, my men will be coming behind you, using your machine as a shield where possible. I have to say, sir, they are all jolly excited about going into action with you.'

One tank, thought Halford. Would he had a hundred and one of the things. That would provide proper shelter from the German guns. And with the tanks' own weapons blazing, that number would be able to keep German heads down while the infantry advanced.

'Well, let's hope we justify their excitement,' said Halford, scratching at his armpit through the layers. The lice, the real victors of the Western Front, had wasted no time locating fresh meat.

'First time over the bags?' Cross asked. 'I mean, not that you'll be going over the bags. But first time in an attack?'

Halford nodded. 'We are all first-timers. Just like our tanks. What's the phrase? Baptism of fire.'

Cross nodded. 'One thing I know, sir, is that despite the best-laid plans, which these do not appear to be' – he held up the scribbled orders and they both laughed, a hollow sound to their ears – 'it soon descends into chaos out there. So, if I might venture some advice, from what little I know, you'd best fix a single objective and go for that. Then always keep your attention on the next objective – the next shell hole, the next trench, the next strip of wire, the next machine-gun nest. Don't try and take in the whole battle. The big picture is, well, just too big. Leave that to the experts.'

'How long have you . . .?'

'Since July,' said Cross. 'Since day one of the offensive here. That makes me a veteran. Listen, I'll get someone to lay white tape along Chop Alley. So if anything happens to the man walking in front, you have something to follow in the dark.' He, too, consulted his watch. 'Less than two hours to go until the guns start. Which means about fifty minutes till we form up and move forward. Think you can get some sleep?'

Halford thought of his men, snoozing on the ground around the tank, or curled up around the engine and gearbox. 'I have to write to my parents. Not that I can say much except platitudes. *Am in X about to go into battle at Y. Don't worry about me. Spirits good. Love to all . . .*' Cross didn't say anything. Every man wrote the same kind of letter. Very few told the truth and those that did rarely escaped the censor. 'But I'll try and get forty winks.'

The gas curtain of the dugout was thrown back. A thuggish face thrust inside. The cap told them it was a military policeman. 'You seen Claude Levass? Frenchman? Attached to Heavy Branch?'

'Not for a day or so,' said Halford. 'Why?'

The policeman grunted and disappeared, to be replaced by a second face. Halford recognized it as belonging to Major Hoffman, also of the Heavy Branch Support Team. 'Halford. How are you?'

'Well, sir.'

'Don't let me interrupt your planning. What fuel are you using in your car?'

'Fuel? I got some from the Engineers.'

'Don't put that French muck in. Just got word that it's contaminated.'

'With what?'

'Rainwater.'

'Jesus Christ,' said Halford. As if they didn't have enough problems.

'There'll be fresh supplies arriving within thirty minutes. Someone, somewhere has kicked someone else up the backside to get replacement petrol. All tins will have "G" for "Good" written on the side. Anything else, you ditch. Understood? That bloody fool Levass has brought up thousands of gallons that will cause the Daimlers to misfire.'

'Sir.' No wonder they were looking for poor Levass. He was responsible for saddling them with poor-quality fuel. Men had been shot for far less. But how was he to know the dumps had leaked? Surely he had acted in good faith?

When Hoffman had gone, Cross began to fold the map. 'Well,' he said, 'refuelling. There goes your kip. Twenty winks at best.'

It was a cold, dank dawn that broke over England. At least it felt that way for a doctor in his sixties, sitting in an operations hut at a Royal Naval Air Service base in Kent. The ops hut was a converted cricket pavilion, still festooned with pictures of the teams and plaques that recorded in gilded lettering the captains and chairmen of the club since its founding in 1837.

Watson was the only person in the room. He had been left with a heater and a cup of strong tea by the wing commander, who told him someone would be along shortly for his 'hop'. It made it sound innocuous, but the 'hop' meant a flight over the Channel. Watson was heading for France.

Things had moved swiftly in London once they had arrived at noon the previous day, with Churchill understanding at once that Levass had to be stopped before he did any more damage. However, although he had sent urgent telegrams, he insisted that one of them fly over to present the evidence and make sure Levass did not talk his way out of trouble. Holmes was too unwell and still back in Essex being cared for; Mrs Gregson would be battling against presumptions about her gender. Watson, tired though he was, was the obvious choice. He was allowed a few hours of recuperative sleep at his club then driven down to an airfield in Kent for the cross-Channel flight. Alone. *Back to being just half of the solution.*

The door opened and, accompanied by a blast of cool air, in came a long-limbed young man in a flying helmet. He sported an extravagant ginger moustache, of which, judging from the way it was teased to its maximum length, he was inordinately proud. 'Major Watson?'

Watson stood and held out his hand.

'Captain Adam Goodman. Just getting the old girl wheeled out and we'll be ready to go.' He frowned as he examined Watson. 'Best get you some gloves and a warmer coat too. Gets pretty chilly up there. Flown before, sir?'

Watson shook his head.

'Well, there's nothing to it. Not for you. Just leave all the hard work to me.'

'You've done this often? Over the Channel?'

Goodman looked serious. 'Major, it was made clear to me that you were important enough not to be entrusted to a novice. You have some important work, I believe?'

'Indeed.' *To find and stop a madman*, he thought to himself.

'Trust me, they selected me because this is my back yard. Yes, I've done it dozens of times without mishap. We'll be using a Sopwith One-and-a-Half Strutter, which has an endurance of close to four hours, so we won't have to refuel.'

'Don't you have one with the full complement of two struts?' asked Watson.

Goodman laughed. 'It just describes the long and short struts configuration on the fuselage supporting the top wing. Good crate. Ours is converted to a trainer – so a twin-seater. It's fast and it's safe. We'll get up to a hundred miles an hour if the wind is with us.'

Watson shuddered internally at the thought of such recklessness. From outside he heard a whine and a mechanical stutter, followed by the low grumble of an aero engine catching.

'There,' said Goodman with a grin. 'The fitters are just warming her up and giving her a once-over. I'll get you that kit.' He turned to go and then hesitated. 'Any questions, sir?'

'Yes,' said Watson, licking dry lips. 'Is there a lavatory I can use?'

The thump of the tank's engine starting up cracked through the night sky, reverberating among the stumps of trees and across the wasteland beyond. *Heaven alone knows what it must sound like to the Germans over there*, Halford thought. He imagined the defenders peering with periscopes into the pre-dawn murk, wondering what fresh horror the morning had in store.

He looked back down the track that snaked through what was left of the woods. It was clogged with two rifle companies, stamping and shuffling in the chill air. The dark shapes reminded him of a herd of cattle, their breath and the smoke from a last furtive gasper rising like the steam off the animals' backs. He instantly regretted the analogy, the image leading him to thoughts of the abattoir and what was to come in the next half-hour. The smell, of the massed living and the putrefying dead, also reminded him of the slaughterhouse. You get used to it, they had said. That's what worries me, he had replied. But now, he found, the choking fumes inside the tanks didn't seem quite so bad.

'Water, sir?' It was one of the infantry corporals who had been distributing both water and tots of rum through the ranks. 'Or something stronger?'

Halford smiled and took the water. 'Gets damned hot in there.'

'I'll bet. Just wanted to say, glad to have you with us, sir.'

'Good to have something to hide behind for a change?'

The corporal's teeth showed surprisingly white in the darkness as he smiled. 'Yes, and to have something Fritz don't have. It's a good feeling.'

'We'll do our best.'

'Ready for loading, sir,' shouted his gearsman from the open doorway, his voice all but swallowed by reverberating metal.

'Thank you, Phibbs. Right, *G for Glory*. All aboard. Calling at all stations to Flers.' He tried to keep the tremor from his voice, but he wasn't sure he succeeded. Still, he received a polite chuckle from those around him. The tankmen stirred into action, relieved, no doubt, that the waiting was over.

'Good luck, sir.' It was Cross, the infantry lieutenant. 'Corporal Tench there will be leading you to the start of the crossing.' He pointed at a pale-faced young man who was attaching a lamp to the back of his belt. He switched it on and it glowed red. Halford gave him the thumbs up and took a gulp of water.

'See you in Flers,' he said to Cross.

Cross grinned with everything but his eyes. 'I hear you can do a good brew-up on that thing's engine.'

'I'll have one waiting. Sugar?'

'Two please, sir.'

They shook hands, an awkward and brief moment, and checked their watches. Cross pulled out his Webley revolver. 'We'll be right behind you.'

'Best place,' said Halford, low enough that Tench wouldn't hear.

He stepped through the narrow doorway into the familiar stew of heat, sweat and fumes. From now on, normal conversation would be impossible. He wriggled into the commander's position and nodded to his driver, the perpetually glum but highly talented Sergeant Yates. Both men pulled on their leather helmets and lowered the new-issue goggles with dangling chainmail visors. The idea was to stop the burns from 'bullet splash', the sparks and hot metal that flew around the inside of the tank when it came under fire. Now the crew all looked liked a cross between medieval knights and strange, leather-carapaced insects.

Hatches would have to be shut, but Halford wanted to wait until the last moment to seal himself into this steel world. The viewing prisms were worse than useless, and it was often like driving blind. It was worth risking a bullet through the skull to be sure they were heading in the right direction. He put his face close to the open visor of the tank, hoping for fresh morning air, but, as usual, it was a breeze polluted by effluent and decay that drifted in. Tench was on the road ahead, with the white tapes – much of which had been trampled into the mud – on either side of him. Five thirty. Time to go.

One last drink of water. A final prayer. A wipe of the palms. A valedictory mental message to his loved ones. Little acts, repeated in one form or another a million times along the line.

Halford picked up the spanner from the side of his seat and banged four times. Shut all doors, it said. Then he gave two rat-a-tats with the tool. There was a clash of gear teeth, a curse loud enough to be heard over the engine, more oaths, then an answering clang of the spanner and the driver let in the clutch. *G for Glory* gave a reluctant judder and then, with a mighty creaking and squeaking, the first tank began its long slow roll to war.

The old woman lay at the bottom of the stairs, her neck twisted at an unnatural angle. A terrible domestic accident. Those old slippers on her feet had become tangled with her robe. She had plummeted head first, no doubt screaming as she went. But there were no neighbours near this little cottage on the outskirts of Great Wakering to hear her dying cries. Poor Mary Wallace. Just a few months short of her seventieth birthday. Candles would be lit in church.

It had taken Ilse Brandt, as she now thought of herself once again, some considerable time to arrange the tragic scene quite so artfully, and now her damaged arm was throbbing with pain. After a search through the kitchen she had found a bottle of meat and malt wine, which she had drained. Now she sat, waiting for first light, when she would make her move.

Twenty-four hours had passed since the crossing of the Broomway. They would have found the abandoned lorry very quickly, and would have seen the blood stains from that bitch's lucky shot. Brandt had stolen a bicycle, but not pedalled too far, barging in on the old woman with a tale of having fallen off her bike into a ditch. It was the best way of explaining her ragged appearance, the blood down her arm and the bruise on her face.

The woman had patched up her arm and as she cleaned the wound, it was obvious to Brandt that her suspicions were aroused. No fall from a bicycle would make such a gouge in the flesh. She had insisted on fetching the local doctor. That was when it became necessary to snap her neck.

She had hidden the bicycle and laid low, not stirring. She had heard army boots on the road outside and various vehicles racing by, but she suspected they had assumed she had fled the immediate vicinity on the bicycle, which she had dragged into the kitchen. There had been a knock at the door at midday, but she kept completely still and out of sight. She moved around only after dark, feeding on cold cuts from the larder.

If only the signalling rendezvous with the submarine had worked out. How different things would have been. Still, it was no use having regrets. She would never get anything done.

She knew that soon she would have to go through the woman's wardrobe and find something that might be the kind of clothes a

Miss Deane or a Miss Pillbody would wear. Something that didn't smell of mothballs or old age. She would use rouge or powder to hide the bruise from the stone that had struck her. Then she would head, not to London, but back north once more. She would report to Silber, the postal censor, in person. She knew the secret of Elveden now. Landships. It sounded fantastical. But that was why she had had to get off the island. It was surprising how many people would discuss the indiscretion that had them incarcerated. She had thought Sherlock Holmes's vision of the landships the ravings of an old man, but when Watson arrived he, too, had talked of them. And so had that damned redhead.

Her arm throbbed once more at the mere thought of Mrs Gregson. If only she'd shot her and then stripped her clothes off. Or killed them all out on the Broomway. What, was she going soft? No, following the poles was a two-person job. She had needed the Gregson woman. Still, one day they might meet again, and then she would put everything right. But first, she had to share what she had learned. It might be a day or two before she could deliver it to Silber. But the news of the existence of these armoured 'landships' would reach Germany soon enough after that. After all these weeks, what was the rush?

FORTY-NINE

The going was painfully laboured. The route to Chop Alley was slow, the road clogged with men and machines moving to their own assembly points, and the guide tapes had been laid running next to the communication trenches, just inviting *G for Glory* to slither in sideways. To make matters worse, it had started to rain and the road was slippery, even for the tracks. Negotiating a corner took four of the crew working in absolute unison with steering, gears and differentials. It was a slow creep rather than a smooth turn, and felt as cumbersome as it must have looked. Halford knew the four-miles-an-hour calculation was now wildly optimistic. He doubted they were running at more than two. Perhaps it would improve as they moved onto no man's land.

He followed the red light of Tench towards the front, aware of the thin line of grey that suggested dawn – and the opening barrage – wasn't far off. In some places he could see the road was blocked by the curious, some openly laughing at the great steel monster that was rolling their way. Tench was gesticulating wildly for them to get out of its path.

Then, over the space of perhaps a hundred yards, the infantry fell away. The white tapes also came to end. That was no man's land ahead, Halford was certain. He instructed Sergeant Yates to speed up and the machine gave an eager lurch. For a tank, anyway. Halford indicated that all visors, doors and escape hatches should be closed and they sealed themselves in. Now he was looking at the red guide light through a glass prism.

Which meant he had to peer hard when the beacon wobbled and then moved wildly from side to side. He pressed his face forward, just in time to see Tench stagger and slump to the ground. He'd been hit.

'Stop!' Halford yelled, banging the spanner as hard as he could. *G for Glory* groaned, juddered to a halt and slipped into neutral.

Halford pushed up the visor. Ahead was indeed the no man's land he had heard so much about, as featureless as a black lake. He doubted whether there would be many more landmarks out there, even when dawn did put in an appearance.

He could make out the prone shape of poor Tench, lying motionless a few feet from the track that would have squashed him into the ground. Another figure, an officer, was crouching over him, removing the still glowing guide light.

'What are you doing?'

'Follow me!' the man cried, looping the lamp through his own belt before dragging Tench to one side.

Brave chap, Halford thought. He wouldn't want to be out there, exposed to sniper fire with a glowing red light that almost invited 'Shoot me'.

Halford leaned back in his seat, pulled the visor hatch shut, gave the order to engage gears and they crept forward again. Over the engine he could hear the crump of the occasional shell, and there was a whiff of gas a few moments later. But the clumsy gas masks with their fogged eyepieces meant viewing through the prisms or periscopes would be almost impossible. He could see the officer ahead of them slipping on his respirator, though. The tankmen would just have to try to power through without.

A ping. Then another ping, as if they were being fired at by a boy's peashooter. Then a louder bang and a shout. Halford turned in his seat. One of the gunners was clutching his arm. A round had come through the thinner metal of the sponson.

'You all right?' he mouthed over the relentless clattering of the Daimler.

The gunner nodded. 'Don't worry about me, sir.'

Christ, Halford thought. The side sponsons weren't bullet proof after all.

It was then the tank lurched onto its side, slithering out of the horizontal, throwing half the men against hot pipes and metal surfaces. The engine gave a strangled screech and stalled. A strange ticking silence came over the interior as each man, stunned, tried to reorient themselves. They had toppled into a crater.

'Fuck,' someone said. 'How did that happen?'

Both Yates, the driver, and Halford, peered through the prisms to see how the guiding officer had brought them to this pickle. There was the crack of shattering glass and Yates was pushed back, his face full of splinters from the prism and a messy hole punched into the bridge of his nose.

'We have to get her out of here,' said Halford, as more rounds screeched off the frontal armour. 'Get the boards under the tracks.'

'But Ralph—' said a shaken Phibbs, pointing to the slumped shape of the driver.

'I can bloody well drive,' snapped Halford, heaving the dead man from his position.

Phibbs tried the port sponson door, but it was wedged against the mud of the crater and would move only an inch. He staggered up the slanting floor, grabbing at handholds as he went, and managed to push open the starboard sponson's hatch. There were strange noises rending the rain-sodden night now – snaps, crackles, whistles, whooshes and booms – preliminary, probing attacks from both sides until the dawn onslaught proper.

Four of the men had already de-tanked when another figure came inside. Halford recognized him as Levass. It had been he who had picked up Tench's red light. He had led them to the edge of this deep shell crater and marooned them. He who had . . . had he shot Yates through the observation slit? And killed poor Tench in the bargain? But that would mean this man was a traitor at best, a deranged monster at worst.

'What the hell are you doing?' Halford asked.

'Abandon tank,' Levass instructed.

'Certainly not. We have a machine-gun position to knock out.'

'You will never make it across in this machine.'

'Not with you in front of us. Get out of my car.'

The sound of the gunshot filled the tank, snapping at their eardrums. It took a long time for the ringing to die away, about the same as for each of the three remaining tankmen to realize they hadn't been shot. Levass had put a bullet from his pistol through the engine.

'I think you had better go,' said Levass. 'This tank must not fall into enemy hands. Now!'

He waved the pistol around and Halford and the others all came to the same conclusion at once. That Levass was utterly insane. Without a word they filed out into the drizzle, heading back to their own lines and the infantry who had been deprived of their precious cover by this madman.

*

As he bolted the door after them, Claude Levass was well aware they would all think him crazy at best, a deranged traitor at worst. But this was no more insane than pitching your best weapon at the Germans only to have its secrets discovered. The corrupted fuel had been intended to stop them dead in their tracks, before they engaged the Germans. But someone had discovered it far too soon. In fact, the poor quality of the machines had almost done his job for him in many cases. Of the forty-nine landships scheduled to attack, only about half were free of problems. And, he reckoned, if this one was seen to have failed on the opening gambit of the offensive, then perhaps the strategists might think again and pull the machines back to Yvranch, saving the march of the tanks for another day. The burning of *G for Glory* would be visible for miles, a visual signal that the landships had been unleashed too soon.

Of course, he was finished. But at the very least, Levass would have his day in court to tell the top brass how pig-headed and short-sighted they had been. And Cardew? Well, Cardew could take the blame for what happened at Elveden and the men in that tank. He was in no position to argue. The tiny quantities of the drug he had given the engineer to make him suggestible and pliant – the Mexicans called the Datura extract *Esclavo de los Dioses*, 'Slave of the Gods' – had been used in larger doses by the Aztecs to convince their human sacrifices that they were dying for a good cause. But even in the smaller dose, it must have disturbed the balance of Cardew's mind. Why else would he have killed himself in such a melodramatic way?

Which reminded him. Levass took one of the sachets of powder he always carried with him from his top pocket and emptied the contents onto his tongue. It was bitter, but as soon as he swallowed he felt the rush of warmth around his body, the glow of inner strength from the drug. He did the same with two further packets, far more than he usually ingested. *But this is an unusual day*, he thought, as he opened the hatch to let the two carrier pigeons fly free.

Levass had unscrewed the cap of the first can of petrol and sloshed it over the front of the interior and was working on pouring the second over the engine when he heard the clanging noise. Several bullets had hit the tank – it was evidently becoming visible in the strengthening light – so he thought it must be a particularly large calibre round. Then it came again, a rhythmic rat-tat-tat. Someone was hammering at the sponson door.

Levass put down the half-empty can and drew his pistol once more. He turned the metal lever and pushed open the door, straining against gravity. The tank was at such an angle that he could just see the head and shoulders of the new arrival. It was Major Watson, a metal bar in his hand.

'A word, Levass?' he asked, as casually as if they had met in the bar at his club.

A machine gun chattered. There was answering rifle fire. The attack on the German position had started, without the benefit of *G for Glory*.

'I'm going to burn this,' Levass said. 'You might want to get away.'

'That's as maybe, but I am feeling rather exposed out here. Can I climb up?'

'Are you armed?'

'My pistol is holstered.' He made a show of tossing the bar away.

Levass grunted and stepped back, leaving the major to struggle with the mass of the door and the tricky ascent unaided. Levass was more intent on keeping his own pistol trained on him.

'You are alone?' the Frenchman asked.

'Very alone,' said Watson, as he clambered inelegantly inside. 'I'd hoped never to see the inside of one of these monsters again. In fact, I had hoped never to see no man's land again.' He caught his breath. The petrol fumes stung his eyes and he rubbed at them. 'Yet here I am.'

The access door clanged shut under its own weight. Watson was reminded of the 'special' cells at Wandsworth Hospital, the horrible finality of the crash of metal on metal, closing in the deranged and damaged occupants for yet another endless night.

'What do you want, Watson?' demanded Levass.

Watson gasped his breath back before he answered. He was getting too old for this. 'You have led me a merry dance since I arrived in France, you know. Been searching for you up and down the line. Luckily, one of the engineers spotted you following the tapes behind this tank.'

'And you didn't bring the police? Someone to arrest me?'

Watson pointed to the rear of the tank. 'Oh, they are out there. Not the police, military or otherwise, but some officers to deliver you to the provost marshal. They let me come in ahead, just to save any . . . unpleasantness.' There were those who wanted to shoot Levass on sight and have done with it. Watson thought it should all be done with due legal process.

'I want a French court martial,' Levass said.

Even in the dim light, Watson could see the Frenchman's pin-pricked pupils. The man was on some kind of narcotic. He had to be careful. Reasonable. 'This is a British tank. Let it be and we'll see.'

'It has to burn,' Levass said. There was strange, metallic quality his the voice.

'Burn this, and I'm afraid they'll take you straight to the Tower. And I want to know what other tricks you have been up to with the other tanks. Lives are going to be lost—'

'Thousands of lives are going to be lost in future because this great invention will be thrown away.'

Watson sighed. 'It is not your decision.'

'No, it is the decision of the blunderers and the . . .' Levass lapsed into rapid French, not all of which Watson could follow.

'Levass. It's over. I—'

The tank bucked like an angry stallion. The ground shook beneath their feet and the metal walls began to resonate. The Allied barrage had started. The noise of the guns was amplified by the vibrating steel hull into a continuous, oppressive thundering. The air thickened and it seemed as if someone was trying to crush Watson's chest.

'Levass. I don't know how' – he struggled for support as the tank slid into the crater a little more – 'how accurate the guns are. We could be blown to pieces where we stand.'

Levass was thrown backwards as a shockwave punched into *G for Glory*. The petrol can overturned and gurgled away its contents, pooling at the lower side of the stricken machine. Now the air was thick with its vapour.

'Look, you can convince them to call off the tanks when you get out.' Watson knew this was a desperate invention, but he was sweating now and not from the residual heat of the engine. The shells were falling so thick and fast there were no individual explosions.

'They won't listen.'

'They won't be able to hear you at all if you are dead. You might still make a difference. What you say isn't entirely nonsense. Your method of saying it, however . . .'

Levass holstered the pistol. 'Perhaps you are right.'

The machine-gun fusillade hit the exposed front of *G for Glory* like a furious drum roll. The rounds could not penetrate the armour, but the hot metal and sparks they sent buzzing around the interior like manic fireflies ignited the spilled petrol. Watson looked on in horror as the fuel at Levass's feet made a whoosing sound and a wall of flame engulfed him. Soon the rest of the petrol caught, almost masking the burning man's screams, as the inside of the tank crackled into a lethal inferno.

FIFTY

Sherlock Holmes was sleeping. He looked, in repose, like any other patient, his face relaxed, freed from the struggle of his day-to-day existence and some of the ravages of time. He was in a private room at St Bart's, the place where, many, many years before, he had met a lath-thin and nut-brown ex-army officer, and they had decided to share rooms. The start of a great adventure that, Mrs Gregson suspected, only the death of one or the other would curtail for good.

She reached over and dabbed at a line of spittle that had formed at the corner of his mouth, and the former detective stirred slightly. It was almost dawn on Friday 15 September 1916, and she had been there all night, snoozing in the chair. It was a way of keeping the faith for Watson. She had not been able to go with him to France – there had been no room in the aeroplane, for a start – so she had set about making sure his old friend received the best possible care.

She was worried about Watson, of course, but knew better than to try to stop him going. He had wanted this finished off. After requisitioning the motor cycle with a wave of the pistol, the pair had driven to London, contacting MI5 en route to make sure that Langdale Pike – a gossip columnist and skilled double agent – rolled up all the known German contacts and agents in London. If Ilse Brandt had made it to the capital, she would find the channels to Germany had been closed down.

That still left her at large, of course, and dangerous, but apparently her knowledge of Thetford and its machines would soon be redundant.

'How is he?'

Mrs Gregson jumped to her feet, startled by the voice. It was Winston Churchill.

'Thought I'd pop in. Just on my way to a sitting. Bloody Orpen wants to adjust my portrait. I look too glum, he said. No wonder, I said. And I'm not going to be smiling today. Did you hear the news?'

She shook her head.

'They have squandered my landships by launching them in tiny numbers. Tiny.'

She wondered if this was Winston distancing himself from their deployment. He had gone to some lengths to make sure the tanks had got to France, after all. 'So the secret is out?'

'To the Germans? I suspect so, my dear. But thank you for all your work these months. I know it hasn't been easy. I haven't been easy.' He thought for a moment. 'Have you news of Major Watson?'

'No.'

'Early days yet,' Churchill grunted, and then pointed at the slumbering Holmes. 'So how is he?'

'On the mend, sir. There was a chance of pneumonia after the crossing of the Broomway.' Watson had briefed Churchill about their 'escape' from the island and the reasons why it had been imperative they get off Foulness, before the MP had sent him to Kent and an RNAS aeroplane bound for Yvranch and the tank HQ. 'And Major Watson is adamant that he can reverse the effects of the anaemia that befuddled him.'

'Yes. Feel a bit bad about that.' Churchill said it as if regret was a new emotion to him. 'Incarcerating him, I mean.'

'So they'll close Foulness? Now that the secret of the tanks is out?'

Winston squinted at her, as if smoke from his customary cigar were in his eyes. 'I think it might still have its uses, Mrs Gregson. This damned war isn't over yet. There'll be other secrets to keep.'

'I remembered something during the night. Something the woman said to me when she was pointing a gun at my head.'

'Hhmm?'

'She said I wouldn't be the first woman the *Sie Wölfe* had killed.'

'*Sie Wölfe?*' Churchill thought for a moment. 'She Wolves?'

'I think so. It suggests some sort of organization. It suggests—'

'So there is more than one of her?'

Mrs Gregson suppressed a shudder at the thought.

'Leave that with me,' said Churchill. 'I'll put the word out with the intelligence people, see if it raises any flags. Right. I'd best be going. If there is anything I can do—'

'There is one thing,' she said.

'Yes?'

'Get Major Watson back as quickly as you got him out there. He's not a young man any more and . . .'

Churchill put his hat on. 'Don't worry. I'll get him back for you.'

'For both of us,' she said, glancing at Holmes.

'For both of you.'

FIFTY-ONE

The pain was intense. It was as if the flames were still licking at his back, singeing his hair and blistering his skin. Watson was lying on his front on the bed, naked, arms dangling either side of the mattress, his modestly protected by a sheet draped over his buttocks. His back and thighs were slathered in an unguent of some description. From the smell of phenol, he was fairly sure it was a tannic acid-based ointment. Personally, he would have prescribed Dakin's hypochlorite, but he had been in no position to dictate the course of his own treatment.

His last memory before he woke up, many yards from the burned-out and eviscerated hulk of *G for Glory* was opening the heavy, heavy door as the fire engulfed him. His best guess was that a shell had ignited and hurled him free. At least some of the munitions had certainly detonated at some time, judging by the holed hull of the tank. It looked as if steel-eating maggots had bored through it. *G for Glory* wouldn't be giving up her secrets. Levass would have been pleased with that, at least.

How had the attack gone? It was now getting towards dusk, which meant the day's pattern of gain and loss should have emerged. Once night fell, the opposing armies had a habit of staying put. It was like a savage game of musical chairs and when the music stopped, the players dug in and counted their dead and the feet and yards of ground captured or given.

He remembered the two men crouched over him, the jab of the needle, the warm flood of morphia, and that, a few blurred images apart, was all he had to go on regarding his situation.

He shifted his head. This was an advanced makeshift hospital of the kind he recognized from his time at Plug Street the previous year. A former industrial building, most likely a few miles from the front, still blessed with a roof, filled with steel beds and staffed by male orderlies and the odd nurse. It reeked of disinfectant and suppuration. Emergency operations would be performed here, but its main role was to stabilize the wounded and move them along. Once his back had healed a little, that would no doubt happen to him. Except in his case the evacuation line would keep moving – ambulance, train, boat, train – until he was back in London.

He wondered if anyone knew exactly where he was. The chaos of war meant there was no paperwork to say where he had been taken. His situation might not emerge for several days or weeks. No doubt Mrs Gregson would be worried. And Holmes. Poor Holmes. He hoped they were giving him blood and beef tea as he had instructed. It would be good to have the old Holmes back. They could discuss the cases that had still to see the light of day – 'The Illustrious Client', 'The Sussex Vampire', 'Shoscombe Old Place' – at least a dozen more adventures, the rough drafts and notes of which were all safely stored in the vaults of Cox & Co. Bank at Charing Cross.

A locus of pain opened up at the top of his spine, and soon his neck was burning and itching. But he knew he mustn't scratch the skin. The exposed parts of his flesh had suffered the most. He would need some more morphia soon. Enough to numb the worst of it. And maybe to take him back into a world where the only light was gas, the only transport was a hansom cab, the air was thick with the sulphurous odour of the London particulars and two men in the prime of life ran rings around Scotland Yard. *'Am dining at Goldini's Restaurant, Gloucester Road, Kensington. Please come at once and join me there. Bring with you a jemmy, a dark lantern, a chisel and a revolver. S. H.'*

Ah, how that cheered him. But that world was gone for ever, and not just physically. Nothing would ever be the same, even if they miraculously recovered their youth. There was a darkness over the world now, and it was difficult to see how it could ever glow bright again. The thought squeezed a tear out of the corner of his eye. *Self-pity, Watson,* said the voice in his head, *has there ever been such a wasted emotion? Whatever is to come won't be like the old times. But if our maker spares us, we shall owe it to him to make sure we embrace the days he has gifted us. No, it won't be like it was before. But it'll do us, Watson, it will do us handsomely.*

He had decided the voice was bogus, but at that moment it was as welcome as spring sunshine across a wintery land.

In the corner of his vision he saw the elaborate headdress of a nurse. He raised an arm and began, haltingly, to speak. 'Nurse . . .?'

She spun towards him. *'Ja, wie kann ich helfen?'*

For a moment he thought his brain had failed him. 'Nurse?'

'Ja? Sprechen Sie Deutsch?'

German? For the first time he looked around with eyes unglazed by drugs, at the uniforms hanging next to the beds, the newspaper the lad opposite was reading. German. He was in a German hospital.

'Sind Sie alles in Ordnung? Is everything all right? I'm sorry, I do speak English,' she said, crouching down so he could see her face. It was pretty, moon-like, smooth save for dimpled cheeks. When she smiled, he could see she was in the habit of snapping thread with her teeth. She had stitched a lot of wounds. 'Just not too good, I am afraid. How can I help?' She put a hand on his forehead. 'You have gone quite pale.'

'This is a German hospital?' he asked.

'Ja, of course.'

'Where?'

'A town called Bapaume.'

He had seen it on maps. It was well behind the lines. German lines. 'And I'm a prisoner?'

She shrugged. 'I suppose you are. But first, you are a patient. Now, what is wrong? You called me over.'

His throat had lost all moisture and in a scratchy voice he asked for some water. She fetched him an enamel mug full to the brim and he swallowed the entire contents. 'Thank you, Nurse. My neck is hurting somewhat. I don't think the rest is far behind. I might need some morphia.'

The man in the next bed said something and she hissed a torrent of words back, silencing him. He was no doubt complaining about her talking in a foreign tongue to an enemy.

She flashed Watson a smile that was almost apologetic. She was a *Frontschwester*, one the Germans' front-line nurses, the equivalent of the British QAs. And no doubt she broke as many young men's hearts as they did. 'You're a doctor now, are you?'

He laughed and regretted it. When the spasm had gone, he said, 'Actually I am, Nurse. Royal Army Medical Corps.' He supposed all the insignia had been burned off his uniform.

'Oh. Well, Doctor, then welcome.' He did not correct her regarding his title, it was probably best she thought of him as a medical man than as a combatant. 'If you don't mind me saying so, aren't you a little . . .'

'Old?'

'Mature. A little mature to be at the front?'

He would have nodded his agreement if he could have, but the pain in his neck was like a steel band that had been heated in a forge. 'It's a long story. I hope I never see no man's land and the trenches again.'

She registered the expression on his face as the area over his shoulders began to prickle unpleasantly. 'I'll fetch some morphia. And, don't worry, you won't be seeing the front again soon. We're being evacuated back tomorrow. Your side managed some gains. We are within range of your bigger guns now.'

'Where are we being moved to?'

She looked surprised. 'Well, I don't know where we'll end up, but once your back has healed sufficiently, you are going to Germany.'

The pain faded, to be replaced by a rushing sound in his ears as blood thumped through narrow vessels and the truth dawned on him. The steel band now gripped his temples. He had to face the reality of his situation. He was heading east. For Major John H. Watson, MD, the war to end all wars was about to take a very unexpected turn indeed.

EPILOGUE

KRIEGSGEFANGENEN SENDUNG
GEÖFFNET – ZENSIEREN No. AP 2121

7 January 1917
To: Major John H. Watson
Inmate: Krefeld Offizierlager

Dear Major Watson,

What a thrill it was to receive the news that you were alive
and well. The best (belated) Christmas present I have ever had.
Mr Holmes has said he will also write to you now we have some
vague address. And I shall send parcels through the Red Cross.
But I have news.

■■■■■■■■■■■■■■■■■■■■■■■■■■■■■■■■■■■■

■■■■■■■■■■■■■■■■■■■■■■■■■■■■■■■■■■■■

■■■■■■■■■■■■■■■■■■■■■■■■■■■■■

And you remember the old friend we crossed the Broomway with?
Well, we have made contact with her again. It was Mr Holmes's idea.
When he was well enough he 'debriefed me', as he put it, until my
head spun. Then he placed an advertisement in the newspapers in
one port after another – Dover, Plymouth, Portsmouth, Liverpool. He

said she so loves the sea, she'll be near it. It was to say that there was a particular mechanical doll for sale – an autoperipatetikos like the one she had broken – in mint condition. He felt sure she would be looking for a replacement. And it was for a bargain price. And yes, she came to meet the buyer in Liverpool and Mr Holmes, myself and two nice gentlemen from Mr Coyle's company were there to greet her. So we were all reunited. She is staying with friends at the moment in London, not far from the Tower of London. We aren't certain what will happen to her in the future, but she is in good hands – so all is well that ends well.

I hope that cheers you.

And I want you to know that you are sorely missed. I have been knitting. It does not come naturally, but I can manage socks and mittens. I am sure the winters are cold over there.

Let us hope the war is over soon and we can all be together. Dinner at The Connaught (as they call the Coburg now), says Mr Holmes. Doesn't that sound grand?

I will write again soon, but in the meantime look for my parcels. ~~With all my best wishes~~

With all my love,

Georgina

AUTHOR'S NOTE

Although many of the characters in this novel existed, and tanks were developed at Thetford in Suffolk in circumstances roughly analogous to those depicted here, I have taken many liberties with history. There was no G Company of the Heavy Branch, Machine Gun Corps, although a G Battalion of the new Tank Corps was formed in December 1916. Similarly, I have not replicated the exact geography of the area, although Elveden Hall exists (albeit currently unoccupied) and the story of the maharajah and the Koh-I-Noor is true. You can find out more in Peter Bance's book *Maharajah Duleep Singh: Sovereign, Squire, Rebel* (Coronet), which contains photographs of the hall. It is available at the Elveden shops (see www.elveden.com).

For details of the tank's inception, development and deployment, David Fletcher and Tony Bryan's monograph on the *British Mark 1 Tank 1916* (Osprey) was invaluable in describing the layout of the first machines. I also drew on Patrick Wright's *Tank* (Viking). I am particularly indebted to *Band of Brigands: The Extraordinary Story of the First Men in Tanks* by Christy Campbell, which put me on the trail of the *Notes for Tank Commanders*, the original of which is in the wonderful Bovington Tank Museum (www.tankmuseum.org) in Dorset. I also used *Tanks and Trenches*, edited by David Fletcher (The History Press). Reading many of the accounts of the early tanks, it will come as no surprise to discover that men really did lose their sanity in these metal beasts – carbon monoxide disoriented them and, in some cases, the combination of noise, heat and fumes sent them over the edge completely. One tank commander really did use his revolver to shoot the engine of his tormentor. The bravery of the men who drove those first tanks into battle, with little experience of war or the machines, is wholly admirable. The tank, though, was not the super-weapon the Allies had hoped for, mainly because the element of surprise was squandered in the mud of the Somme and because the early versions were so primitive and unreliable (although some tanks did make it across no man's land on 15 September and helped liberate a village or two).

There were later successes, notably at Cambrai in 1917, but the tank did not really come into its own as a fighting machine until the next war when, of course, its initial, devastating successes came in the hands of German crews and commanders. And, as Colonel-General Heinz Guderian said in his book *Panzer Marsch!*, published in 1937: 'The higher the concentration of tanks, the faster, greater and more sweeping will be the success – and the smaller our own losses . . .'

I'd like to thank Frances Armstrong at the Elveden Estate (elveden.com) and Brian Dawson of Nature Break Wildlife Cruises (wildlifetrips.org.uk). The latter showed me the Broomway and the fascinating island of Foulness and the little community of Churchend. His company offers walks, boat rides and even tractor rides along the Broomway to the island.

My thanks go to Maxine Hitchcock and Clare Hey for their exemplary editing and enthusiasm; Yvonne Holland for saving me from myself so many times; and to Sue Stephens, James Horobin and Kerr MacRae and all at Simon & Schuster for continuing support, even when it involves listening to jazz. David Miller, Alex Goodwin, Susan d'Arcy, Katie Haines, Jonathan Kinnersely, Gary Cook and Barry Forshaw have all offered sterling back-room work in various capacities. Finally, thank you to Guy Barker, whose various attempts to turn me into a lyricist at least offered a welcome respite from the writing trenches.

Robert Ryan